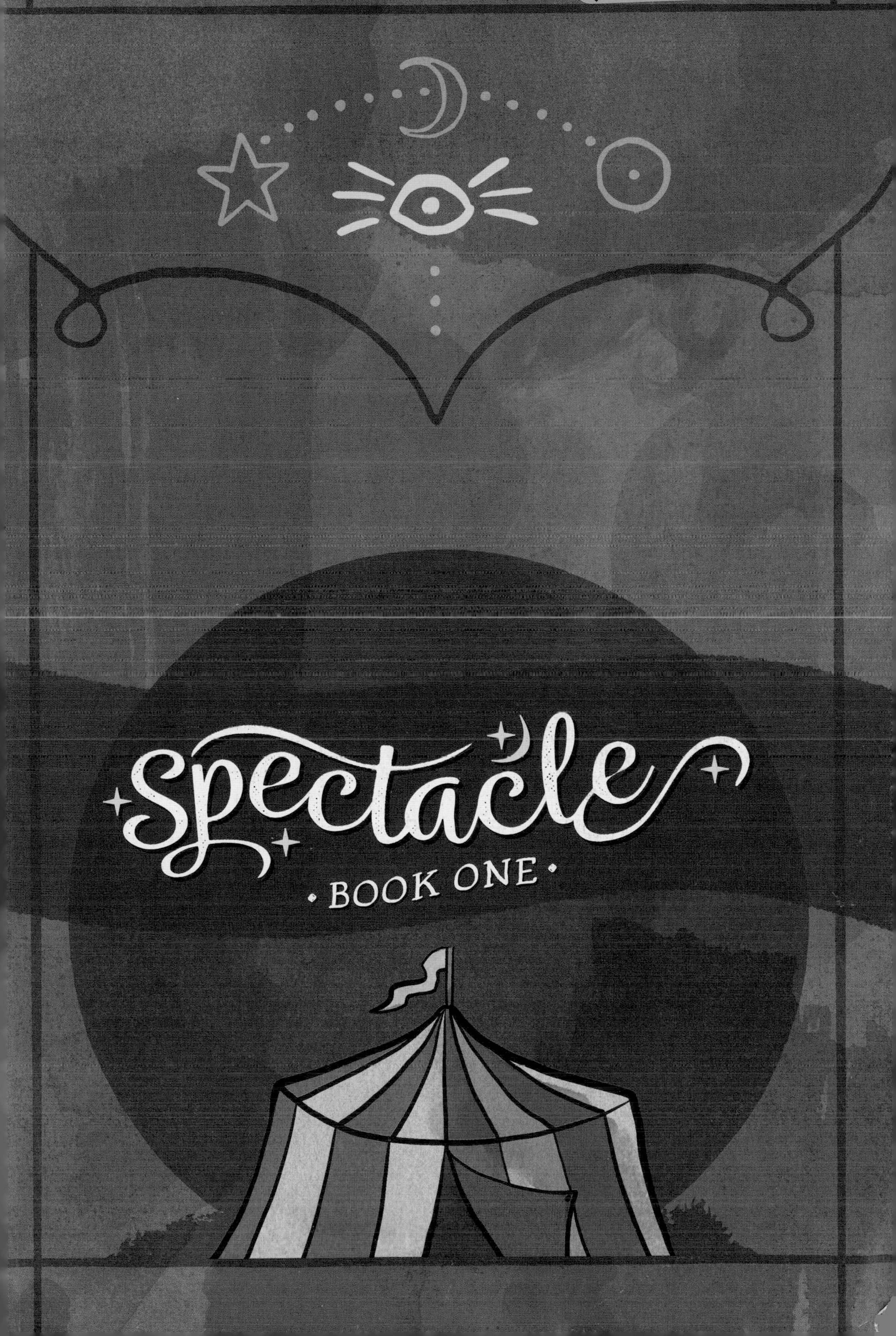
Spectacle
• BOOK ONE •

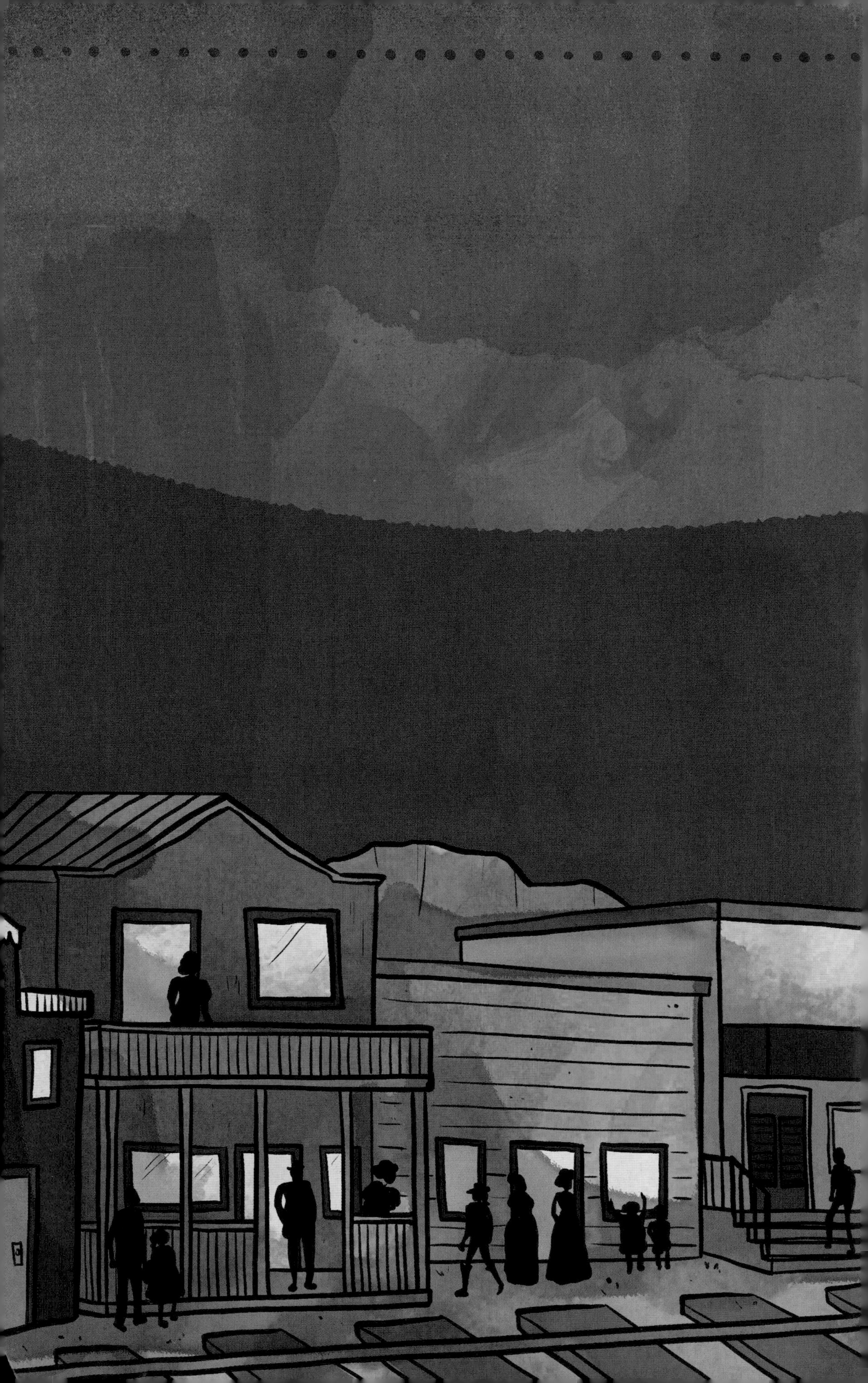

Spectacle

BOOK ONE

- MEGAN ROSE GEDRIS -

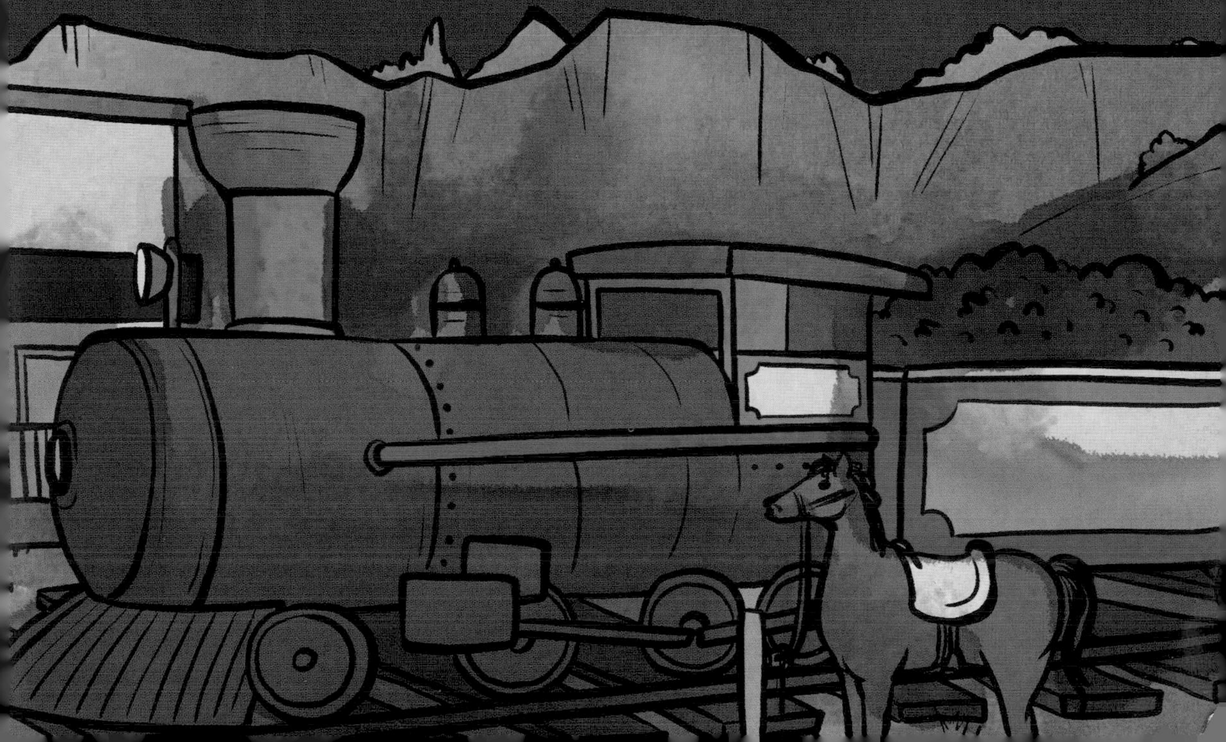

Designed by Hilary Thompson
Edited by Ari Yarwood

PUBLISHED BY ONI PRESS, INC.
Joe Nozemack, founder & chief financial officer
James Lucas Jones, publisher
Charlie Chu, v.p. of creative & business development
Brad Rooks, director of operations
Rachel Reed, marketing manager
Melissa Meszaros, publicity manager
Troy Look, director of design & production
Hilary Thompson, senior graphic designer
Kate Z. Stone, junior graphic designer
Angie Knowles, digital prepress lead
Ari Yarwood, executive editor
Robin Herrera, senior editor
Desiree Wilson, associate editor
Alissa Sallah, administrative assistant
Jung Lee, logistics associate

1319 SE Martin Luther King, Jr. Blvd.
Suite 240
Portland, OR 97214

onipress.com
facebook.com/onipress
twitter.com/onipress
onipress.tumblr.com
instagram.com/onipress

rosalarian.com
twitter.com/rosalarian

First Edition: May 2018
ISBN: 978-1-62010-492-7
eISBN: 978-1-62010-493-4

1 2 3 4 5 6 7 8 9 10

Library of Congress Control Number: 2017956258

Printed in China.

Chapter One

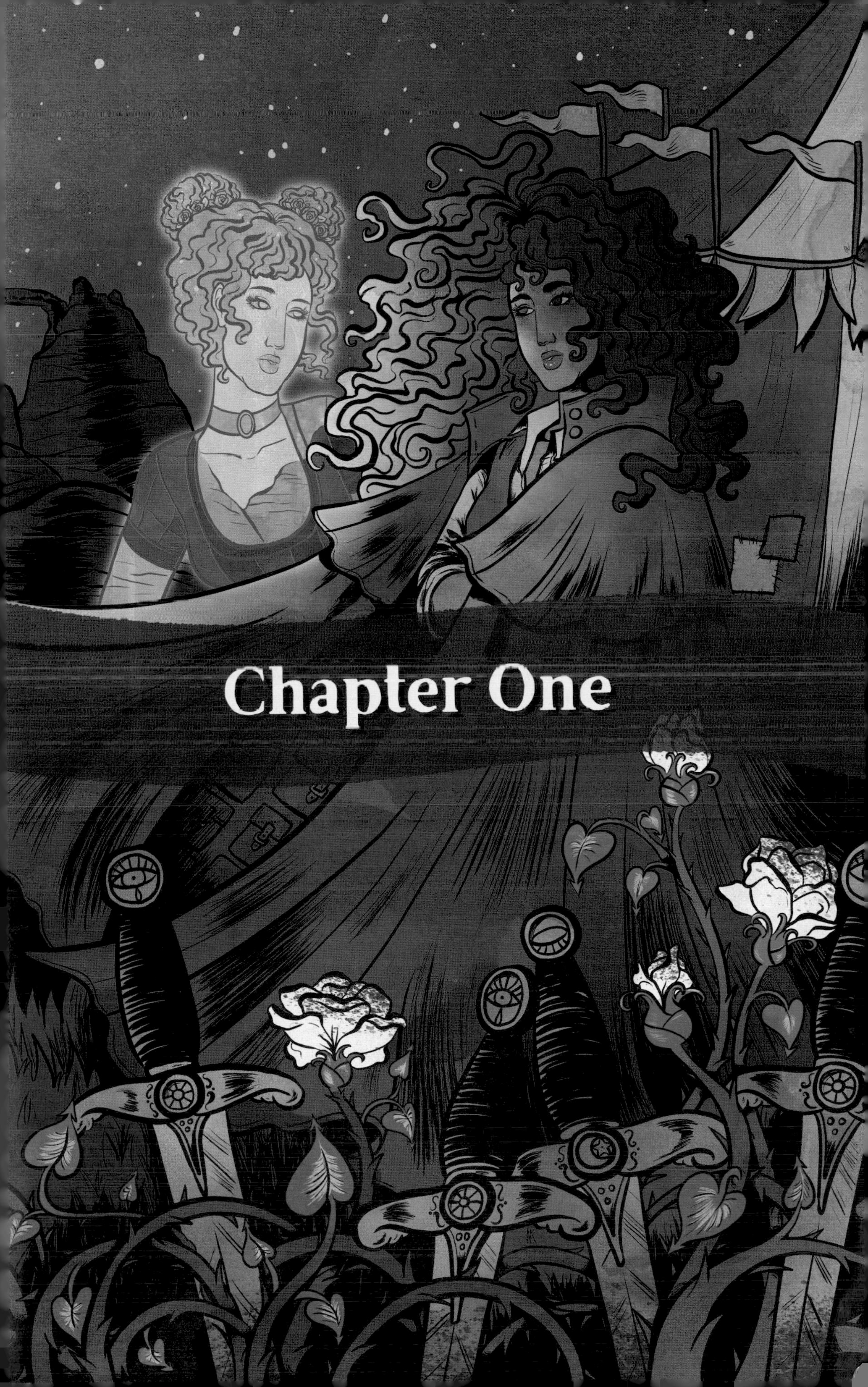

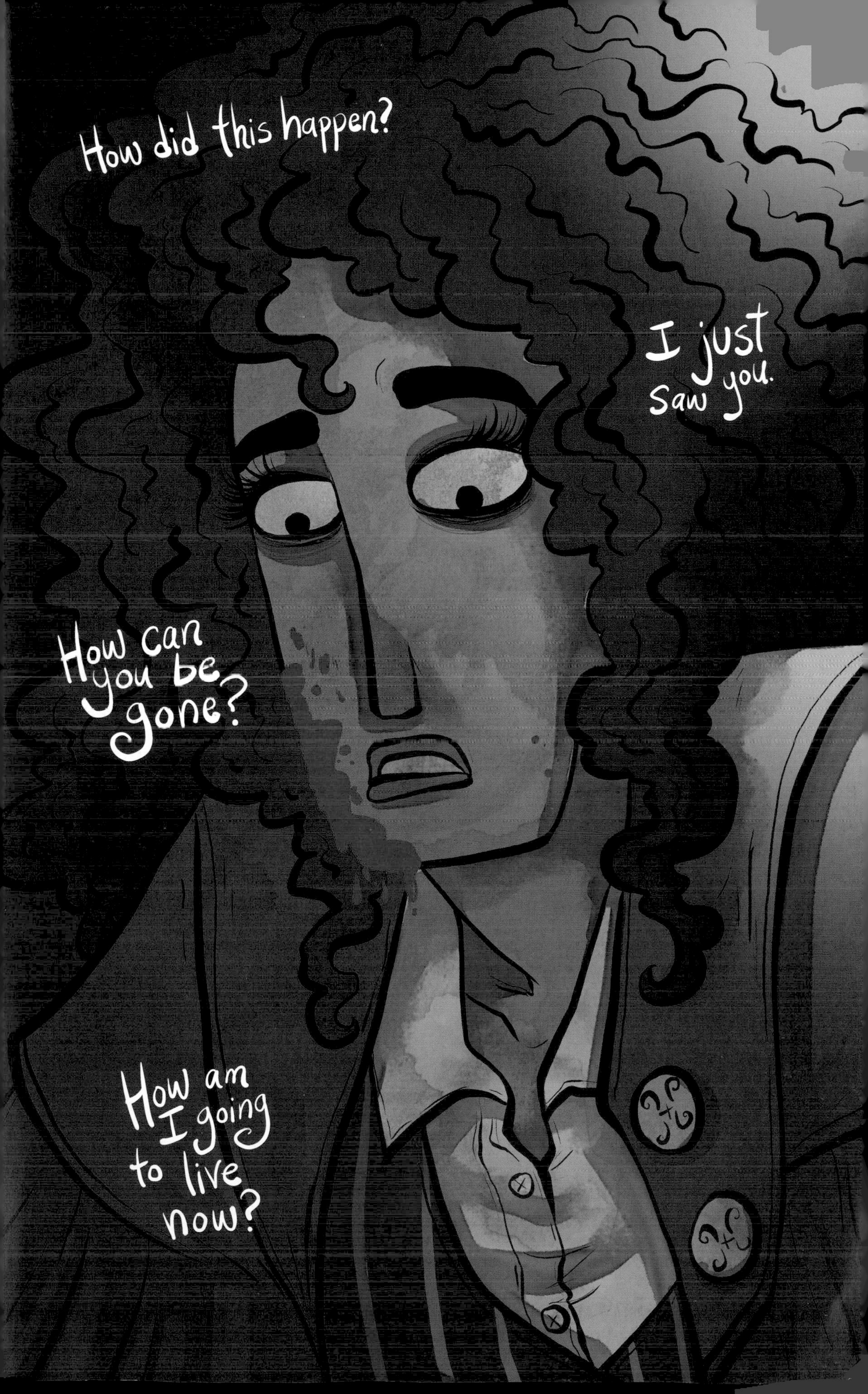
How did this happen?
I just saw you.
How can you be gone?
How am I going to live now?

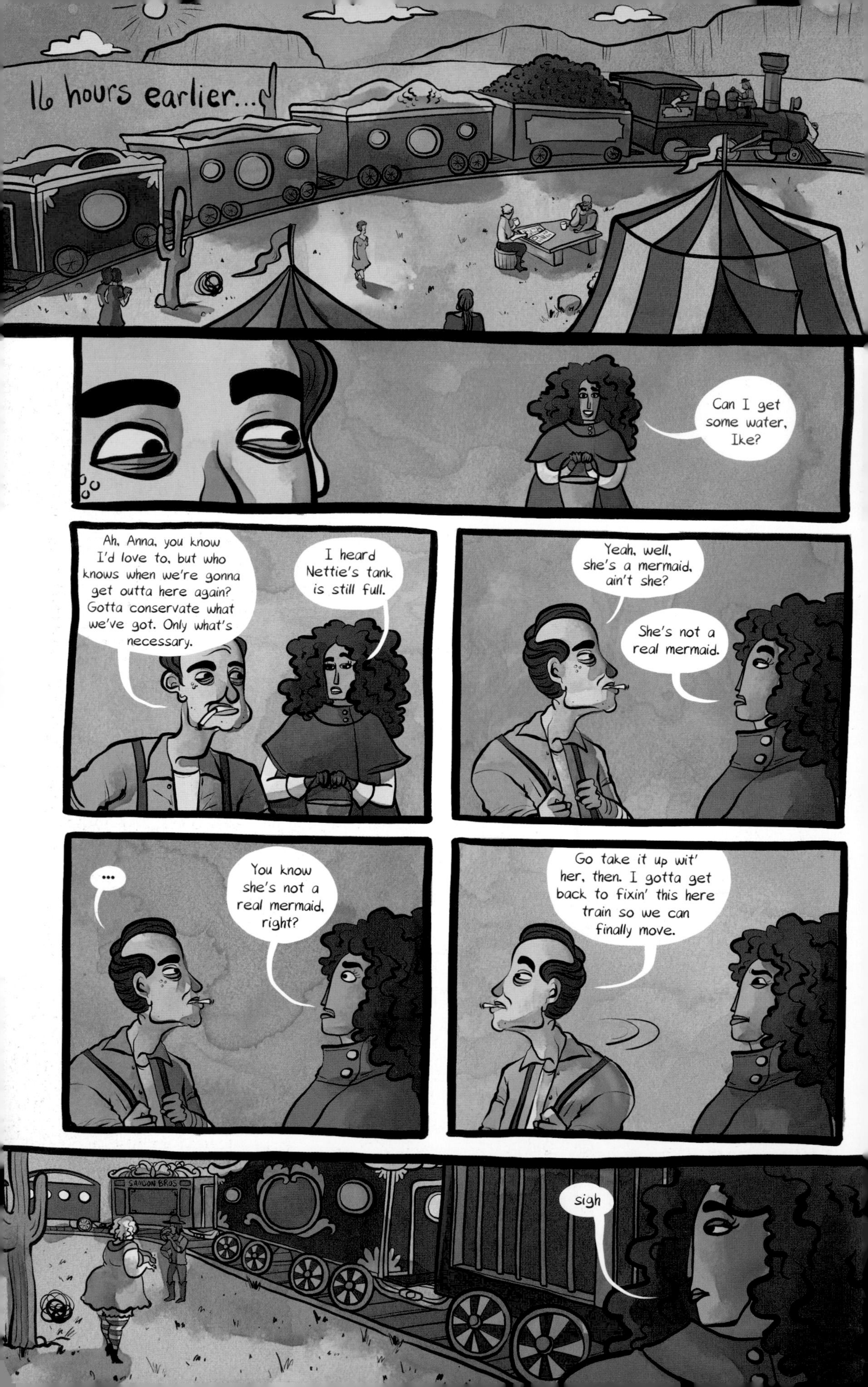
16 hours earlier...
Can I get some water, Ike?
Ah, Anna, you know I'd love to, but who knows when we're gonna get outta here again? Gotta conservate what we've got. Only what's necessary.
I heard Nettie's tank is still full.
Yeah, well, she's a mermaid, ain't she?
She's not a real mermaid.
...
You know she's not a real mermaid, right?
Go take it up wit' her, then. I gotta get back to fixin' this here train so we can finally move.
sigh

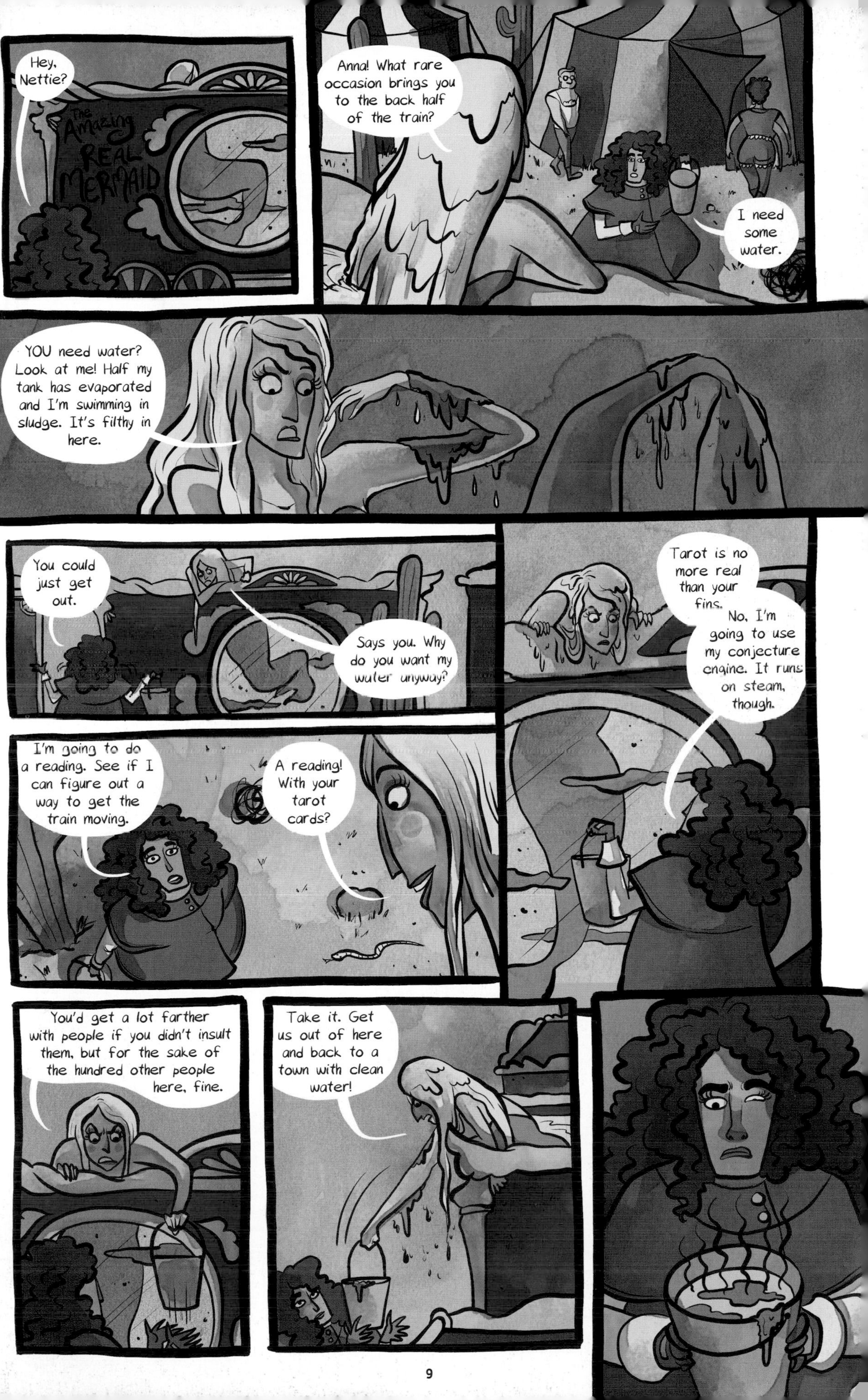
Hey, Nettie?
Anna! What rare occasion brings you to the back half of the train?
I need some water.
YOU need water? Look at me! Half my tank has evaporated and I'm swimming in sludge. It's filthy in here.
You could just get out.
Says you. Why do you want my water anyway?
I'm going to do a reading. See if I can figure out a way to get the train moving.
A reading! With your tarot cards?
Tarot is no more real than your fins.
No, I'm going to use my conjecture engine. It runs on steam, though.
You'd get a lot farther with people if you didn't insult them, but for the sake of the hundred other people here, fine.
Take it. Get us out of here and back to a town with clean water!

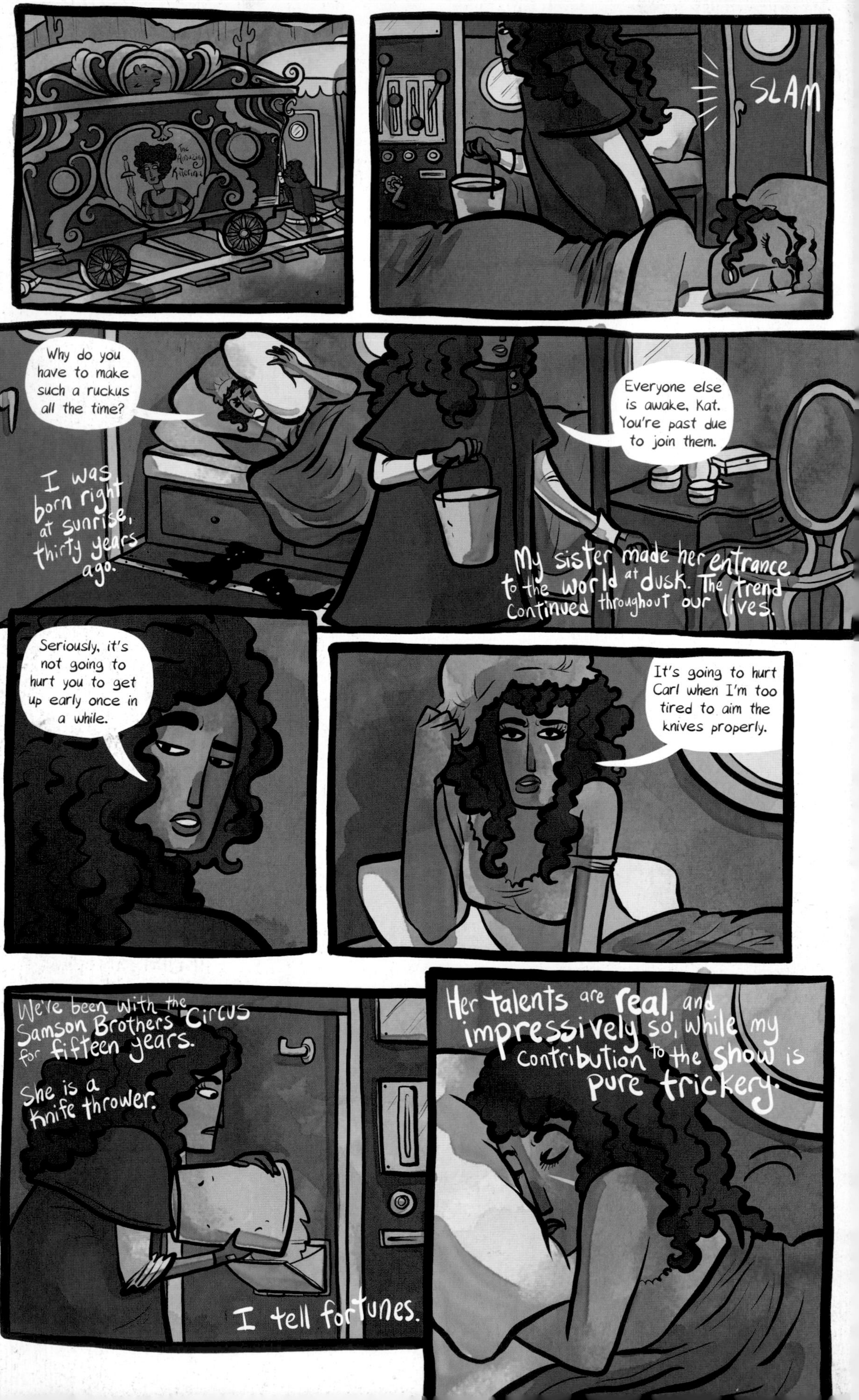
SLAM
Why do you have to make such a ruckus all the time?
I was born right at sunrise, thirty years ago.
Everyone else is awake, Kat. You're past due to join them.
My sister made her entrance to the world at dusk. The trend continued throughout our lives.
Seriously, it's not going to hurt you to get up early once in a while.
It's going to hurt Carl when I'm too tired to aim the knives properly.
We've been with the Samson Brothers Circus for fifteen years.
She is a knife thrower.
I tell fortunes.
Her talents are real, and impressively so, while my contribution to the show is pure trickery.

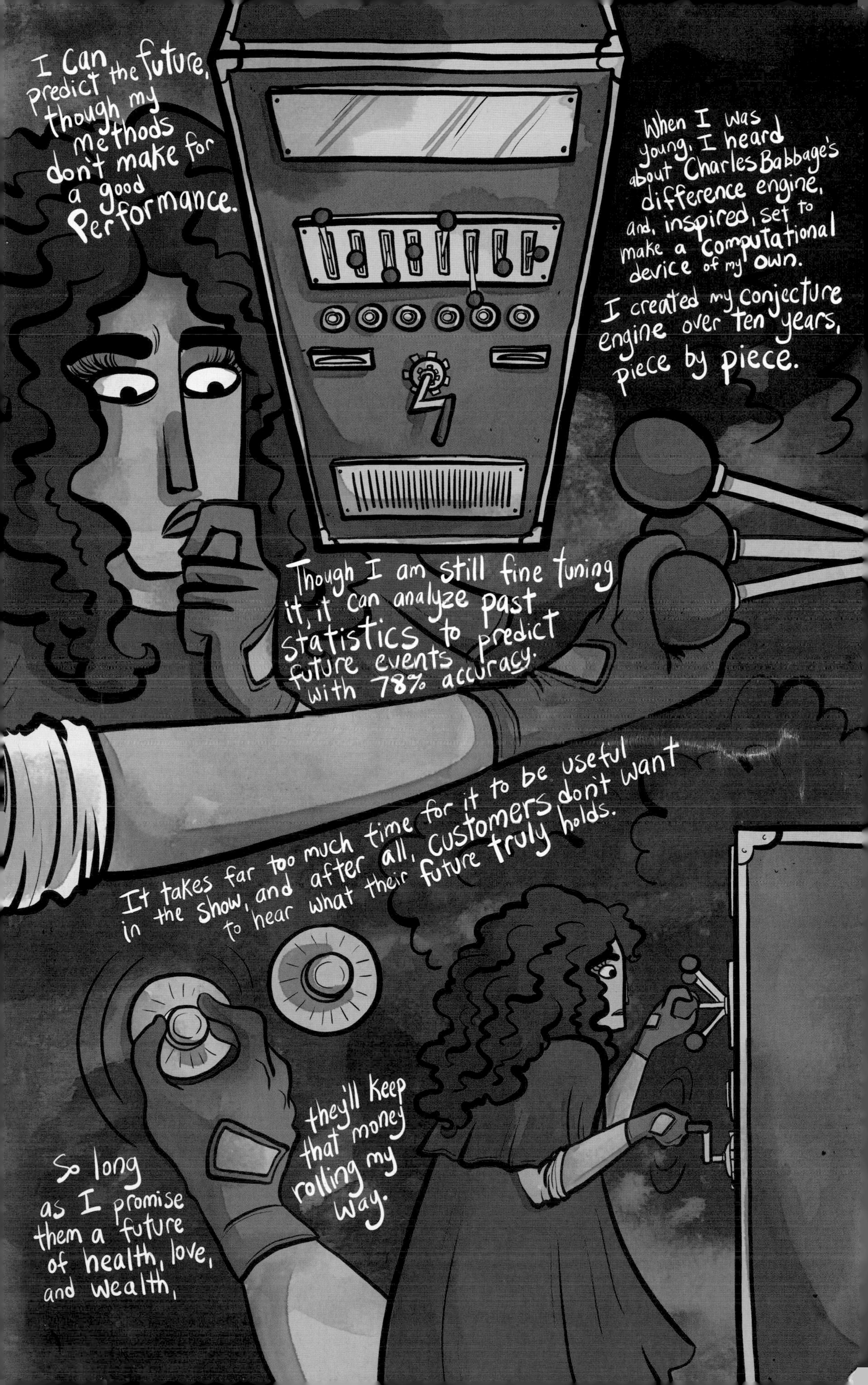
I can predict the future, though my methods don't make for a good Performance.
When I was young, I heard about Charles Babbage's difference engine, and, inspired, set to make a computational device of my own.
I created my conjecture engine over ten years, piece by piece.
Though I am still fine tuning it, it can analyze past statistics to predict future events with 78% accuracy.
It takes far too much time for it to be useful in the show, and after all, customers don't want to hear what their future truly holds.
So long as I promise them a future of health, love, and wealth,
they'll keep that money rolling my way.

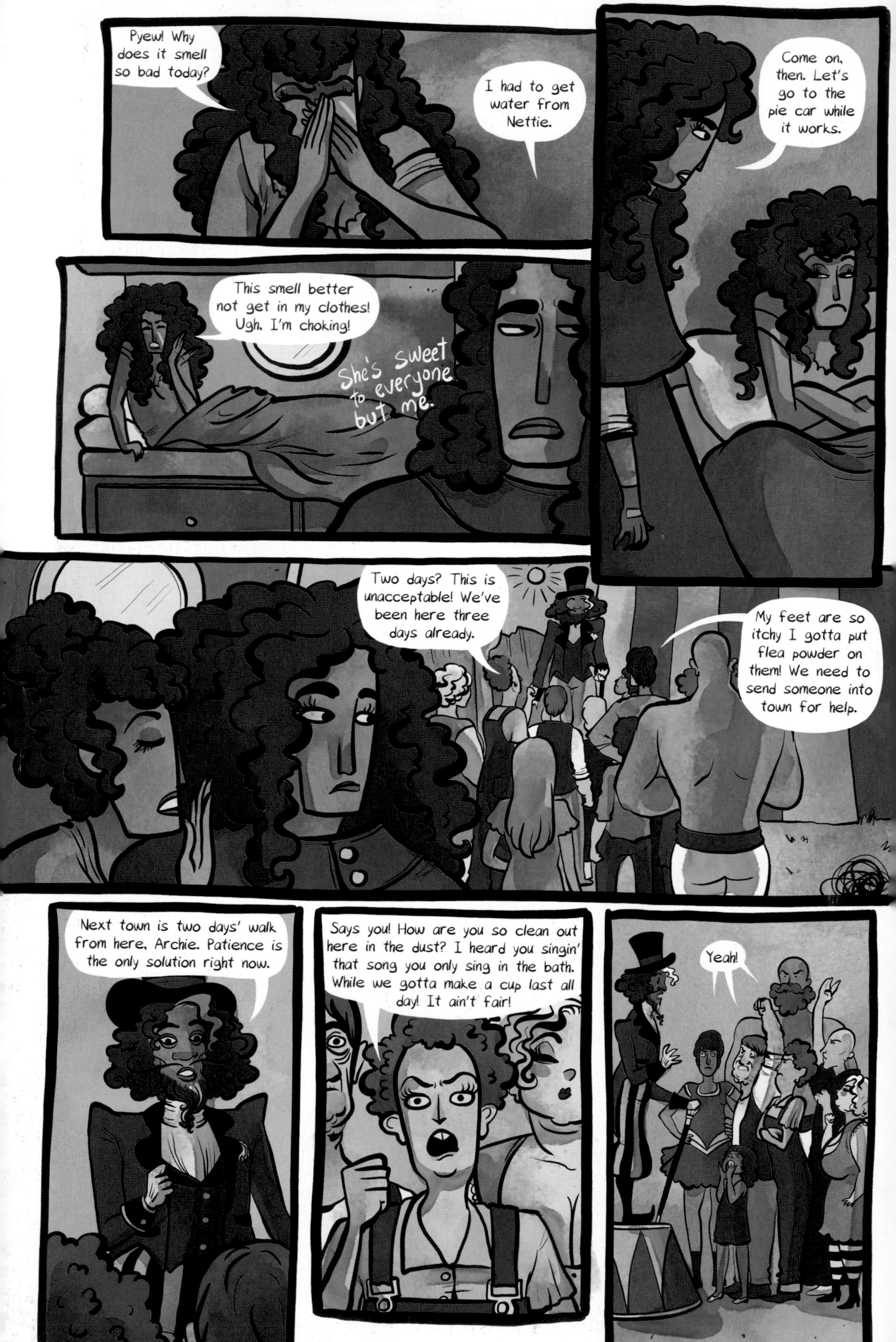
Pyew! Why does it smell so bad today?
I had to get water from Nettie.
Come on, then. Let's go to the pie car while it works.
This smell better not get in my clothes! Ugh, I'm choking!
She's sweet to everyone but me.
Two days? This is unacceptable! We've been here three days already.
My feet are so itchy I gotta put flea powder on them! We need to send someone into town for help.
Next town is two days' walk from here, Archie. Patience is the only solution right now.
Says you! How are you so clean out here in the dust? I heard you singin' that song you only sing in the bath. While we gotta make a cup last all day! It ain't fair!
Yeah!

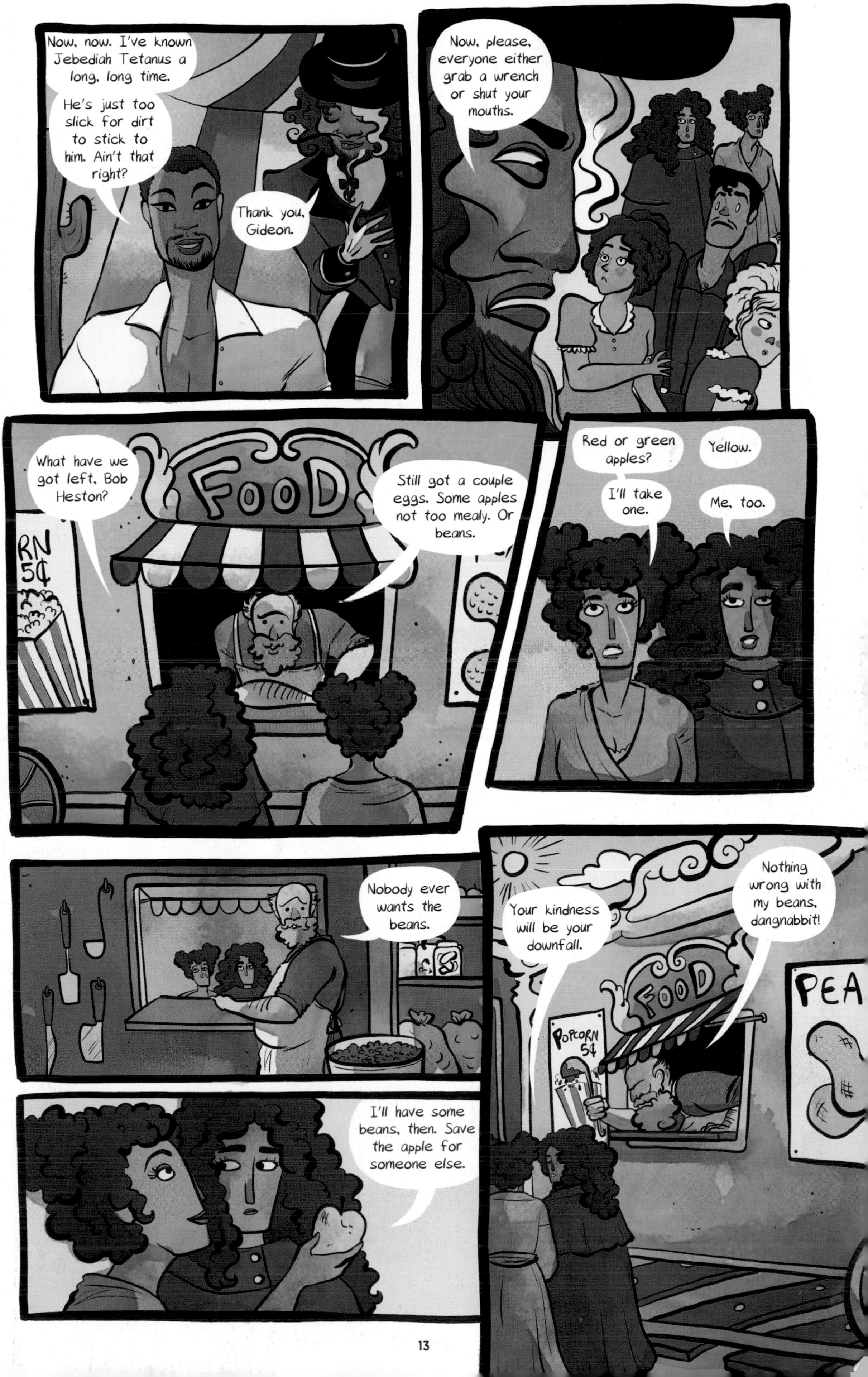
Now, now. I've known Jebediah Tetanus a long, long time.
He's just too slick for dirt to stick to him. Ain't that right?
Thank you, Gideon.
Now, please, everyone either grab a wrench or shut your mouths.
What have we got left, Bob Heston?
FOOD
RN 5¢
Still got a couple eggs. Some apples not too mealy. Or beans.
Red or green apples?
Yellow.
I'll take one.
Me, too.
Nobody ever wants the beans.
I'll have some beans, then. Save the apple for someone else.
Your kindness will be your downfall.
Nothing wrong with my beans, dangnabbit!
FOOD
POPCORN 5¢
PEA

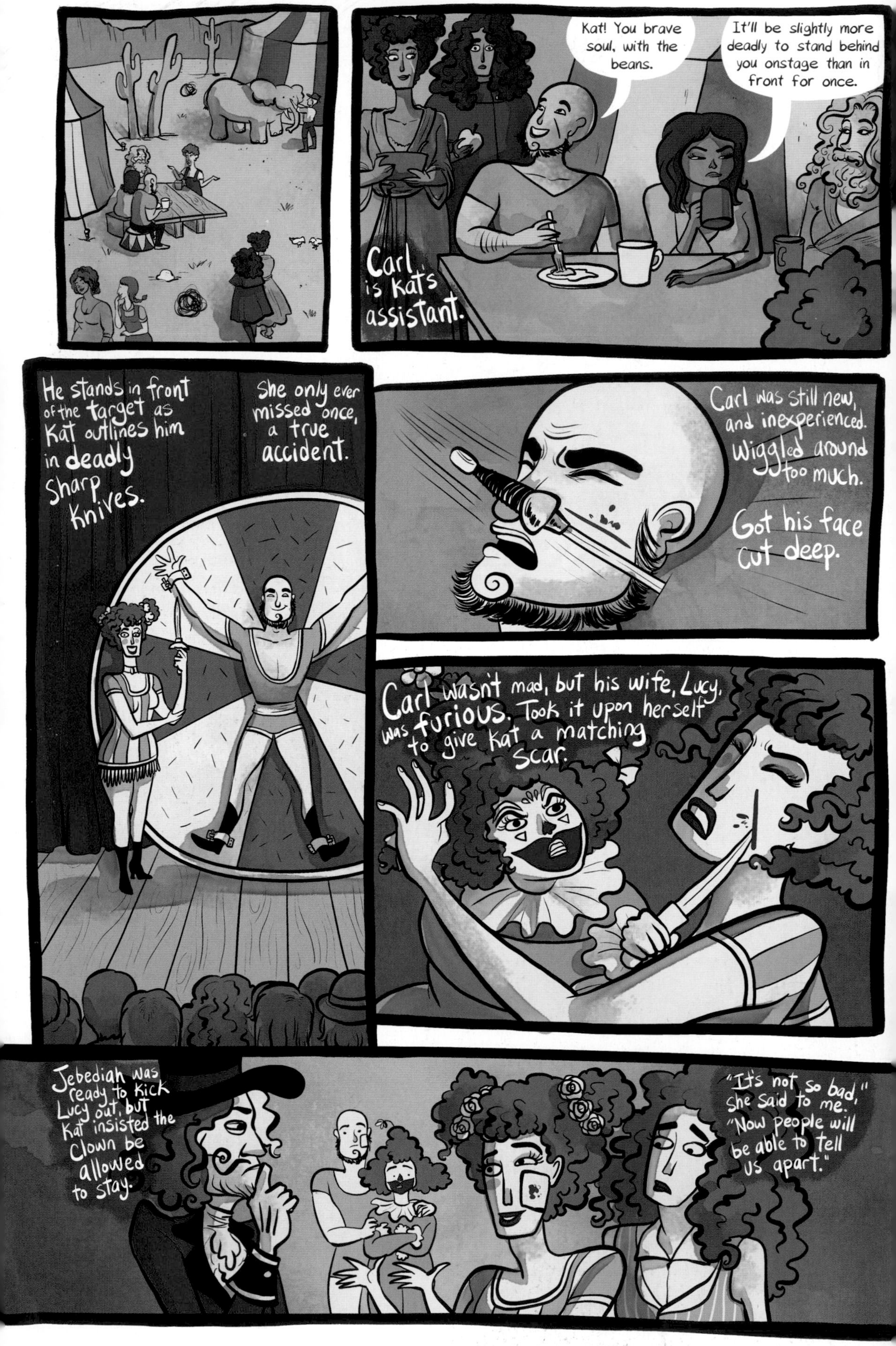
Kat! You brave soul, with the beans.
It'll be slightly more deadly to stand behind you onstage than in front for once.
Carl is Kat's assistant.
He stands in front of the target as Kat outlines him in deadly sharp knives.
She only ever missed once, a true accident.
Carl was still new, and inexperienced. Wiggled around too much.
Got his face cut deep.
Carl wasn't mad, but his wife, Lucy, was furious. Took it upon herself to give Kat a matching scar.
Jebediah was ready to kick Lucy out, but Kat insisted the Clown be allowed to stay.
"It's not so bad," she said to me. "Now people will be able to tell us apart."

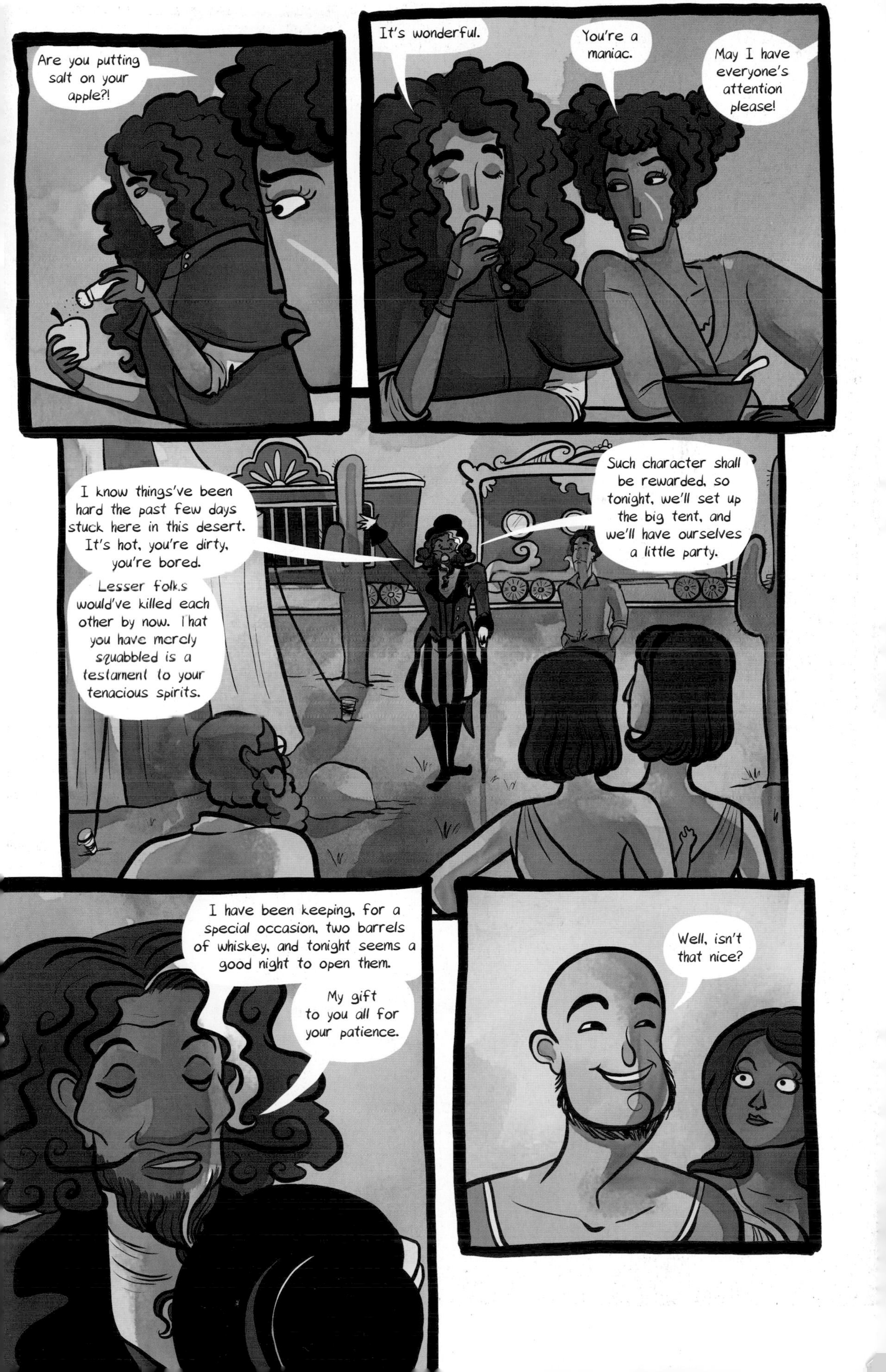
Are you putting salt on your apple?!
It's wonderful.
You're a maniac.
May I have everyone's attention please!
I know things've been hard the past few days stuck here in this desert. It's hot, you're dirty, you're bored.
Lesser folks would've killed each other by now. That you have merely squabbled is a testament to your tenacious spirits.
Such character shall be rewarded, so tonight, we'll set up the big tent, and we'll have ourselves a little party.
I have been keeping, for a special occasion, two barrels of whiskey, and tonight seems a good night to open them.
My gift to you all for your patience.
Well, isn't that nice?

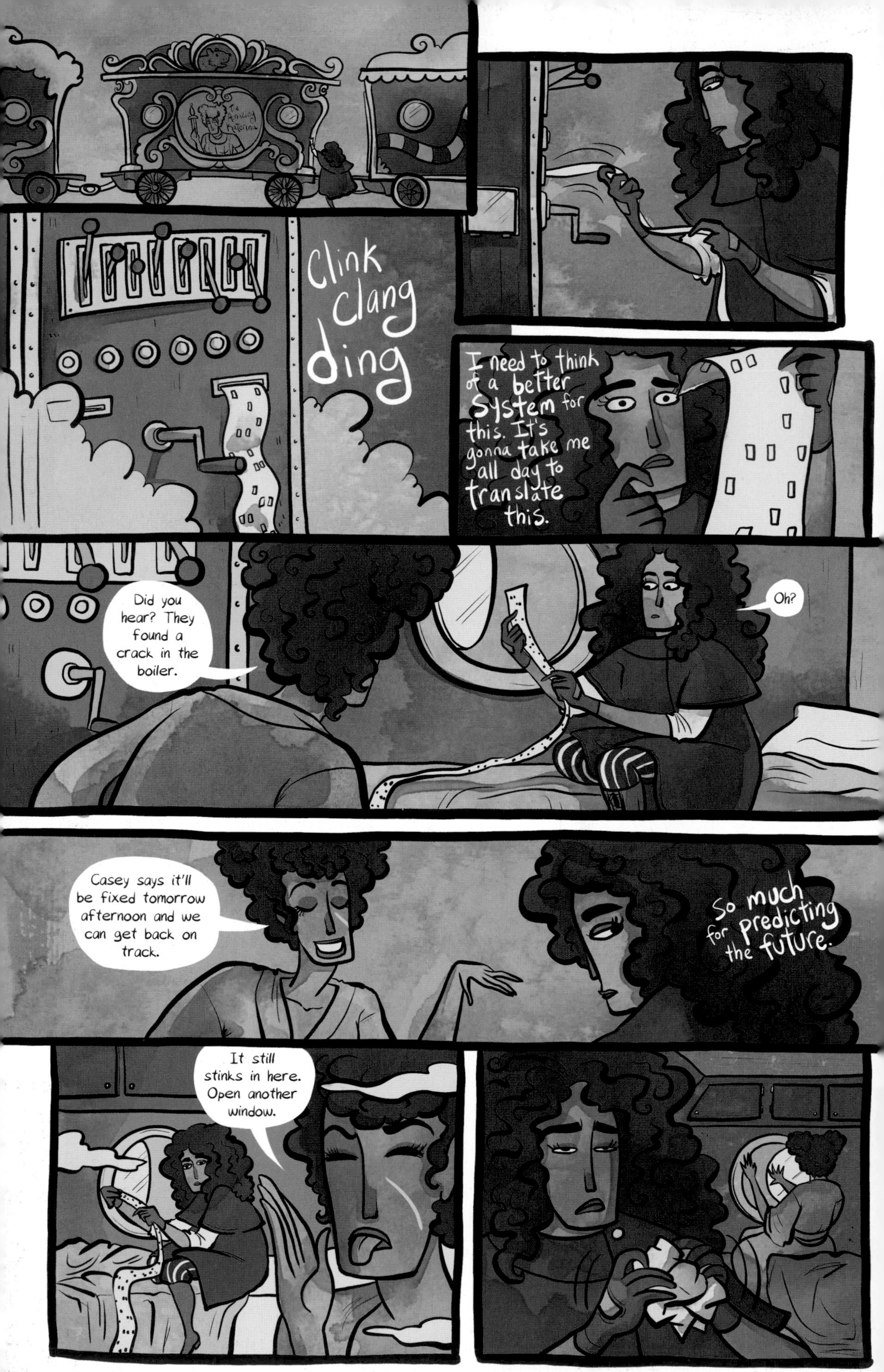
The Amazing Katerina
Clink clang ding
I need to think of a better System for this. It's gonna take me all day to translate this.
Did you hear? They found a crack in the boiler.
Oh?
Casey says it'll be fixed tomorrow afternoon and we can get back on track.
So much for predicting the future.
It still stinks in here. Open another window.

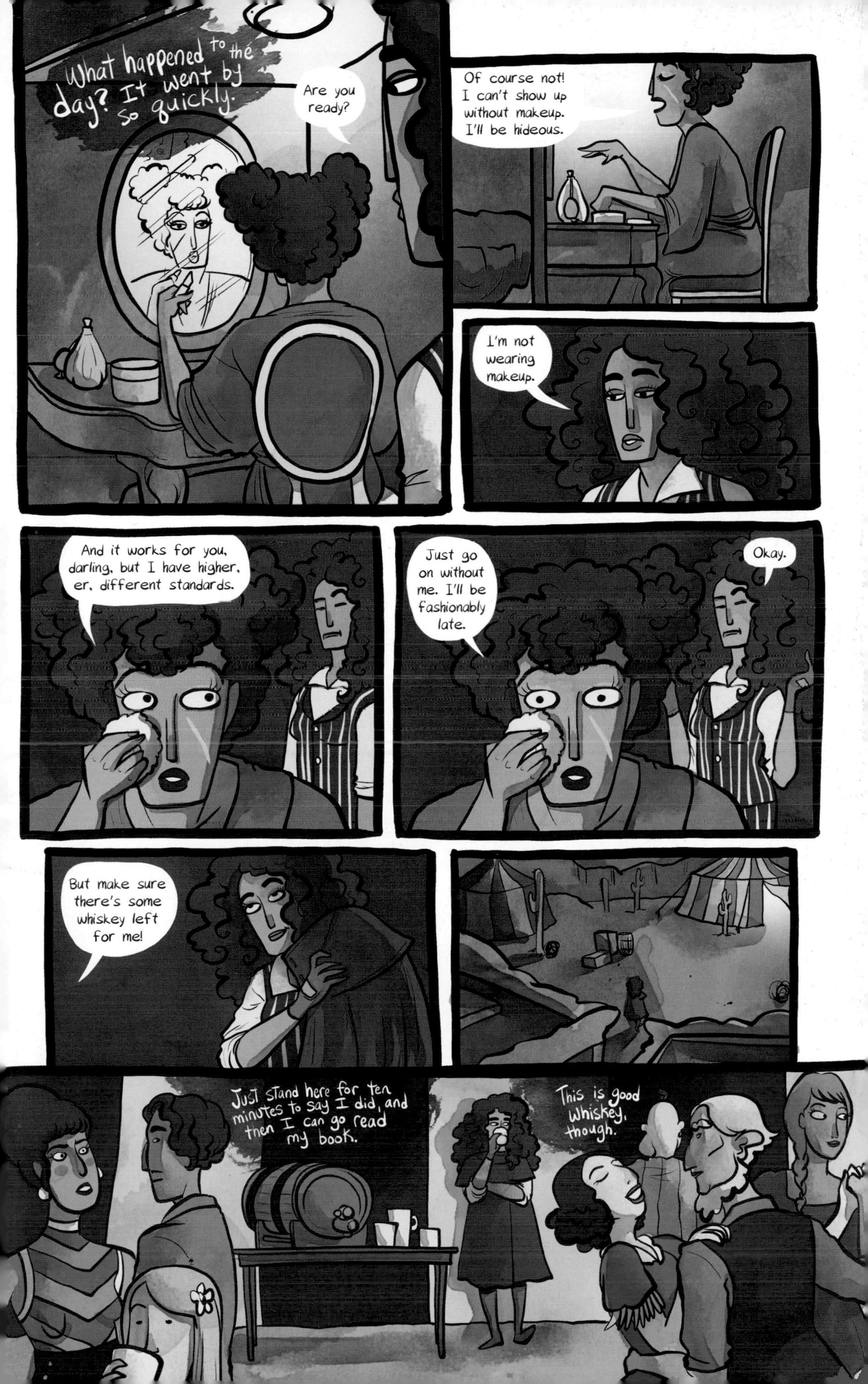
What happened to the day? It went by so quickly.
Are you ready?
Of course not! I can't show up without makeup. I'll be hideous.
I'm not wearing makeup.
And it works for you, darling, but I have higher, er, different standards.
Just go on without me. I'll be fashionably late.
Okay.
But make sure there's some whiskey left for me!
Just stand here for ten minutes to say I did, and then I can go read my book.
This is good whiskey, though.

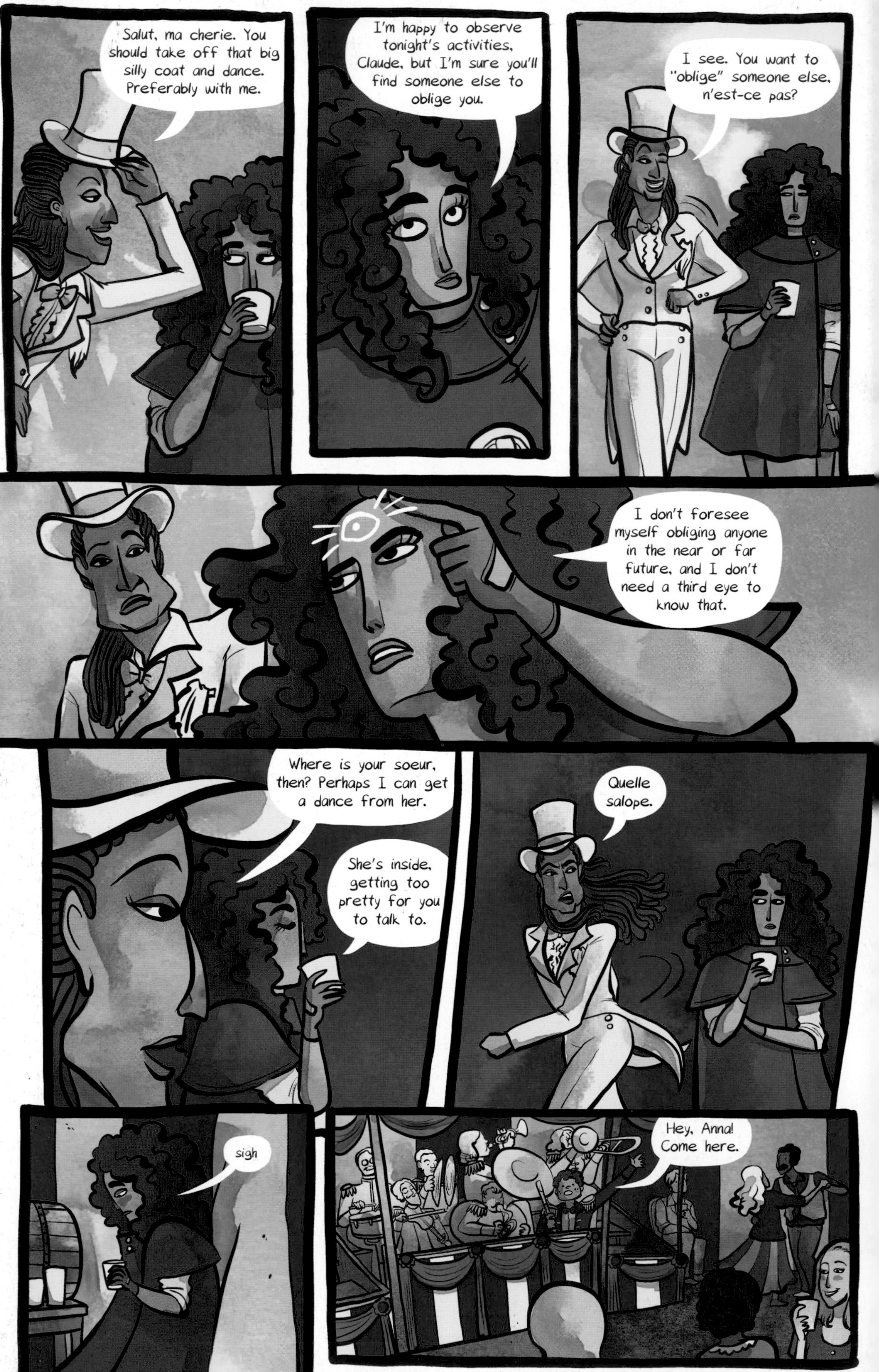
Salut, ma cherie. You should take off that big silly coat and dance. Preferably with me.
I'm happy to observe tonight's activities, Claude, but I'm sure you'll find someone else to oblige you.
I see. You want to "oblige" someone else, n'est-ce pas?
I don't foresee myself obliging anyone in the near or far future, and I don't need a third eye to know that.
Where is your soeur, then? Perhaps I can get a dance from her.
She's inside, getting too pretty for you to talk to.
Quelle salope.
sigh
Hey, Anna! Come here.

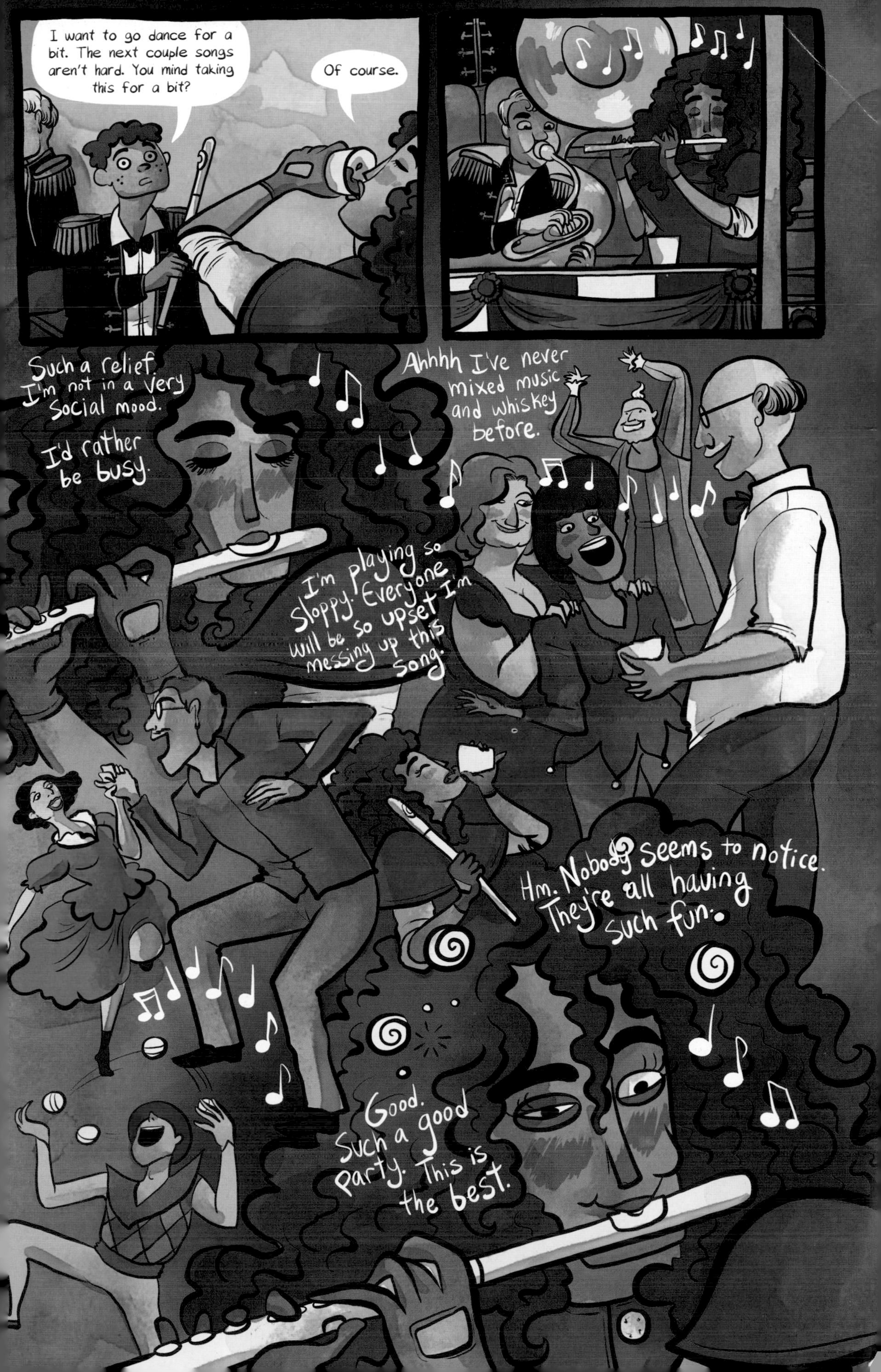
I want to go dance for a bit. The next couple songs aren't hard. You mind taking this for a bit?
Of course.
Such a relief. I'm not in a very social mood.
I'd rather be busy.
Ahhhh I've never mixed music and whiskey before.
I'm playing so sloppy. Everyone will be so upset I'm messing up this song.
Hm. Nobody seems to notice. They're all having such fun.
Good. Such a good party. This is the best.

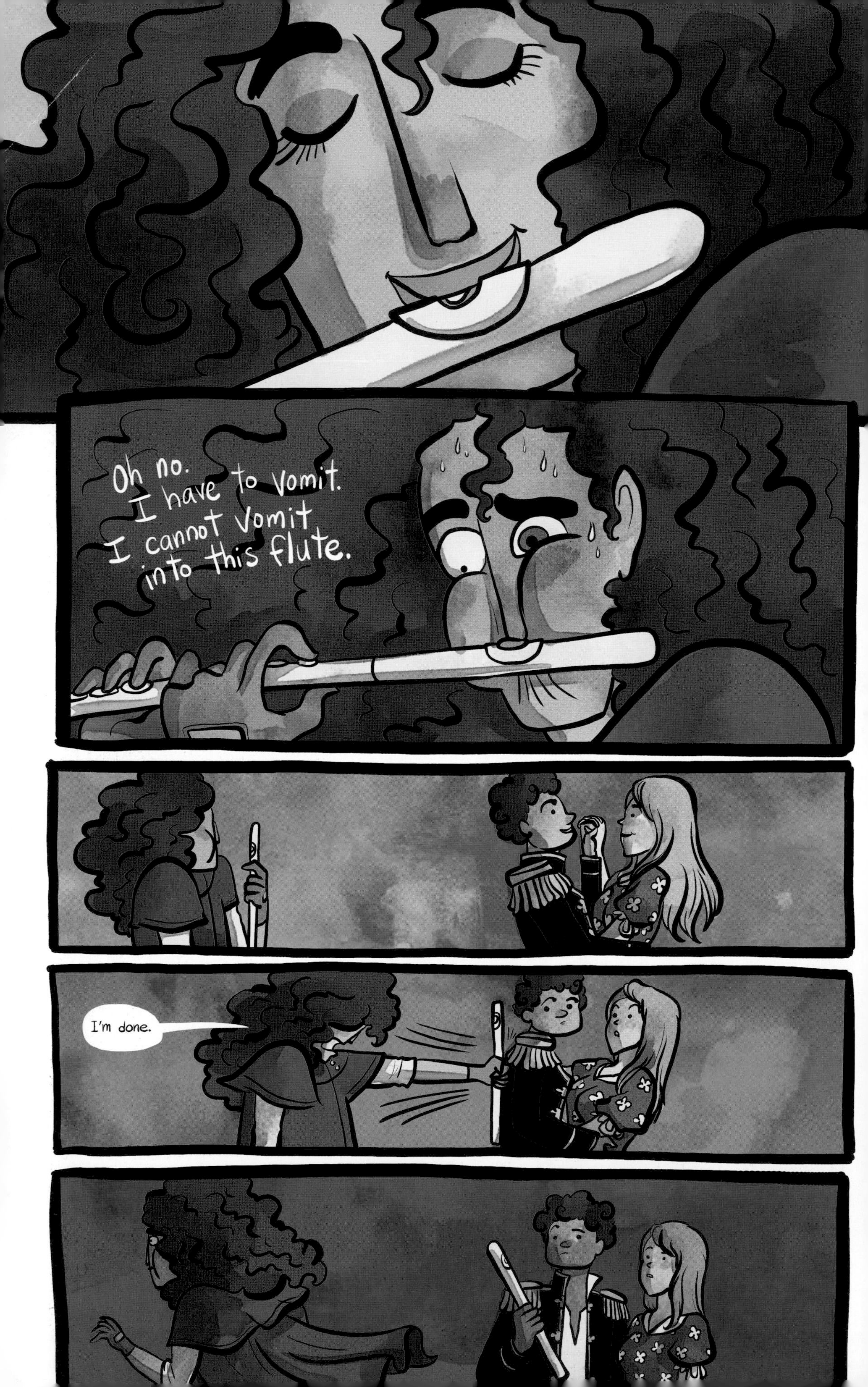
Oh no.
I have to vomit.
I cannot vomit
into this flute.
I'm done.

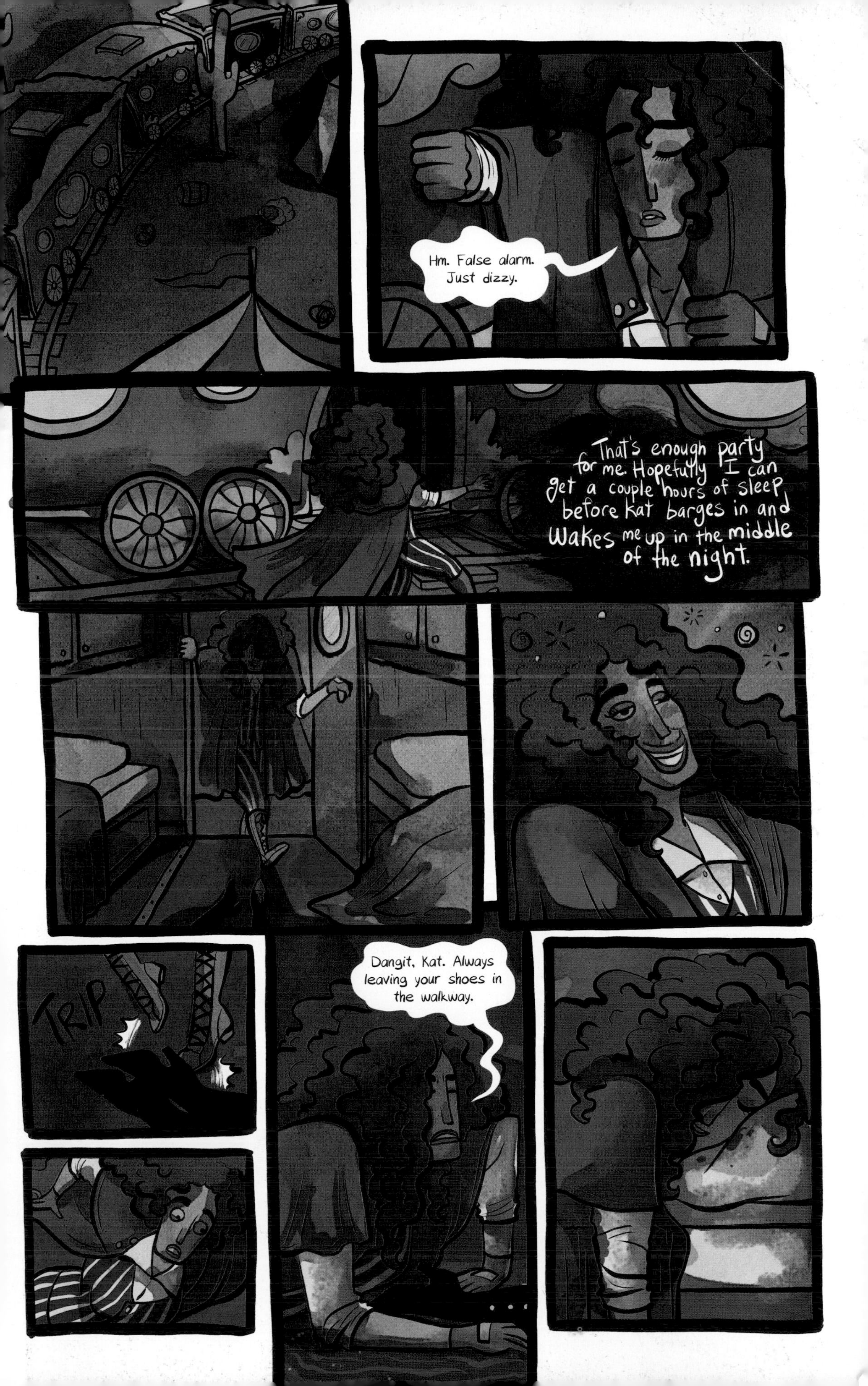
Hm. False alarm. Just dizzy.
That's enough party for me. Hopefully I can get a couple hours of sleep before Kat barges in and wakes me up in the middle of the night.
TRIP
Dangit, Kat. Always leaving your shoes in the walkway.

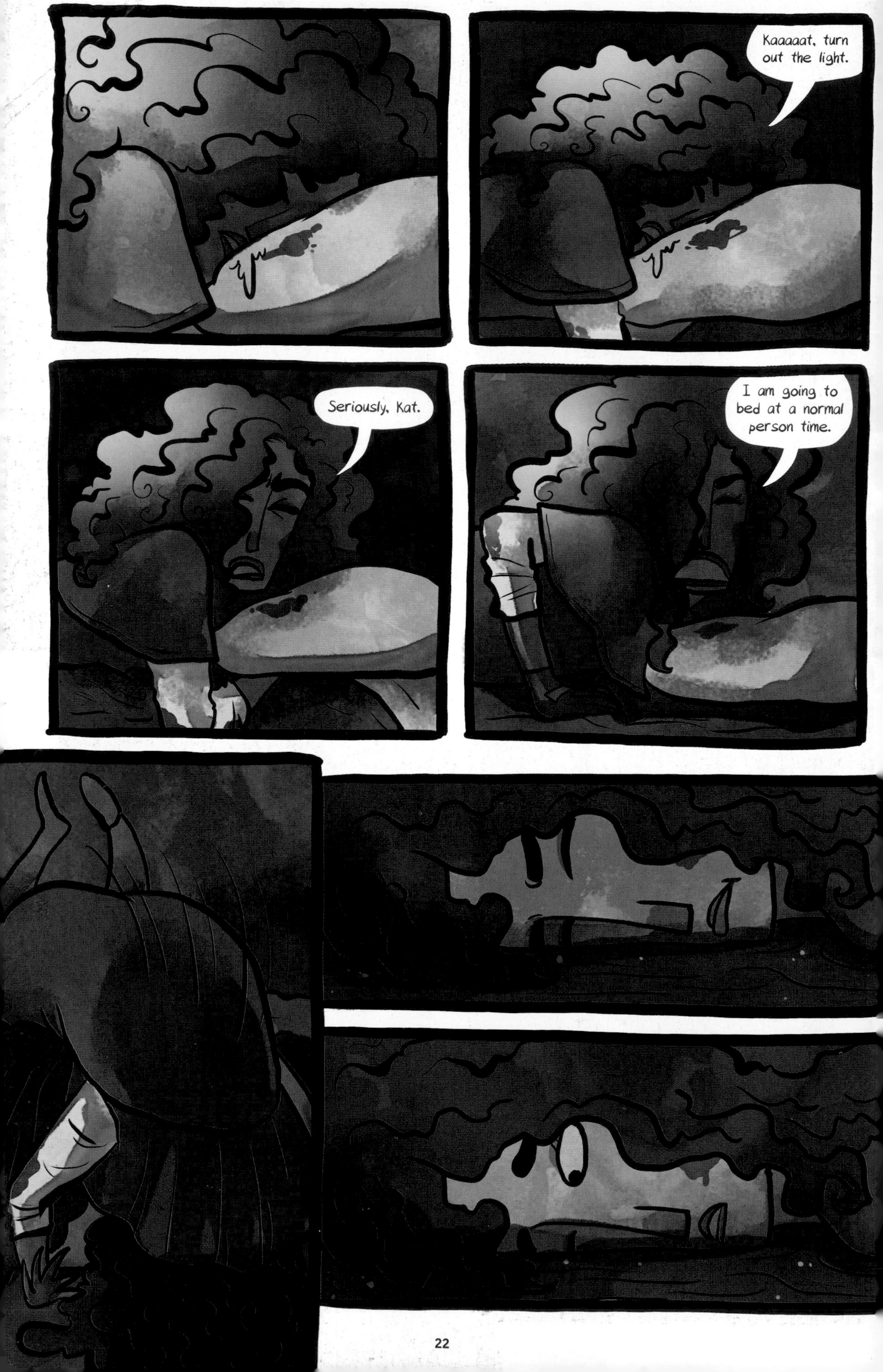
Kaaaaat, turn out the light.
Seriously, Kat.
I am going to bed at a normal person time.

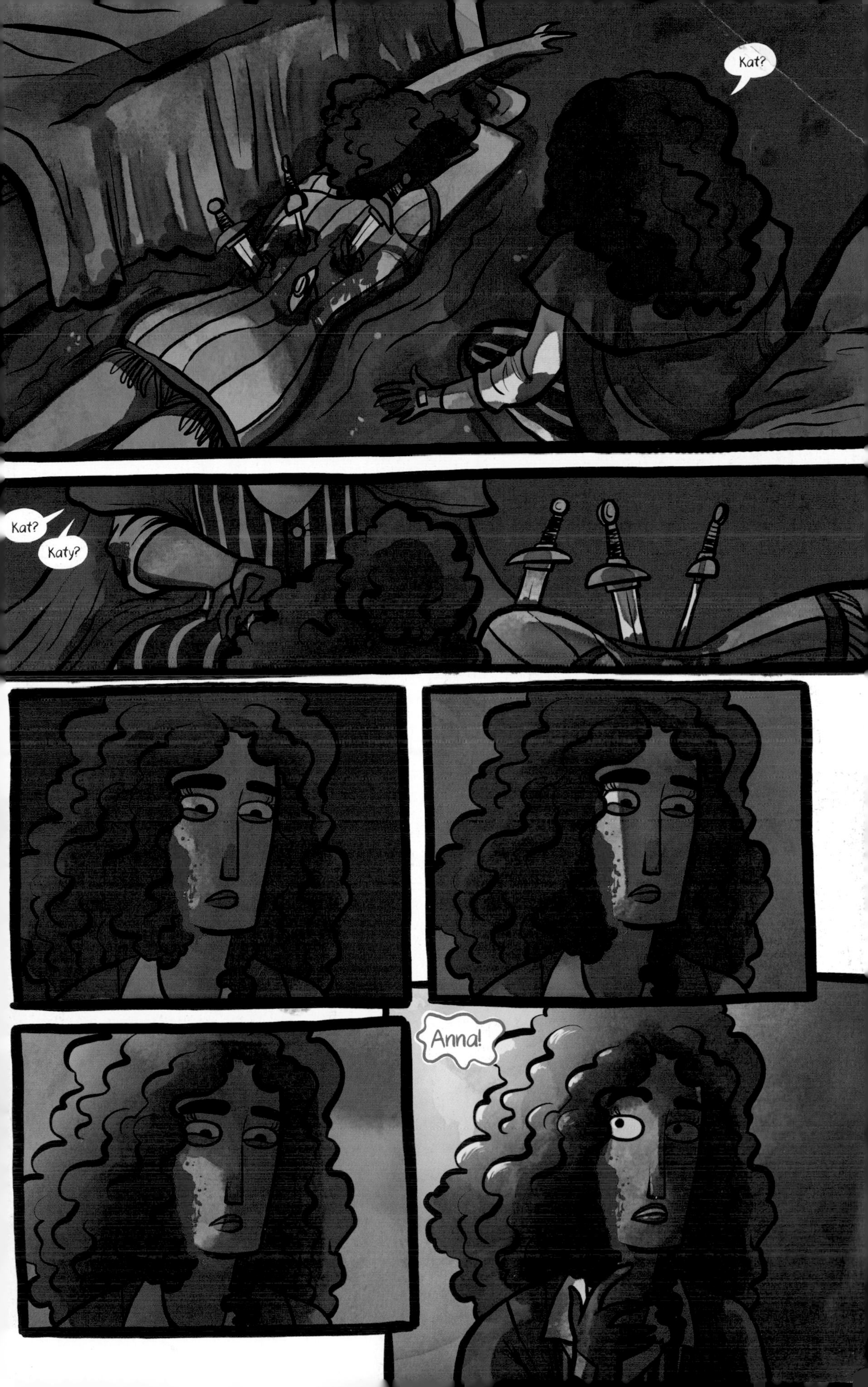
Kat?
Kat?
Katy?
Anna!

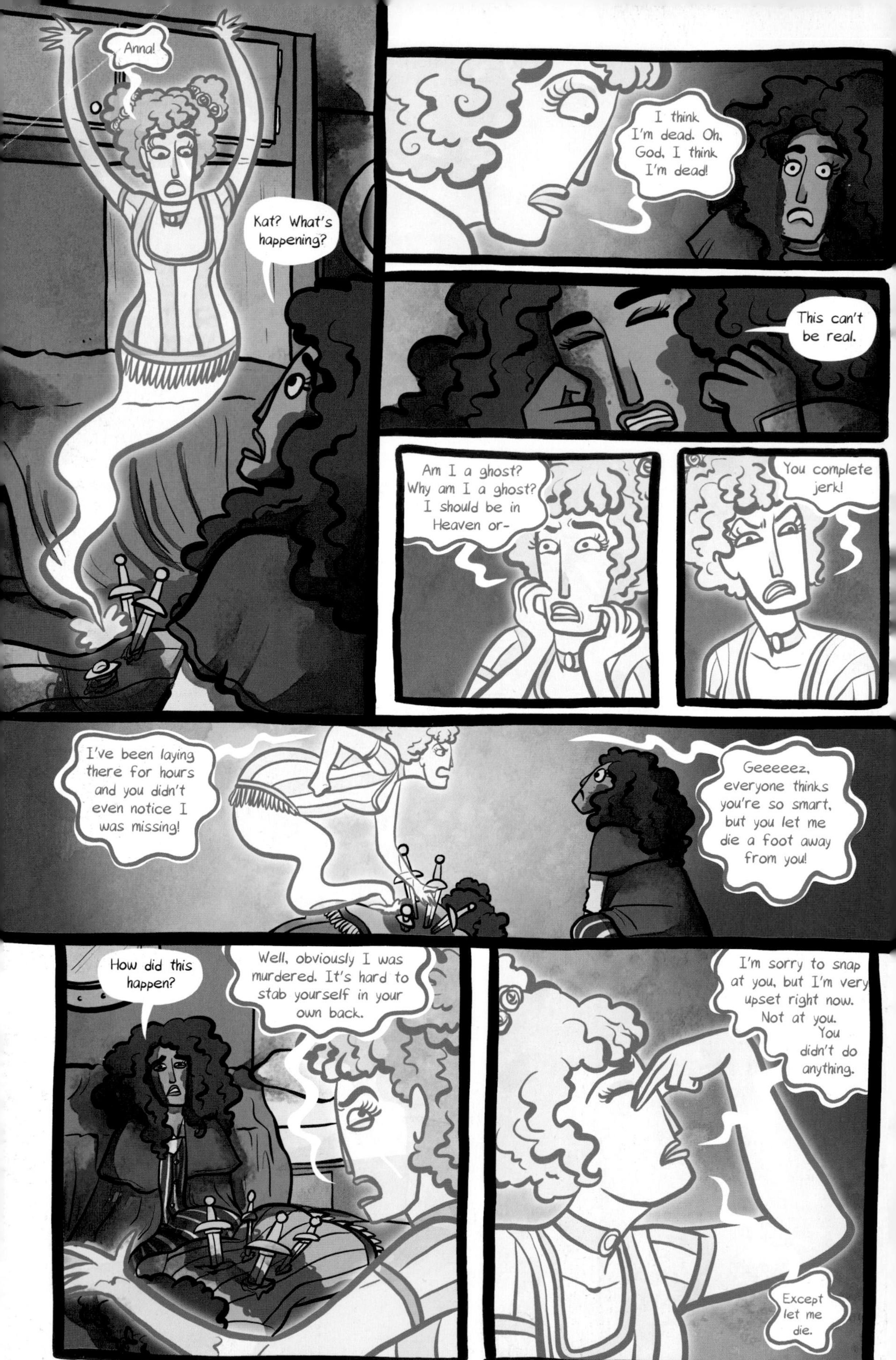
Anna!
Kat? What's happening?
I think I'm dead. Oh, God, I think I'm dead!
This can't be real.
Am I a ghost? Why am I a ghost? I should be in Heaven or-
You complete jerk!
I've been laying there for hours and you didn't even notice I was missing!
Geeeeez, everyone thinks you're so smart, but you let me die a foot away from you!
How did this happen?
Well, obviously I was murdered. It's hard to stab yourself in your own back.
I'm sorry to snap at you, but I'm very upset right now. Not at you. You didn't do anything.
Except let me die.

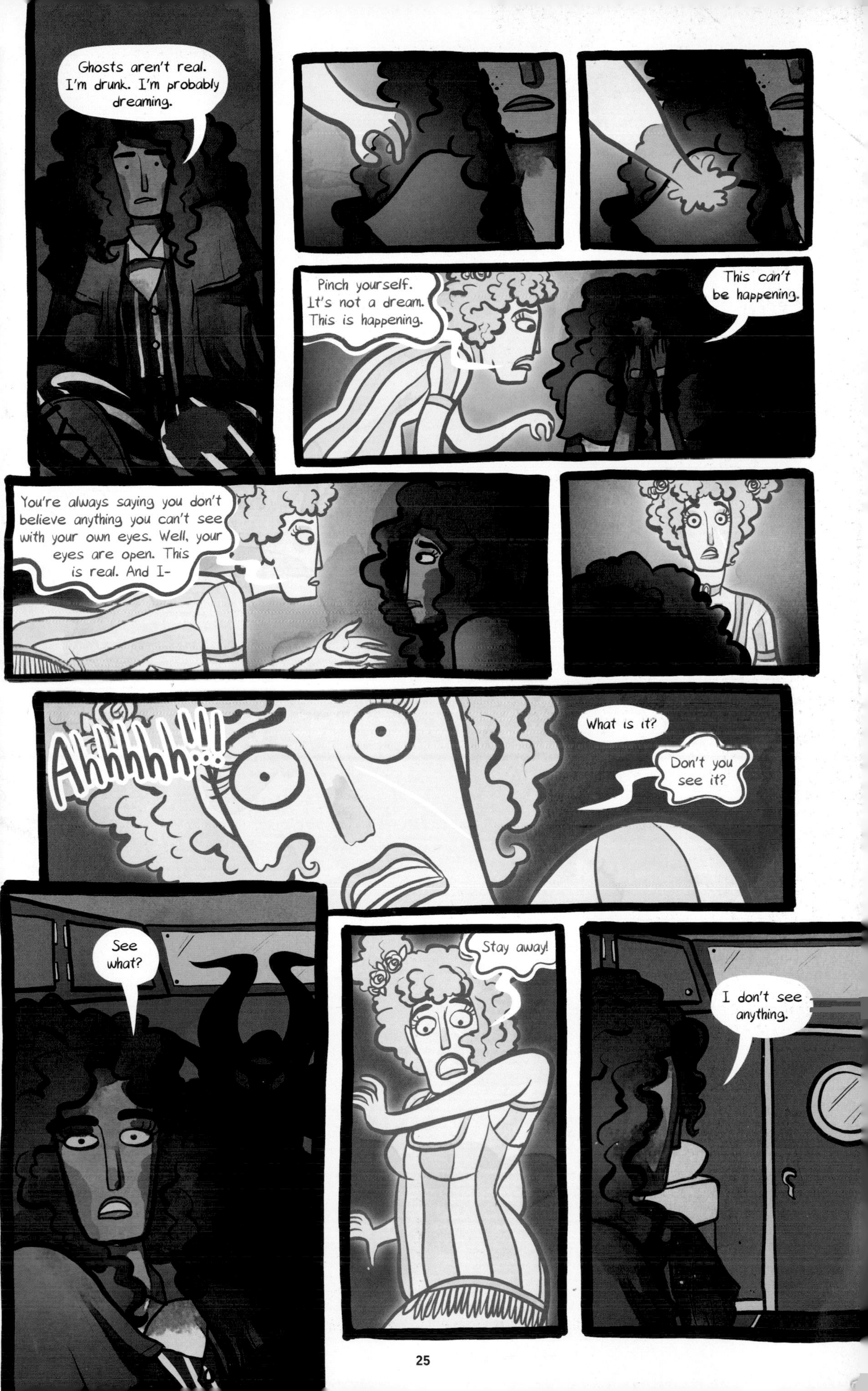

Ghosts aren't real. I'm drunk. I'm probably dreaming.
Pinch yourself. It's not a dream. This is happening.
This can't be happening.
You're always saying you don't believe anything you can't see with your own eyes. Well, your eyes are open. This is real. And I-
Ahhhhh!!!
What is it?
Don't you see it?
See what?
Stay away!
I don't see anything.

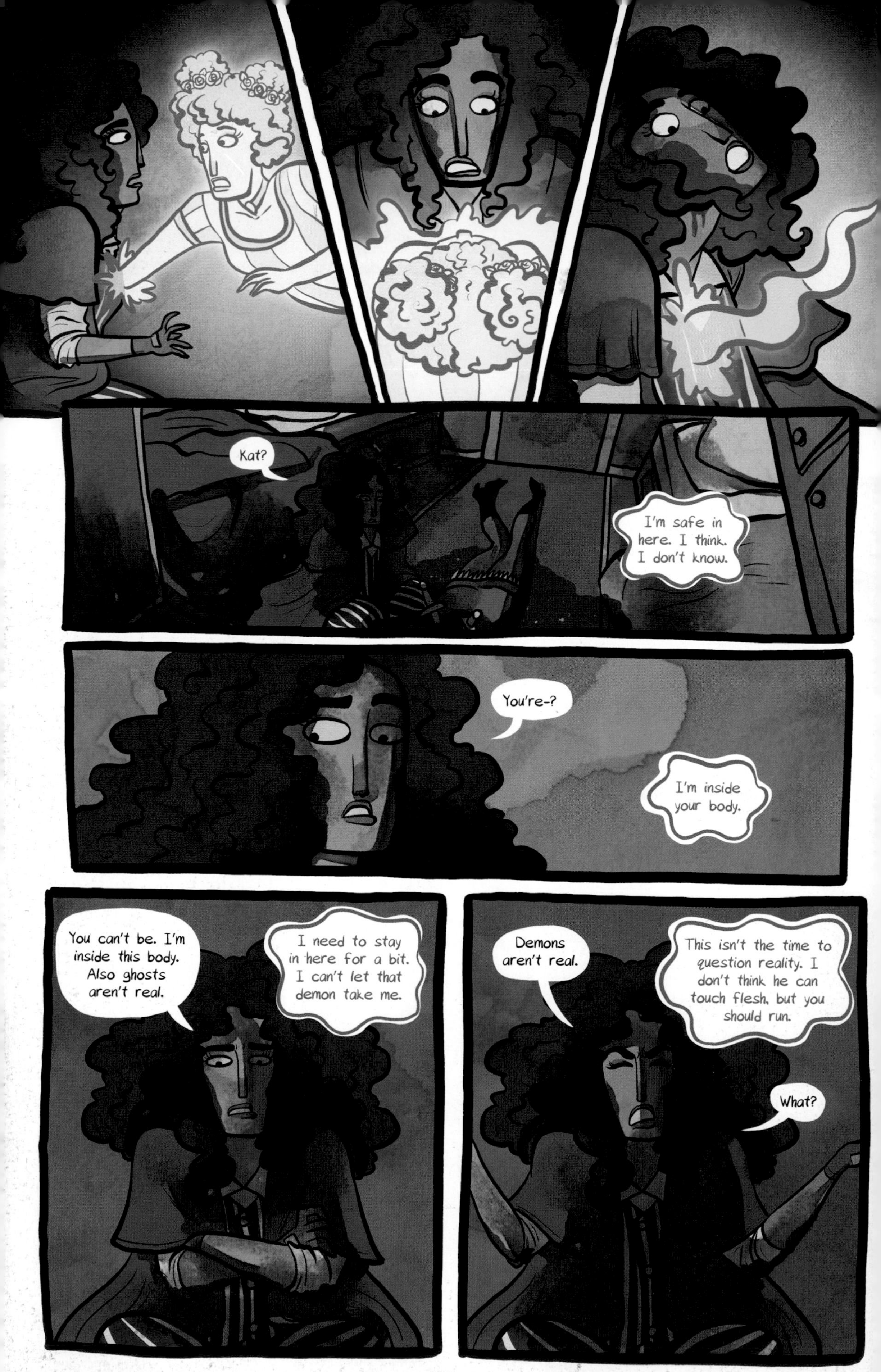
Kat?
I'm safe in here. I think. I don't know.
You're-?
I'm inside your body.
You can't be. I'm inside this body. Also ghosts aren't real.
I need to stay in here for a bit. I can't let that demon take me.
Demons aren't real.
This isn't the time to question reality. I don't think he can touch flesh, but you should run.
What?

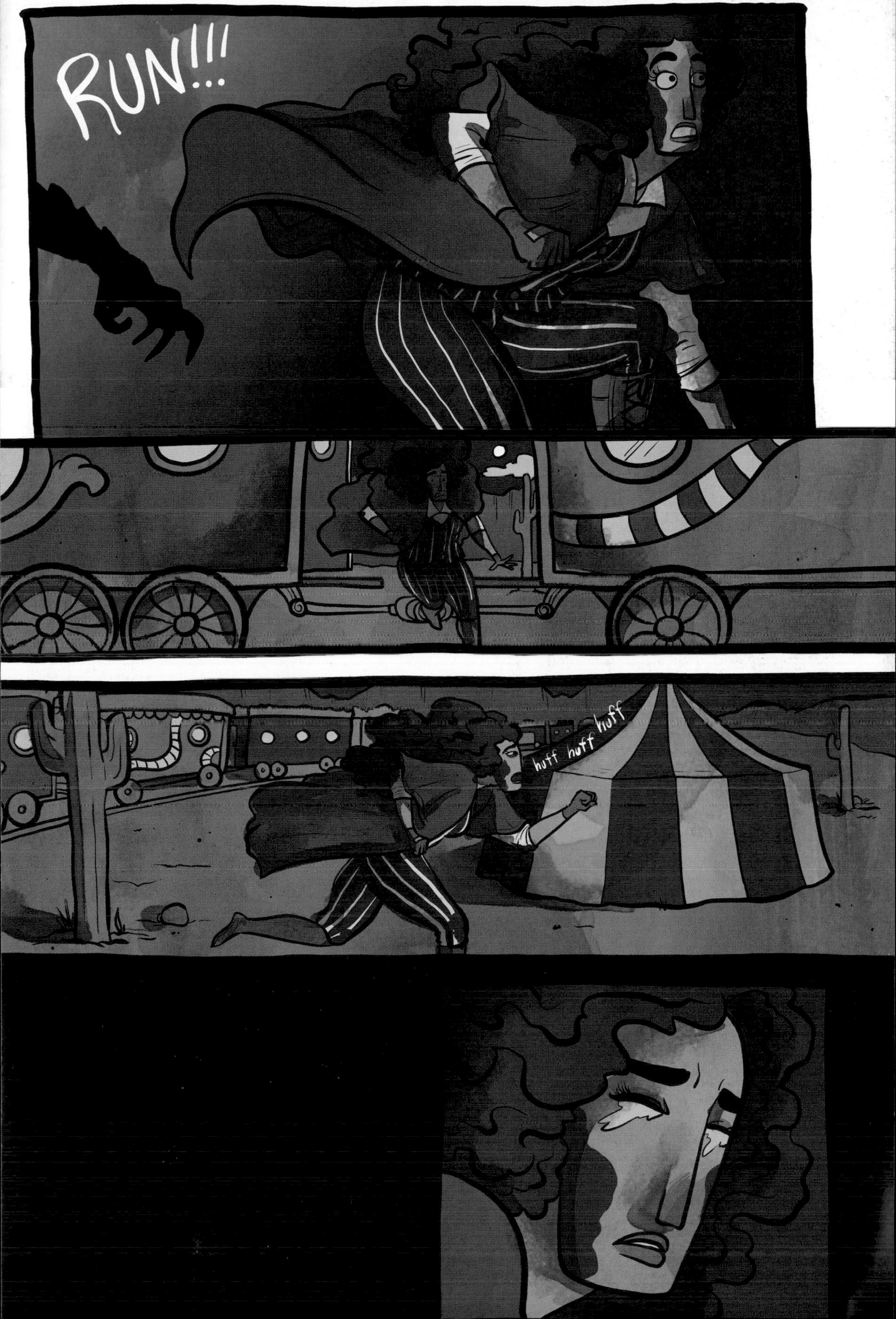
RUN!!!
huff huff huff

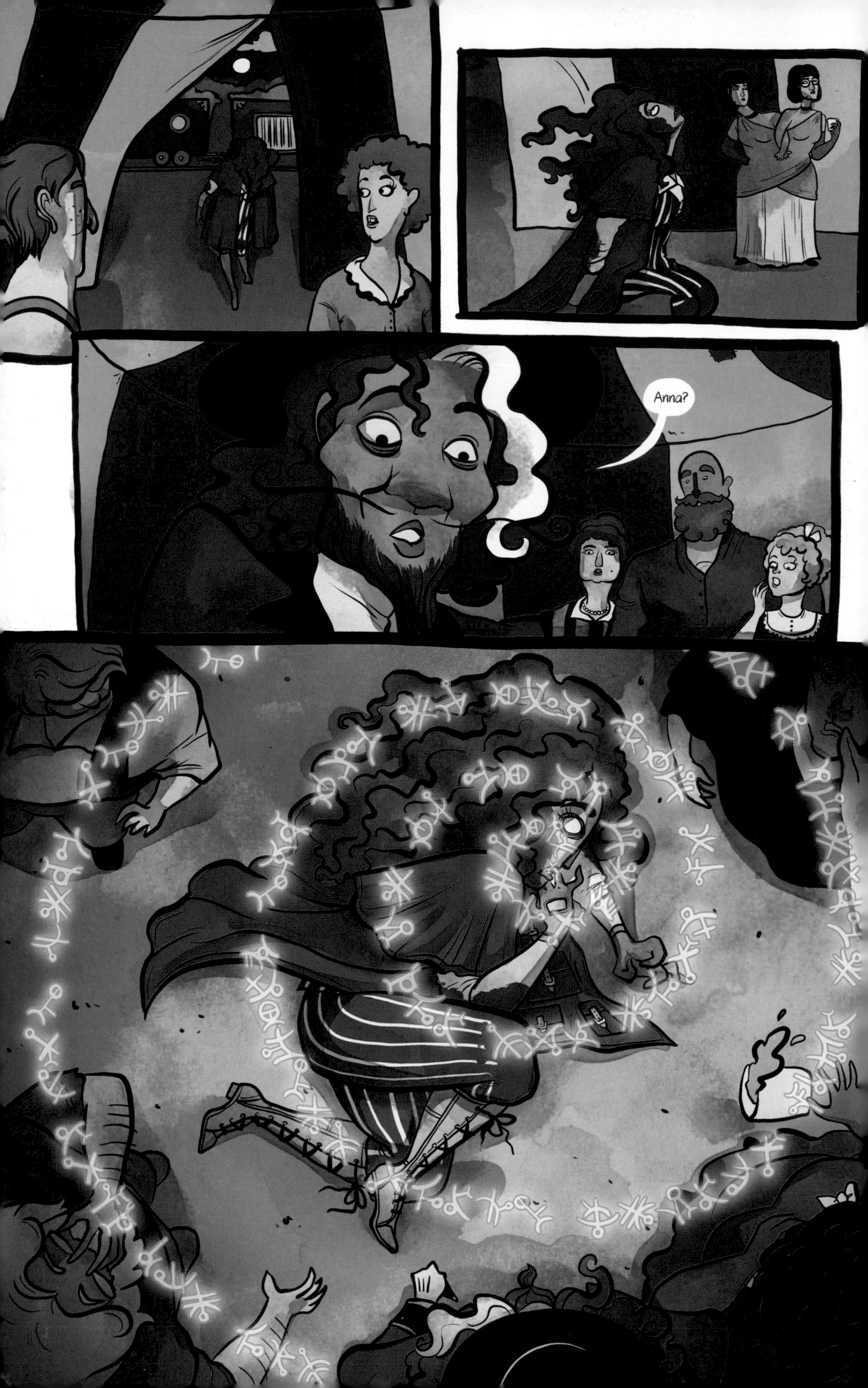
Anna?

Chapter Two

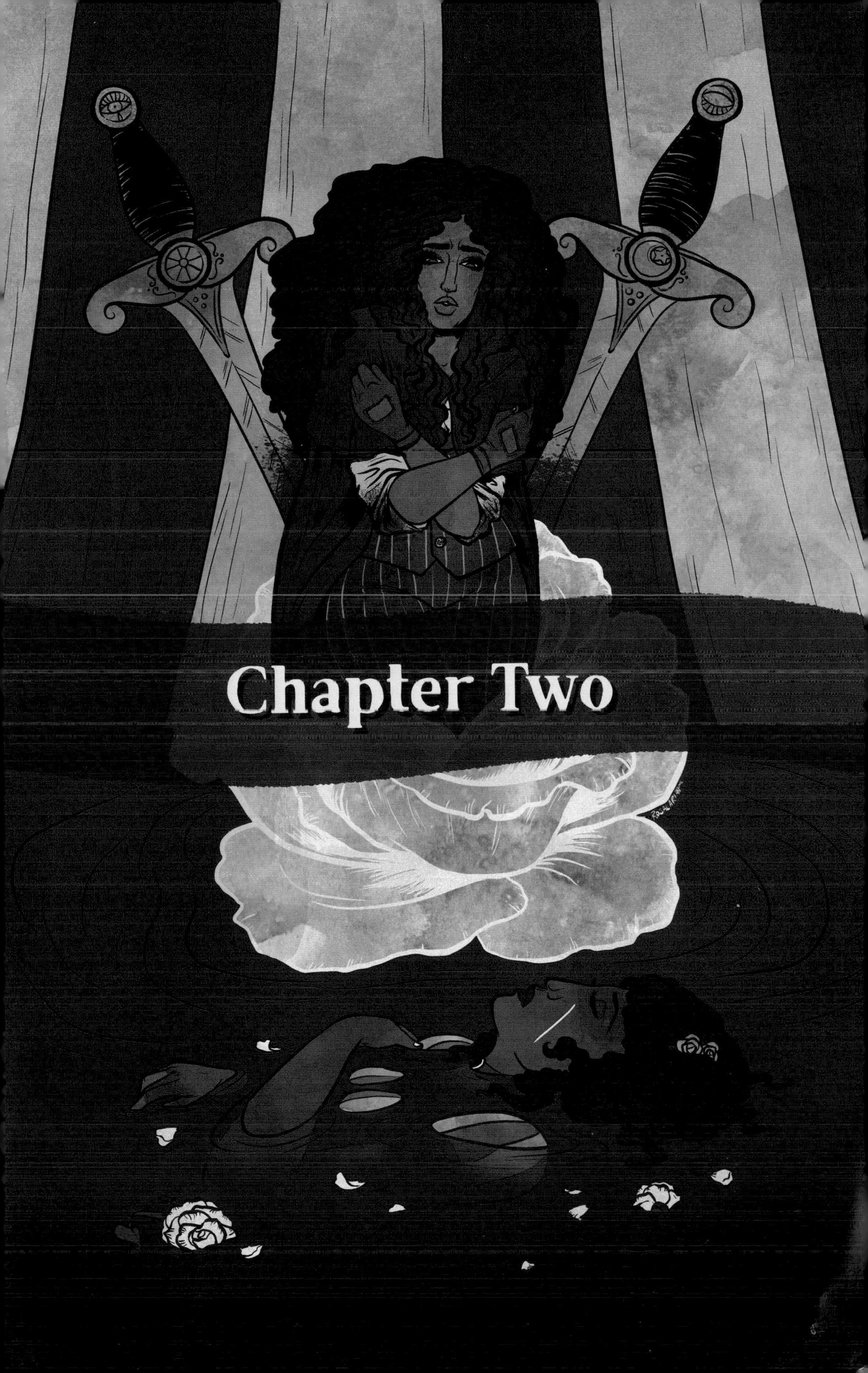

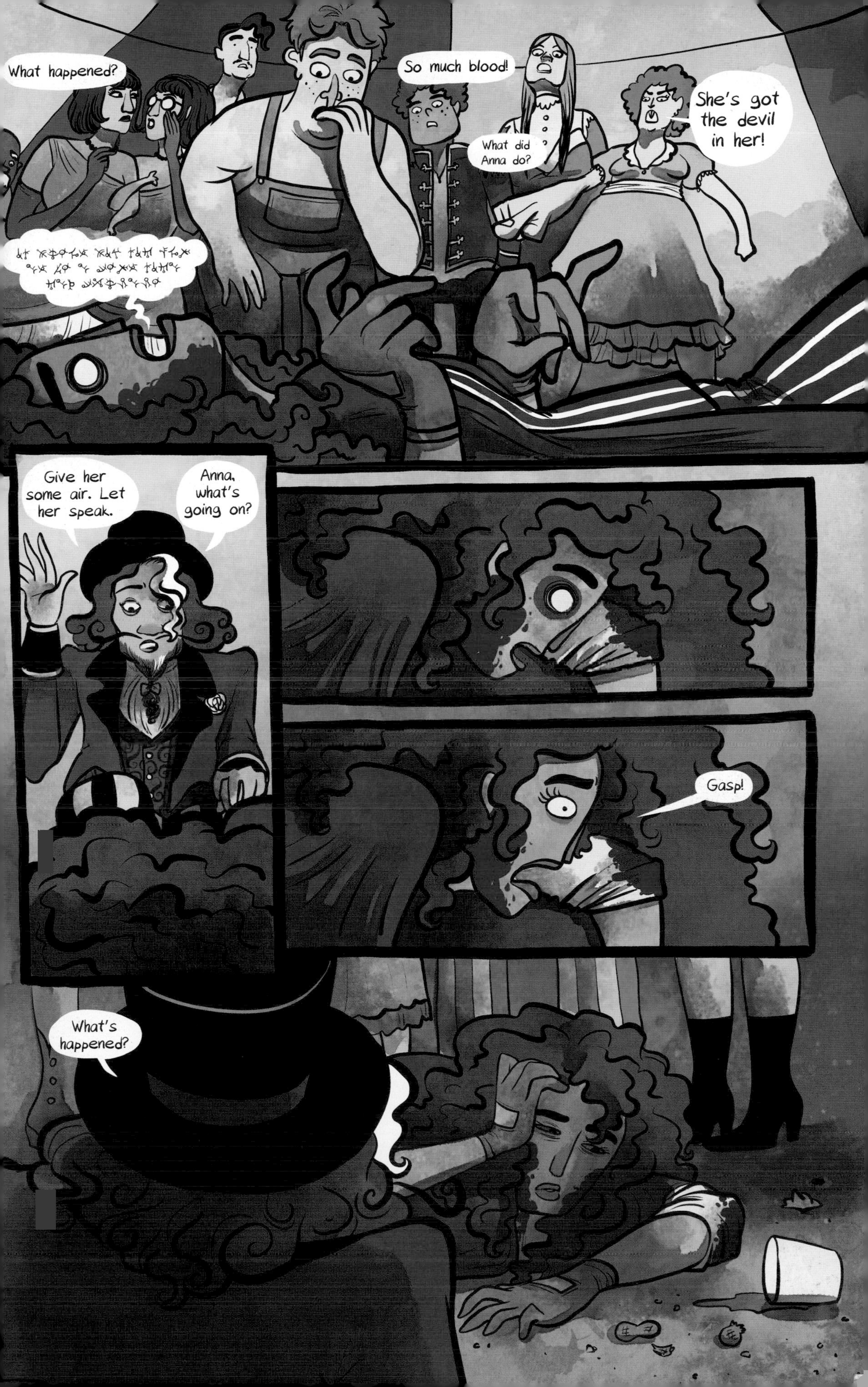
What happened?
So much blood!
What did Anna do?
She's got the devil in her!
Give her some air. Let her speak.
Anna, what's going on?
Gasp!
What's happened?

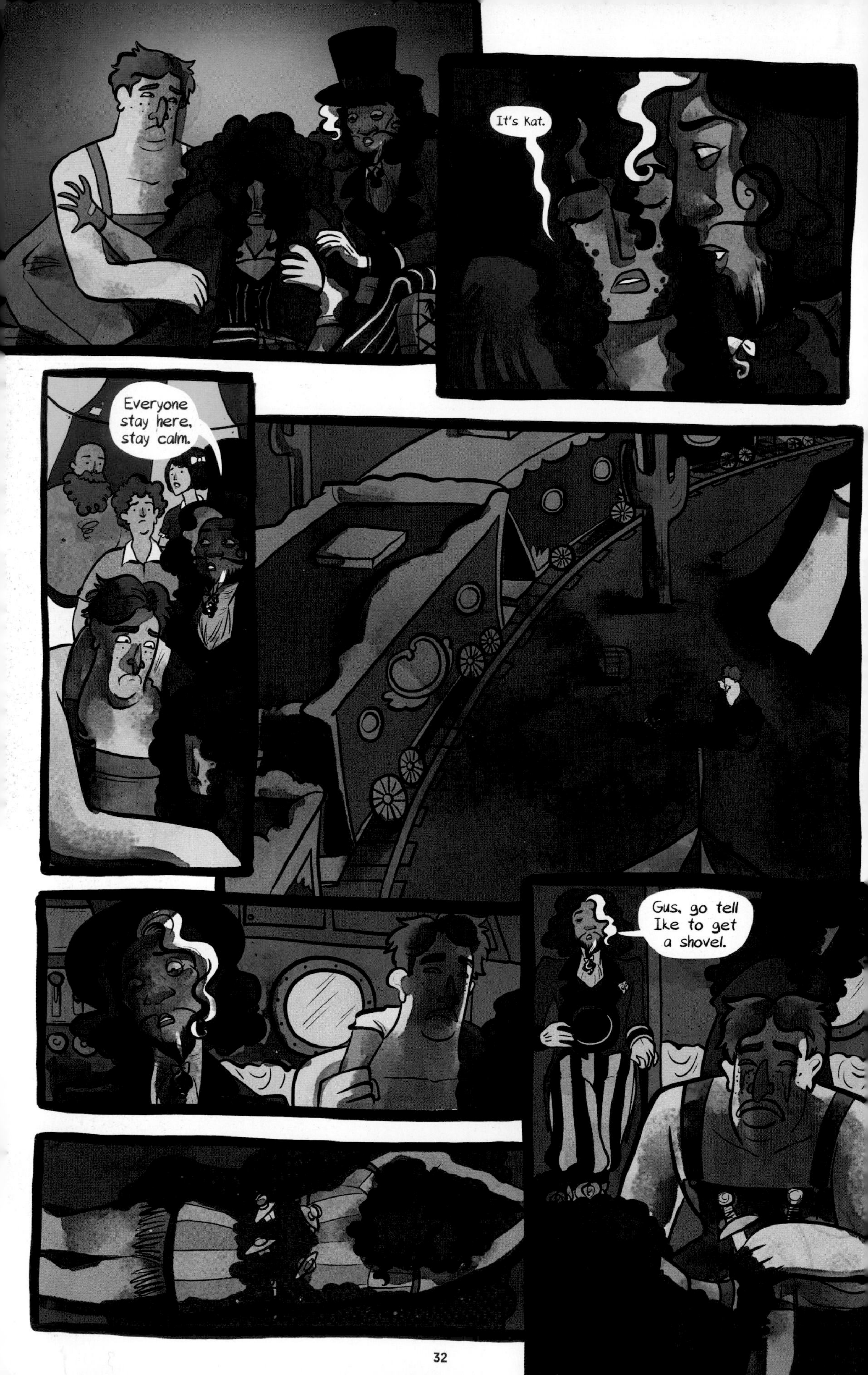
It's Kat.
Everyone stay here, stay calm.
Gus, go tell Ike to get a shovel.

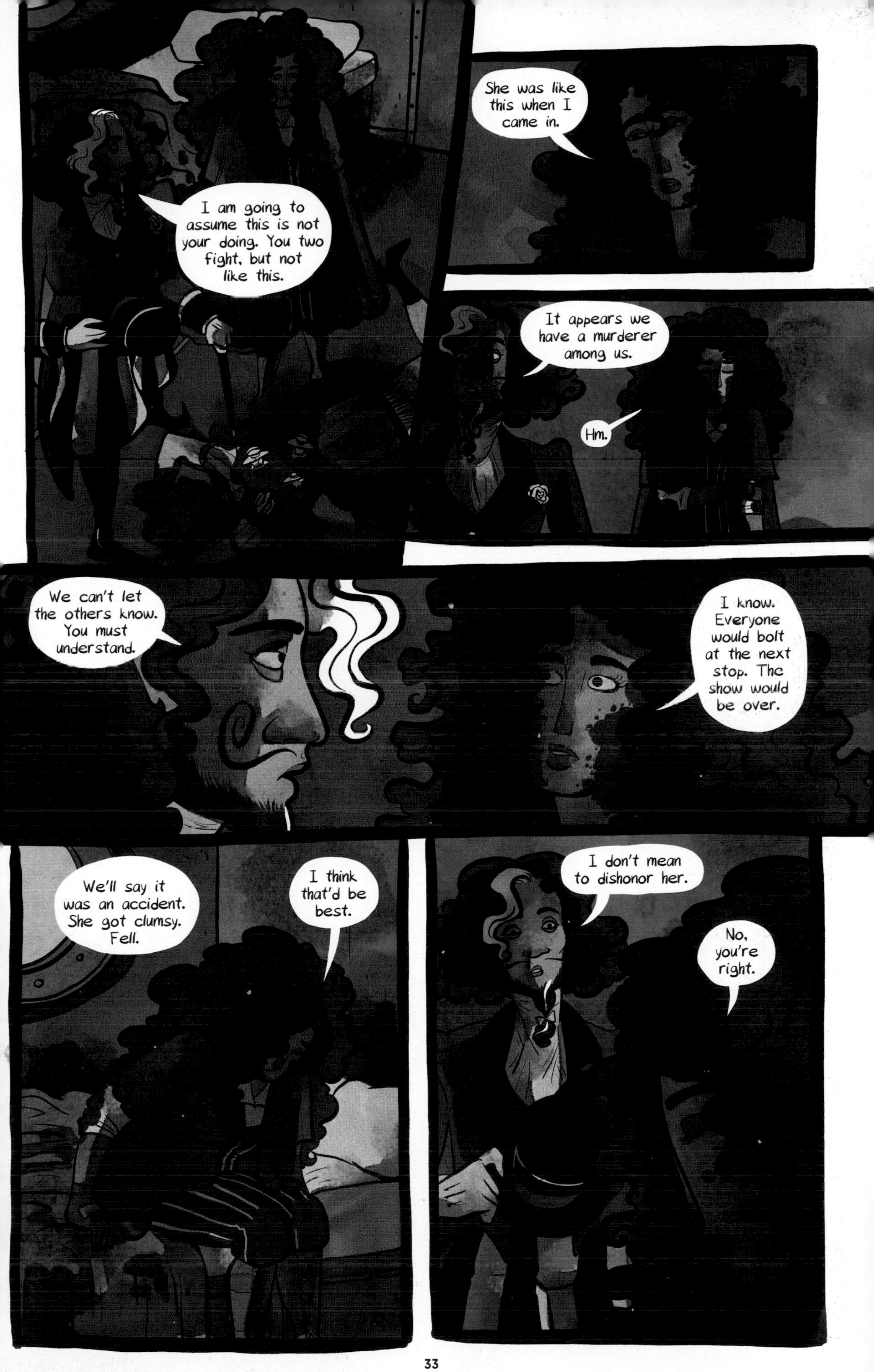
I am going to assume this is not your doing. You two fight, but not like this.
She was like this when I came in.
It appears we have a murderer among us.
Hm.
We can't let the others know. You must understand.
I know. Everyone would bolt at the next stop. The show would be over.
We'll say it was an accident. She got clumsy. Fell.
I think that'd be best.
I don't mean to dishonor her.
No, you're right.

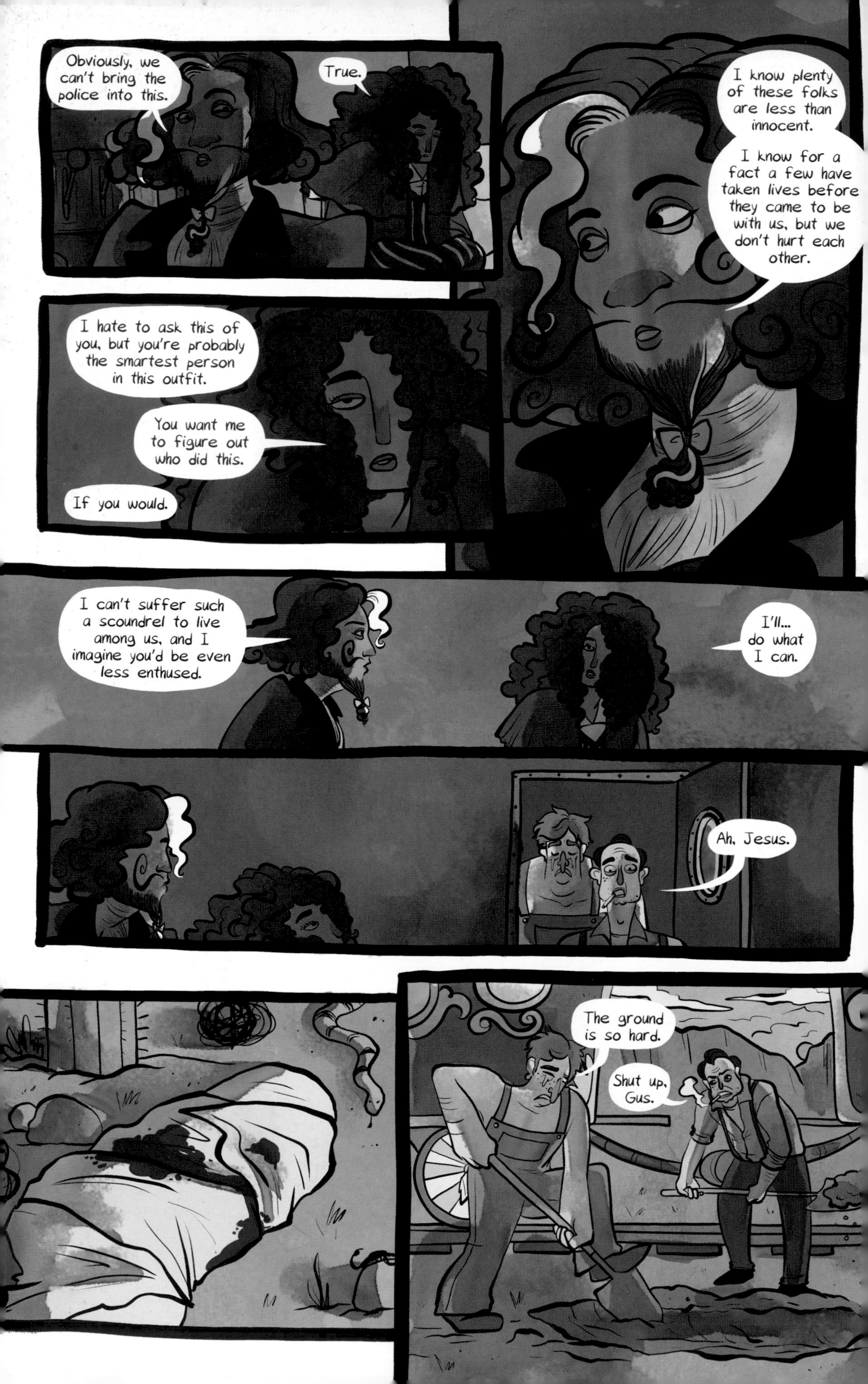
Obviously, we can't bring the police into this.
True.
I know plenty of these folks are less than innocent.
I know for a fact a few have taken lives before they came to be with us, but we don't hurt each other.
I hate to ask this of you, but you're probably the smartest person in this outfit.
You want me to figure out who did this.
If you would.
I can't suffer such a scoundrel to live among us, and I imagine you'd be even less enthused.
I'll... do what I can.
Ah, Jesus.
The ground is so hard.
Shut up, Gus.

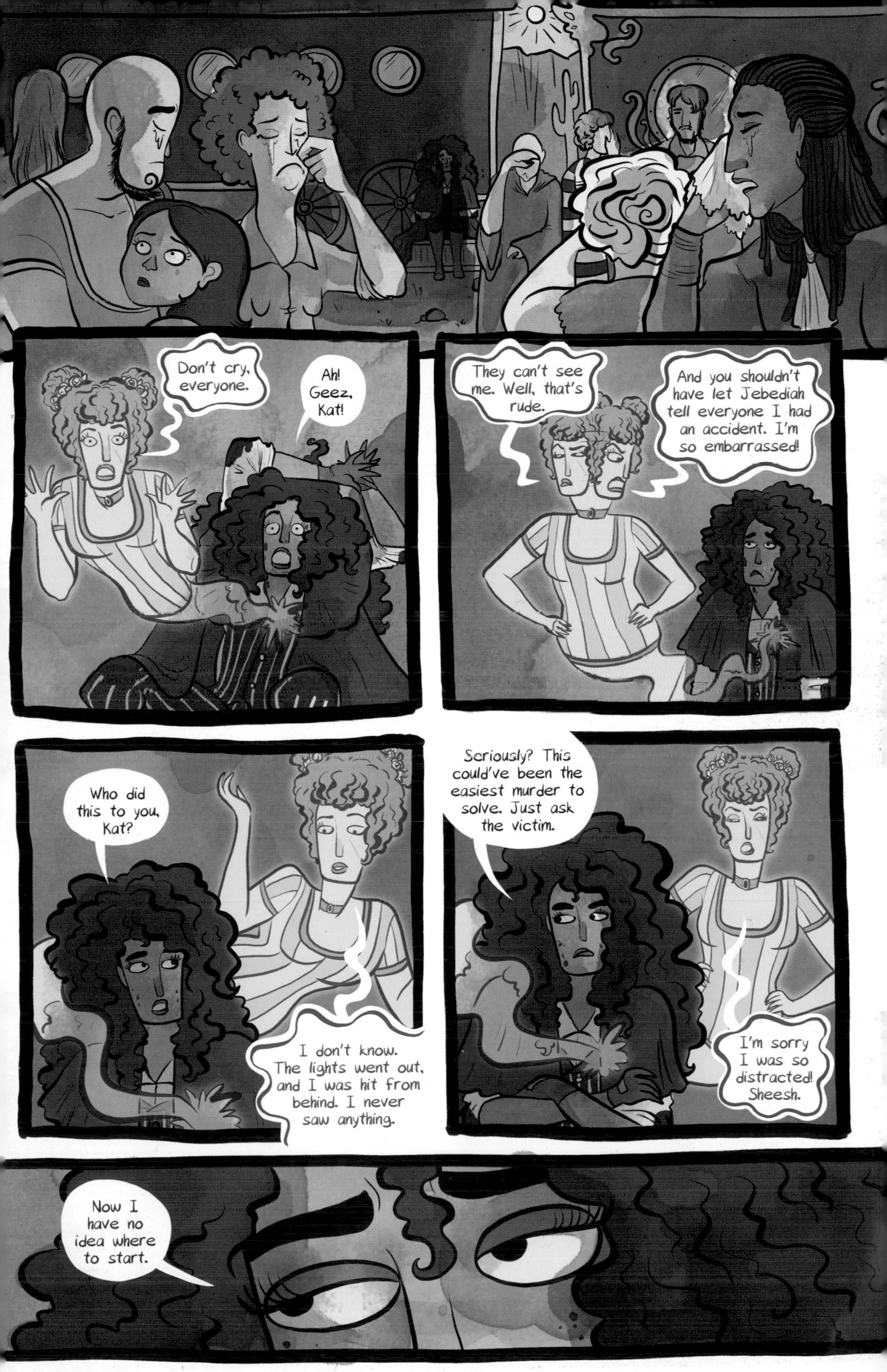
Don't cry, everyone.
Ah! Geez, Kat!
They can't see me. Well, that's rude.
And you shouldn't have let Jebediah tell everyone I had an accident. I'm so embarrassed!
Who did this to you, Kat?
I don't know. The lights went out, and I was hit from behind. I never saw anything.
Seriously? This could've been the easiest murder to solve. Just ask the victim.
I'm sorry I was so distracted! Sheesh.
Now I have no idea where to start.

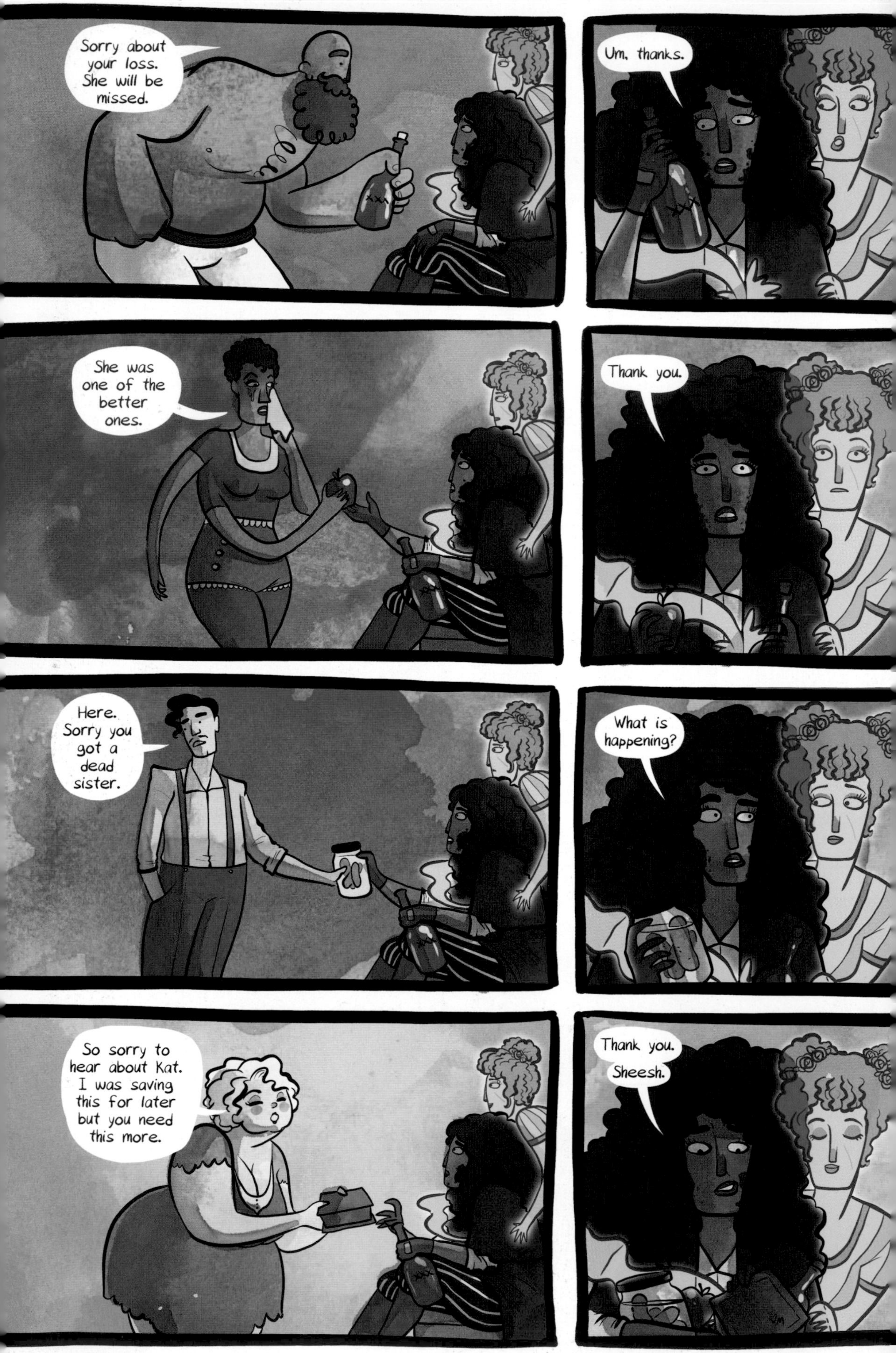
Sorry about your loss. She will be missed.
Um, thanks.
She was one of the better ones.
Thank you.
Here. Sorry you got a dead sister.
What is happening?
So sorry to hear about Kat. I was saving this for later but you need this more.
Thank you.
Sheesh.

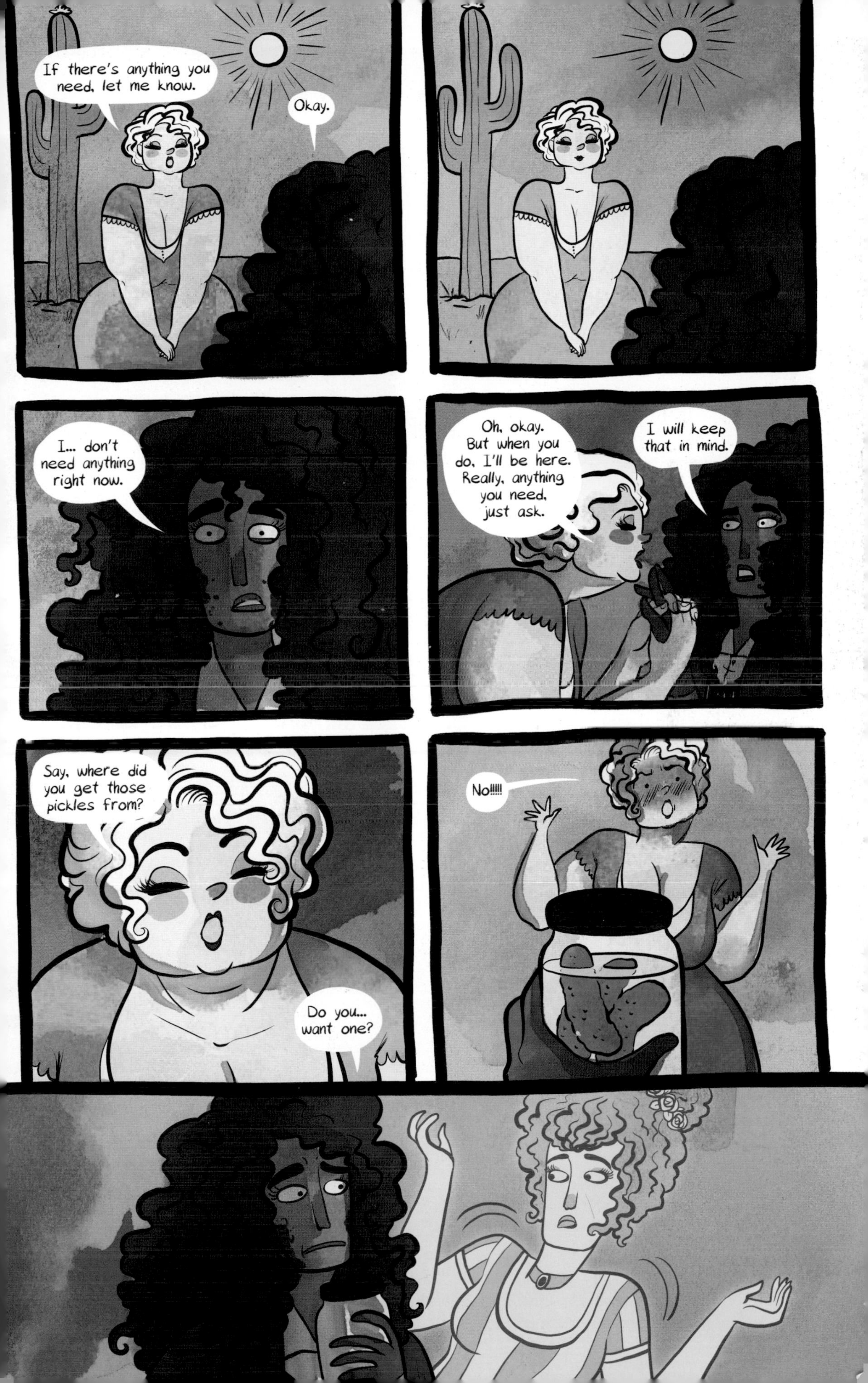
If there's anything you need, let me know.
Okay.
I... don't need anything right now.
Oh, okay. But when you do, I'll be here. Really, anything you need, just ask.
I will keep that in mind.
Say, where did you get those pickles from?
Do you... want one?
No!!!!

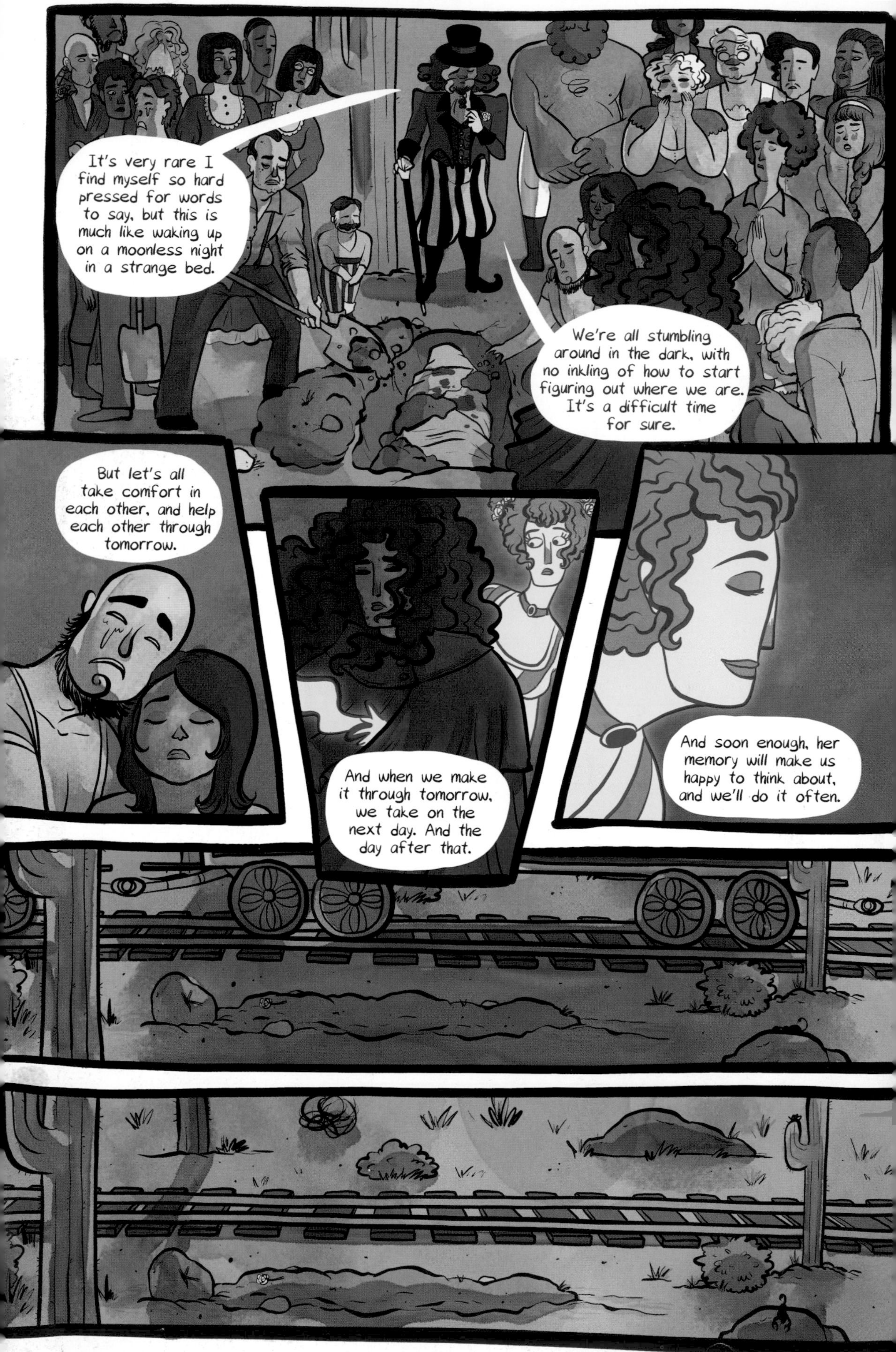
It's very rare I find myself so hard pressed for words to say, but this is much like waking up on a moonless night in a strange bed.
We're all stumbling around in the dark, with no inkling of how to start figuring out where we are. It's a difficult time for sure.
But let's all take comfort in each other, and help each other through tomorrow.
And when we make it through tomorrow, we take on the next day. And the day after that.
And soon enough, her memory will make us happy to think about, and we'll do it often.

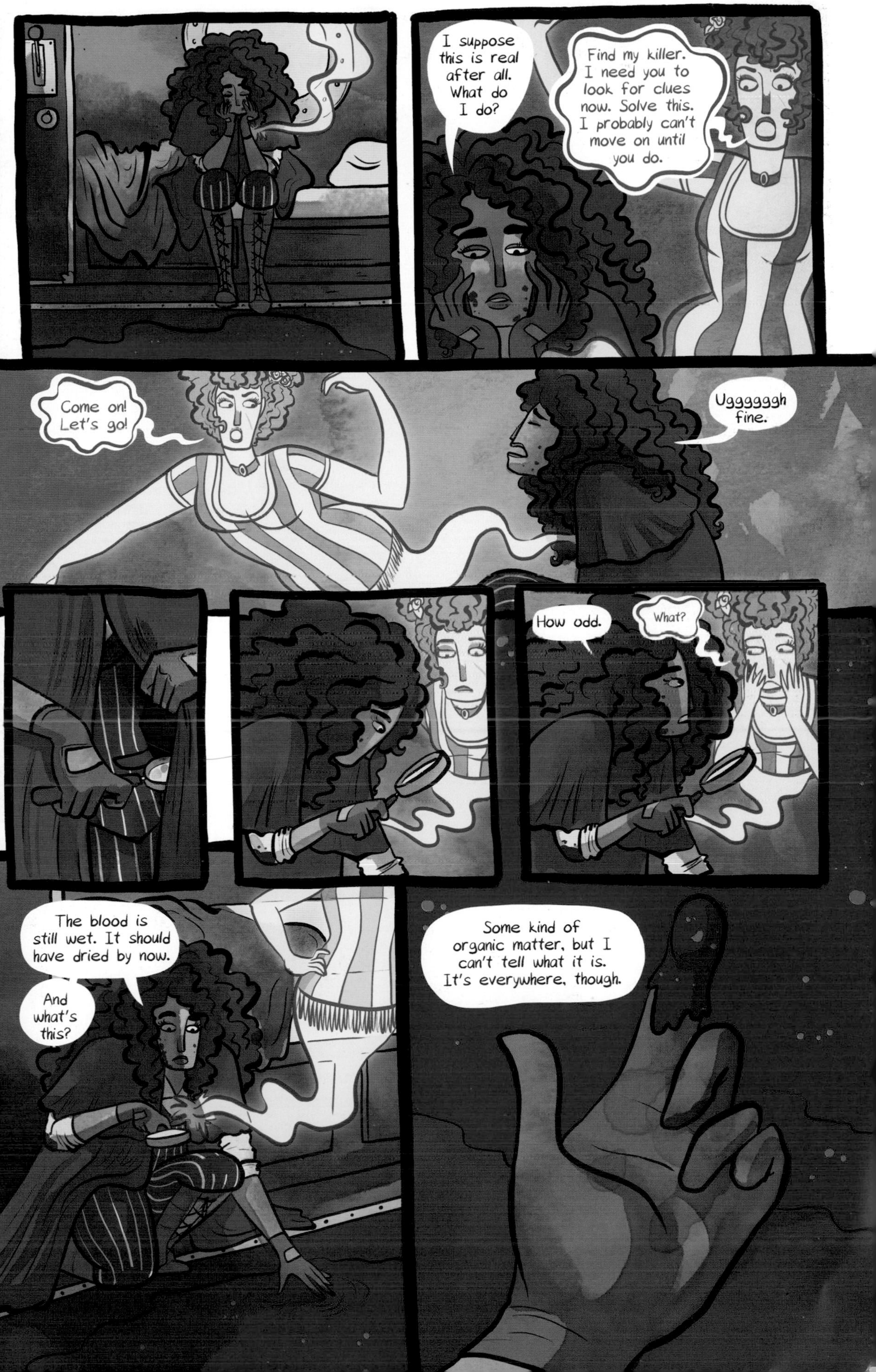
I suppose this is real after all. What do I do?
Find my killer. I need you to look for clues now. Solve this. I probably can't move on until you do.
Come on! Let's go!
Uggggggh fine.
How odd.
What?
The blood is still wet. It should have dried by now.
And what's this?
Some kind of organic matter, but I can't tell what it is. It's everywhere, though.

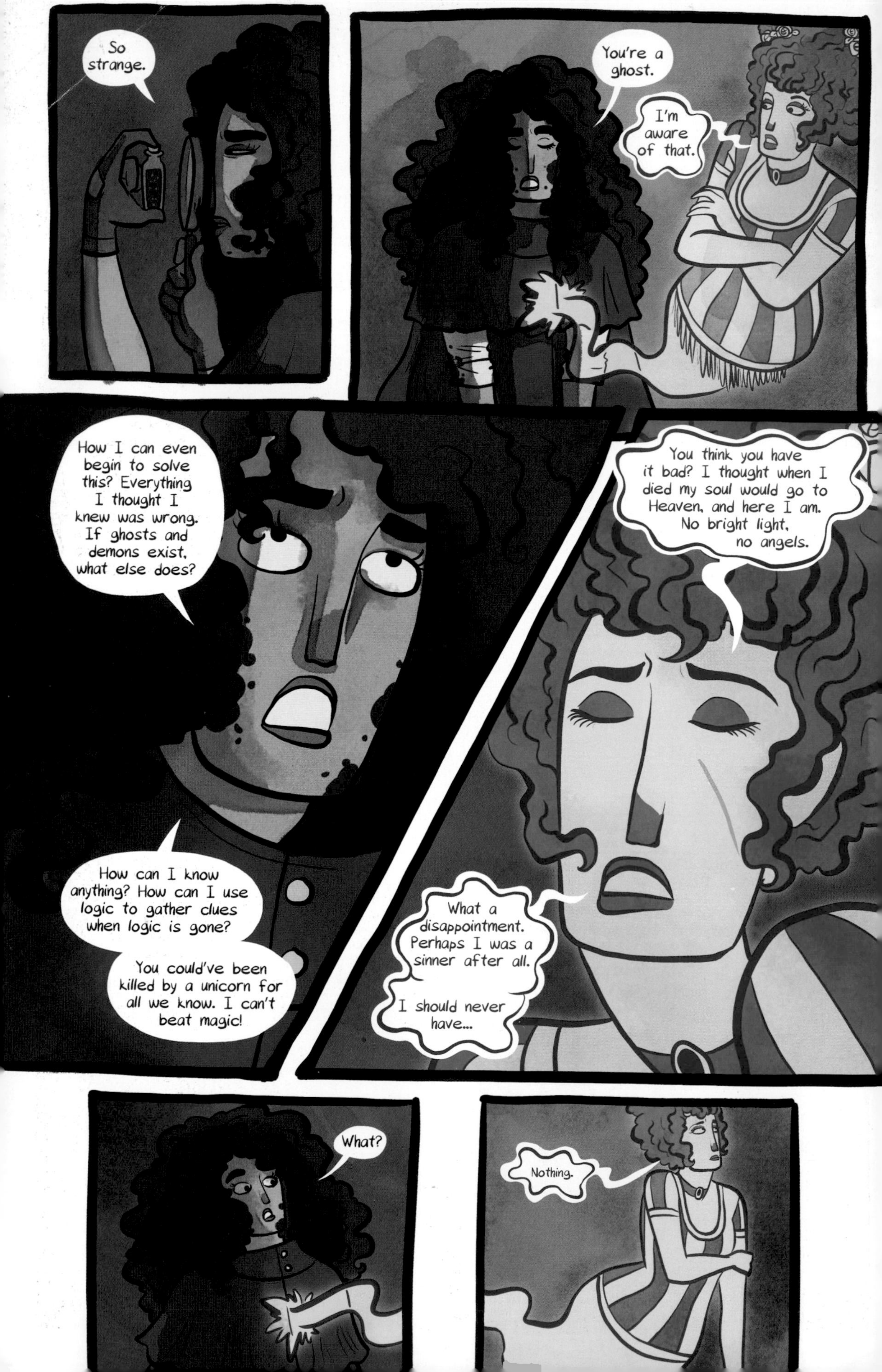
So strange.
You're a ghost.
I'm aware of that.
How I can even begin to solve this? Everything I thought I knew was wrong. If ghosts and demons exist, what else does?
You think you have it bad? I thought when I died my soul would go to Heaven, and here I am. No bright light, no angels.
How can I know anything? How can I use logic to gather clues when logic is gone?
You could've been killed by a unicorn for all we know. I can't beat magic!
What a disappointment. Perhaps I was a sinner after all.
I should never have...
What?
Nothing.

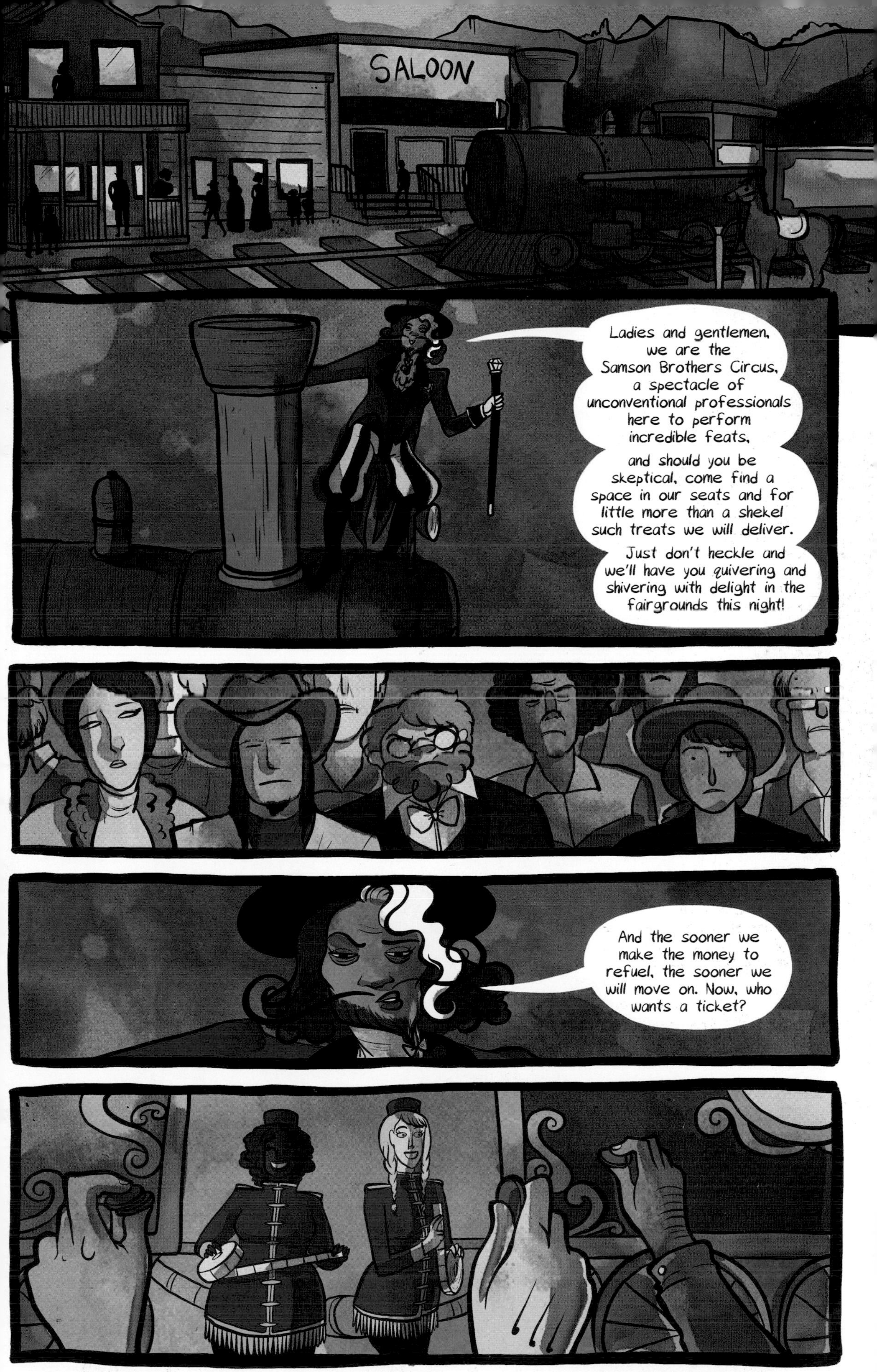
SALOON
Ladies and gentlemen, we are the Samson Brothers Circus, a spectacle of unconventional professionals here to perform incredible feats,
and should you be skeptical, come find a space in our seats and for little more than a shekel such treats we will deliver.
Just don't heckle and we'll have you quivering and shivering with delight in the fairgrounds this night!
And the sooner we make the money to refuel, the sooner we will move on. Now, who wants a ticket?

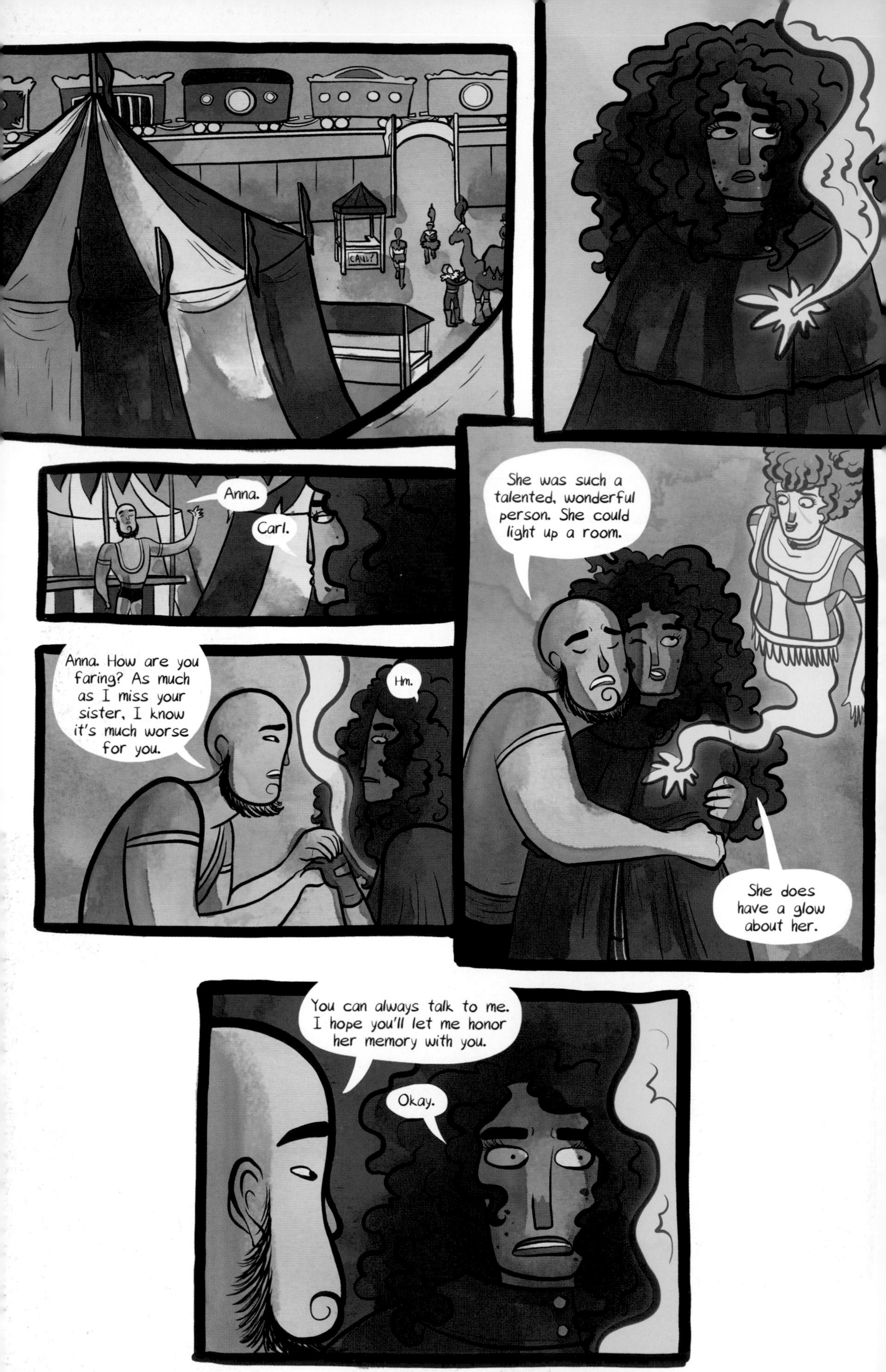
CANDY
Anna.
Carl.
Anna. How are you faring? As much as I miss your sister, I know it's much worse for you.
Hm.
She was such a talented, wonderful person. She could light up a room.
She does have a glow about her.
You can always talk to me. I hope you'll let me honor her memory with you.
Okay.

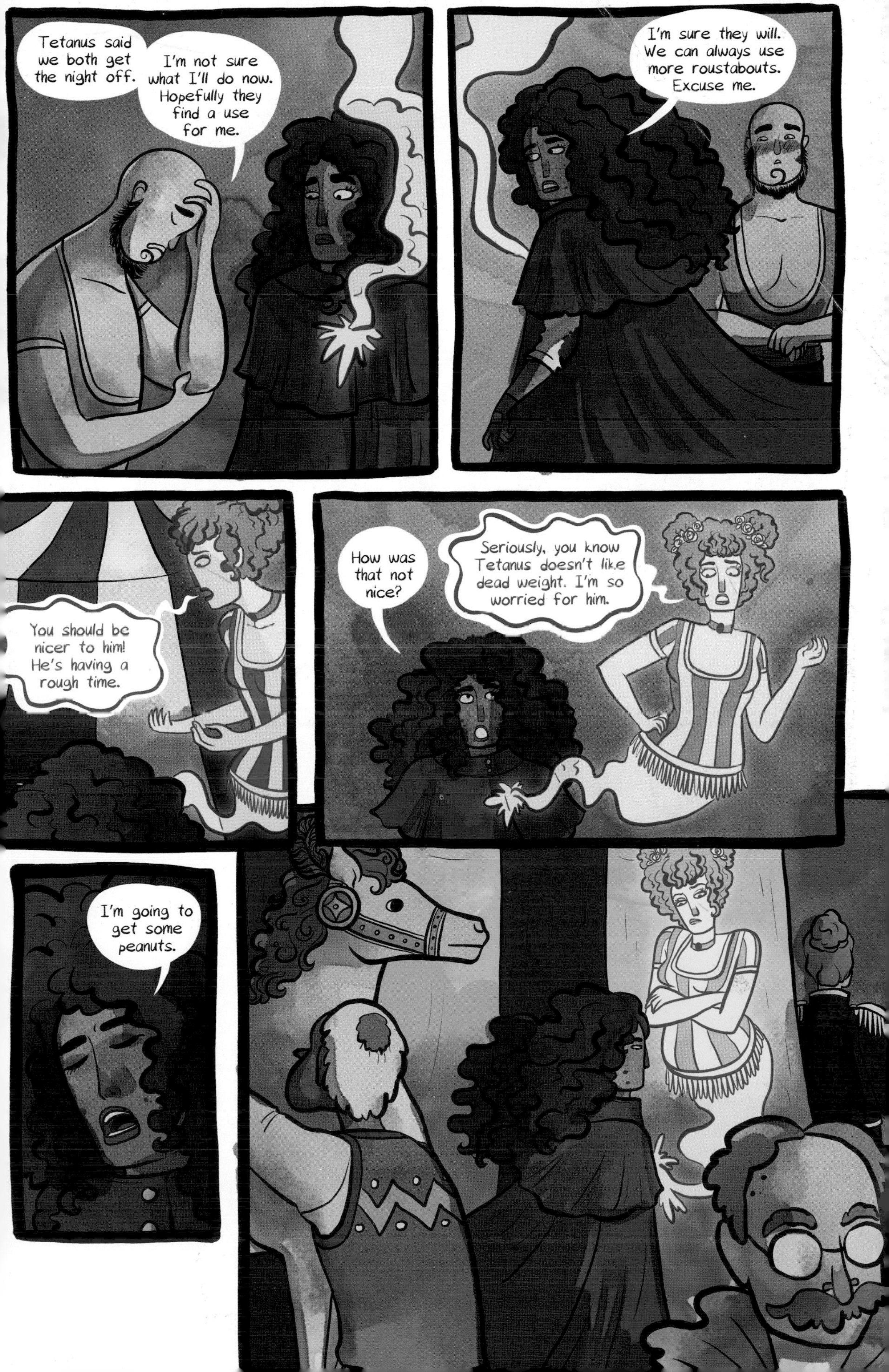
Tetanus said we both get the night off.
I'm not sure what I'll do now. Hopefully they find a use for me.
I'm sure they will. We can always use more roustabouts. Excuse me.
You should be nicer to him! He's having a rough time.
How was that not nice?
Seriously, you know Tetanus doesn't like dead weight. I'm so worried for him.
I'm going to get some peanuts.

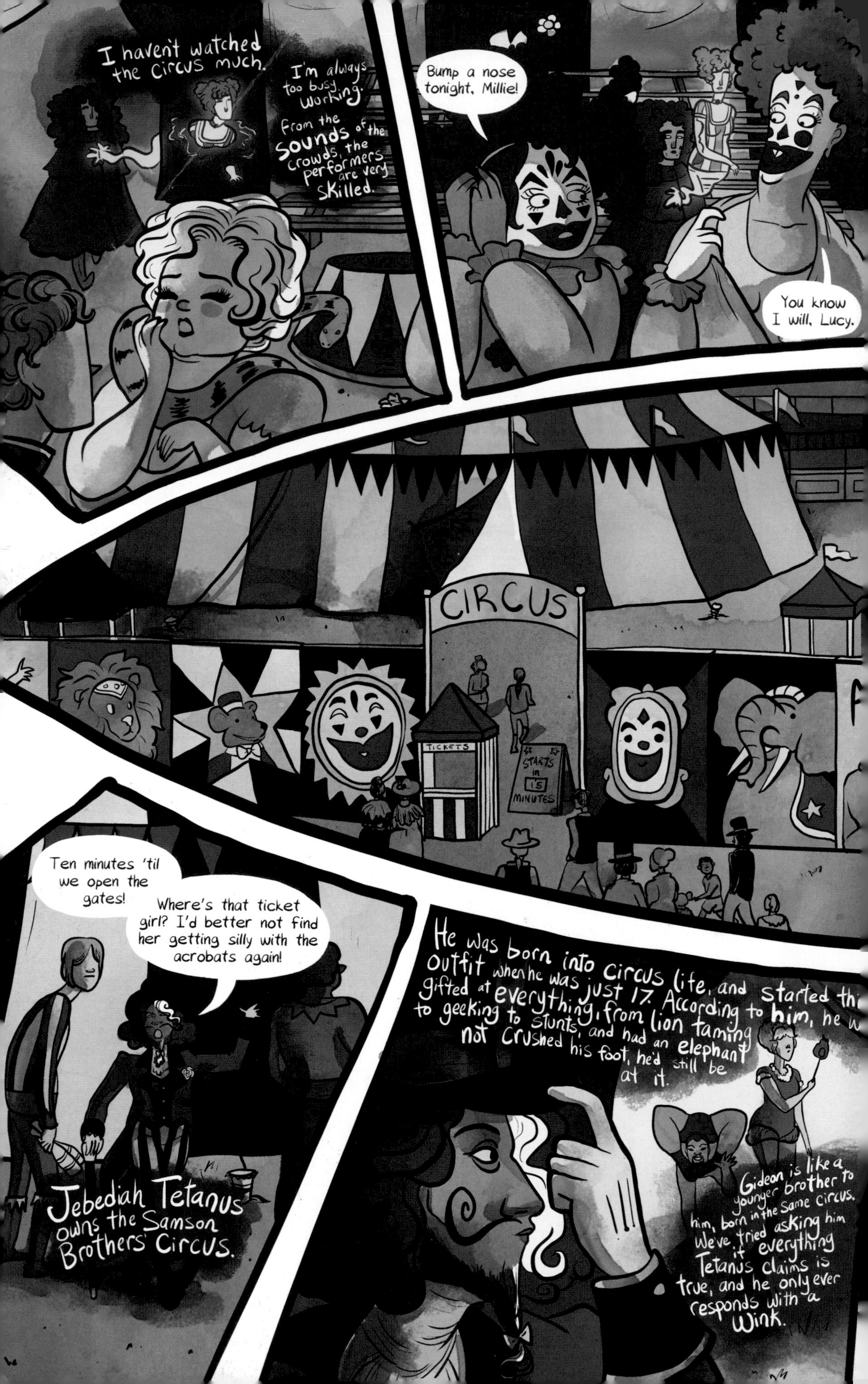

I haven't watched the circus much.
I'm always too busy working.
From the sounds of the crowds, the performers are very skilled.
Bump a nose tonight, Millie!
You know I will, Lucy.
CIRCUS
TICKETS
STARTS in 15 MINUTES
Ten minutes 'til we open the gates!
Where's that ticket girl? I'd better not find her getting silly with the acrobats again!
Jebediah Tetanus owns the Samson Brothers' Circus.
He was born into circus life, and started thi
outfit when he was just 17. According to him, he w
gifted at everything, from lion taming
to geeking to stunts, and had an elephant
not crushed his foot, he'd still be
at it.
Gideon is like a younger brother to him, born in the same circus. We've tried asking him if everything Tetanus claims is true, and he only ever responds with a wink.

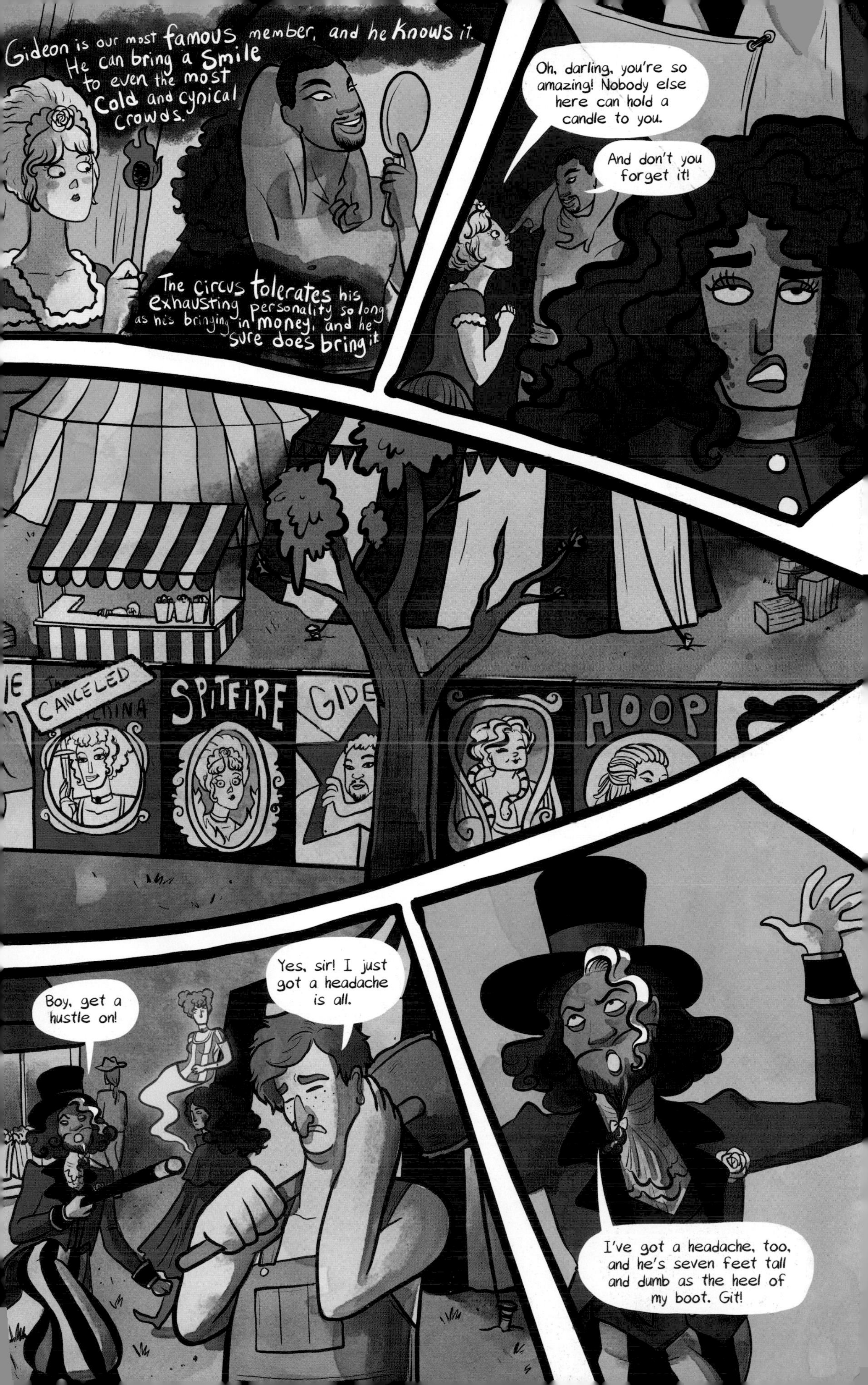
Gideon is our most famous member, and he knows it. He can bring a smile to even the most cold and cynical crowds.
The circus tolerates his exhausting personality so long as he's bringing in money, and he sure does bring it.
Oh, darling, you're so amazing! Nobody else here can hold a candle to you.
And don't you forget it!
CANCELED
SPITFIRE
GIDE
HOOP
Boy, get a hustle on!
Yes, sir! I just got a headache is all.
I've got a headache, too, and he's seven feet tall and dumb as the heel of my boot. Git!

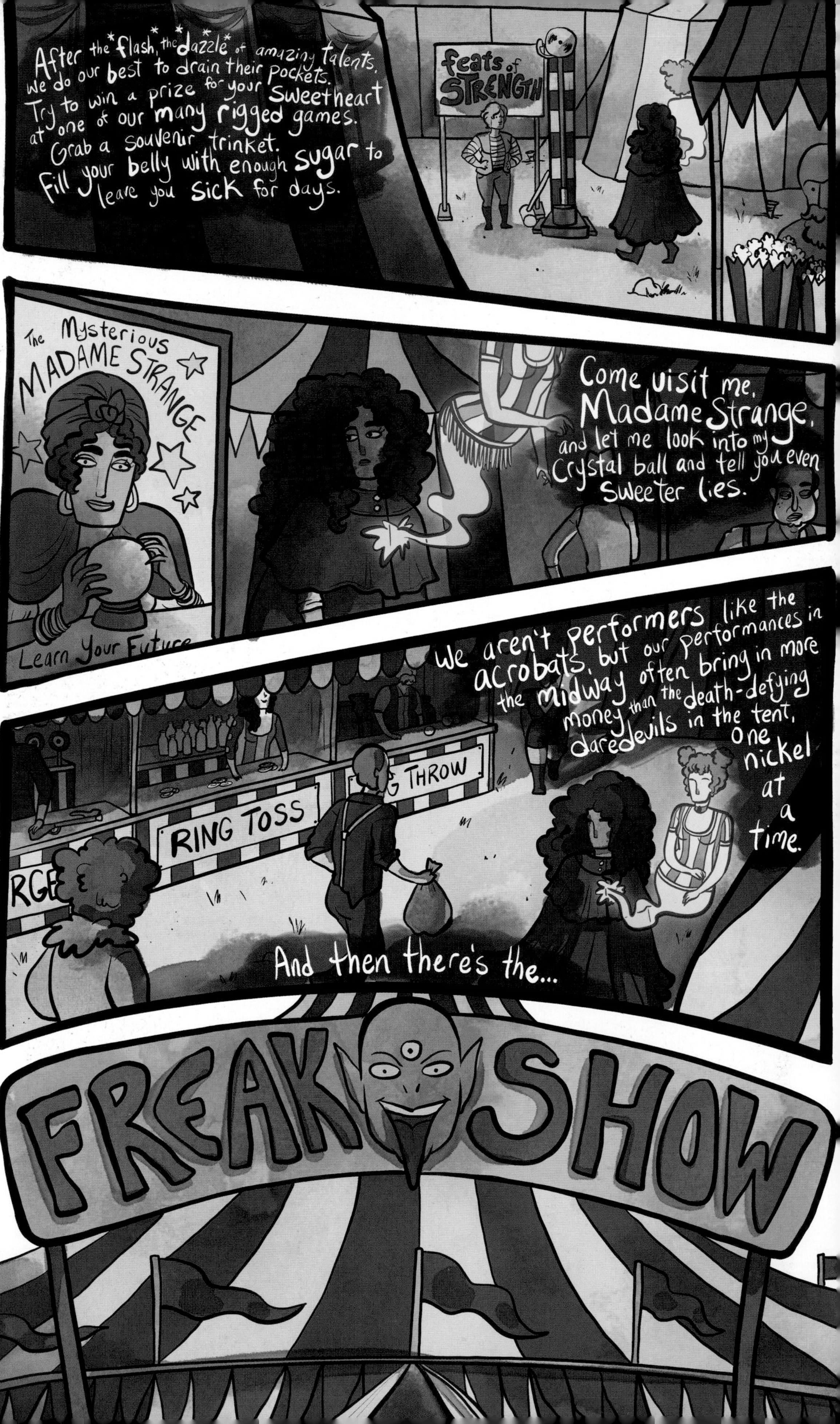
After the flash, the dazzle of amazing talents, we do our best to drain their pockets. Try to win a prize for your sweetheart at one of our many rigged games. Grab a souvenir trinket. Fill your belly with enough sugar to leave you sick for days.
feats of STRENGTH
The Mysterious MADAME STRANGE
Learn Your Future
Come visit me, Madame Strange, and let me look into my crystal ball and tell you even sweeter lies.
We aren't performers like the acrobats, but our performances in the midway often bring in more money than the death-defying daredevils in the tent, one nickel at a time.
RING TOSS
G THROW
RGE
And then there's the...
FREAK SHOW

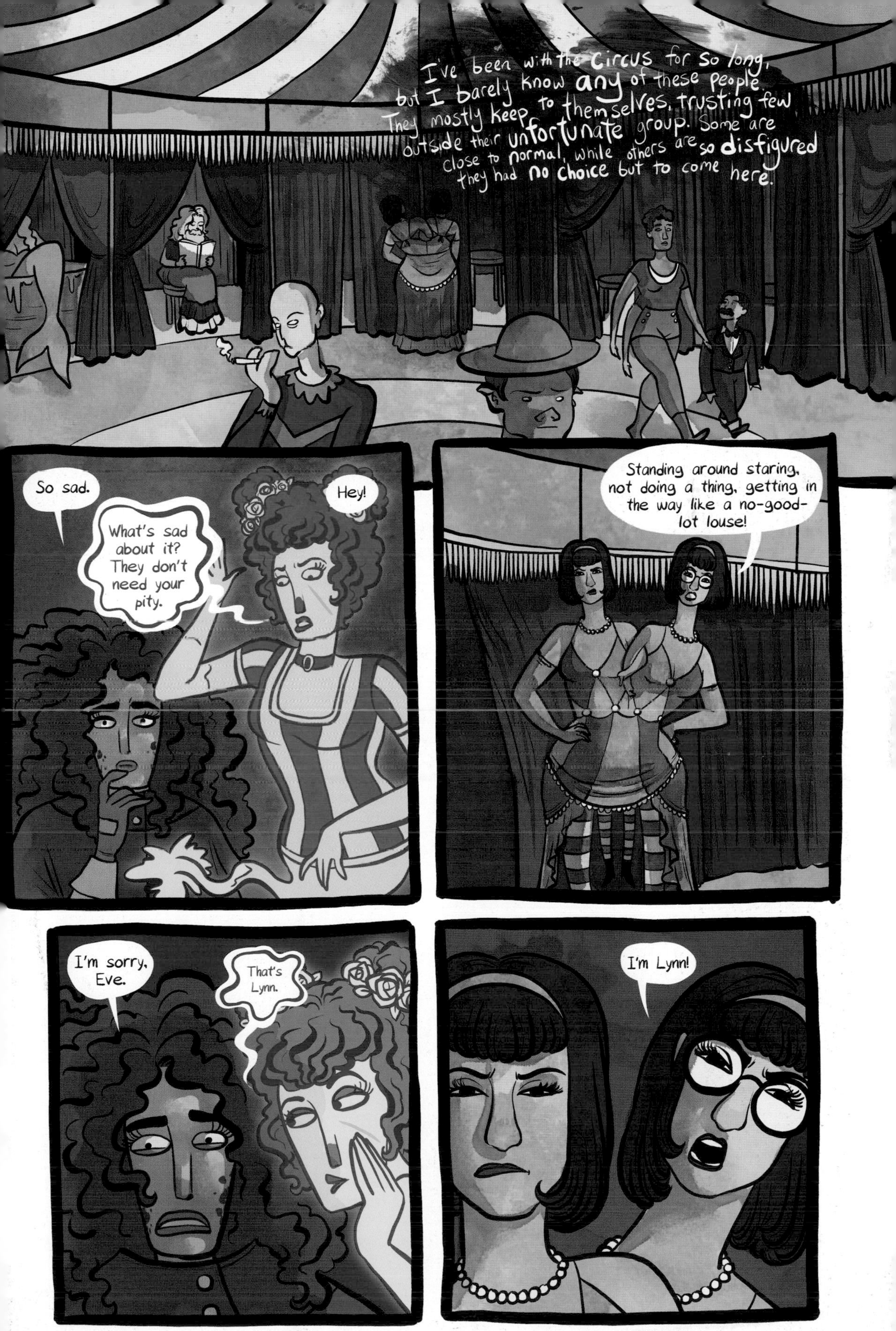
I've been with the circus for so long, but I barely know any of these people. They mostly keep to themselves, trusting few outside their unfortunate group. Some are close to normal, while others are so disfigured they had no choice but to come here.
So sad.
What's sad about it? They don't need your pity.
Hey!
Standing around staring, not doing a thing, getting in the way like a no-good-lot louse!
I'm sorry, Eve.
That's Lynn.
I'm Lynn!

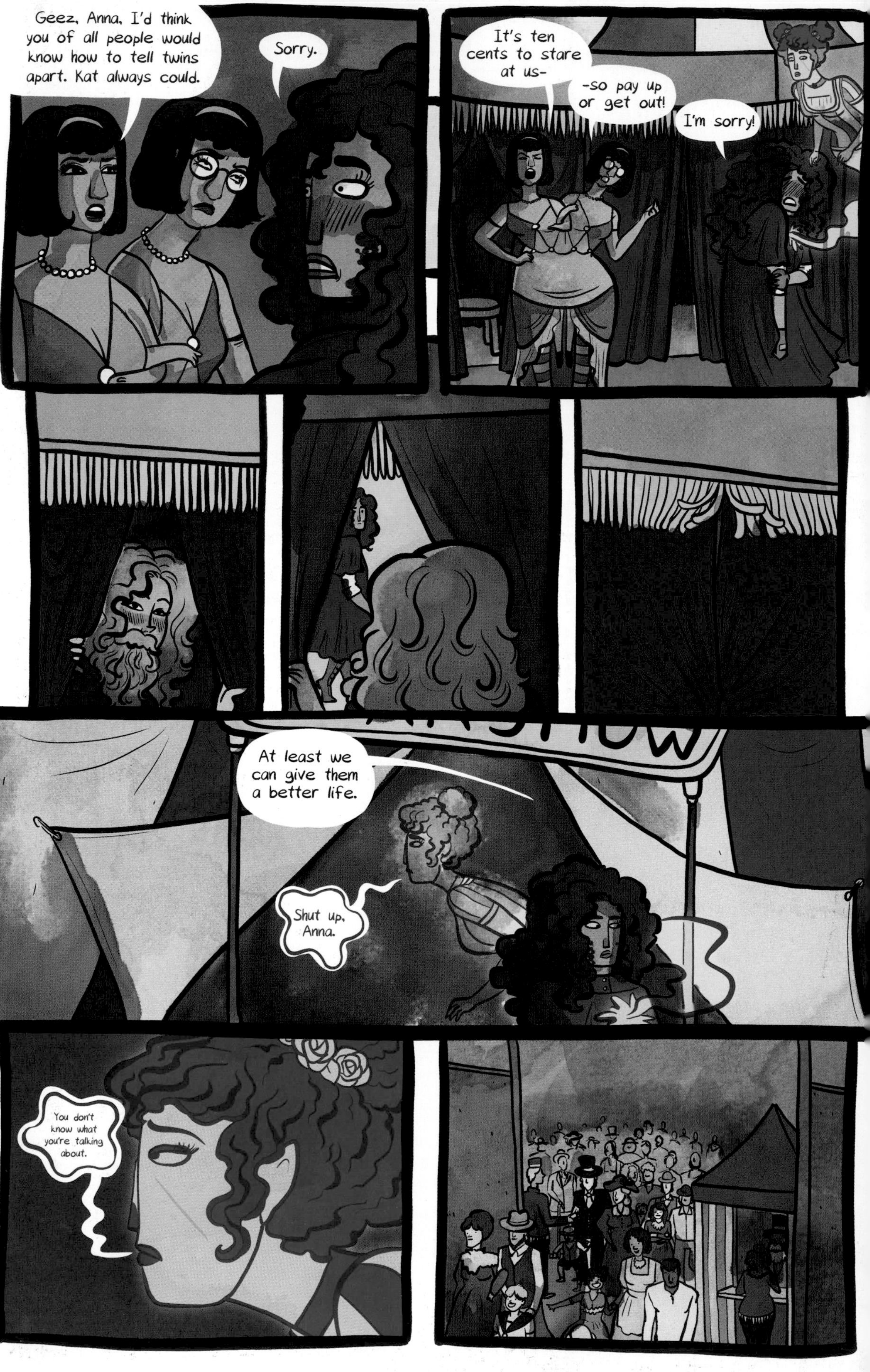
Geez, Anna, I'd think you of all people would know how to tell twins apart. Kat always could.
Sorry.
It's ten cents to stare at us-
-so pay up or get out!
I'm sorry!
At least we can give them a better life.
Shut up, Anna.
You don't know what you're talking about.

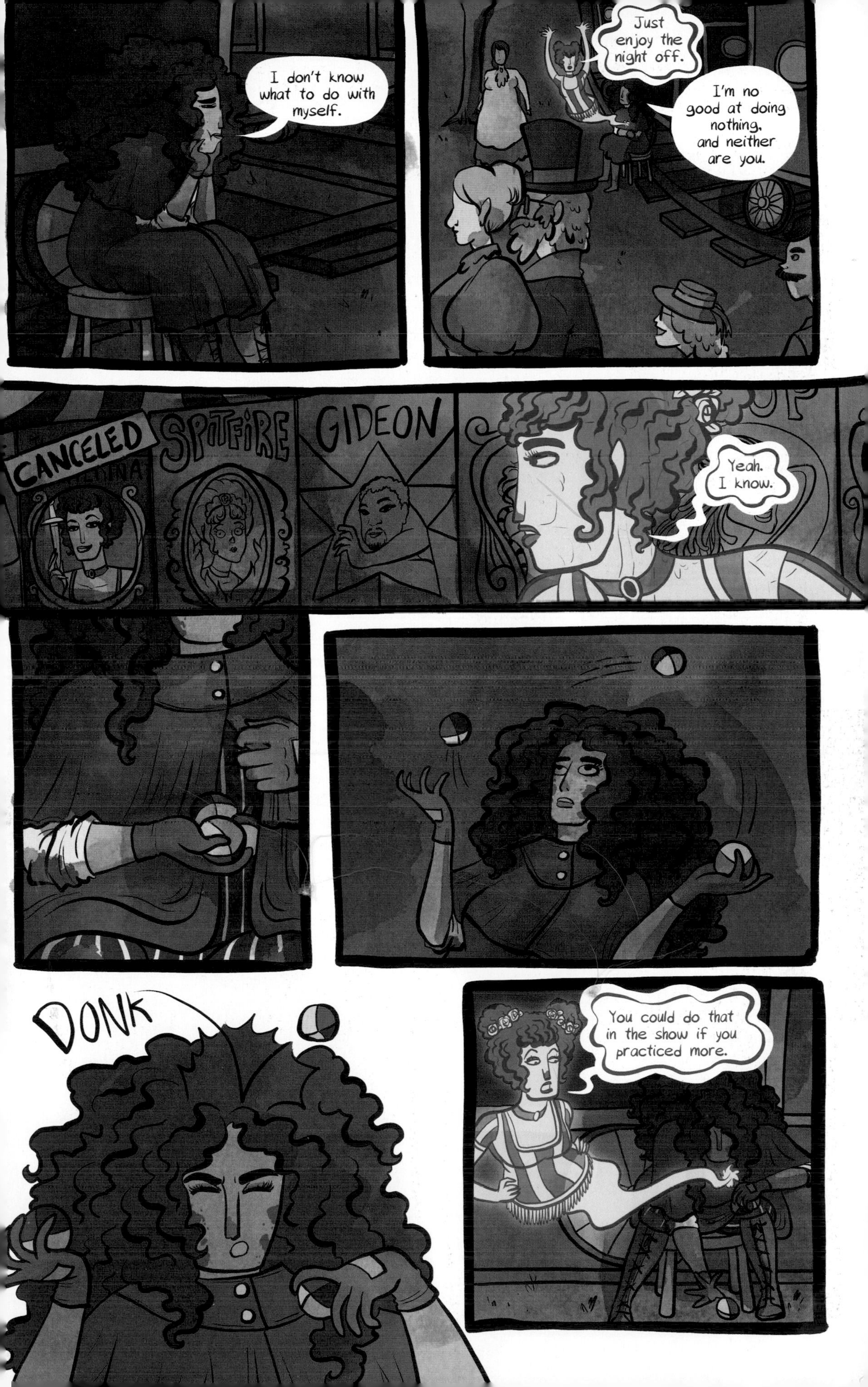

I don't know what to do with myself.
Just enjoy the night off.
I'm no good at doing nothing, and neither are you.
CANCELED
SPITFIRE
GIDEON
Yeah. I know.
DONK
You could do that in the show if you practiced more.

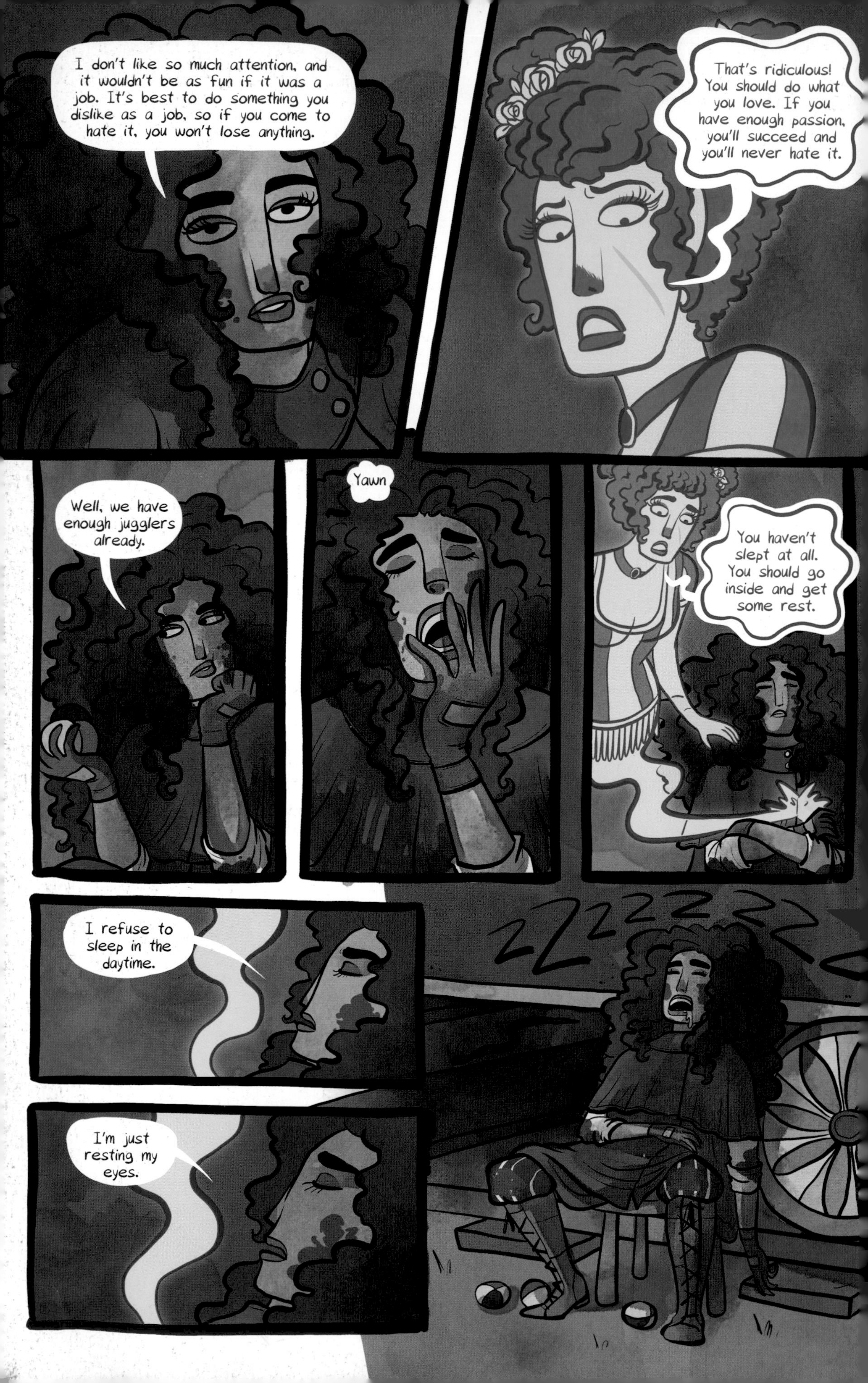
I don't like so much attention, and it wouldn't be as fun if it was a job. It's best to do something you dislike as a job, so if you come to hate it, you won't lose anything.
That's ridiculous! You should do what you love. If you have enough passion, you'll succeed and you'll never hate it.
Well, we have enough jugglers already.
Yawn
You haven't slept at all. You should go inside and get some rest.
I refuse to sleep in the daytime.
I'm just resting my eyes.
ZZZZZZZ

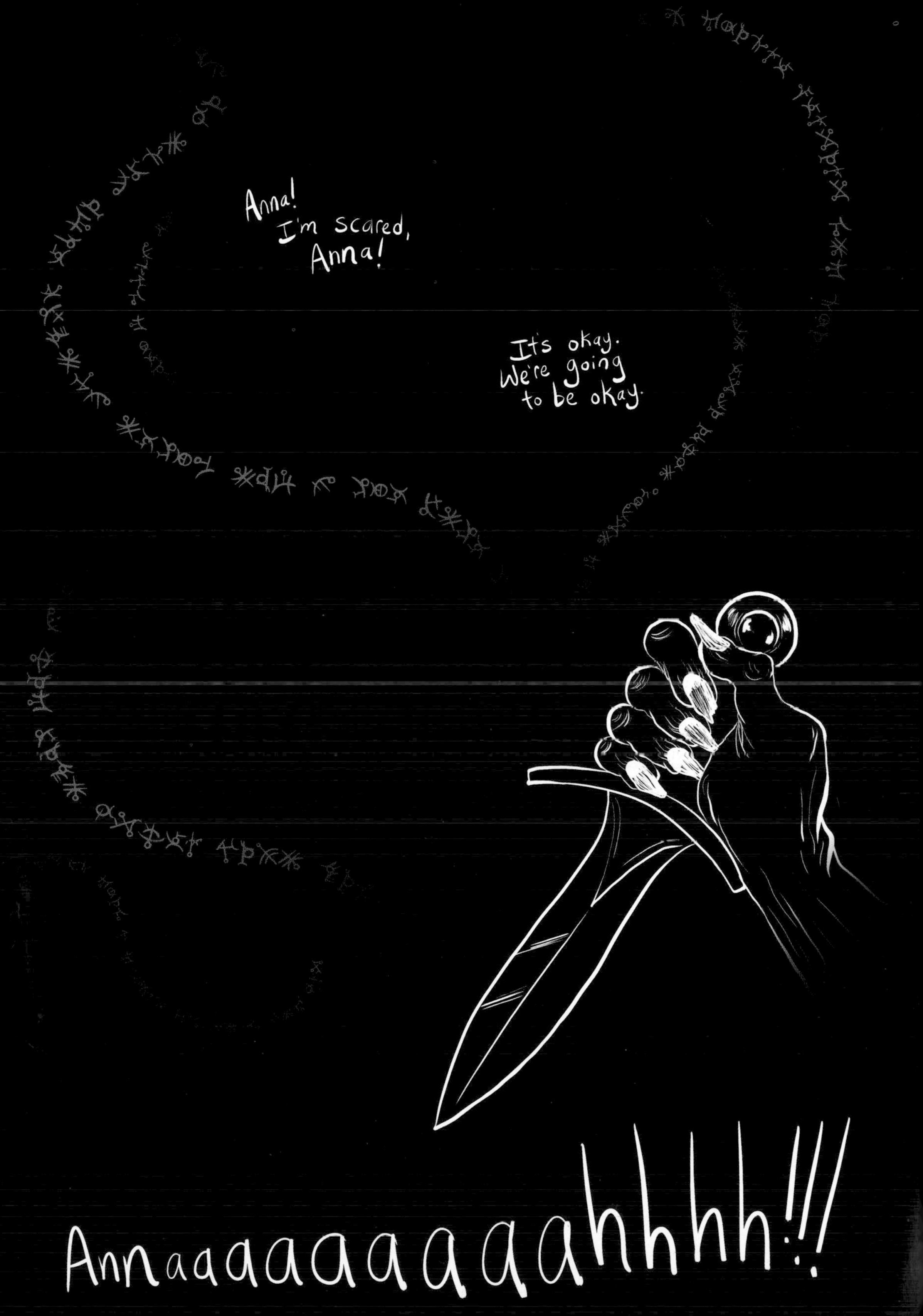
Anna! I'm scared, Anna!
It's okay. We're going to be okay.
Annaaaaaaaaaahhhhh!!!

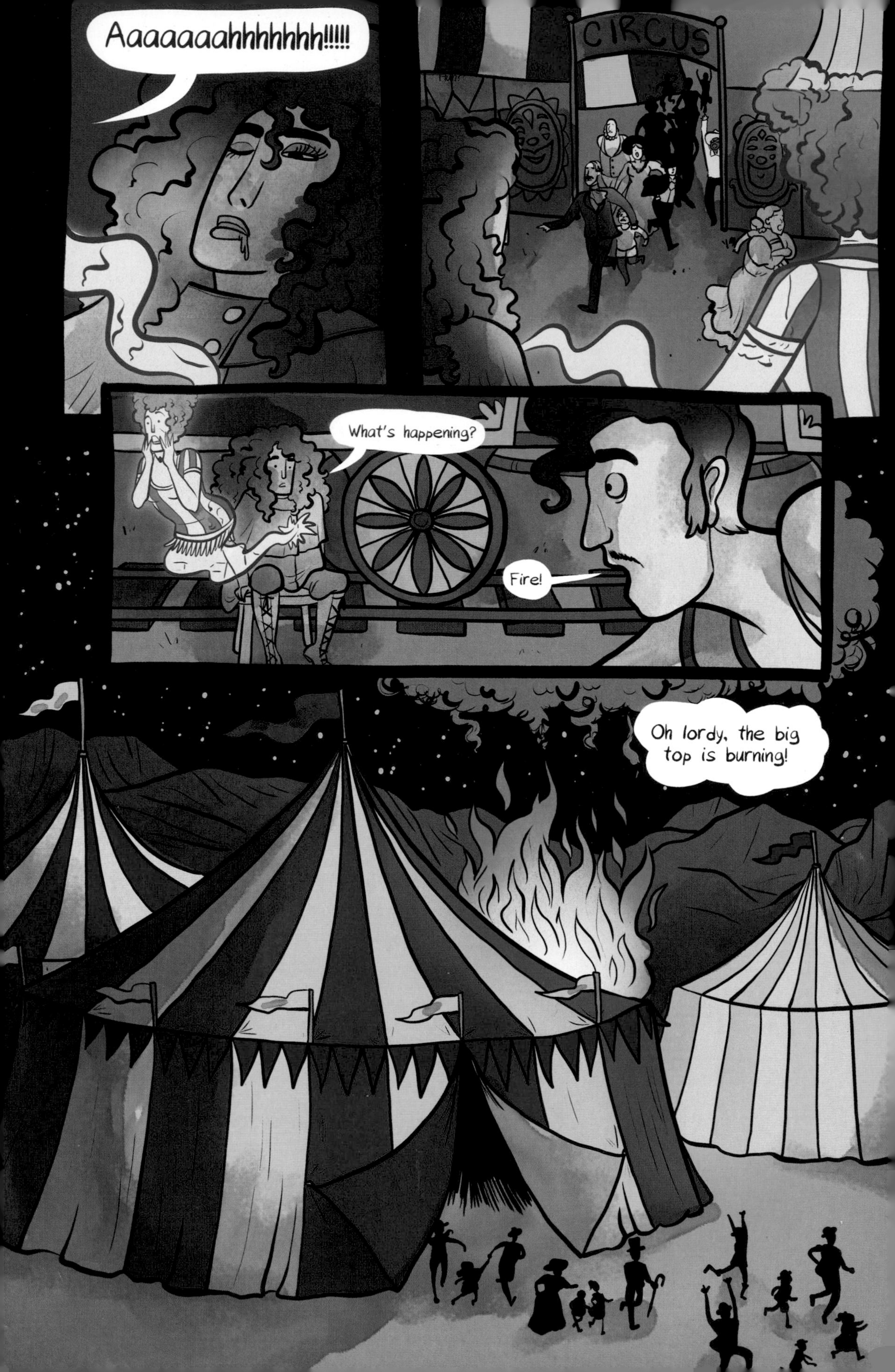
Aaaaaaahhhhhhhh!!!!!
CIRCUS
What's happening?
Fire!
Oh lordy, the big top is burning!

Chapter Three

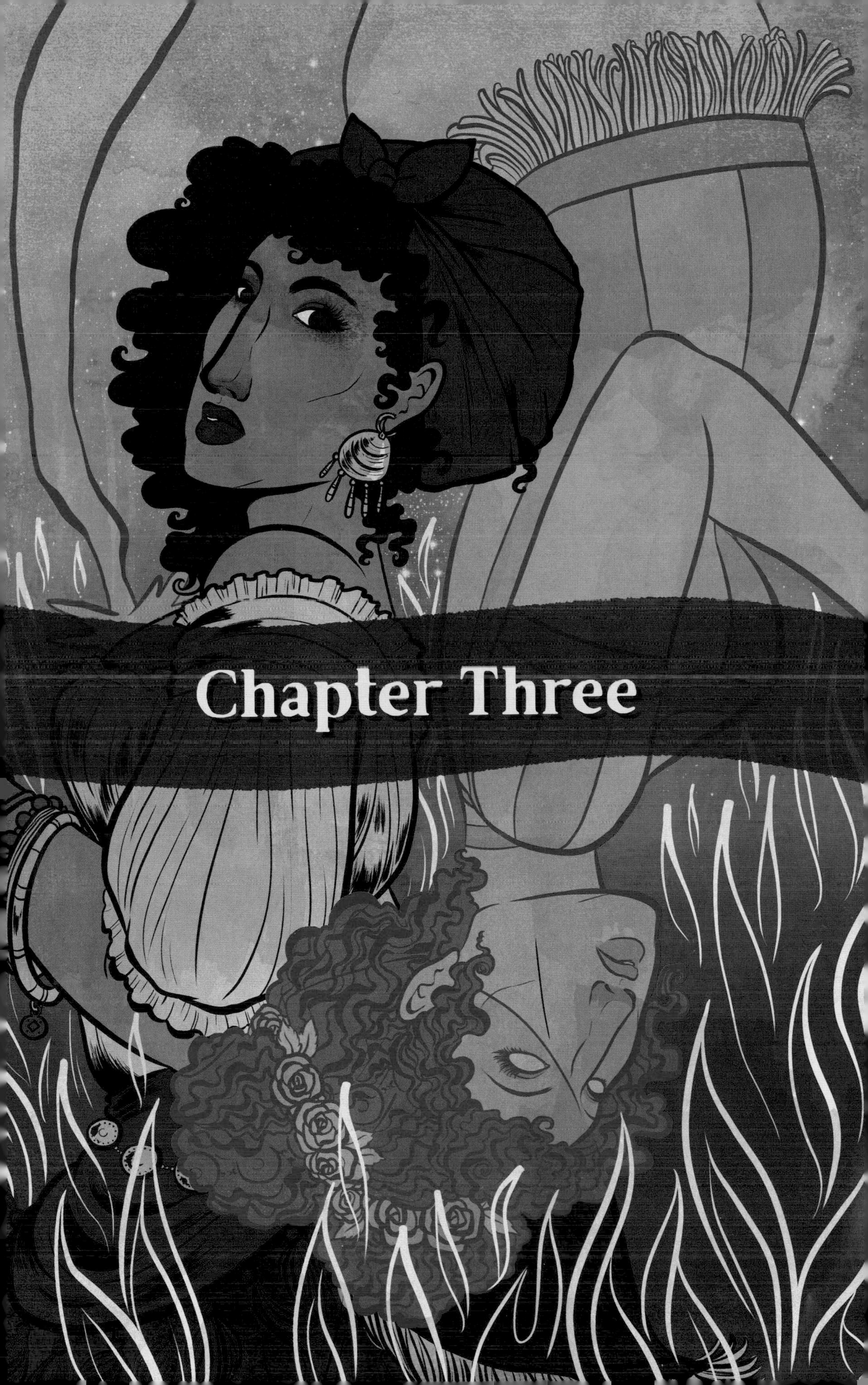

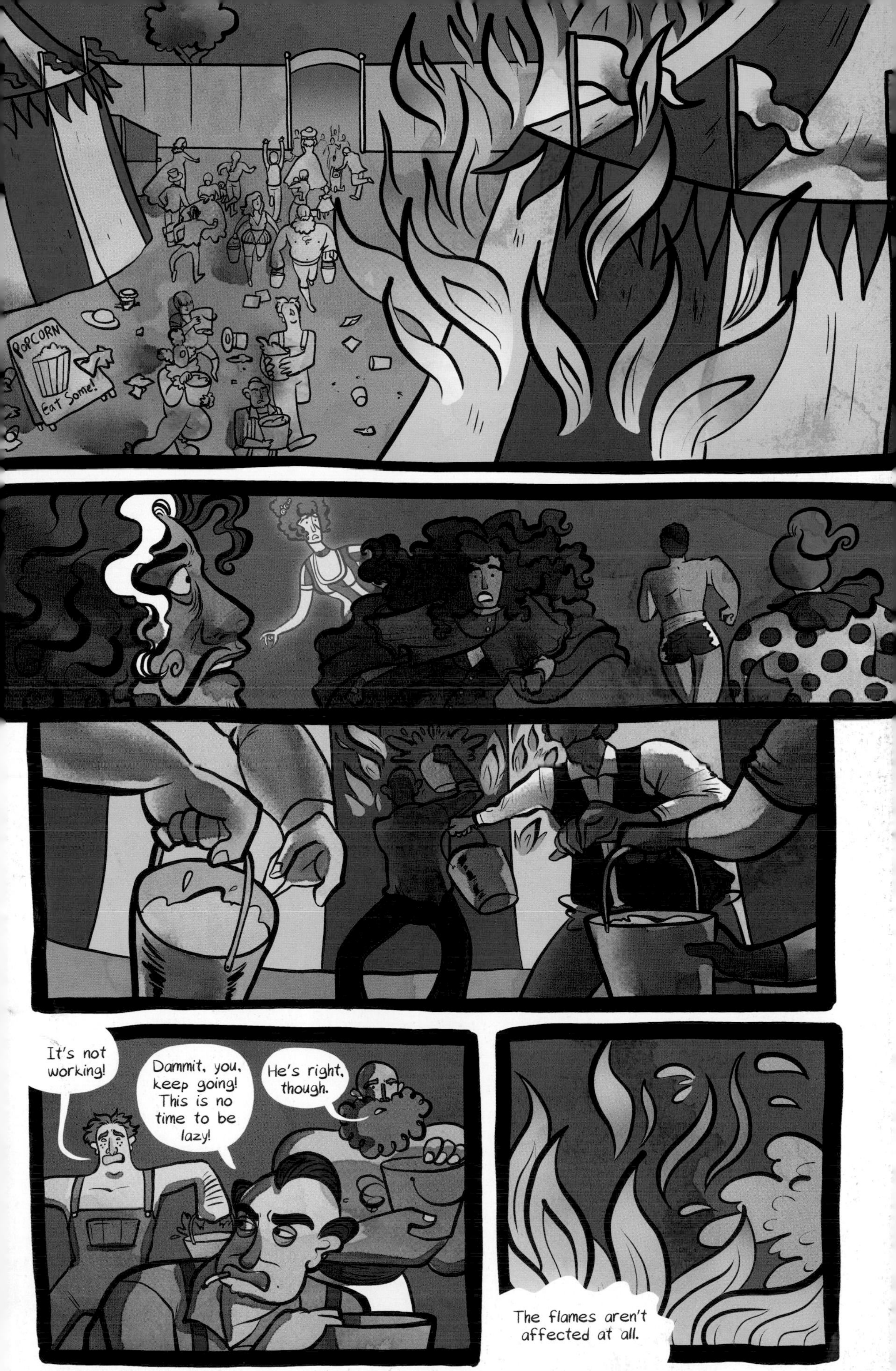
POPCORN
Eat Some!
It's not working!
Dammit, you, keep going! This is no time to be lazy!
He's right, though.
The flames aren't affected at all.

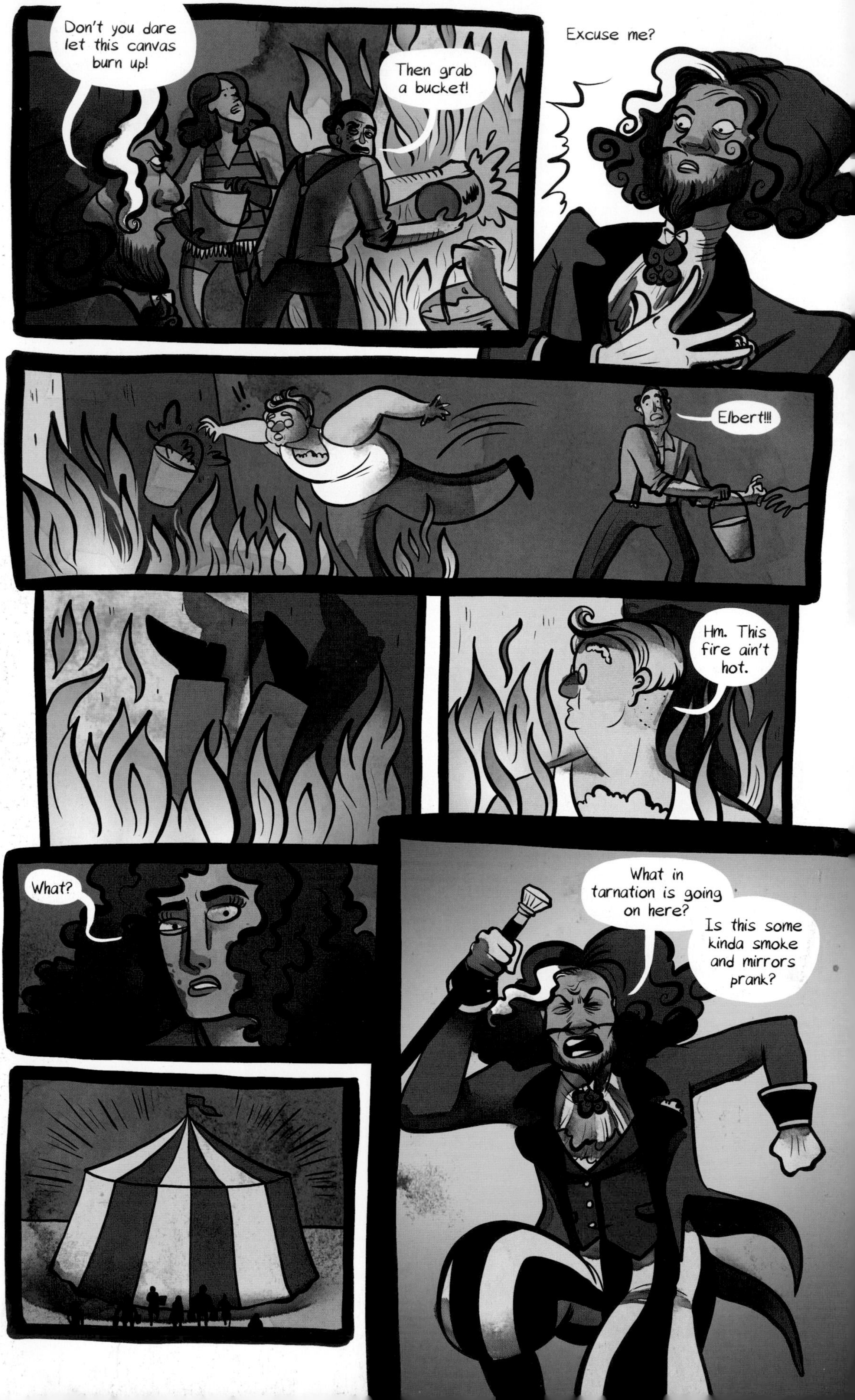
Don't you dare let this canvas burn up!
Then grab a bucket!
Excuse me?
Elbert!!!
Hm. This fire ain't hot.
What?
What in tarnation is going on here?
Is this some kinda smoke and mirrors prank?

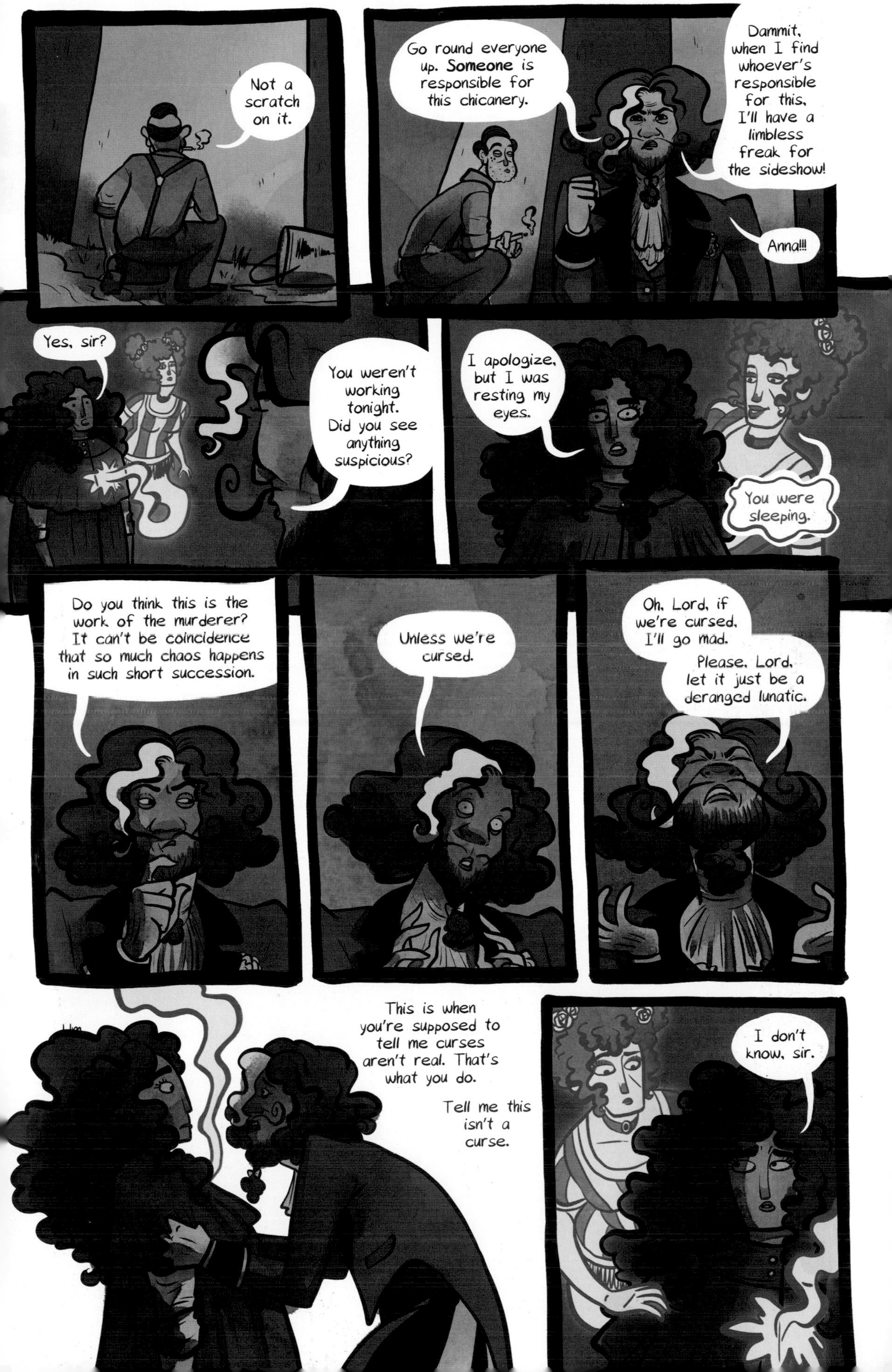
Not a scratch on it.
Go round everyone up. **Someone** is responsible for this chicanery.
Dammit, when I find whoever's responsible for this, I'll have a limbless freak for the sideshow!
Anna!!!
Yes, sir?
You weren't working tonight. Did you see anything suspicious?
I apologize, but I was resting my eyes.
You were sleeping.
Do you think this is the work of the murderer? It can't be coincidence that so much chaos happens in such short succession.
Unless we're cursed.
Oh, Lord, if we're cursed, I'll go mad.
Please, Lord, let it just be a deranged lunatic.
This is when you're supposed to tell me curses aren't real. That's what you do.
Tell me this isn't a curse.
I don't know, sir.

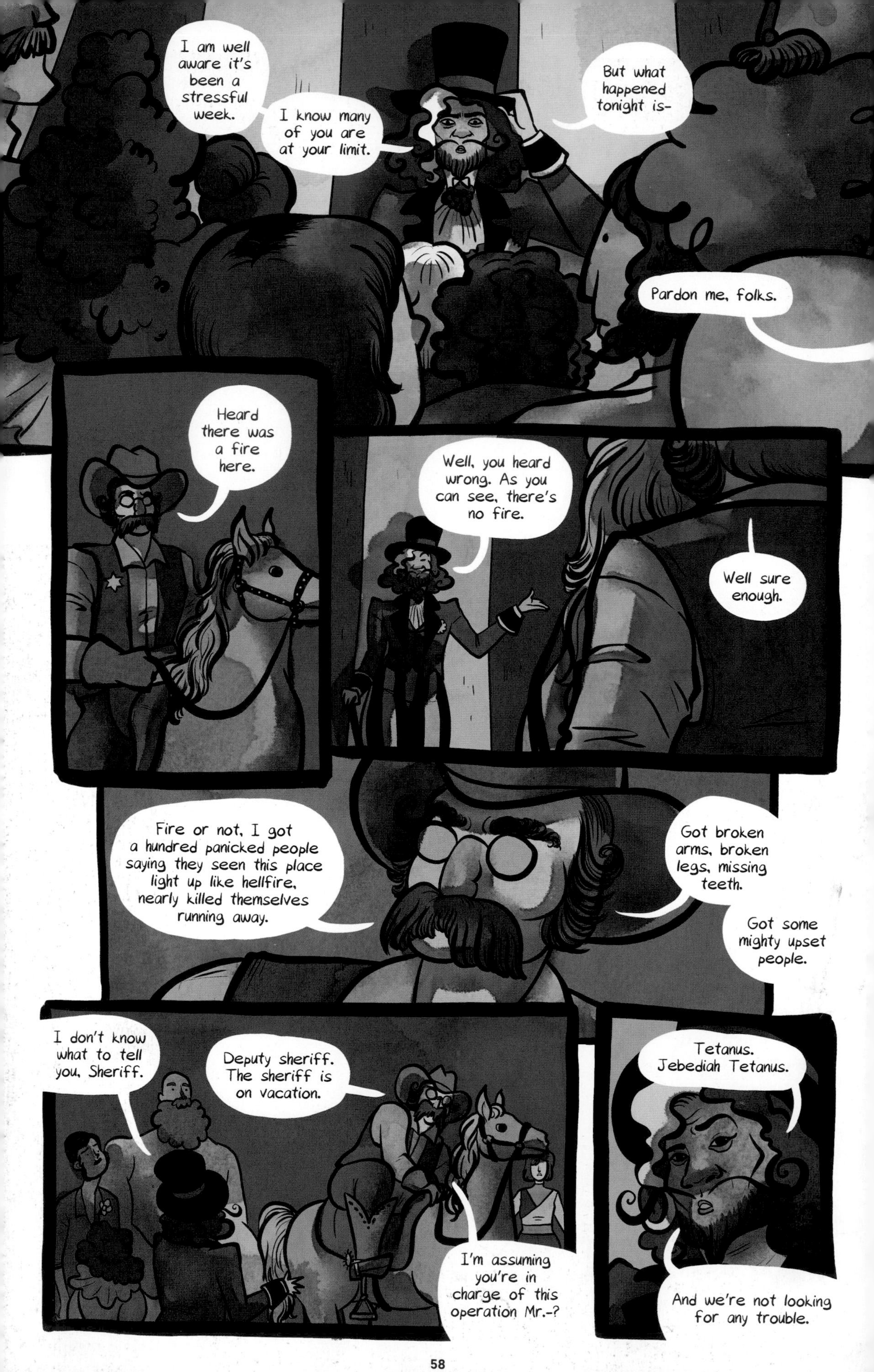
I am well aware it's been a stressful week.
I know many of you are at your limit.
But what happened tonight is-
Pardon me, folks.
Heard there was a fire here.
Well, you heard wrong. As you can see, there's no fire.
Well sure enough.
Fire or not, I got a hundred panicked people saying they seen this place light up like hellfire, nearly killed themselves running away.
Got broken arms, broken legs, missing teeth.
Got some mighty upset people.
I don't know what to tell you, Sheriff.
Deputy sheriff. The sheriff is on vacation.
I'm assuming you're in charge of this operation Mr.-?
Tetanus. Jebediah Tetanus.
And we're not looking for any trouble.

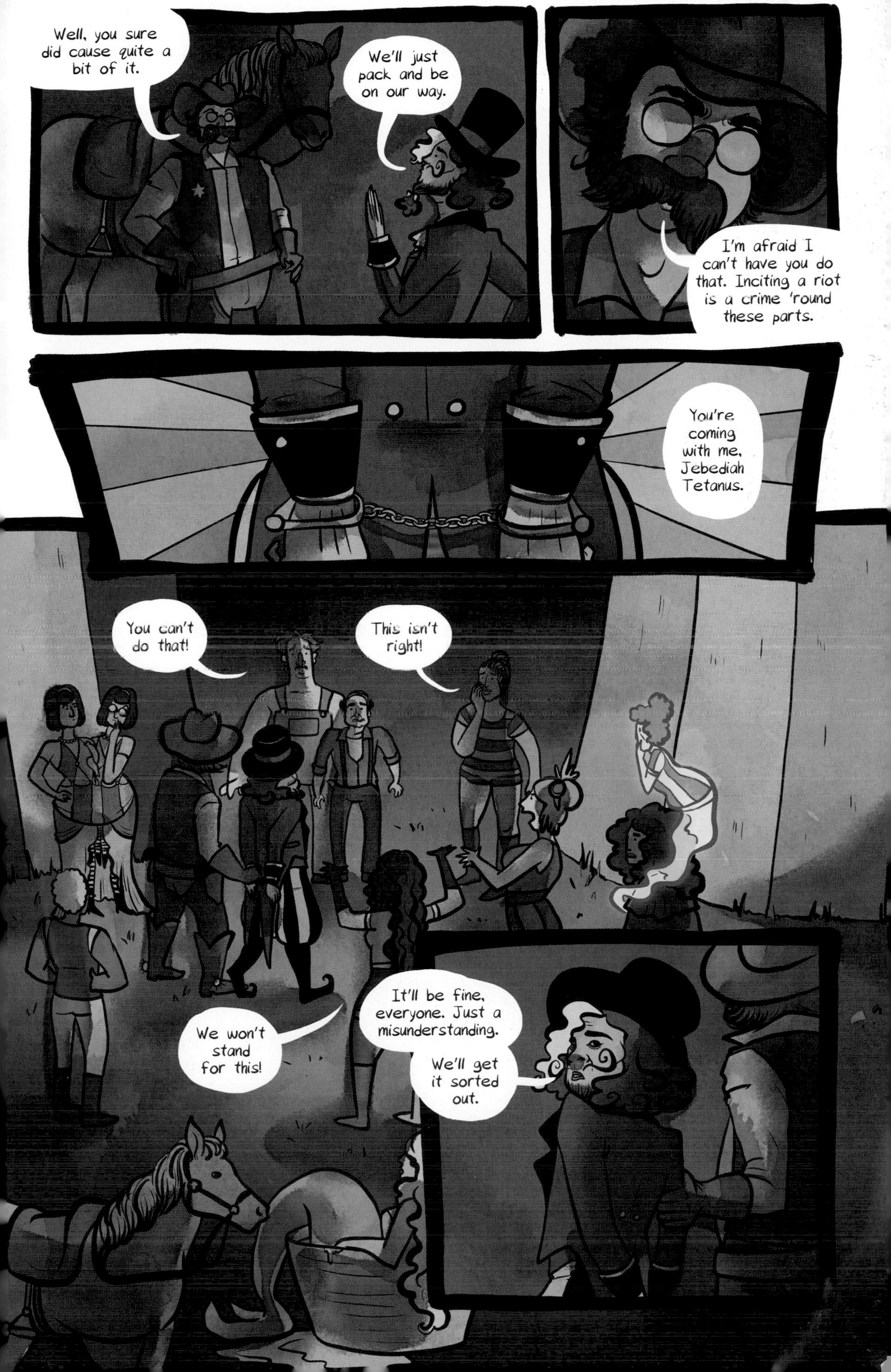
Well, you sure did cause quite a bit of it.
We'll just pack and be on our way.
I'm afraid I can't have you do that. Inciting a riot is a crime 'round these parts.
You're coming with me, Jebediah Tetanus.
You can't do that!
This isn't right!
We won't stand for this!
It'll be fine, everyone. Just a misunderstanding.
We'll get it sorted out.

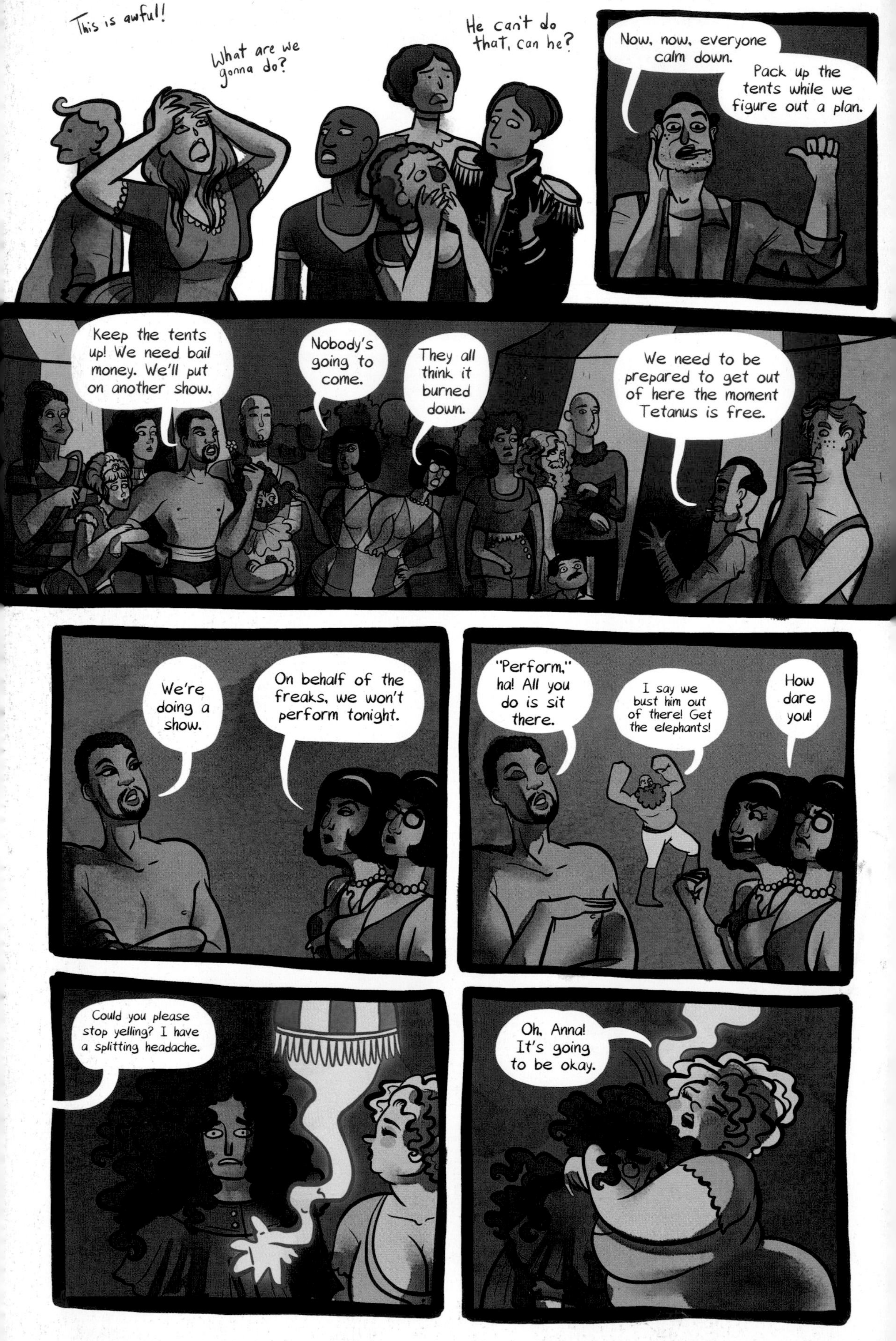
This is awful!
What are we gonna do?
He can't do that, can he?
Now, now, everyone calm down.
Pack up the tents while we figure out a plan.
Keep the tents up! We need bail money. We'll put on another show.
Nobody's going to come.
They all think it burned down.
We need to be prepared to get out of here the moment Tetanus is free.
We're doing a show.
On behalf of the freaks, we won't perform tonight.
"Perform," ha! All you do is sit there.
I say we bust him out of there! Get the elephants!
How dare you!
Could you please stop yelling? I have a splitting headache.
Oh, Anna! It's going to be okay.

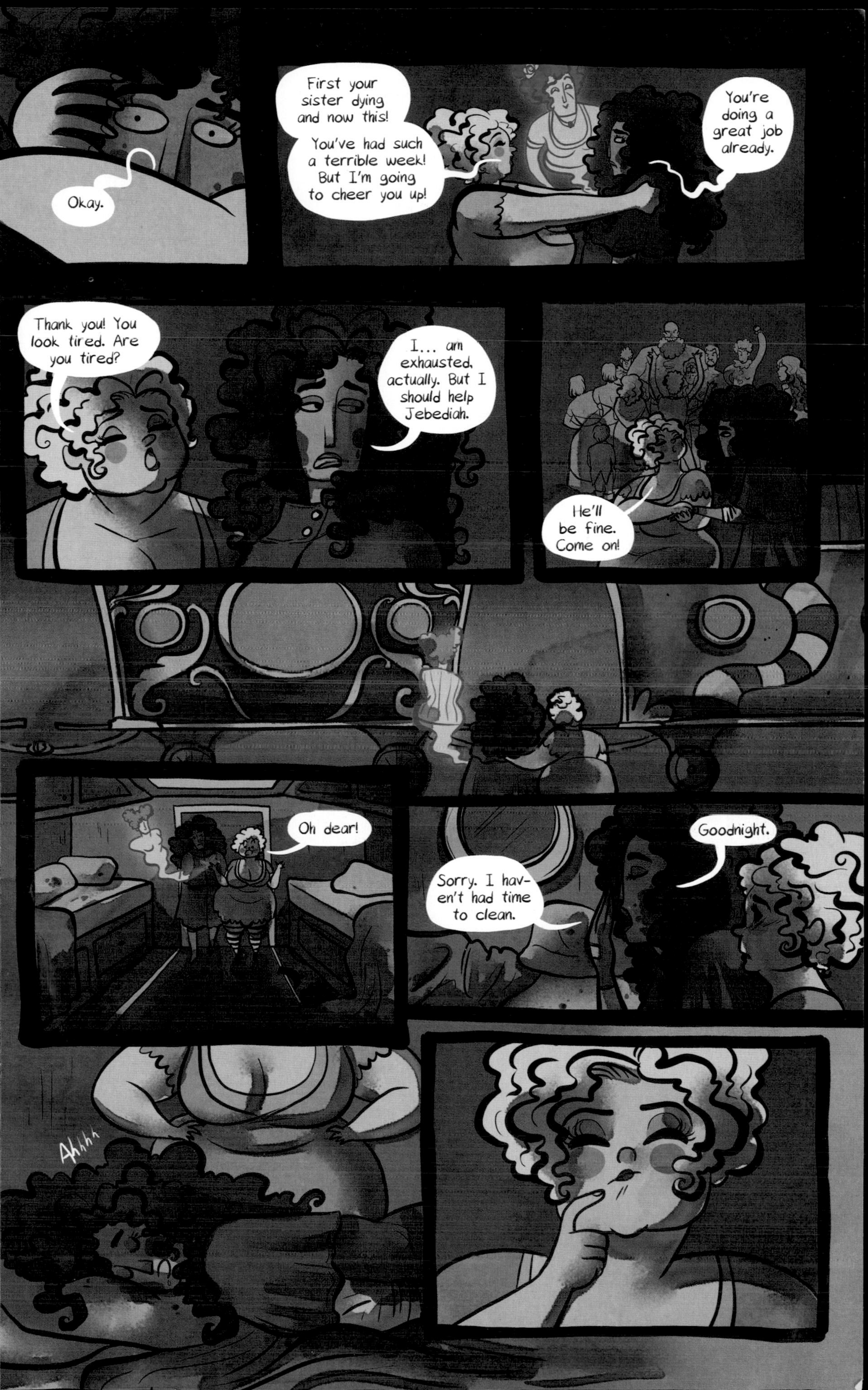
Okay.
First your sister dying and now this!
You've had such a terrible week! But I'm going to cheer you up!
You're doing a great job already.
Thank you! You look tired. Are you tired?
I... am exhausted, actually. But I should help Jebediah.
He'll be fine. Come on!
Oh dear!
Sorry. I haven't had time to clean.
Goodnight.
Ahhhh

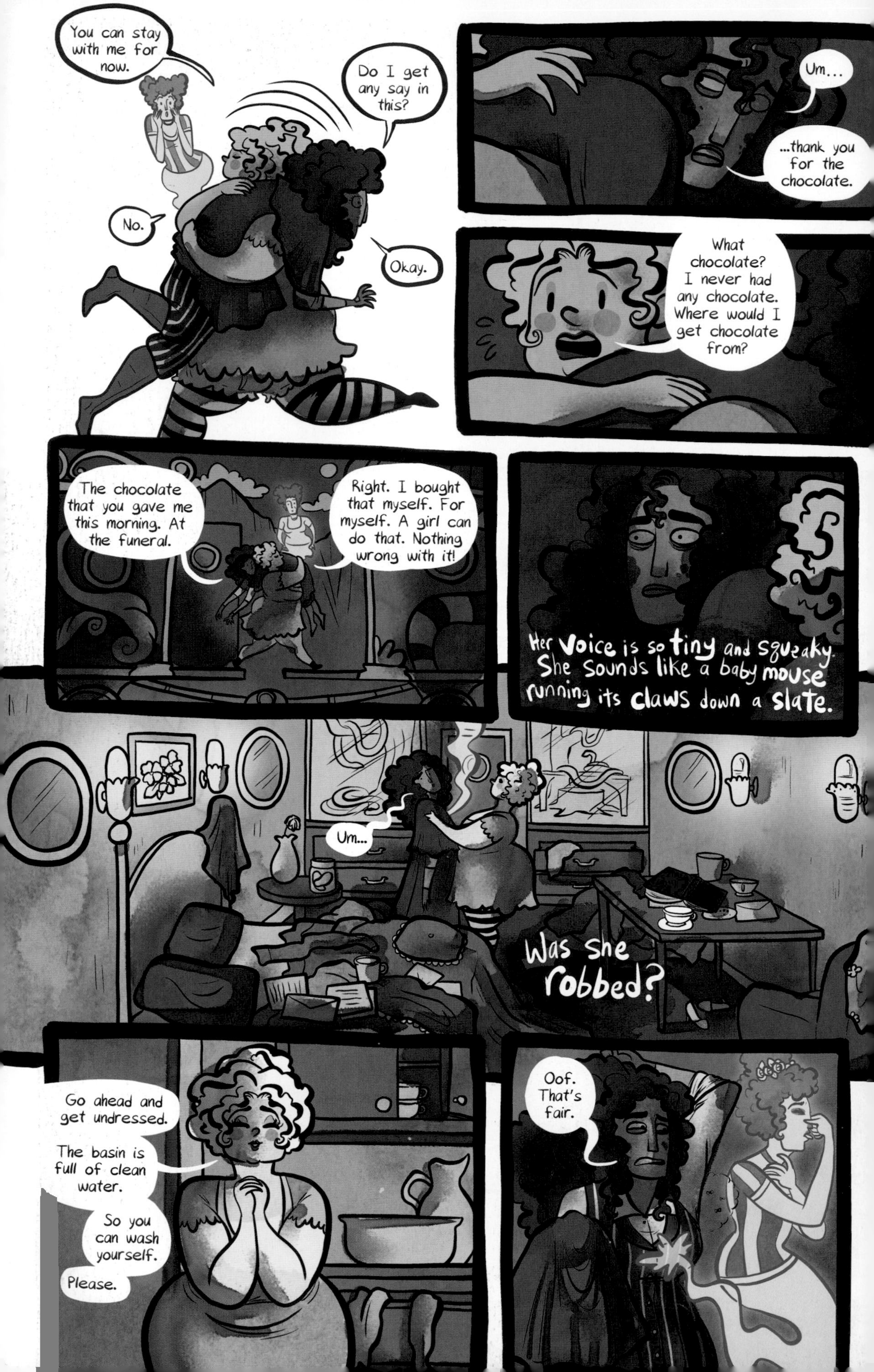
You can stay with me for now.
Do I get any say in this?
No.
Okay.
Um...
...thank you for the chocolate.
What chocolate? I never had any chocolate. Where would I get chocolate from?
The chocolate that you gave me this morning. At the funeral.
Right. I bought that myself. For myself. A girl can do that. Nothing wrong with it!
Her voice is so tiny and squeaky. She sounds like a baby mouse running its claws down a slate.
Um...
Was she robbed?
Go ahead and get undressed.
The basin is full of clean water.
So you can wash yourself.
Please.
Oof. That's fair.

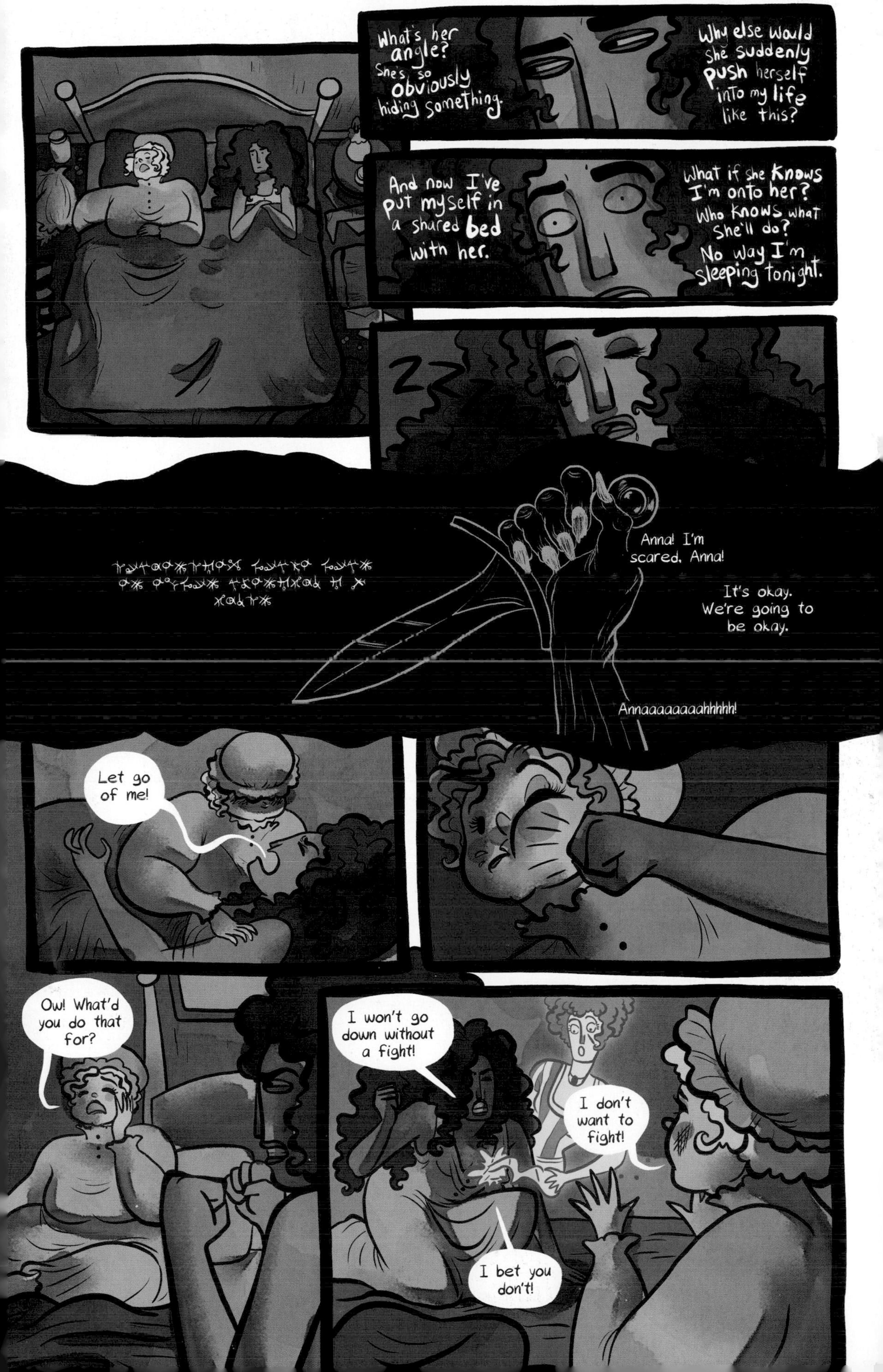

What's her angle? She's so obviously hiding something.
Why else would she suddenly push herself into my life like this?
And now I've put myself in a shared bed with her.
What if she knows I'm onto her? Who knows what she'll do?
No way I'm sleeping tonight.
ZZZ
Anna! I'm scared, Anna!
It's okay. We're going to be okay.
Annaaaaaaaaahhhhh!
Let go of me!
Ow! What'd you do that for?
I won't go down without a fight!
I don't want to fight!
I bet you don't!

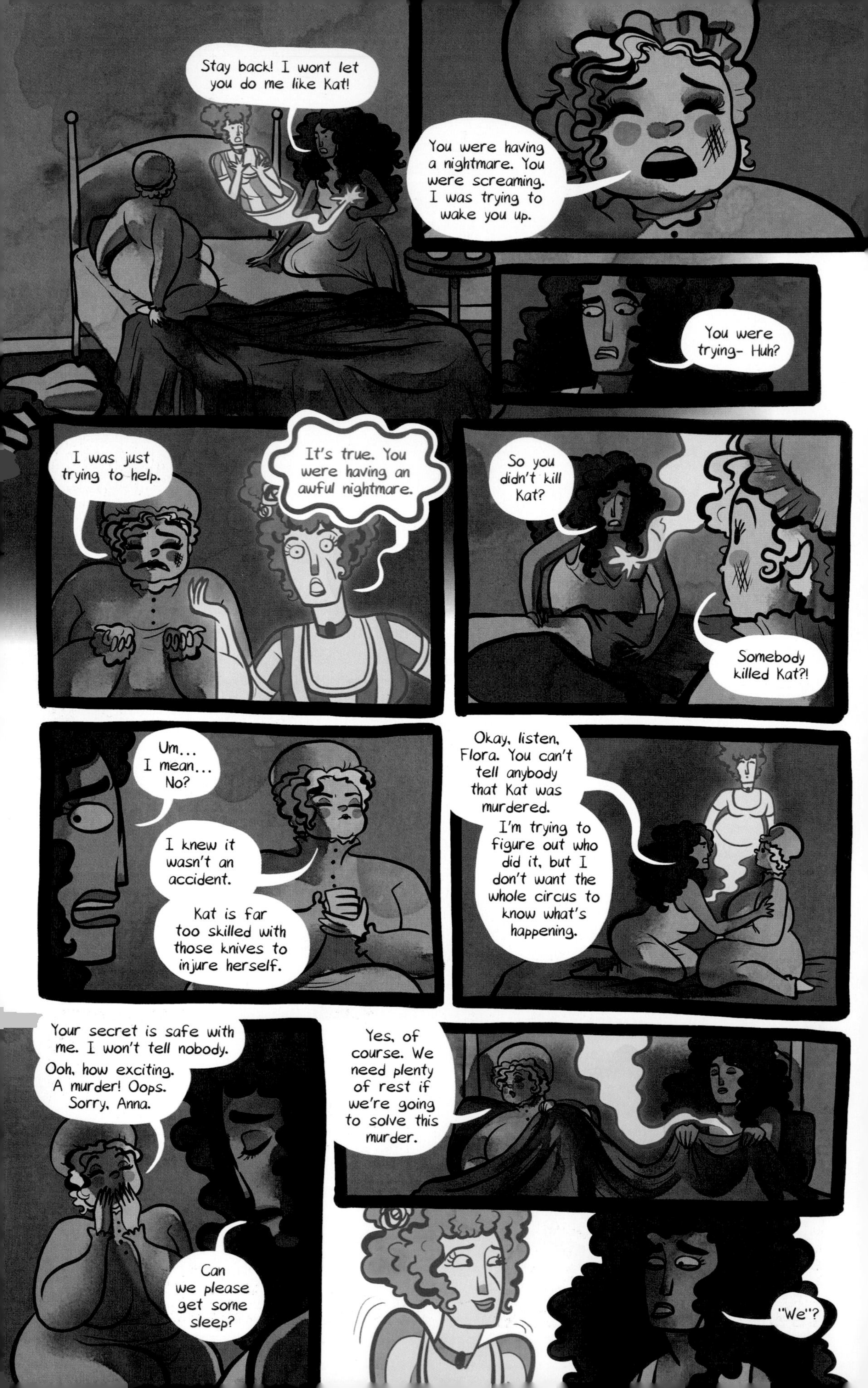
Stay back! I wont let you do me like Kat!
You were having a nightmare. You were screaming. I was trying to wake you up.
You were trying- Huh?
I was just trying to help.
It's true. You were having an awful nightmare.
So you didn't kill Kat?
Somebody killed Kat?!
Um... I mean... No?
I knew it wasn't an accident.
Kat is far too skilled with those knives to injure herself.
Okay, listen, Flora. You can't tell anybody that Kat was murdered.
I'm trying to figure out who did it, but I don't want the whole circus to know what's happening.
Your secret is safe with me. I won't tell nobody.
Ooh, how exciting. A murder! Oops. Sorry, Anna.
Can we please get some sleep?
Yes, of course. We need plenty of rest if we're going to solve this murder.
"We"?

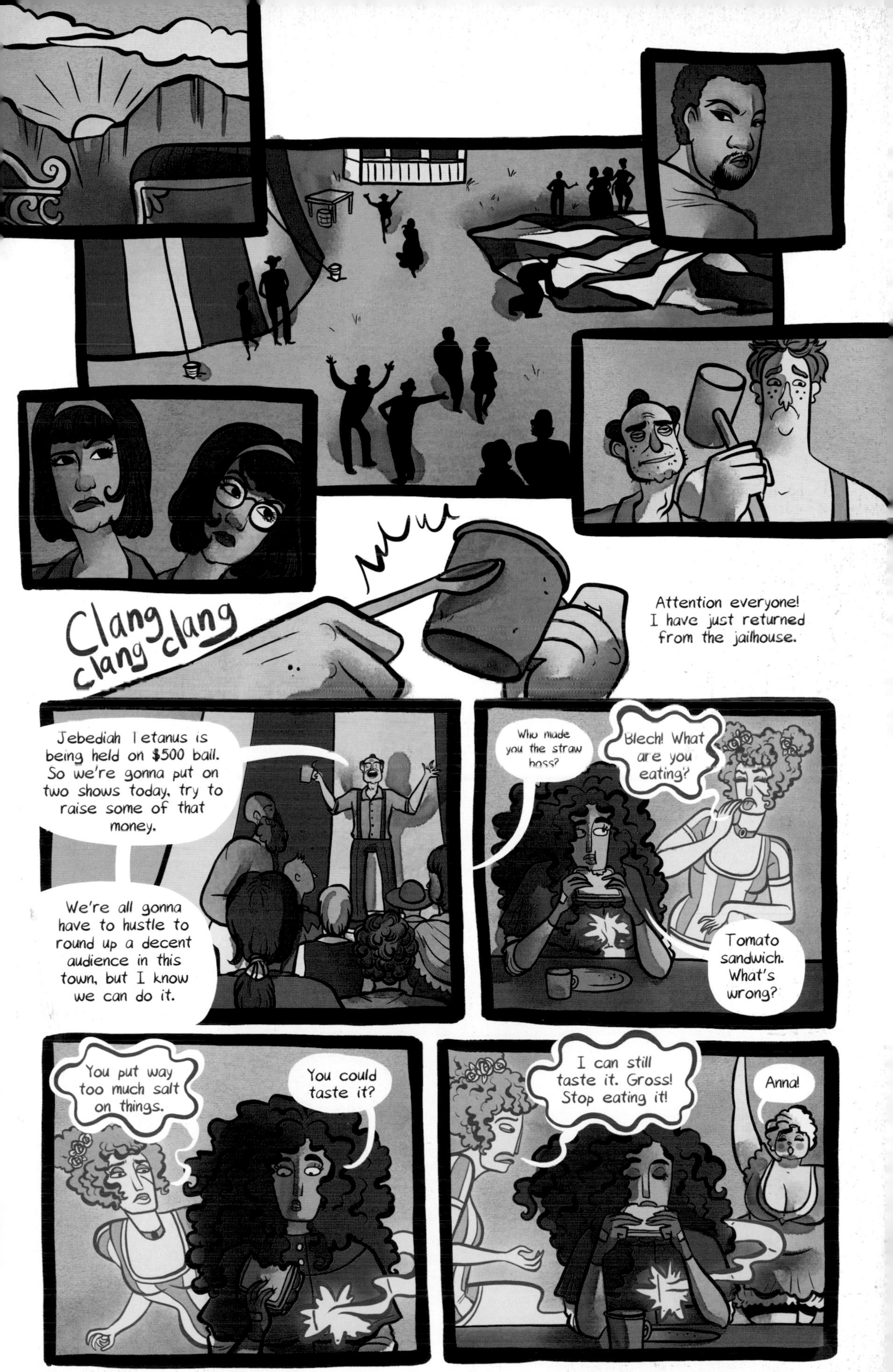
Clang clang clang
Attention everyone! I have just returned from the jailhouse.
Jebediah Tetanus is being held on $500 bail. So we're gonna put on two shows today, try to raise some of that money.
We're all gonna have to hustle to round up a decent audience in this town, but I know we can do it.
Who made you the straw boss?
Blech! What are you eating?
Tomato sandwich. What's wrong?
You put way too much salt on things.
You could taste it?
I can still taste it. Gross! Stop eating it!
Anna!

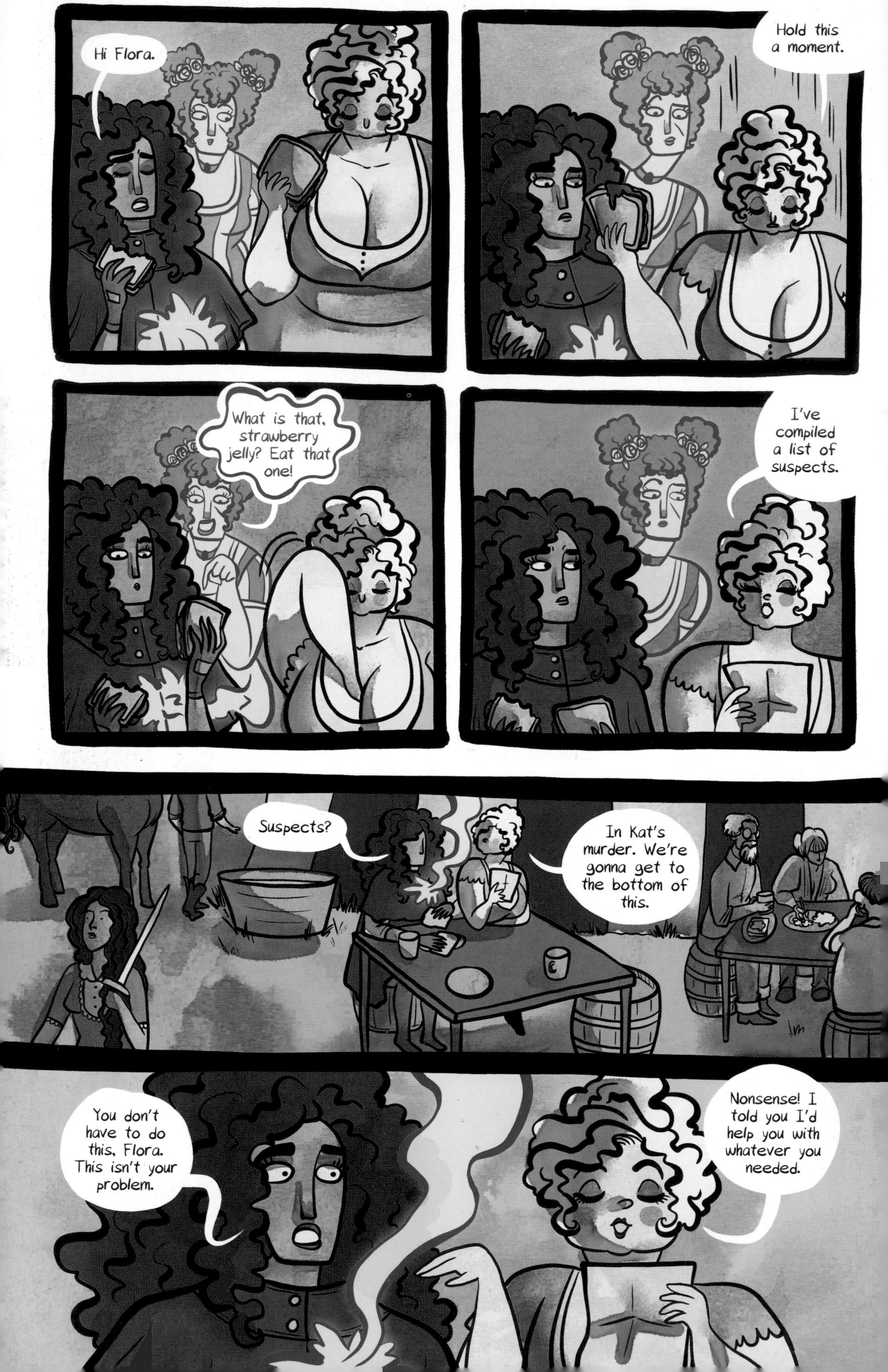
Hi Flora.
Hold this a moment.
What is that, strawberry jelly? Eat that one!
I've compiled a list of suspects.
Suspects?
In Kat's murder. We're gonna get to the bottom of this.
You don't have to do this, Flora. This isn't your problem.
Nonsense! I told you I'd help you with whatever you needed.

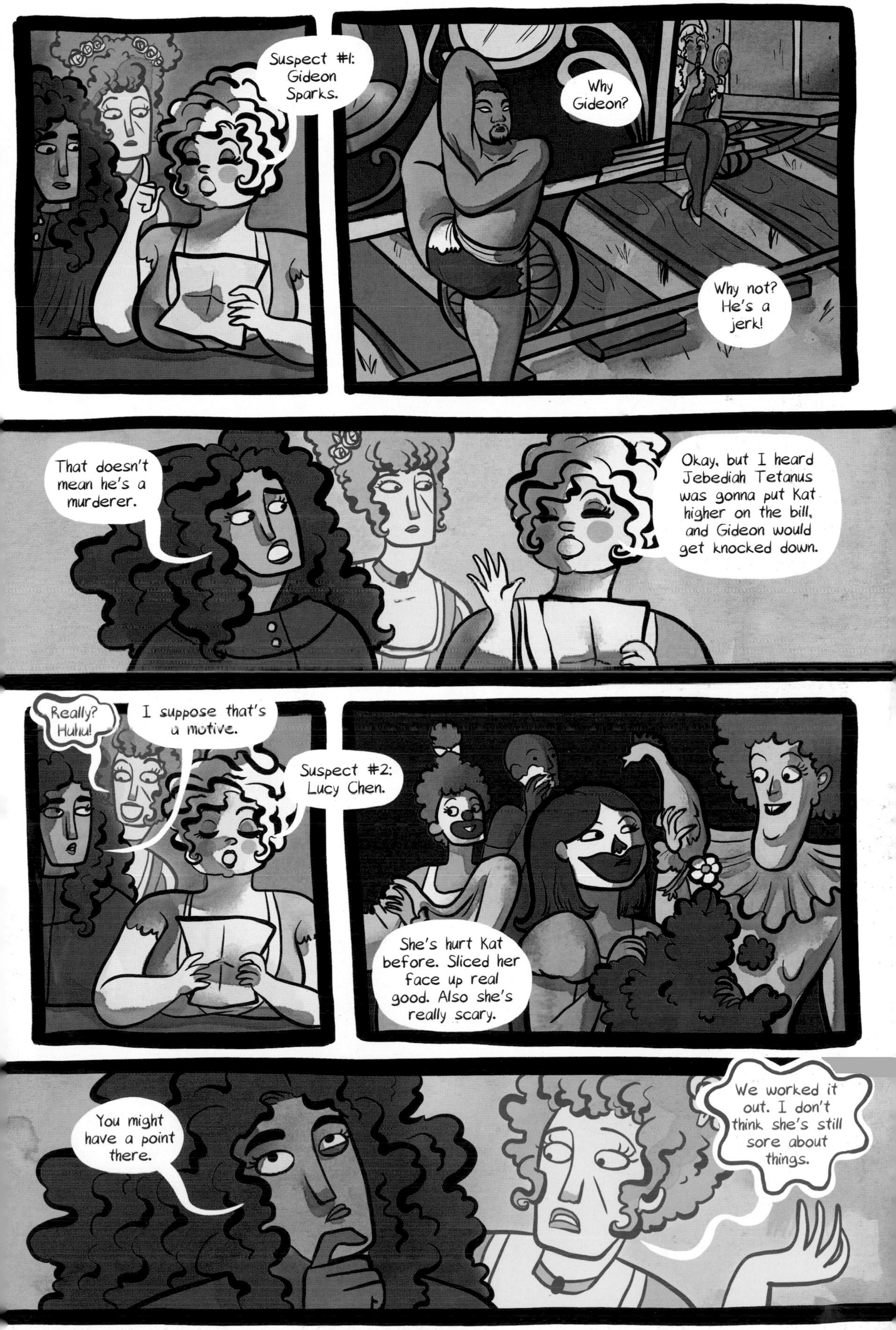
Suspect #1: Gideon Sparks.
Why Gideon?
Why not? He's a jerk!
That doesn't mean he's a murderer.
Okay, but I heard Jebediah Tetanus was gonna put Kat higher on the bill, and Gideon would get knocked down.
Really? Huhu!
I suppose that's a motive.
Suspect #2: Lucy Chen.
She's hurt Kat before. Sliced her face up real good. Also she's really scary.
You might have a point there.
We worked it out. I don't think she's still sore about things.

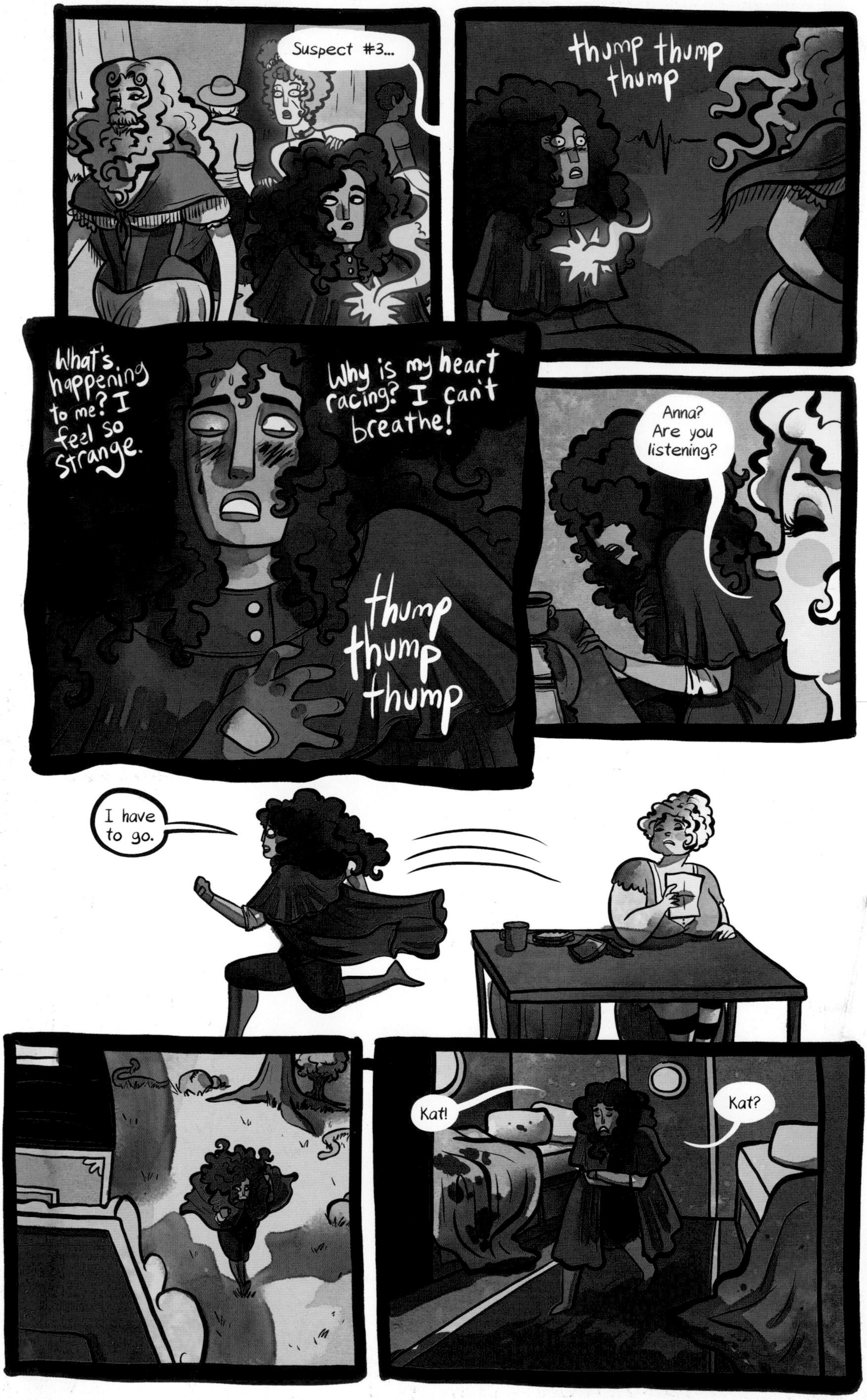
Suspect #3...
thump thump thump
What's happening to me? I feel so strange.
Why is my heart racing? I can't breathe!
thump thump thump
Anna? Are you listening?
I have to go.
Kat!
Kat?

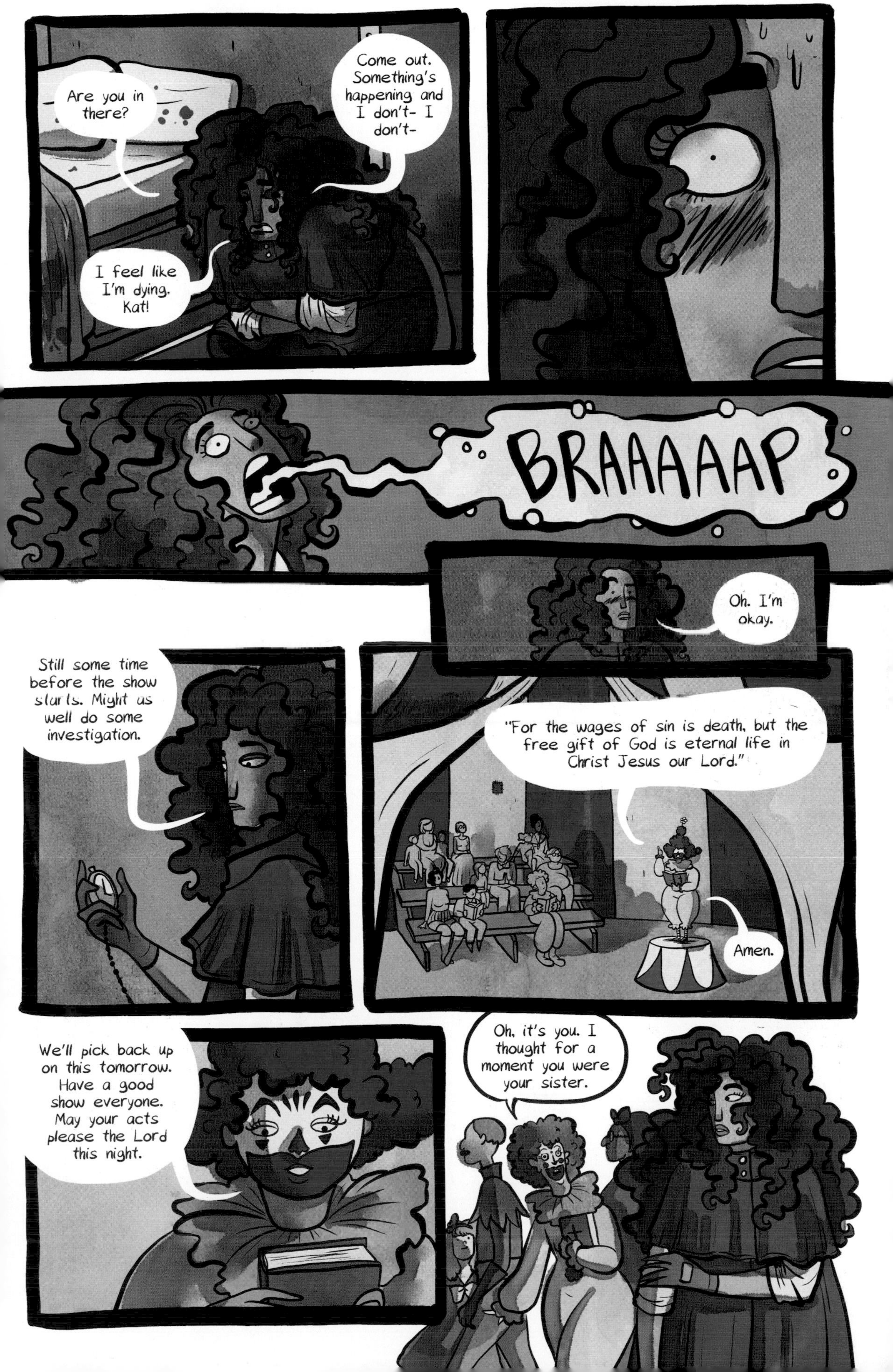
Are you in there?
Come out. Something's happening and I don't- I don't-
I feel like I'm dying. Kat!
BRAAAAAP
Oh. I'm okay.
Still some time before the show starts. Might as well do some investigation.
"For the wages of sin is death, but the free gift of God is eternal life in Christ Jesus our Lord."
Amen.
We'll pick back up on this tomorrow. Have a good show everyone. May your acts please the Lord this night.
Oh, it's you. I thought for a moment you were your sister.

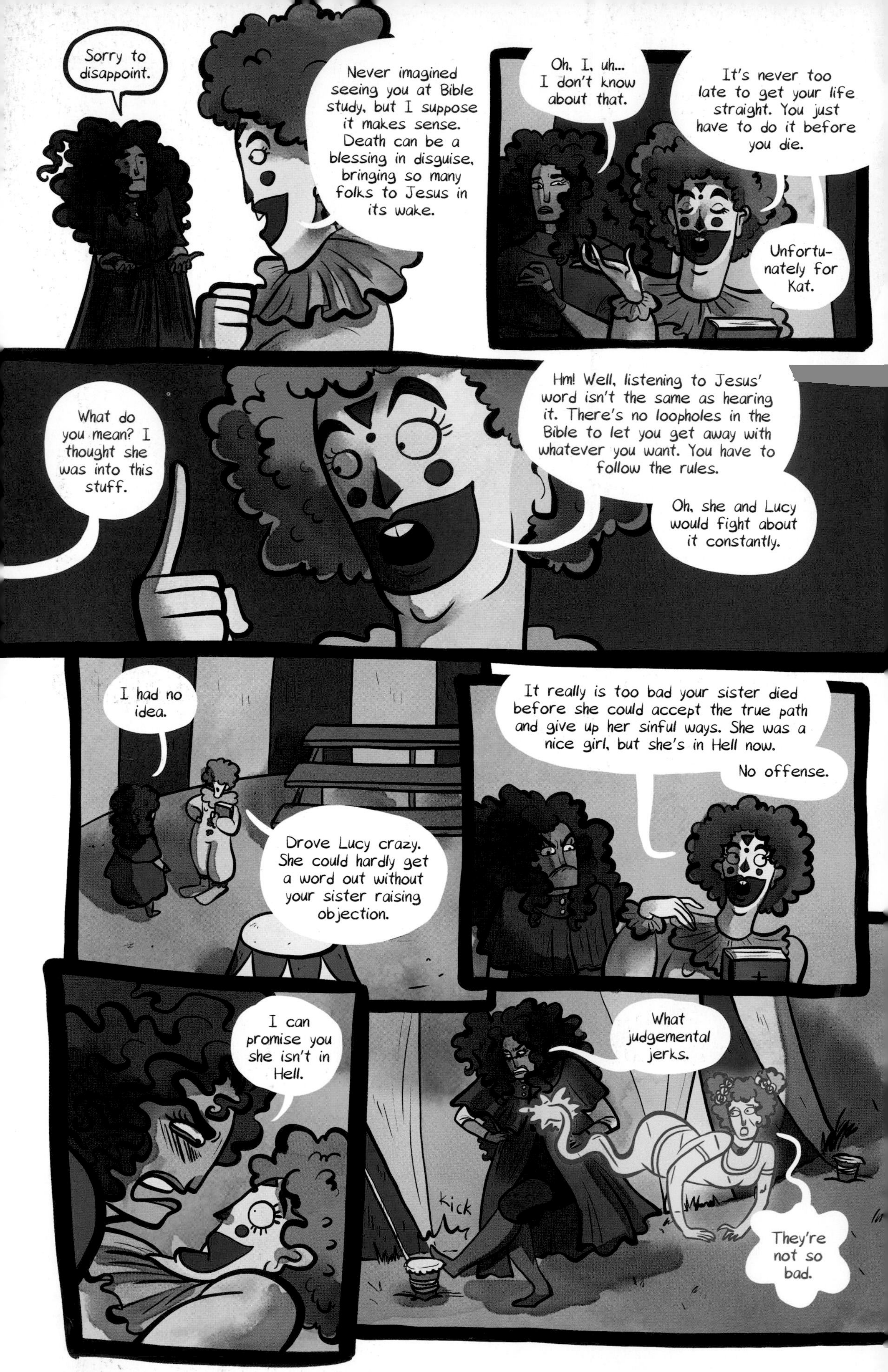

Sorry to disappoint.
Never imagined seeing you at Bible study, but I suppose it makes sense. Death can be a blessing in disguise, bringing so many folks to Jesus in its wake.
Oh, I, uh... I don't know about that.
It's never too late to get your life straight. You just have to do it before you die.
Unfortu-nately for Kat.
What do you mean? I thought she was into this stuff.
Hm! Well, listening to Jesus' word isn't the same as hearing it. There's no loopholes in the Bible to let you get away with whatever you want. You have to follow the rules.
Oh, she and Lucy would fight about it constantly.
I had no idea.
Drove Lucy crazy. She could hardly get a word out without your sister raising objection.
It really is too bad your sister died before she could accept the true path and give up her sinful ways. She was a nice girl, but she's in Hell now.
No offense.
I can promise you she isn't in Hell.
What judgemental jerks.
KICK
They're not so bad.

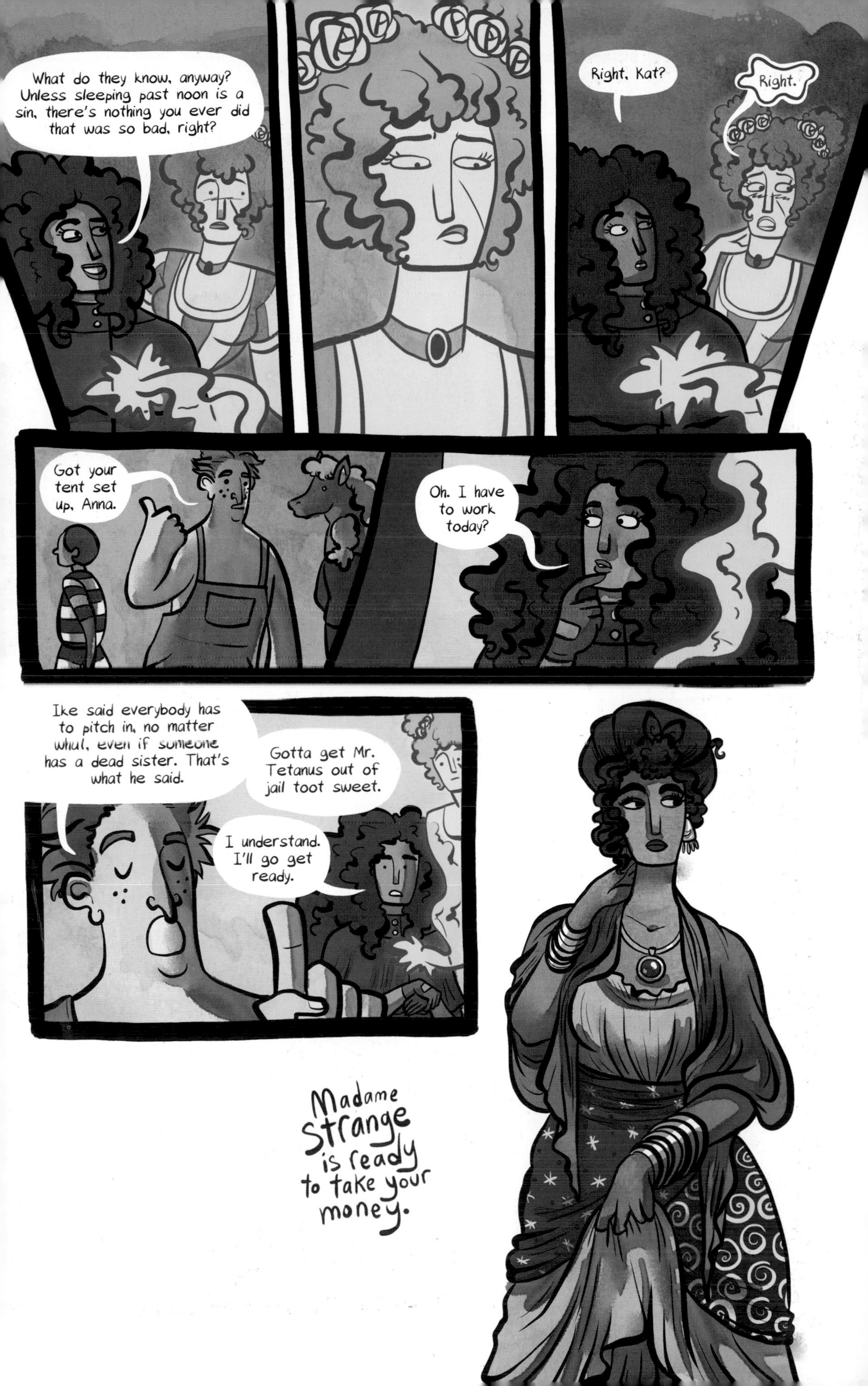
What do they know, anyway? Unless sleeping past noon is a sin, there's nothing you ever did that was so bad, right?
Right, Kat?
Right.
Got your tent set up, Anna.
Oh. I have to work today?
Ike said everybody has to pitch in, no matter what, even if someone has a dead sister. That's what he said.
Gotta get Mr. Tetanus out of jail toot sweet.
I understand. I'll go get ready.
Madame Strange is ready to take your money.

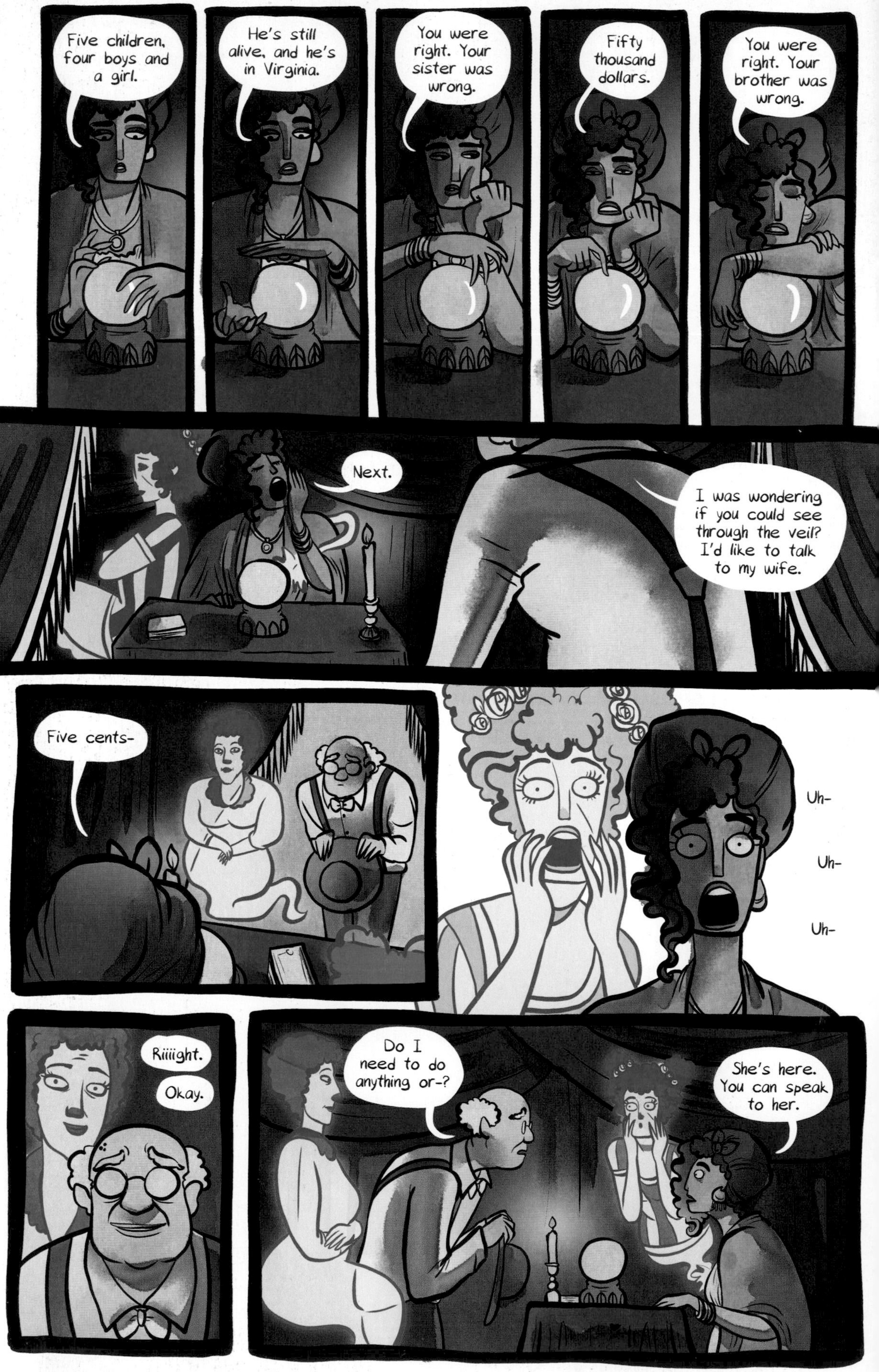

Five children, four boys and a girl.
He's still alive, and he's in Virginia.
You were right. Your sister was wrong.
Fifty thousand dollars.
You were right. Your brother was wrong.
Next.
I was wondering if you could see through the veil? I'd like to talk to my wife.
Five cents-
Uh-
Uh-
Uh-
Riiiight.
Okay.
Do I need to do anything or-?
She's here. You can speak to her.

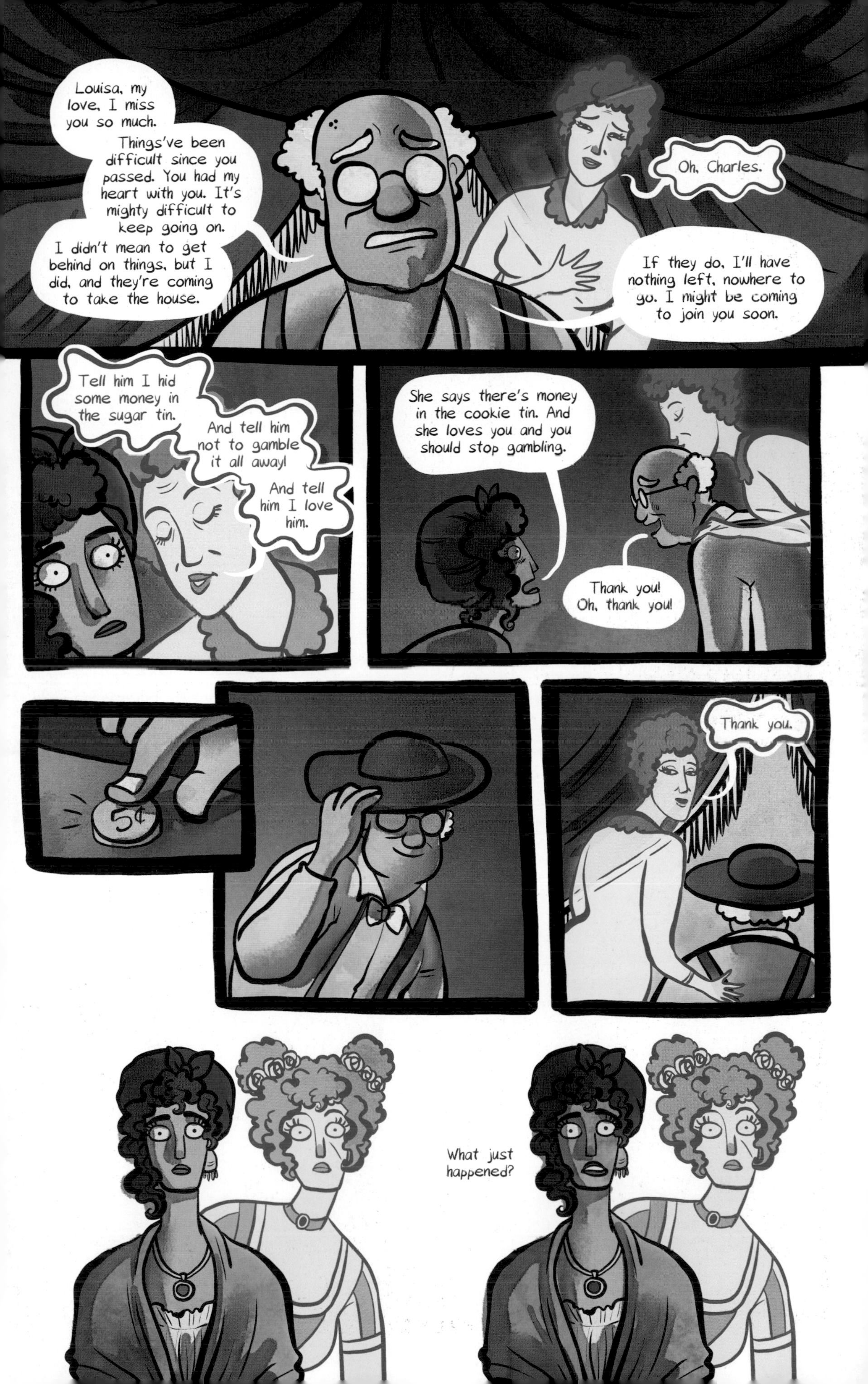
Louisa, my love, I miss you so much.
Things've been difficult since you passed. You had my heart with you. It's mighty difficult to keep going on.
I didn't mean to get behind on things, but I did, and they're coming to take the house.
Oh, Charles.
If they do, I'll have nothing left, nowhere to go. I might be coming to join you soon.
Tell him I hid some money in the sugar tin.
And tell him not to gamble it all away!
And tell him I love him.
She says there's money in the cookie tin. And she loves you and you should stop gambling.
Thank you! Oh, thank you!
5¢
Thank you.
What just happened?

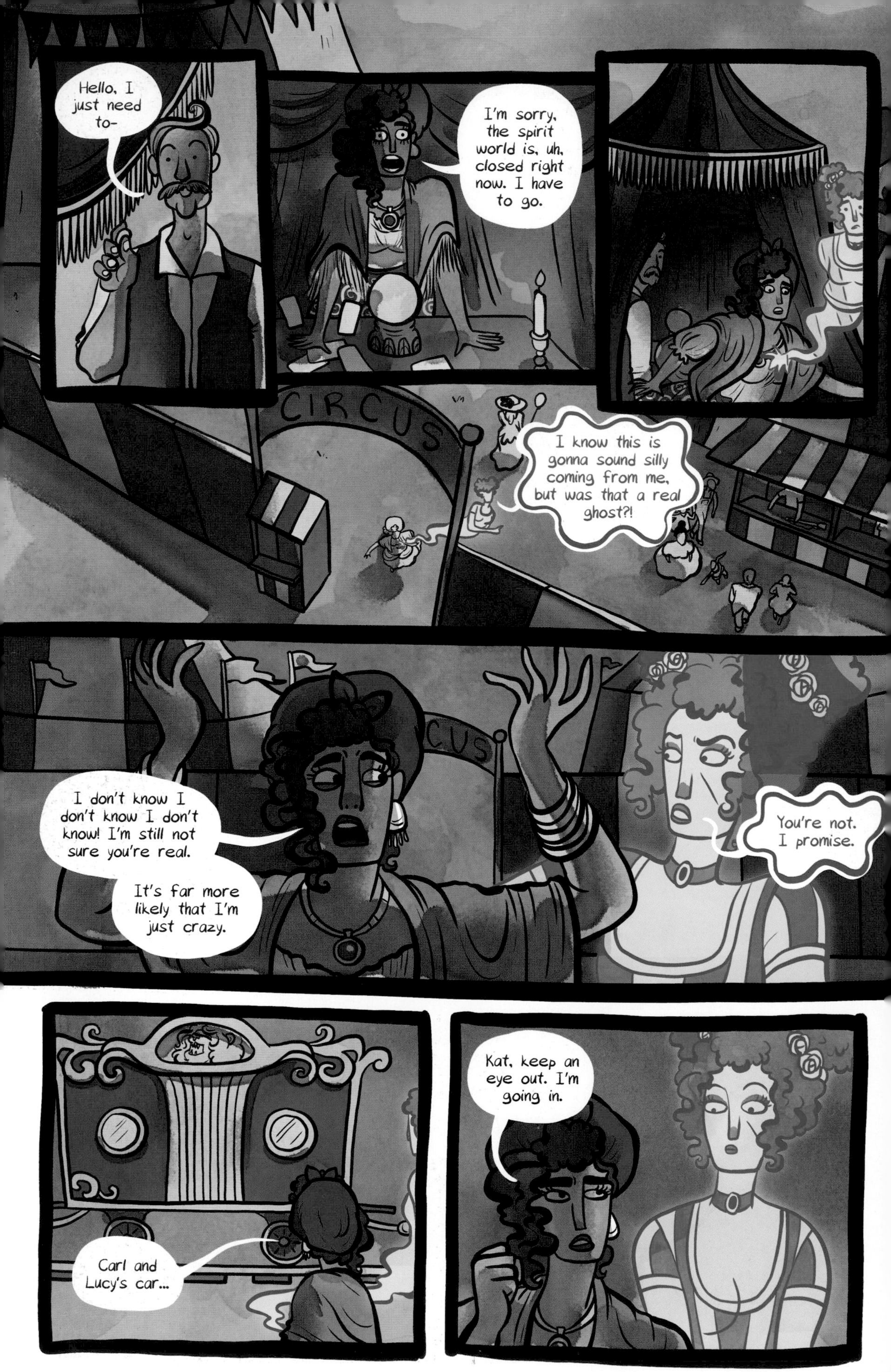
Hello, I just need to-
I'm sorry, the spirit world is, uh, closed right now. I have to go.
CIRCUS
I know this is gonna sound silly coming from me, but was that a real ghost?!
I don't know I don't know I don't know! I'm still not sure you're real.
It's far more likely that I'm just crazy.
You're not. I promise.
Carl and Lucy's car...
Kat, keep an eye out. I'm going in.

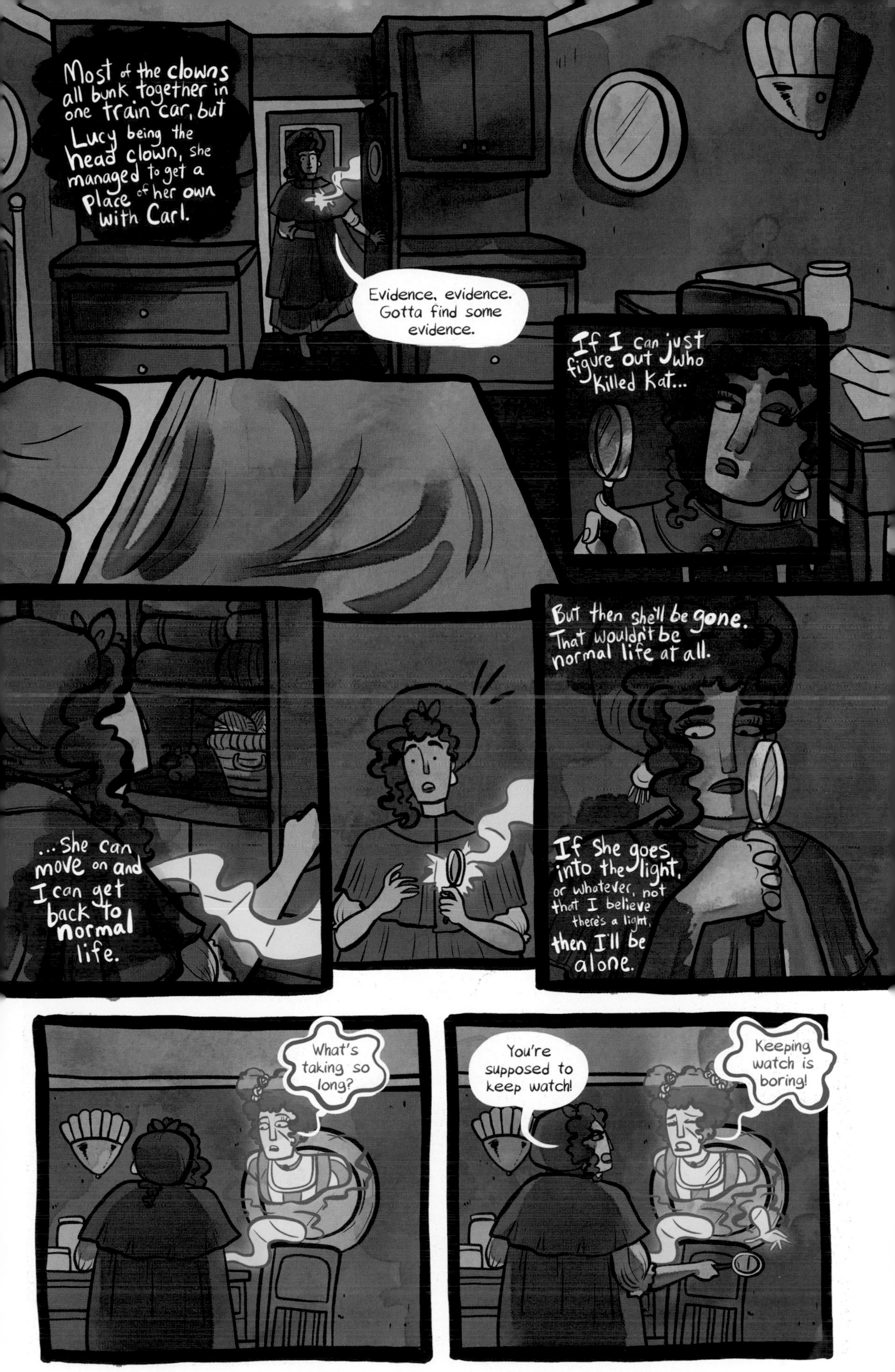

Most of the clowns all bunk together in one train car, but Lucy being the head clown, she managed to get a place of her own with Carl.
Evidence, evidence. Gotta find some evidence.
If I can just figure out who killed Kat...
...she can move on and I can get back to normal life.
But then she'll be gone. That wouldn't be normal life at all.
If she goes into the light, or whatever, not that I believe there's a light, then I'll be alone.
What's taking so long?
You're supposed to keep watch!
Keeping watch is boring!

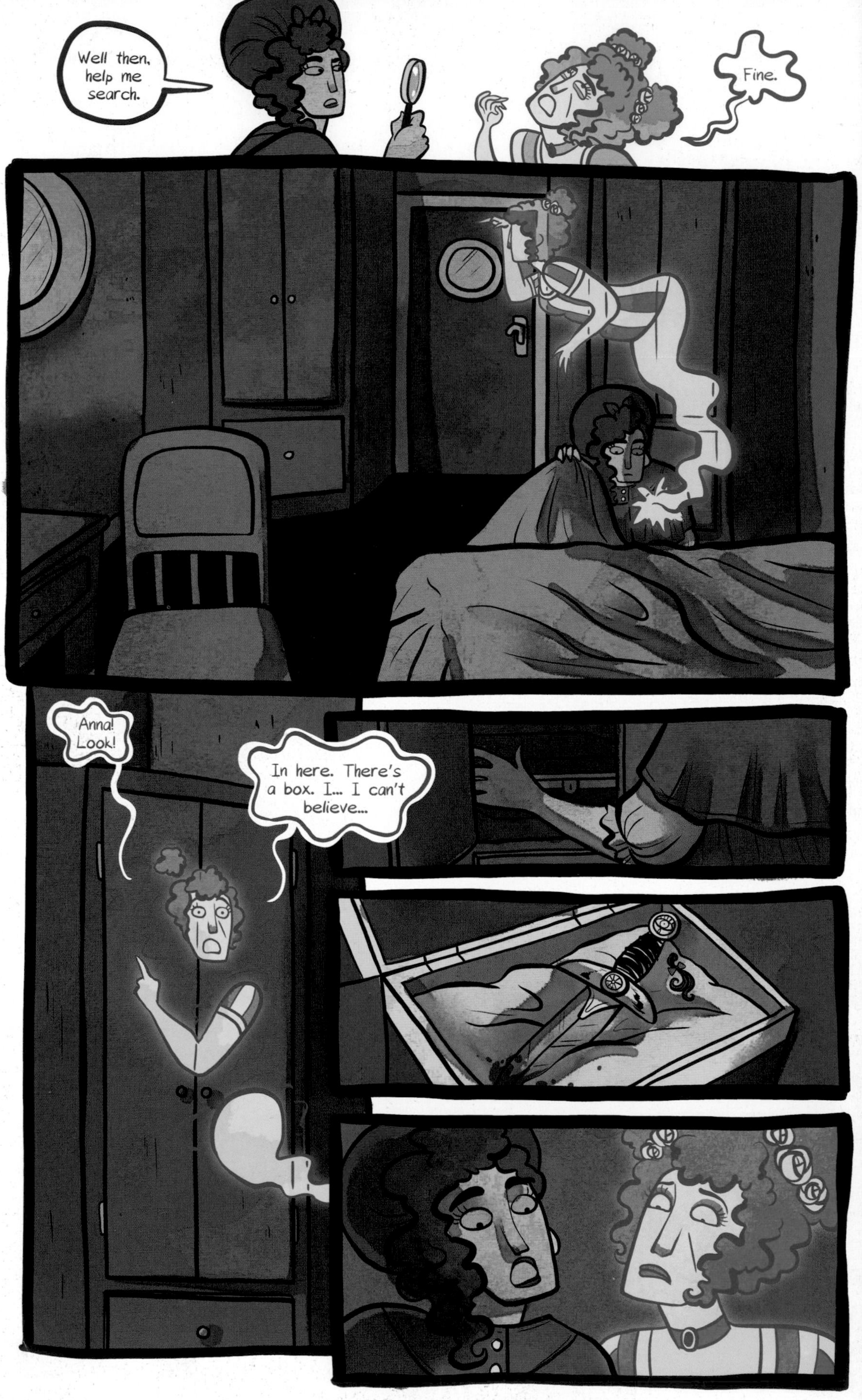
Well then, help me search.
Fine.
Anna! Look!
In here. There's a box. I... I can't believe...

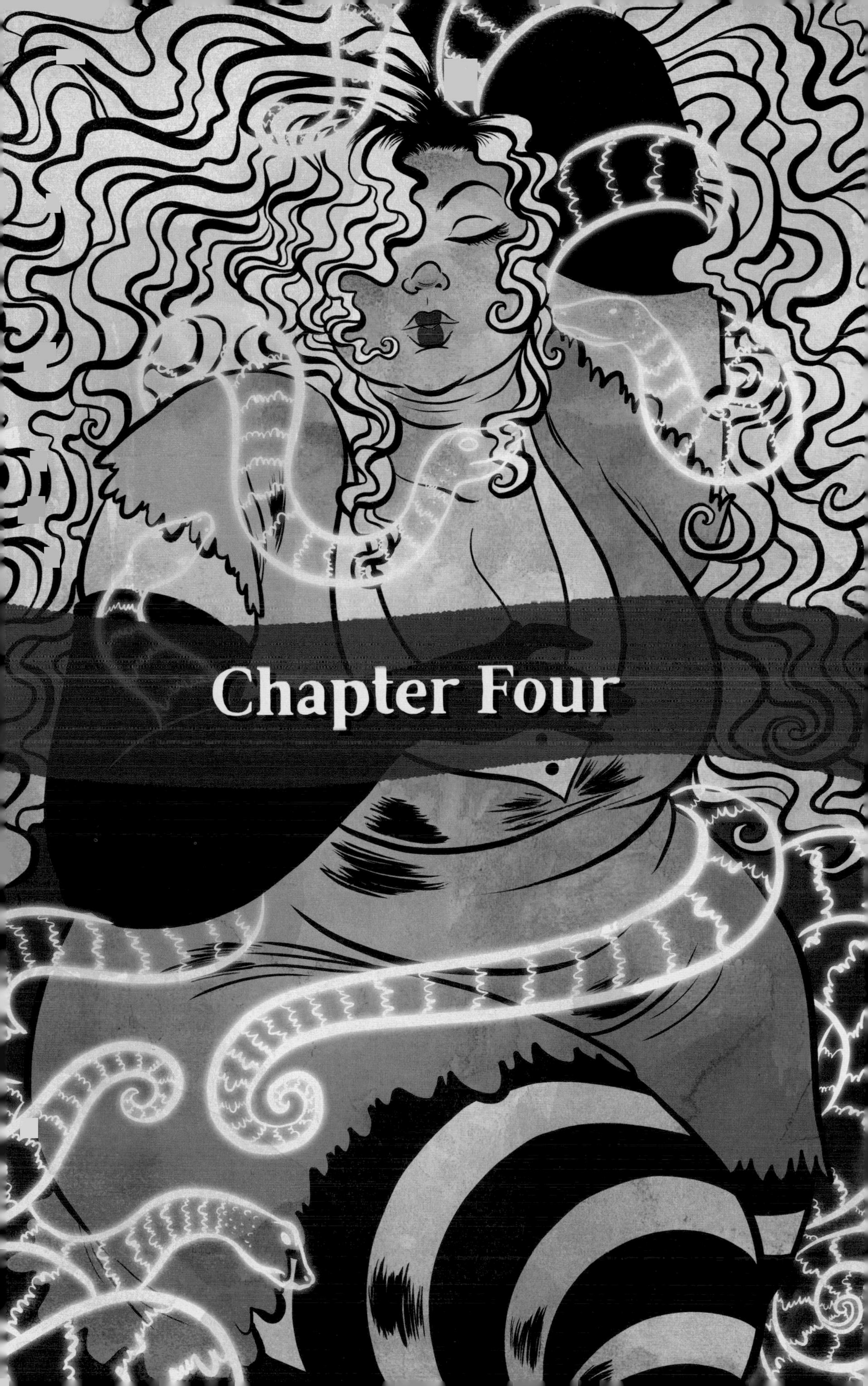

Chapter Four

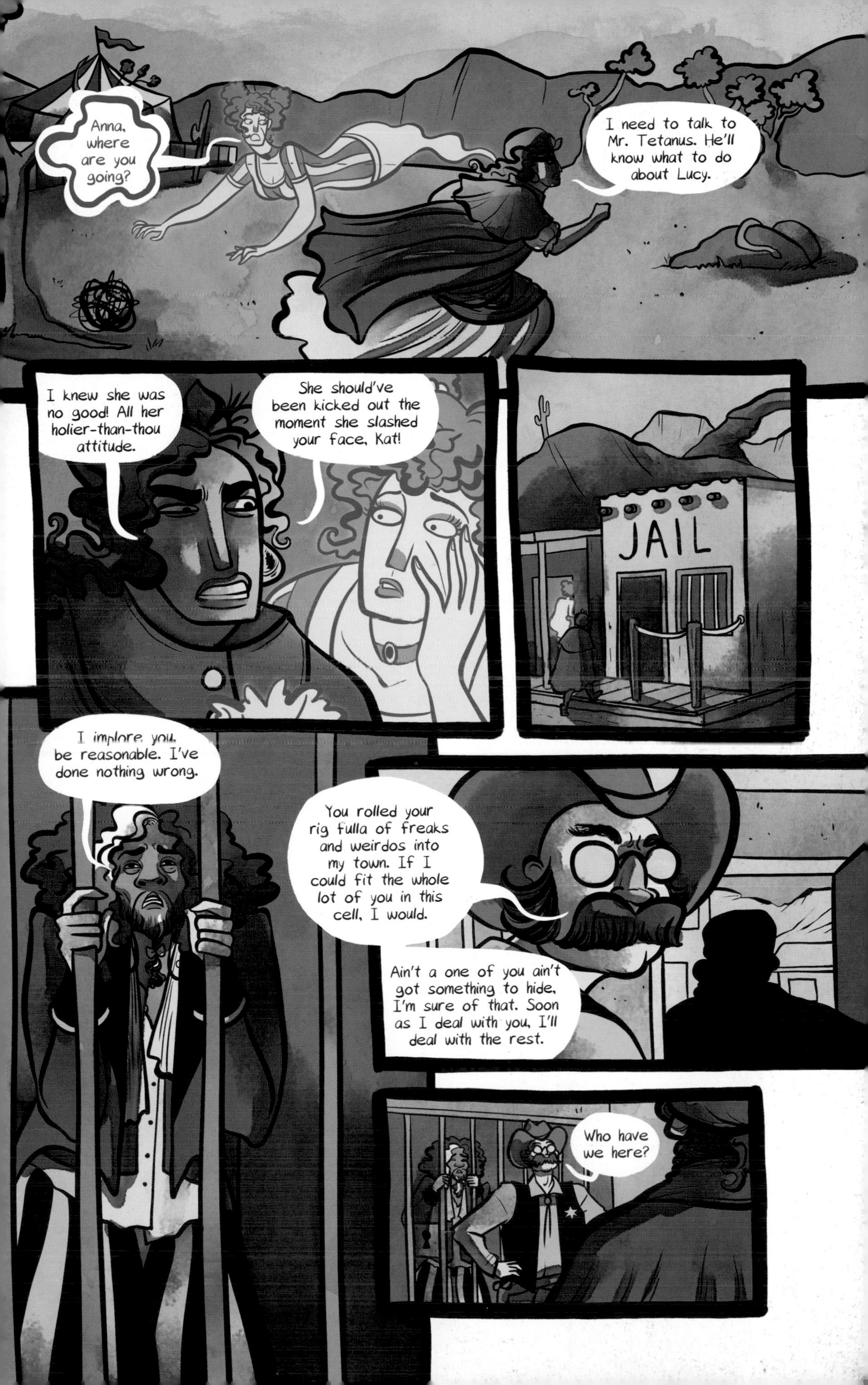
Anna, where are you going?
I need to talk to Mr. Tetanus. He'll know what to do about Lucy.
I knew she was no good! All her holier-than-thou attitude.
She should've been kicked out the moment she slashed your face, Kat!
JAIL
I implore you, be reasonable. I've done nothing wrong.
You rolled your rig fulla of freaks and weirdos into my town. If I could fit the whole lot of you in this cell, I would.
Ain't a one of you ain't got something to hide, I'm sure of that. Soon as I deal with you, I'll deal with the rest.
Who have we here?

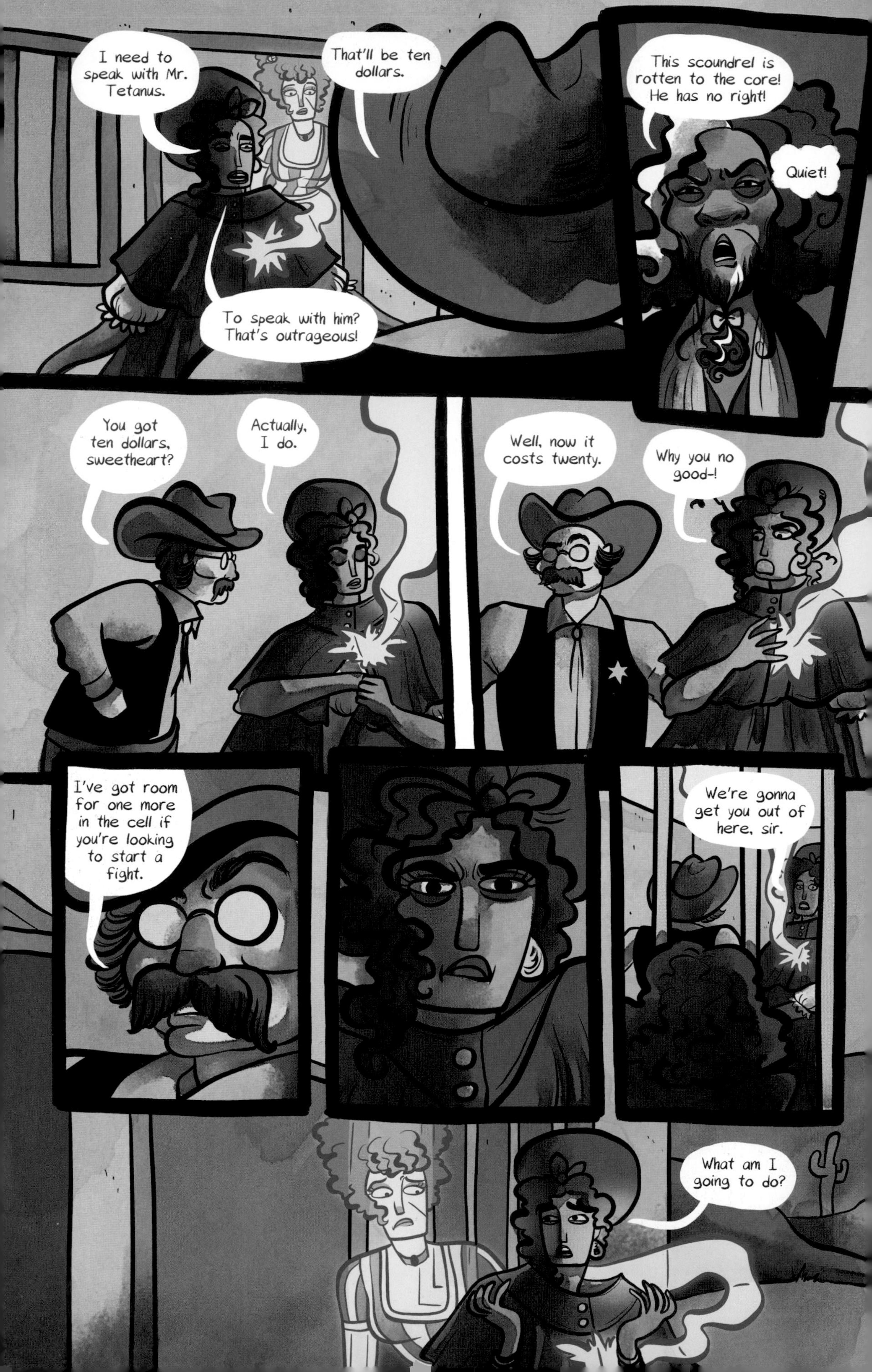

I need to speak with Mr. Tetanus.
That'll be ten dollars.
To speak with him? That's outrageous!
This scoundrel is rotten to the core! He has no right!
Quiet!
You got ten dollars, sweetheart?
Actually, I do.
Well, now it costs twenty.
Why you no good-!
I've got room for one more in the cell if you're looking to start a fight.
We're gonna get you out of here, sir.
What am I going to do?

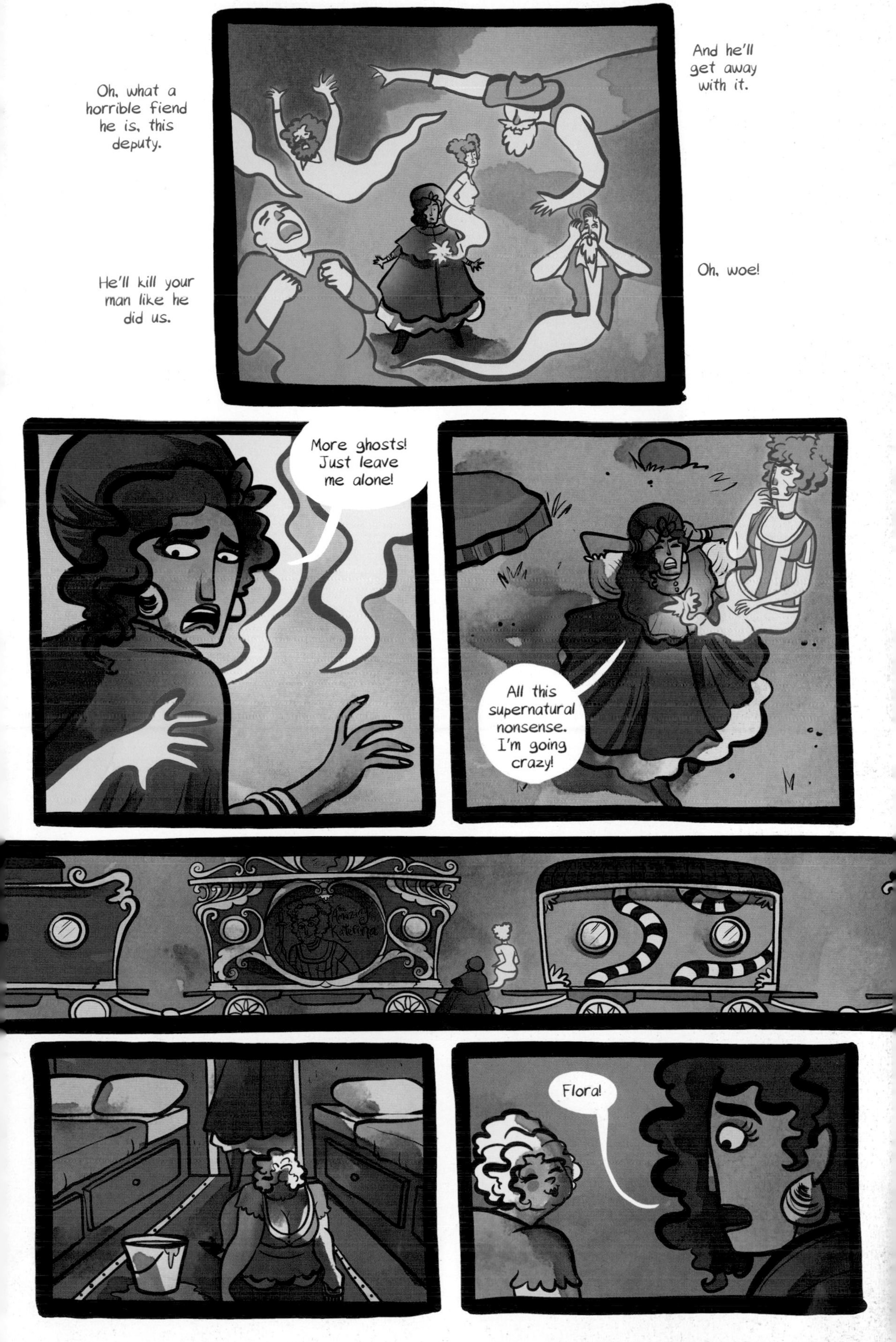
Oh, what a horrible fiend he is, this deputy.
And he'll get away with it.
He'll kill your man like he did us.
Oh, woe!
More ghosts! Just leave me alone!
All this supernatural nonsense. I'm going crazy!
Flora!

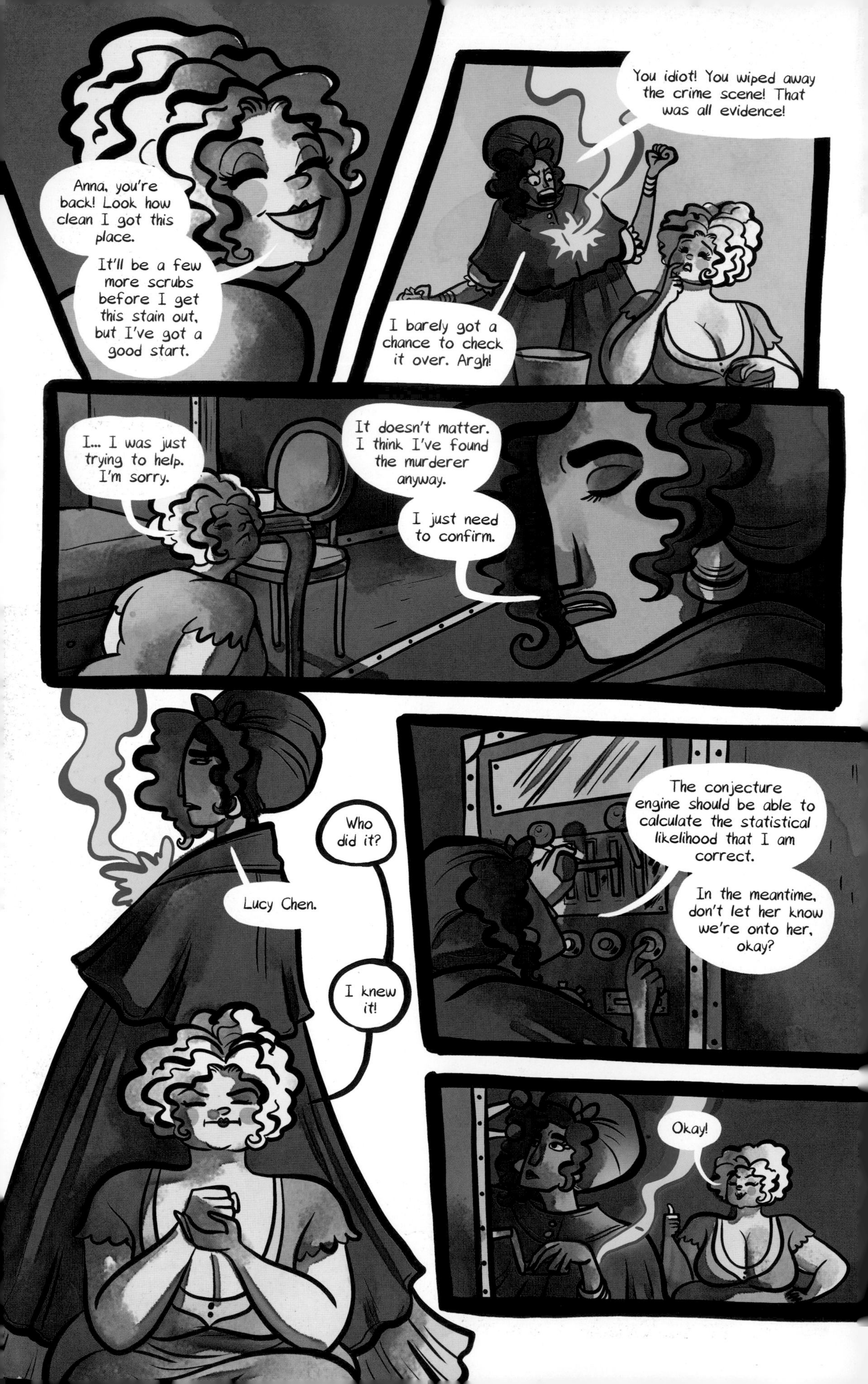
Anna, you're back! Look how clean I got this place.
It'll be a few more scrubs before I get this stain out, but I've got a good start.
You idiot! You wiped away the crime scene! That was all evidence!
I barely got a chance to check it over. Argh!
I... I was just trying to help. I'm sorry.
It doesn't matter. I think I've found the murderer anyway.
I just need to confirm.
Who did it?
Lucy Chen.
I knew it!
The conjecture engine should be able to calculate the statistical likelihood that I am correct.
In the meantime, don't let her know we're onto her, okay?
Okay!

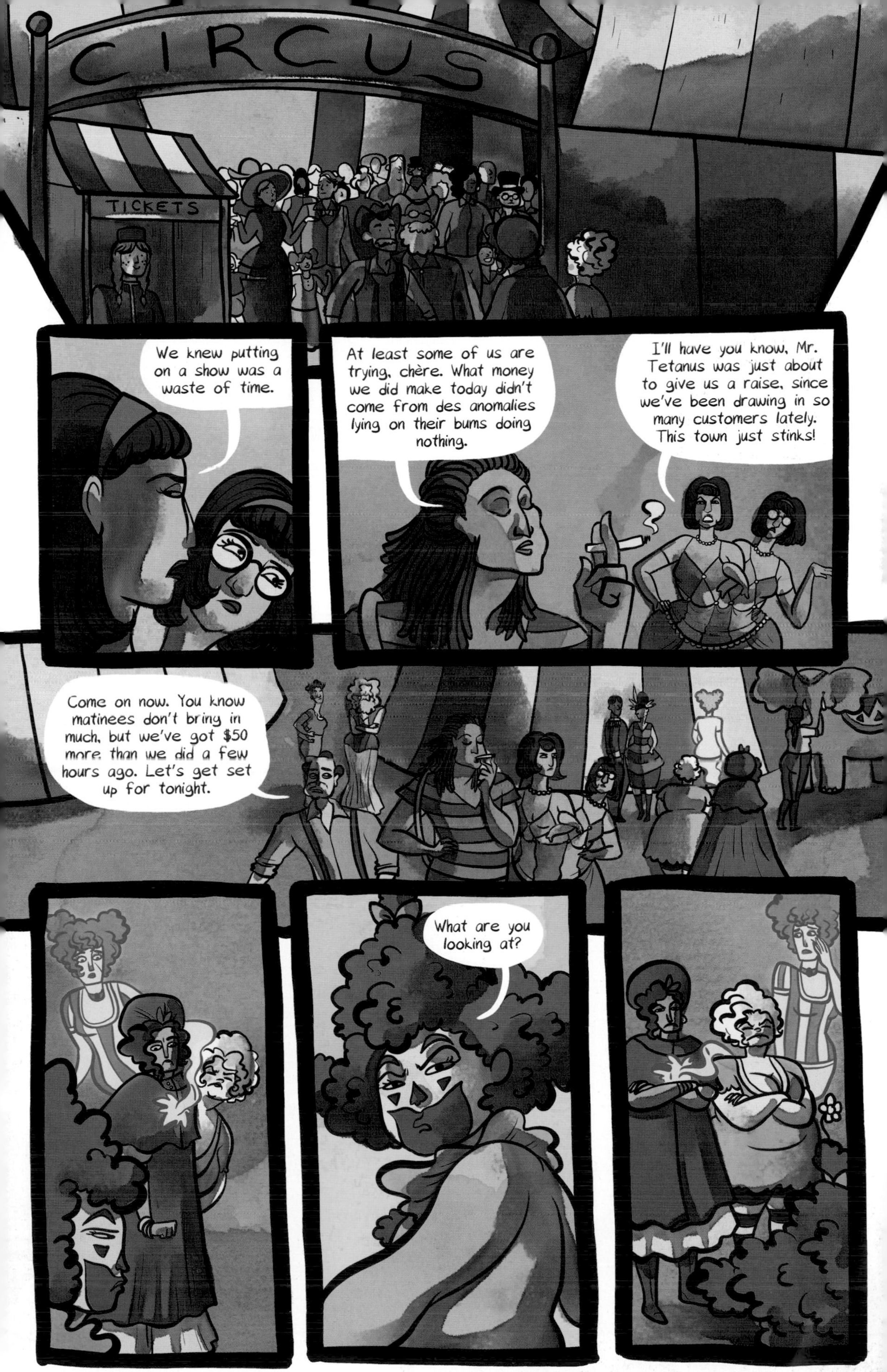
CIRCUS
TICKETS
We knew putting on a show was a waste of time.
At least some of us are trying, chère. What money we did make today didn't come from des anomalies lying on their bums doing nothing.
I'll have you know, Mr. Tetanus was just about to give us a raise, since we've been drawing in so many customers lately. This town just stinks!
Come on now. You know matinees don't bring in much, but we've got $50 more than we did a few hours ago. Let's get set up for tonight.
What are you looking at?

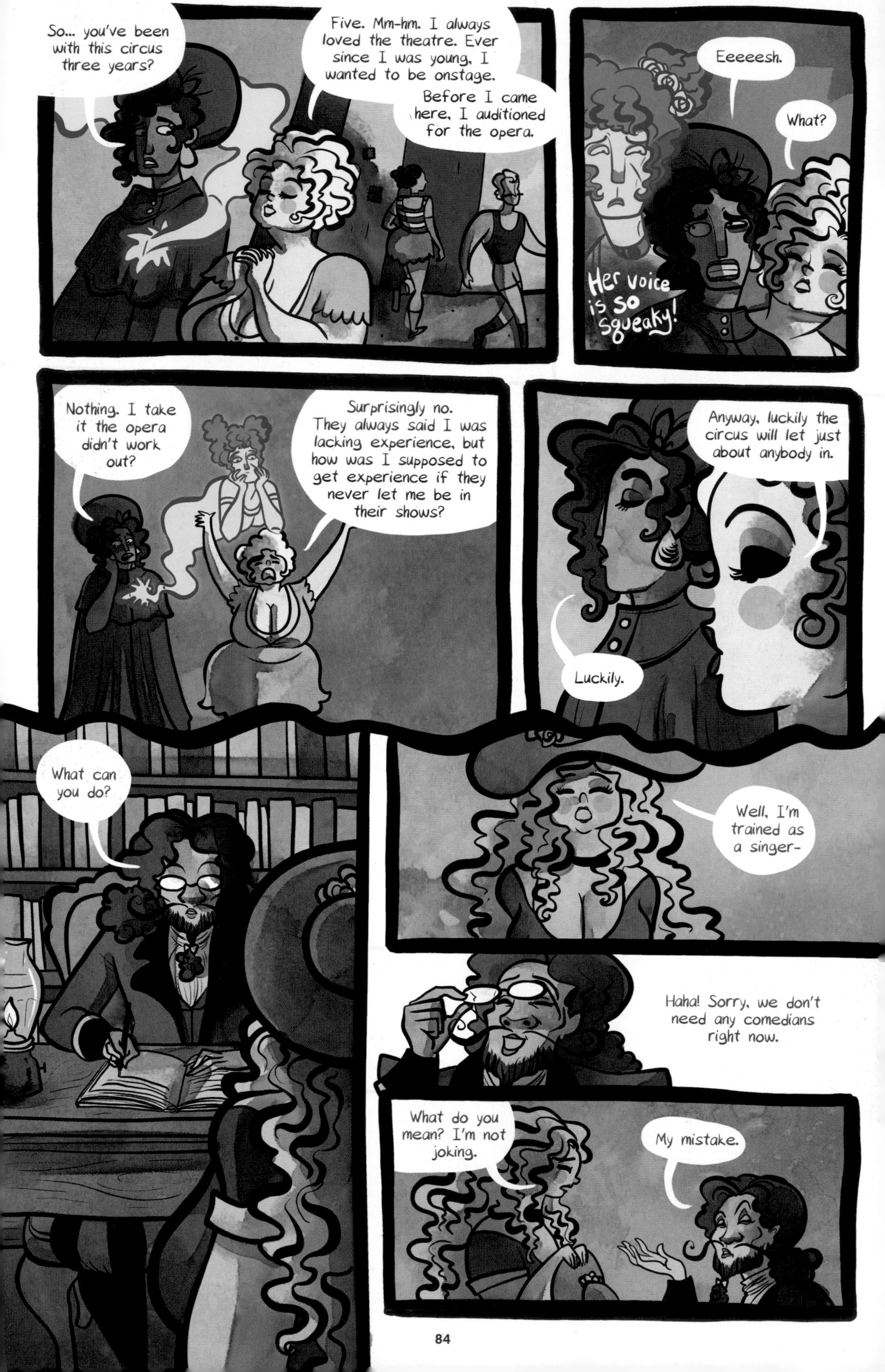
So... you've been with this circus three years?
Five. Mm-hm. I always loved the theatre. Ever since I was young, I wanted to be onstage.
Before I came here, I auditioned for the opera.
Eeeeesh.
What?
Her voice is so squeaky!
Nothing. I take it the opera didn't work out?
Surprisingly no. They always said I was lacking experience, but how was I supposed to get experience if they never let me be in their shows?
Anyway, luckily the circus will let just about anybody in.
Luckily.
What can you do?
Well, I'm trained as a singer-
Haha! Sorry, we don't need any comedians right now.
What do you mean? I'm not joking.
My mistake.

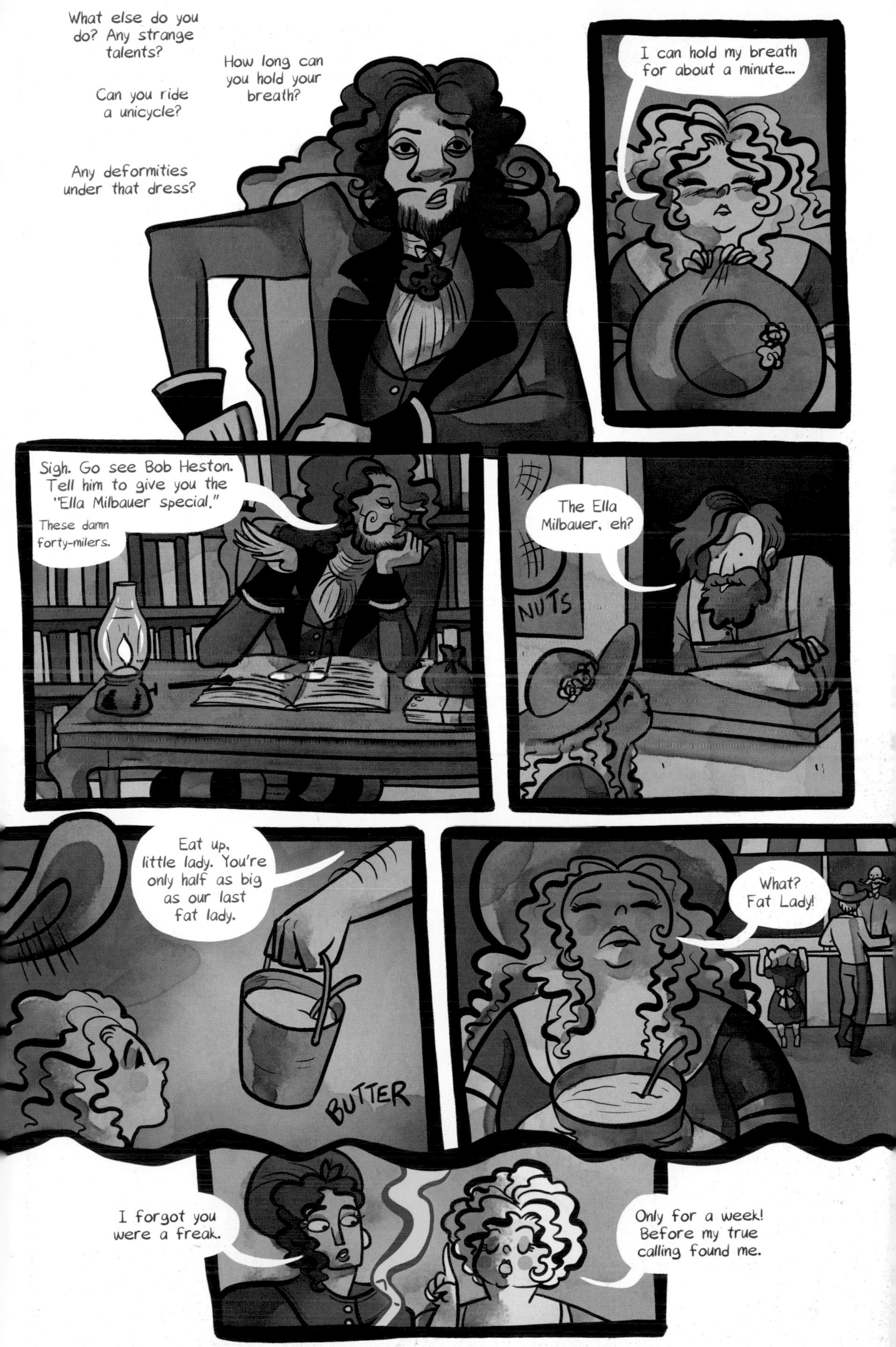
What else do you do? Any strange talents?
Can you ride a unicycle?
Any deformities under that dress?
How long can you hold your breath?
I can hold my breath for about a minute...
Sigh. Go see Bob Heston. Tell him to give you the "Ella Milbauer special."
These damn forty-milers.
NUTS
The Ella Milbauer, eh?
Eat up, little lady. You're only half as big as our last fat lady.
BUTTER
What? Fat Lady!
I forgot you were a freak.
Only for a week! Before my true calling found me.

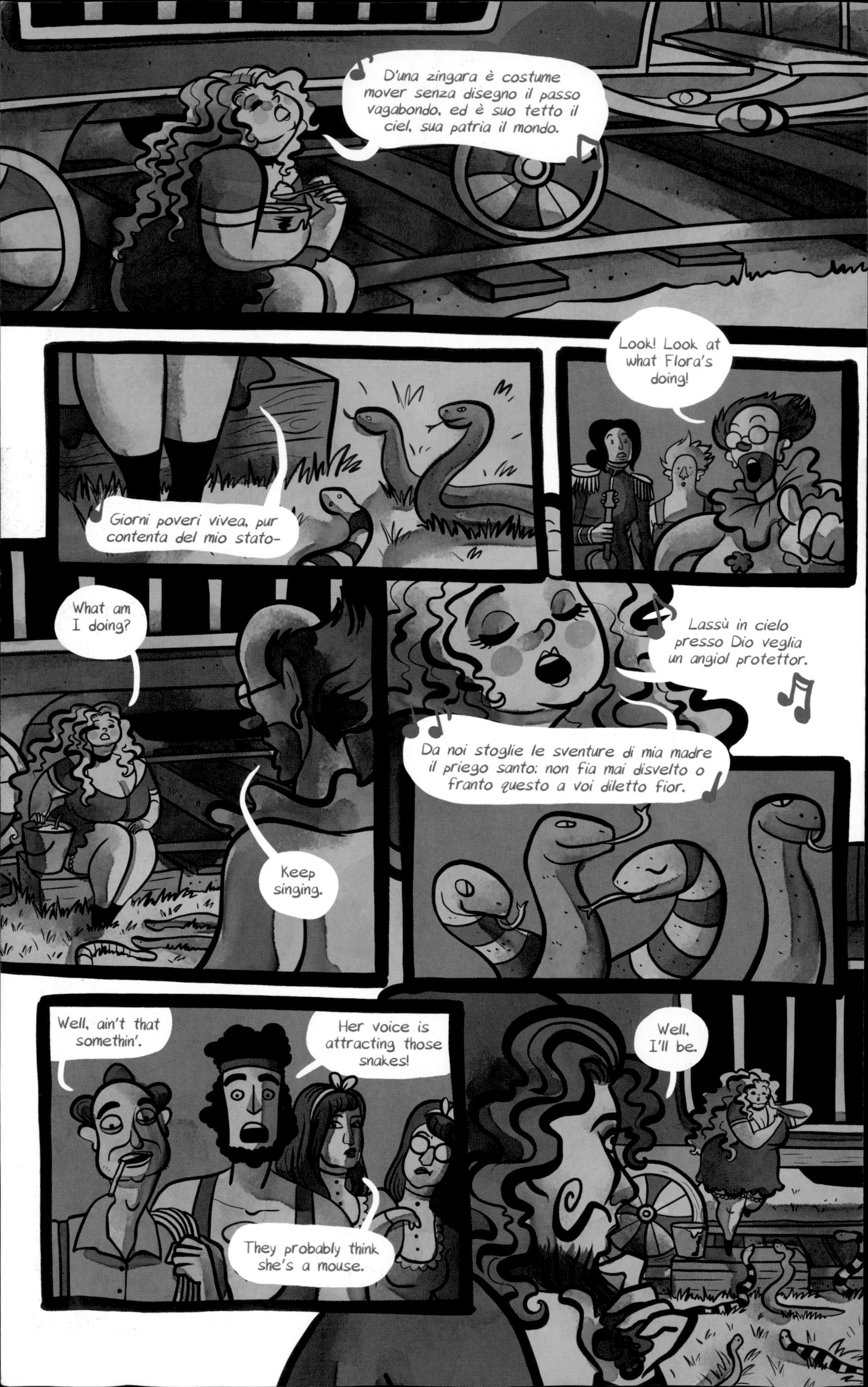
D'una zingara è costume mover senza disegno il passo vagabondo, ed è suo tetto il ciel, sua patria il mondo.
Giorni poveri vivea, pur contenta del mio stato-
Look! Look at what Flora's doing!
What am I doing?
Keep singing.
Lassù in cielo presso Dio veglia un angiol protettor.
Da noi stoglie le sventure di mia madre il priego santo: non fia mai disvelto o franto questo a voi diletto fior.
Well, ain't that somethin'.
Her voice is attracting those snakes!
They probably think she's a mouse.
Well, I'll be.

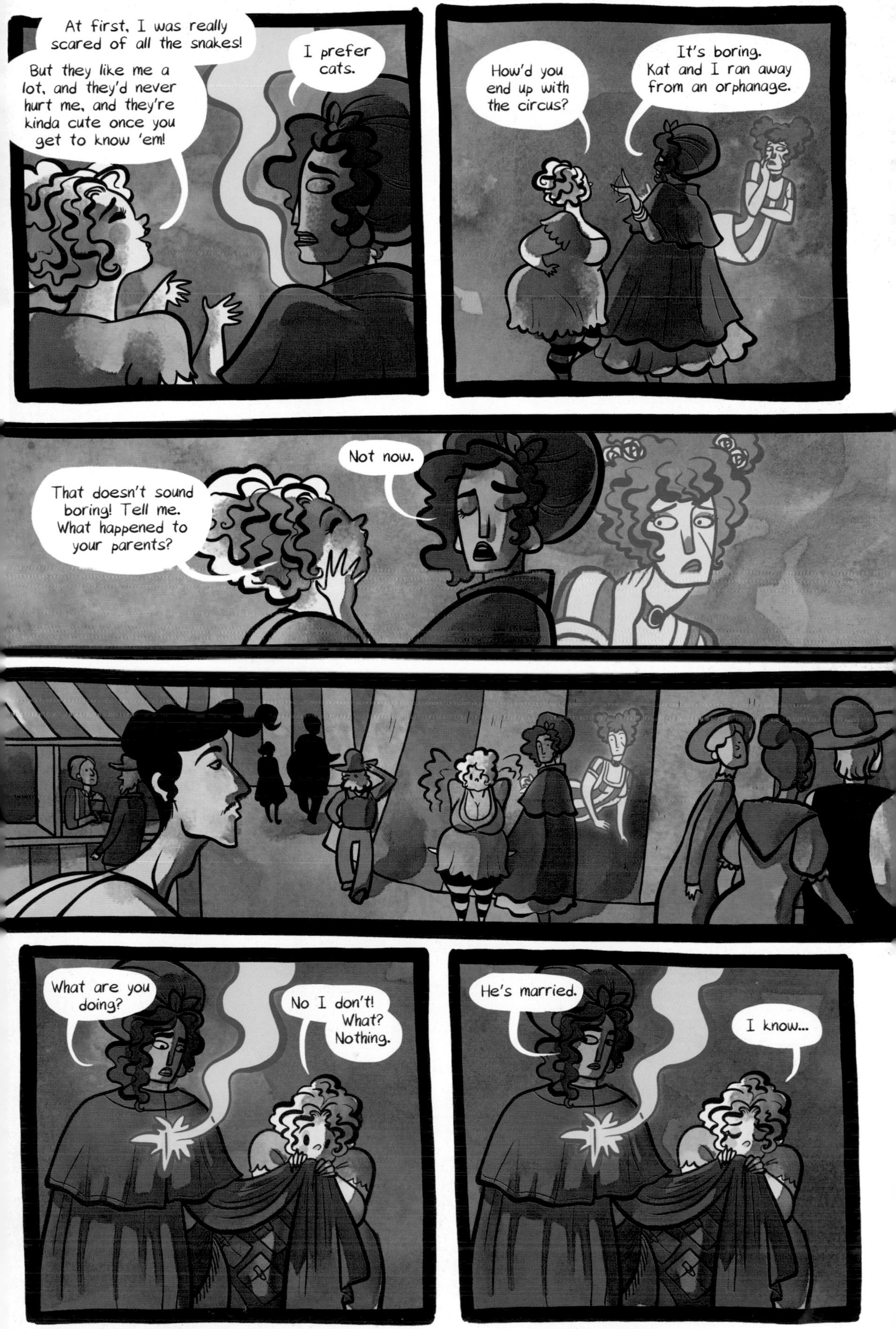
At first, I was really scared of all the snakes!
But they like me a lot, and they'd never hurt me, and they're kinda cute once you get to know 'em!
I prefer cats.
How'd you end up with the circus?
It's boring. Kat and I ran away from an orphanage.
That doesn't sound boring! Tell me. What happened to your parents?
Not now.
What are you doing?
No I don't! What? Nothing.
He's married.
I know...

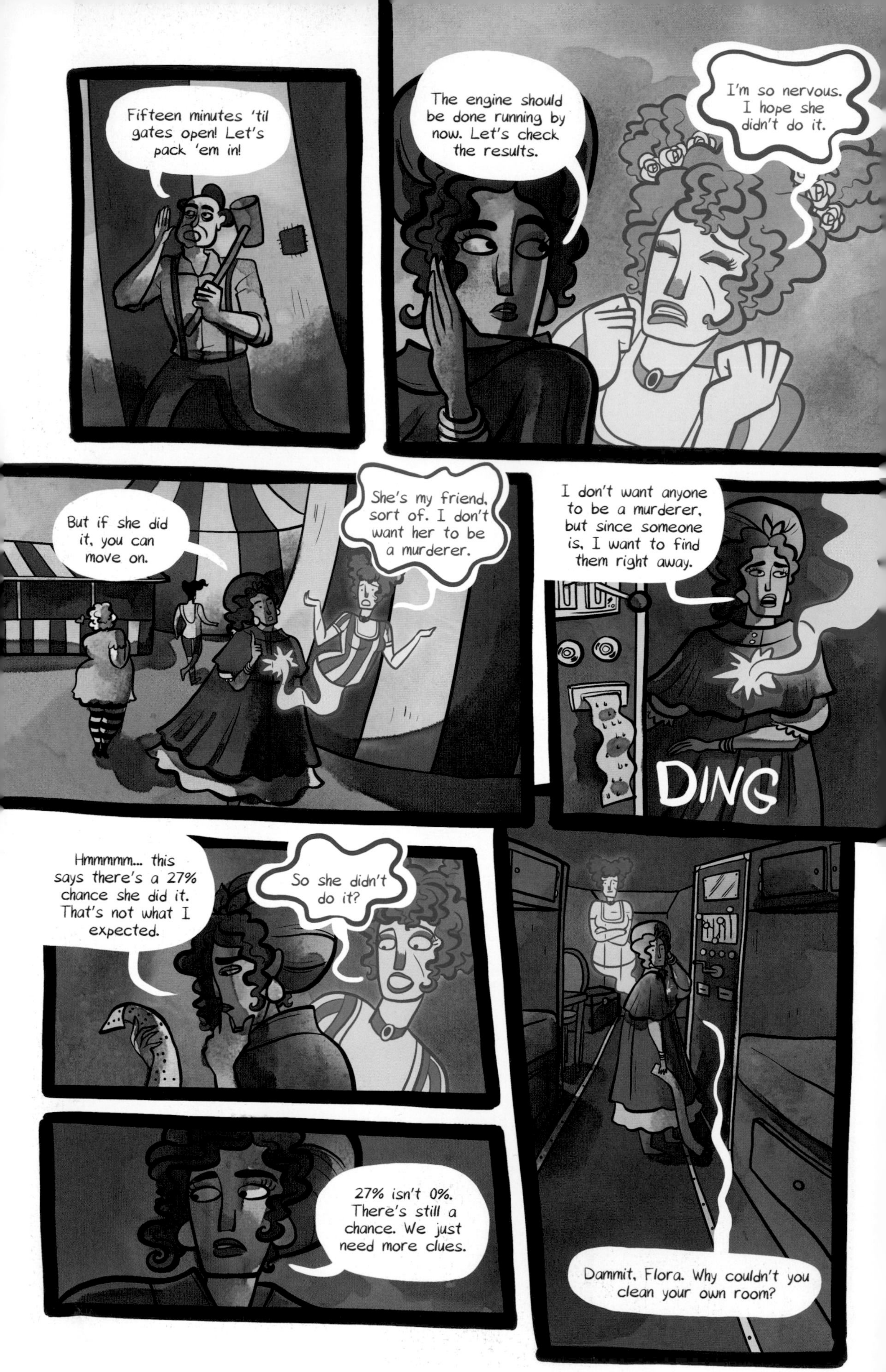
Fifteen minutes 'til gates open! Let's pack 'em in!
The engine should be done running by now. Let's check the results.
I'm so nervous. I hope she didn't do it.
But if she did it, you can move on.
She's my friend, sort of. I don't want her to be a murderer.
I don't want anyone to be a murderer, but since someone is, I want to find them right away.
DING
Hmmmmm... this says there's a 27% chance she did it. That's not what I expected.
So she didn't do it?
27% isn't 0%. There's still a chance. We just need more clues.
Dammit, Flora. Why couldn't you clean your own room?

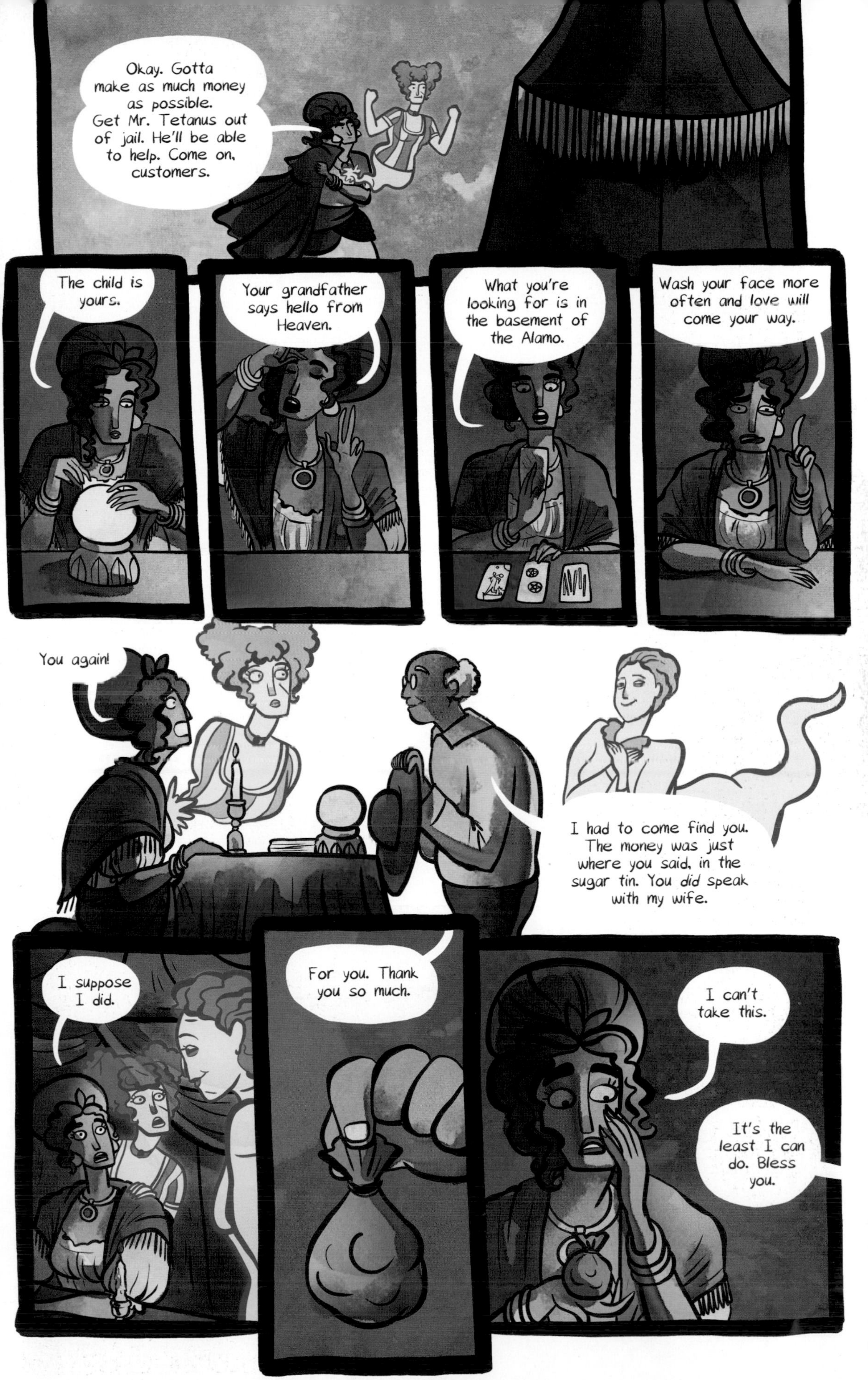
Okay. Gotta make as much money as possible. Get Mr. Tetanus out of jail. He'll be able to help. Come on, customers.
The child is yours.
Your grandfather says hello from Heaven.
What you're looking for is in the basement of the Alamo.
Wash your face more often and love will come your way.
You again!
I had to come find you. The money was just where you said, in the sugar tin. You *did* speak with my wife.
I suppose I did.
For you. Thank you so much.
I can't take this.
It's the least I can do. Bless you.

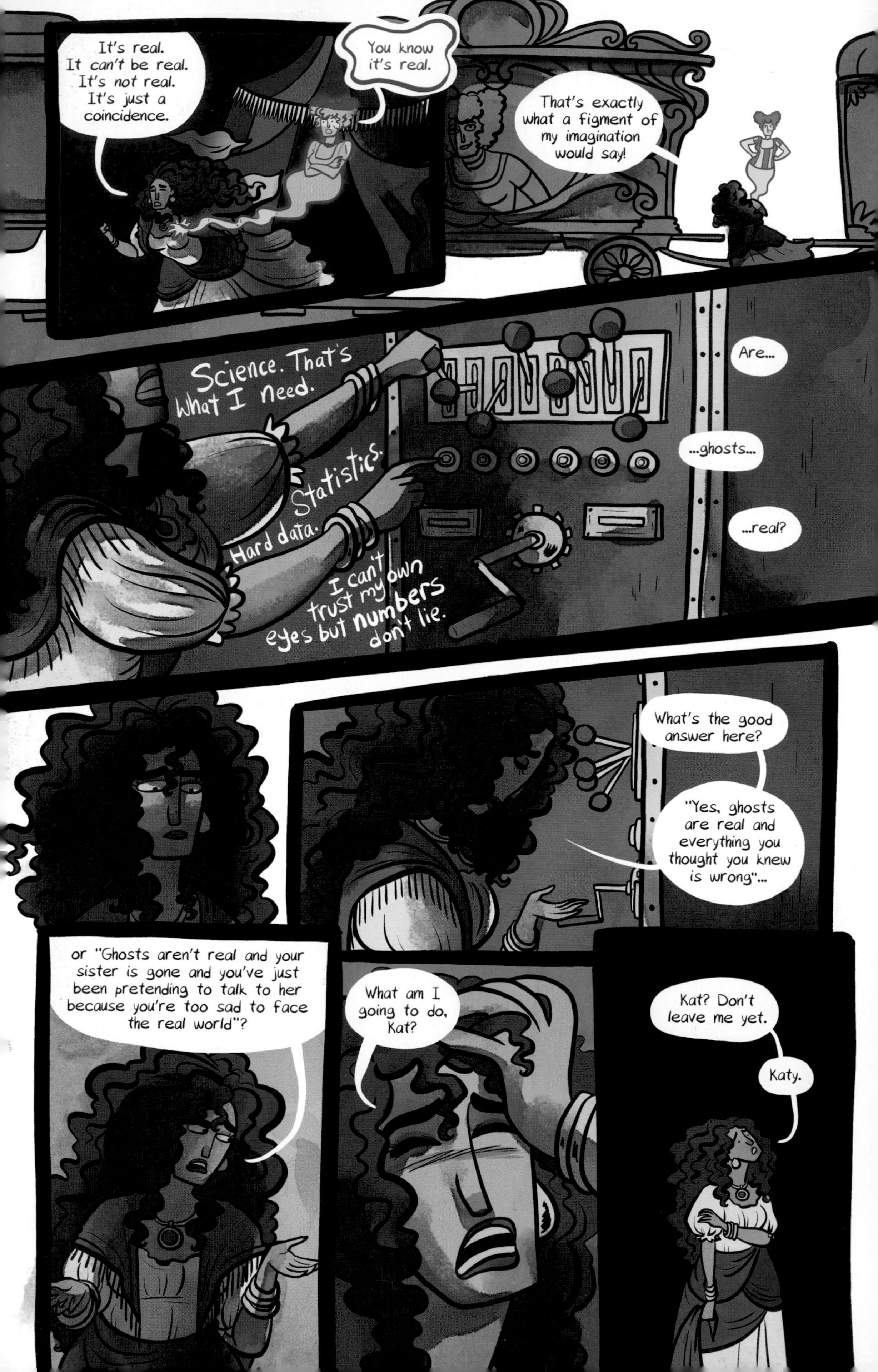
It's real. It can't be real. It's not real. It's just a coincidence.
You know it's real.
That's exactly what a figment of my imagination would say!
Science. That's what I need.
Statistics.
Hard data.
I can't trust my own eyes but numbers don't lie.
Are...
...ghosts...
...real?
What's the good answer here?
"Yes, ghosts are real and everything you thought you knew is wrong"...
or "Ghosts aren't real and your sister is gone and you've just been pretending to talk to her because you're too sad to face the real world"?
What am I going to do, Kat?
Kat? Don't leave me yet.
Katy.

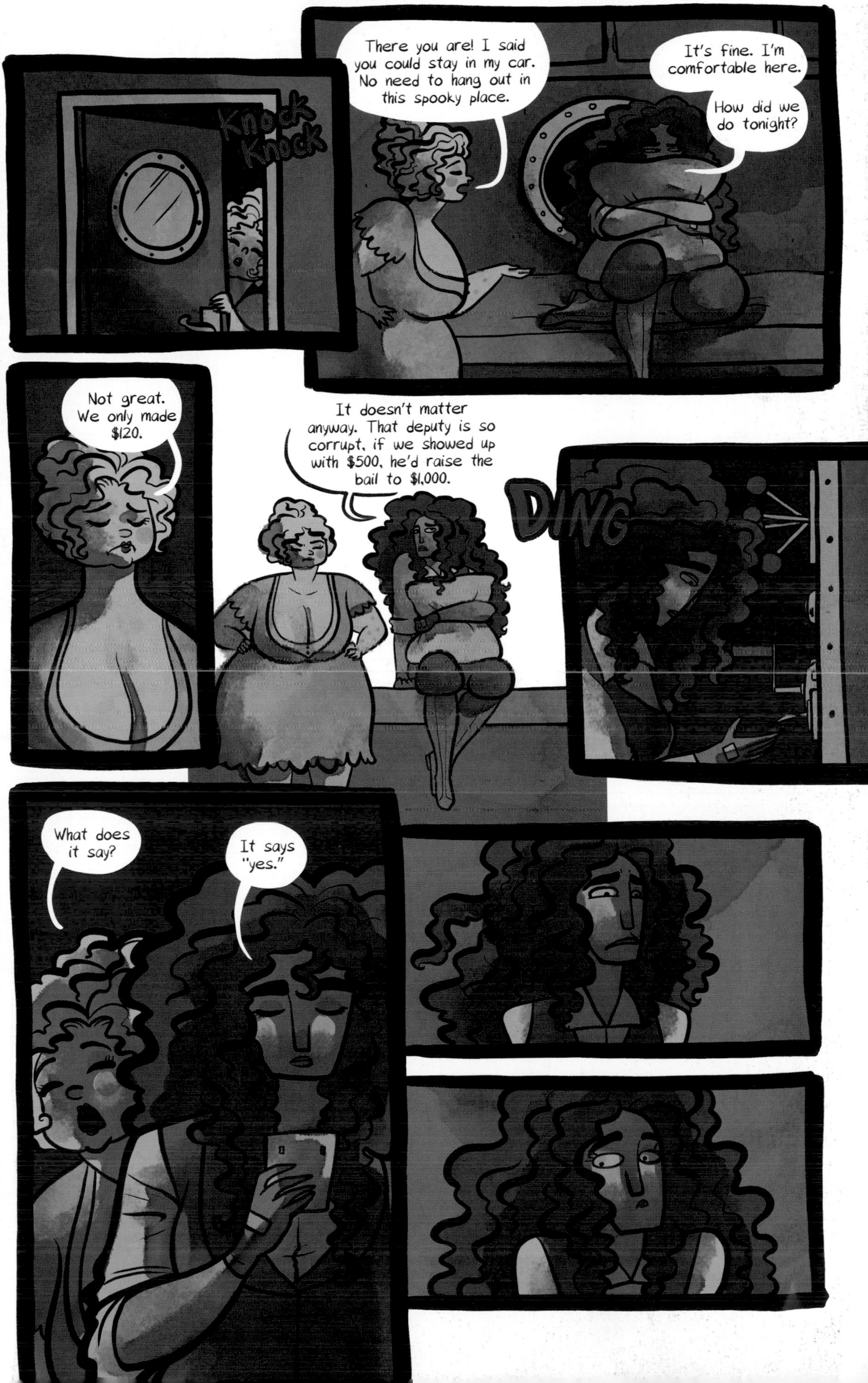
Knock Knock
There you are! I said you could stay in my car. No need to hang out in this spooky place.
It's fine. I'm comfortable here.
How did we do tonight?
Not great. We only made $120.
It doesn't matter anyway. That deputy is so corrupt, if we showed up with $500, he'd raise the bail to $1,000.
DING
What does it say?
It says "yes."

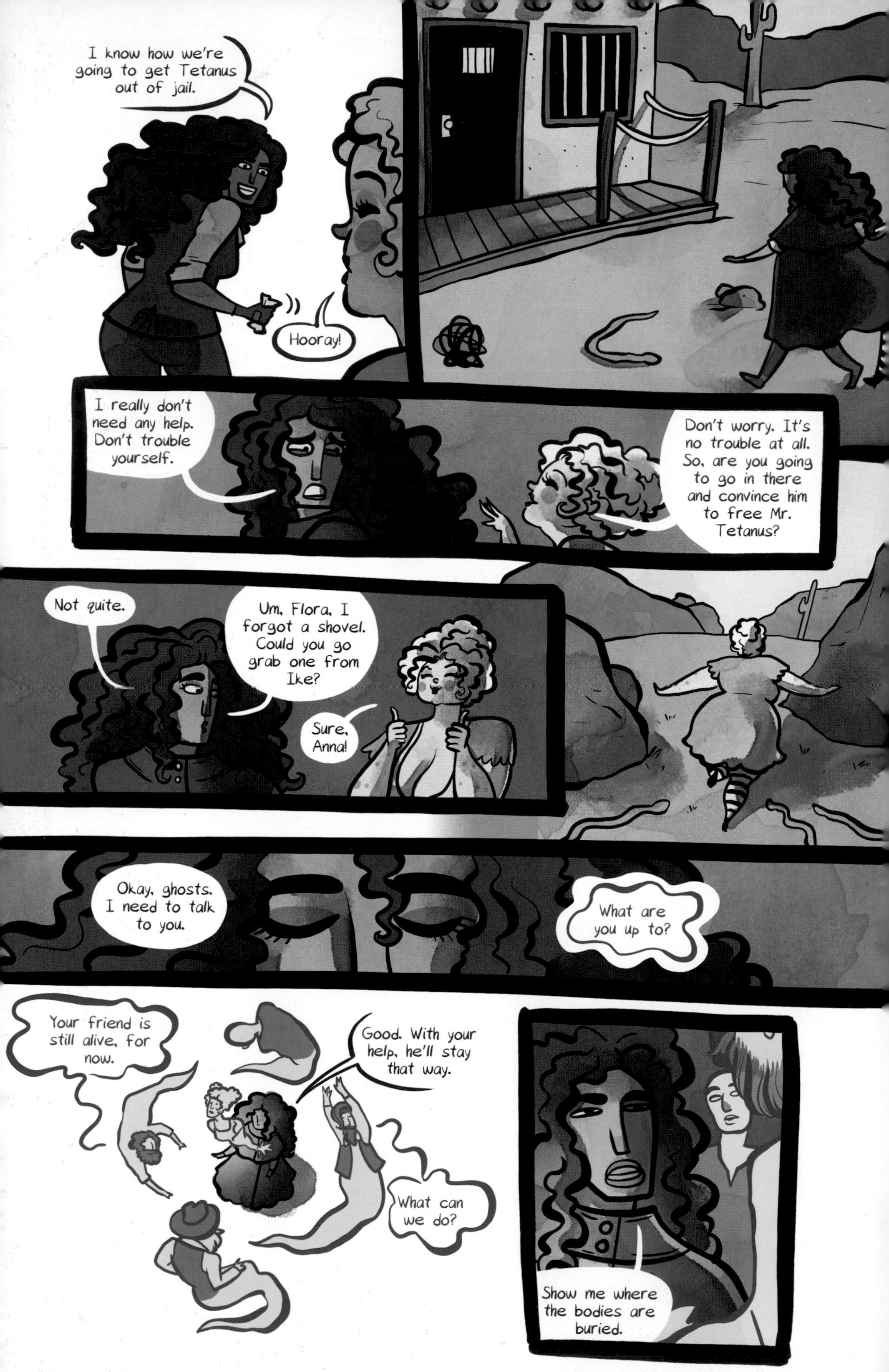
I know how we're going to get Tetanus out of jail.
Hooray!
I really don't need any help. Don't trouble yourself.
Don't worry. It's no trouble at all. So, are you going to go in there and convince him to free Mr. Tetanus?
Not quite.
Um, Flora, I forgot a shovel. Could you go grab one from Ike?
Sure, Anna!
Okay, ghosts. I need to talk to you.
What are you up to?
Your friend is still alive, for now.
Good. With your help, he'll stay that way.
What can we do?
Show me where the bodies are buried.

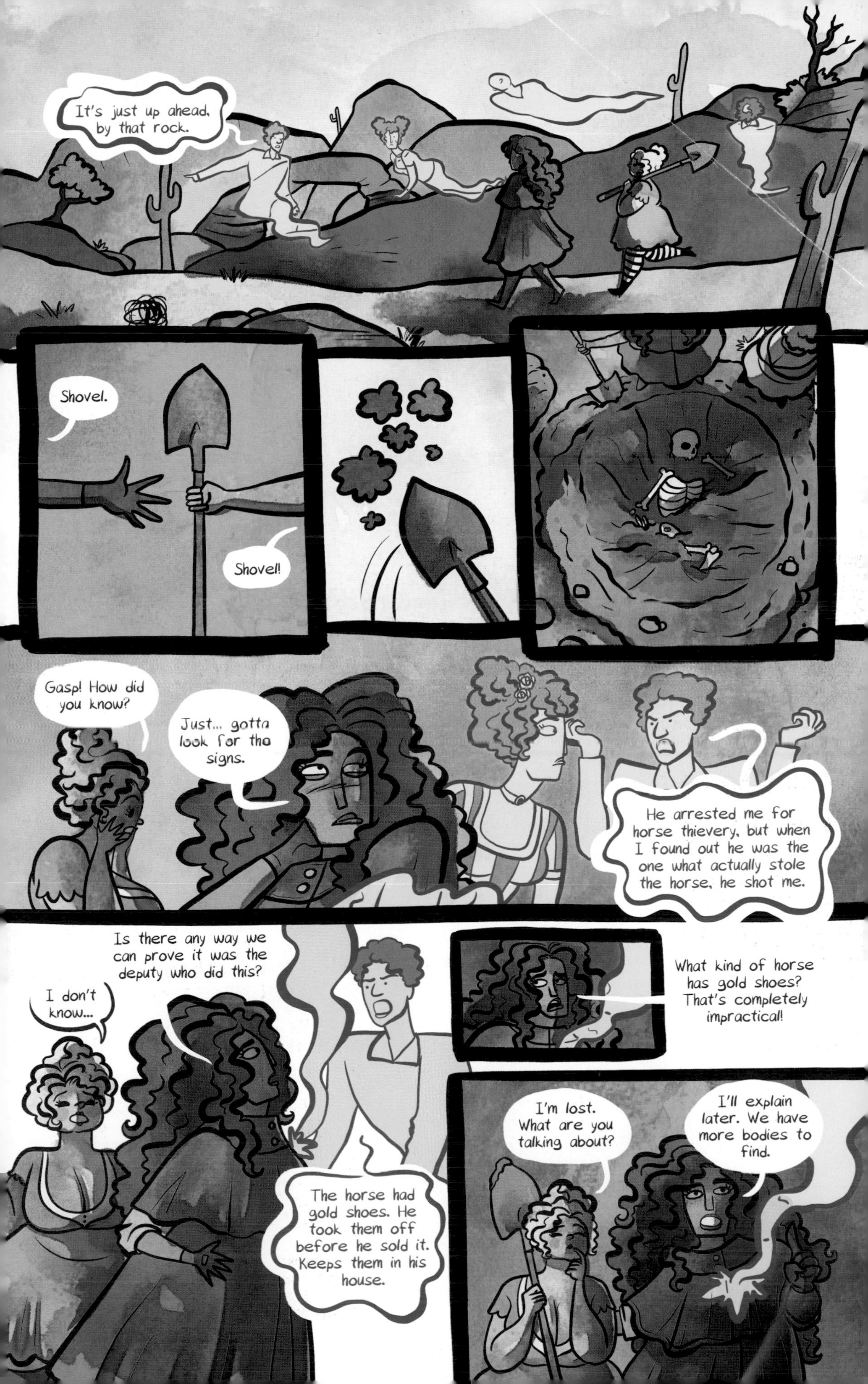
It's just up ahead, by that rock.
Shovel.
Shovel!
Gasp! How did you know?
Just... gotta look for tha signs.
He arrested me for horse thievery, but when I found out he was the one what actually stole the horse, he shot me.
Is there any way we can prove it was the deputy who did this?
I don't know...
The horse had gold shoes. He took them off before he sold it. Keeps them in his house.
What kind of horse has gold shoes? That's completely impractical!
I'm lost. What are you talking about?
I'll explain later. We have more bodies to find.

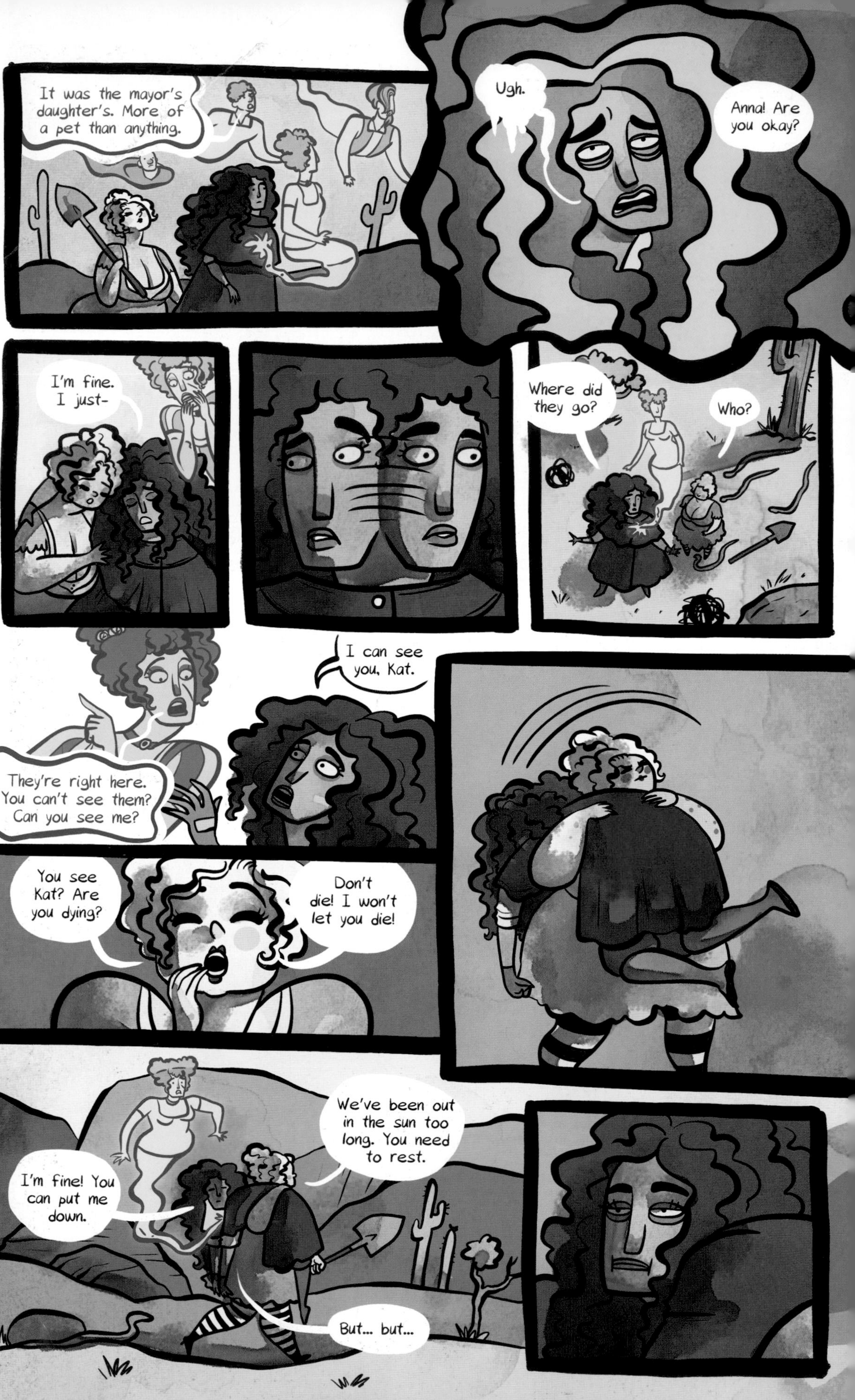
It was the mayor's daughter's. More of a pet than anything.
Ugh.
Anna! Are you okay?
I'm fine. I just-
Where did they go?
Who?
They're right here. You can't see them? Can you see me?
I can see you, Kat.
You see Kat? Are you dying?
Don't die! I won't let you die!
We've been out in the sun too long. You need to rest.
I'm fine! You can put me down.
But... but...

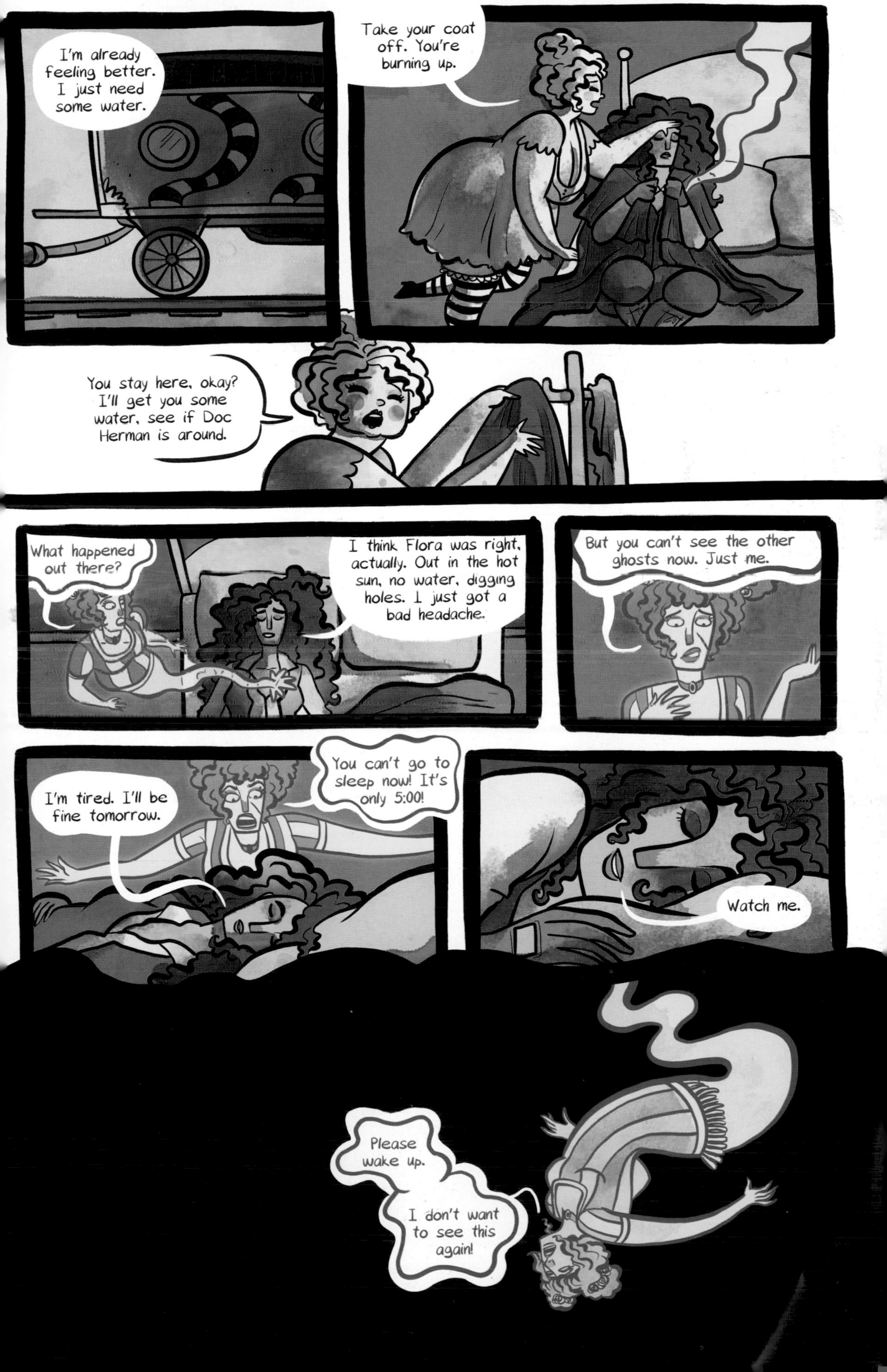
I'm already feeling better. I just need some water.
Take your coat off. You're burning up.
You stay here, okay? I'll get you some water, see if Doc Herman is around.
What happened out there?
I think Flora was right, actually. Out in the hot sun, no water, digging holes. I just got a bad headache.
But you can't see the other ghosts now. Just me.
I'm tired. I'll be fine tomorrow.
You can't go to sleep now! It's only 5:00!
Watch me.
Please wake up.
I don't want to see this again!

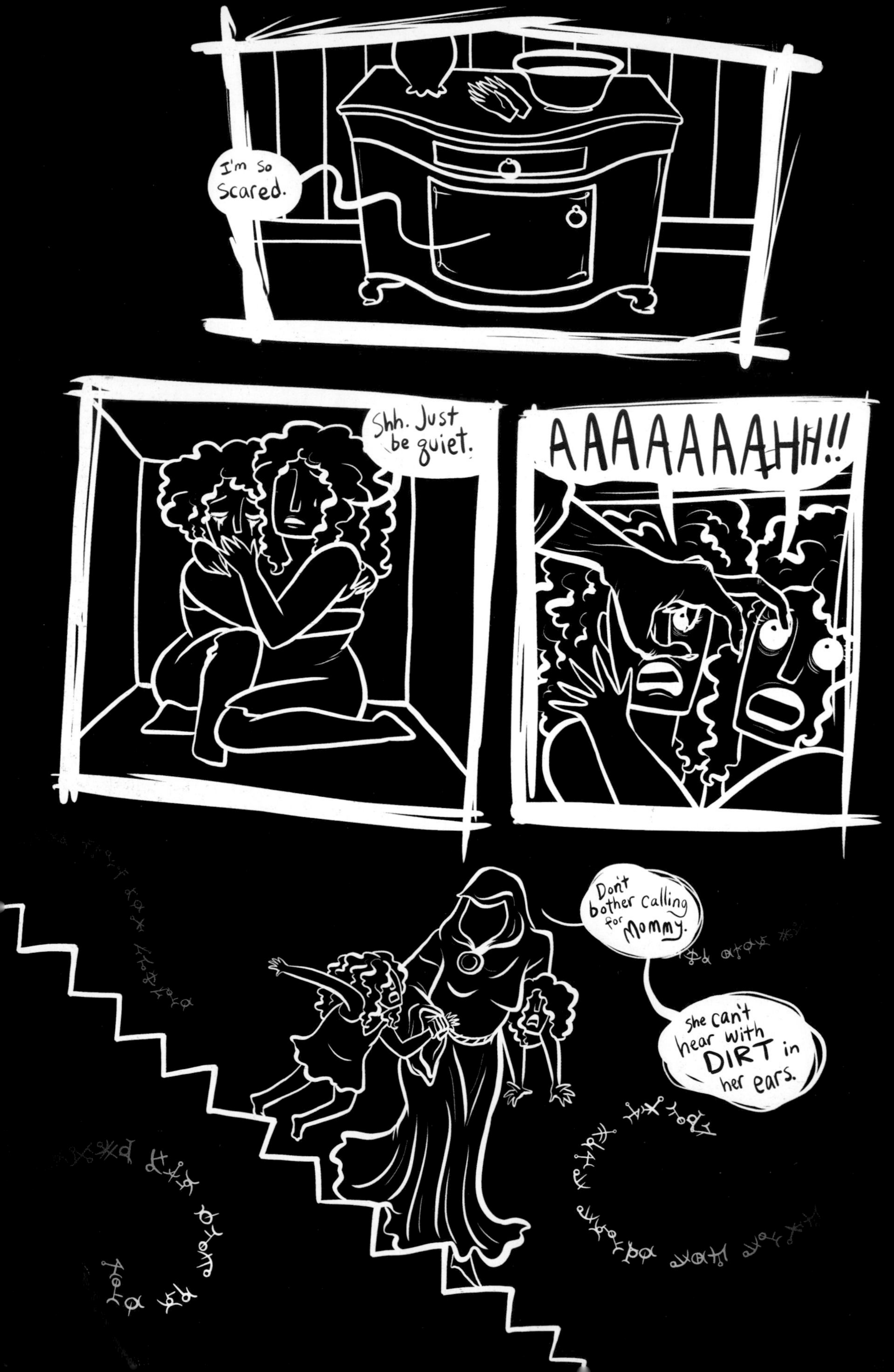
I'm so Scared.
Shh. Just be quiet.
AAAAAAAHH!!
Don't bother calling for Mommy.
She can't hear with DIRT in her ears.

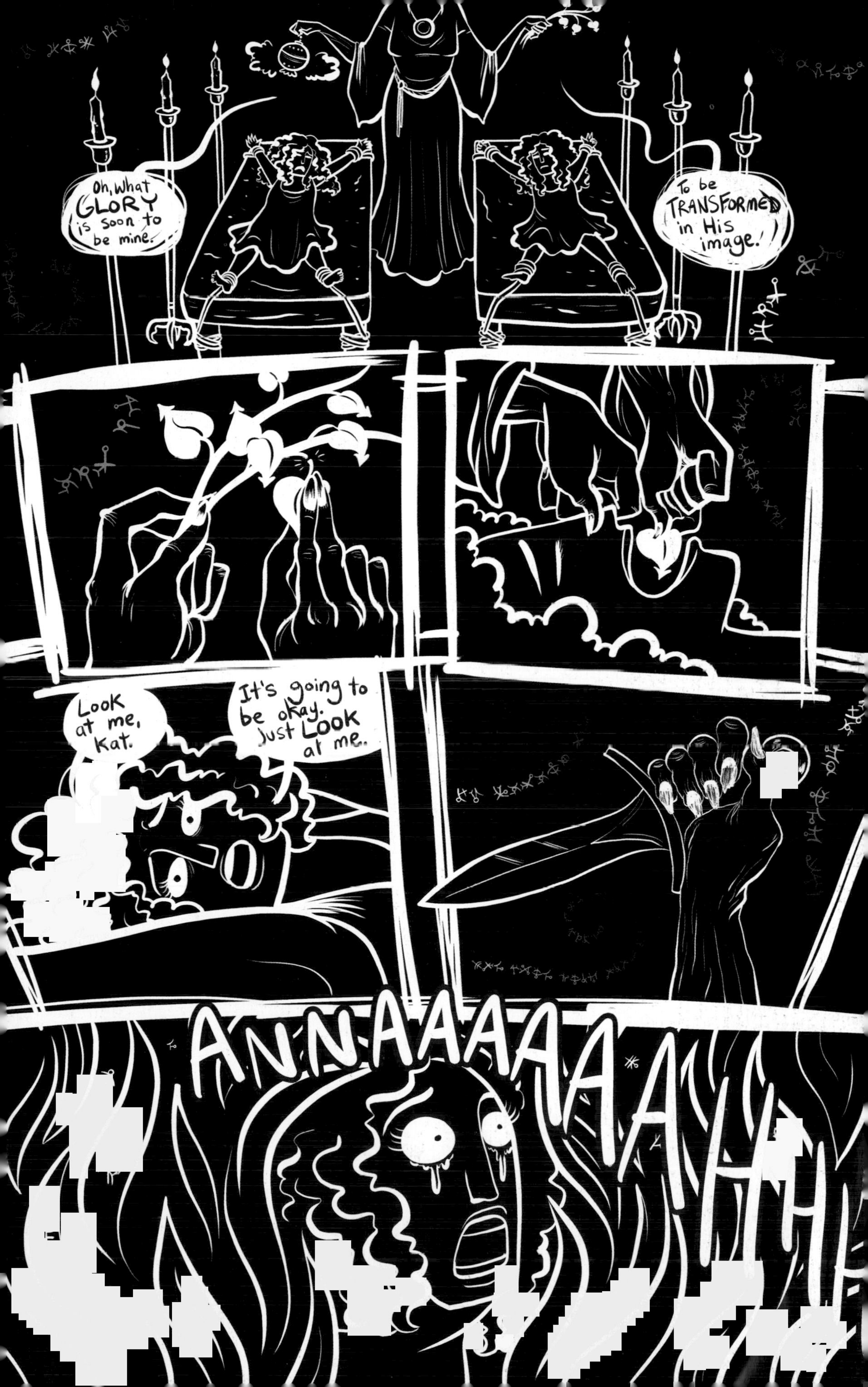
Oh, what GLORY is soon to be mine.
To be TRANSFORMED in His image!
Look at me, Kat.
It's going to be okay. Just LOOK at me.
ANNAAAAAAAAHHH

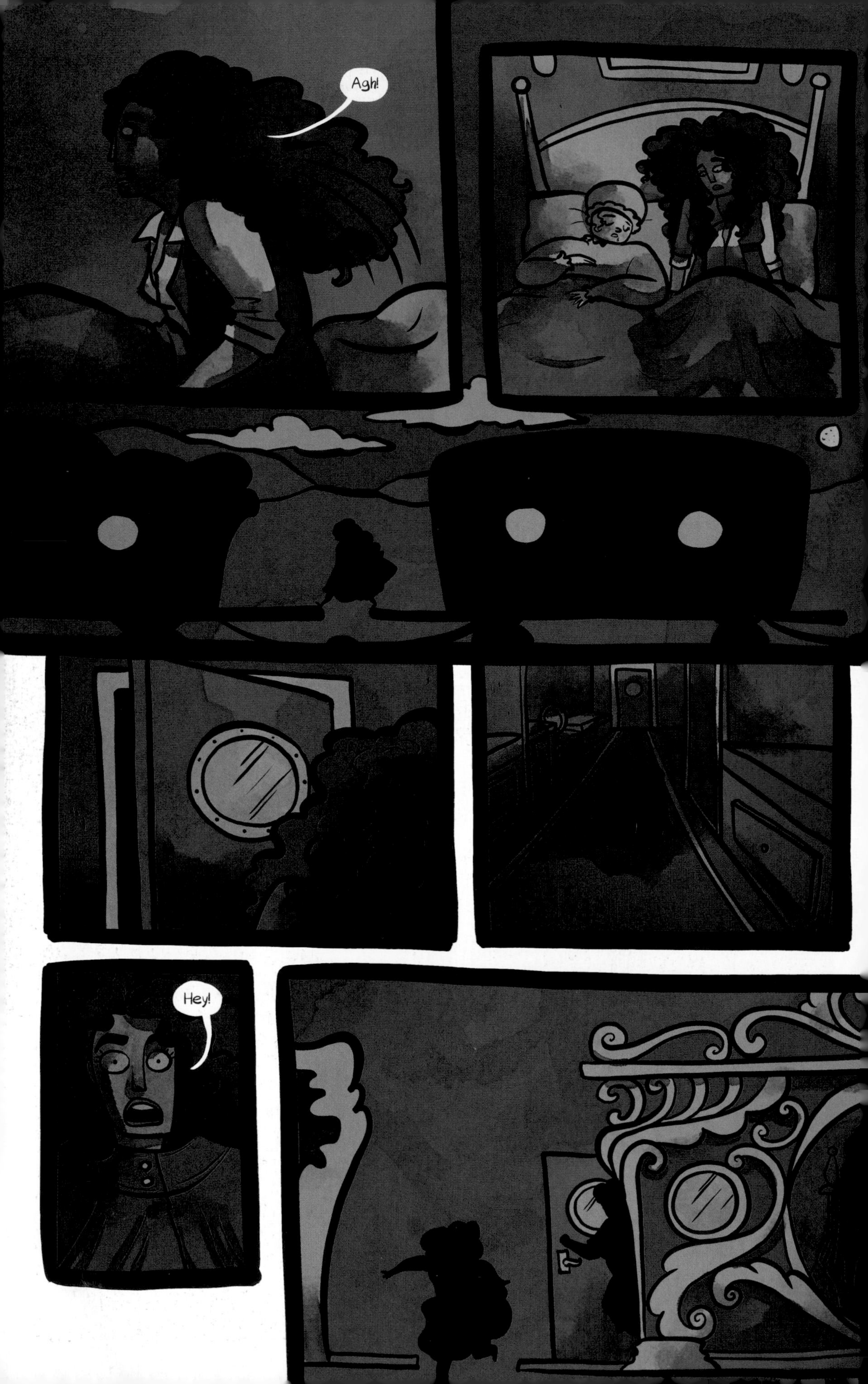
Agh!
Hey!

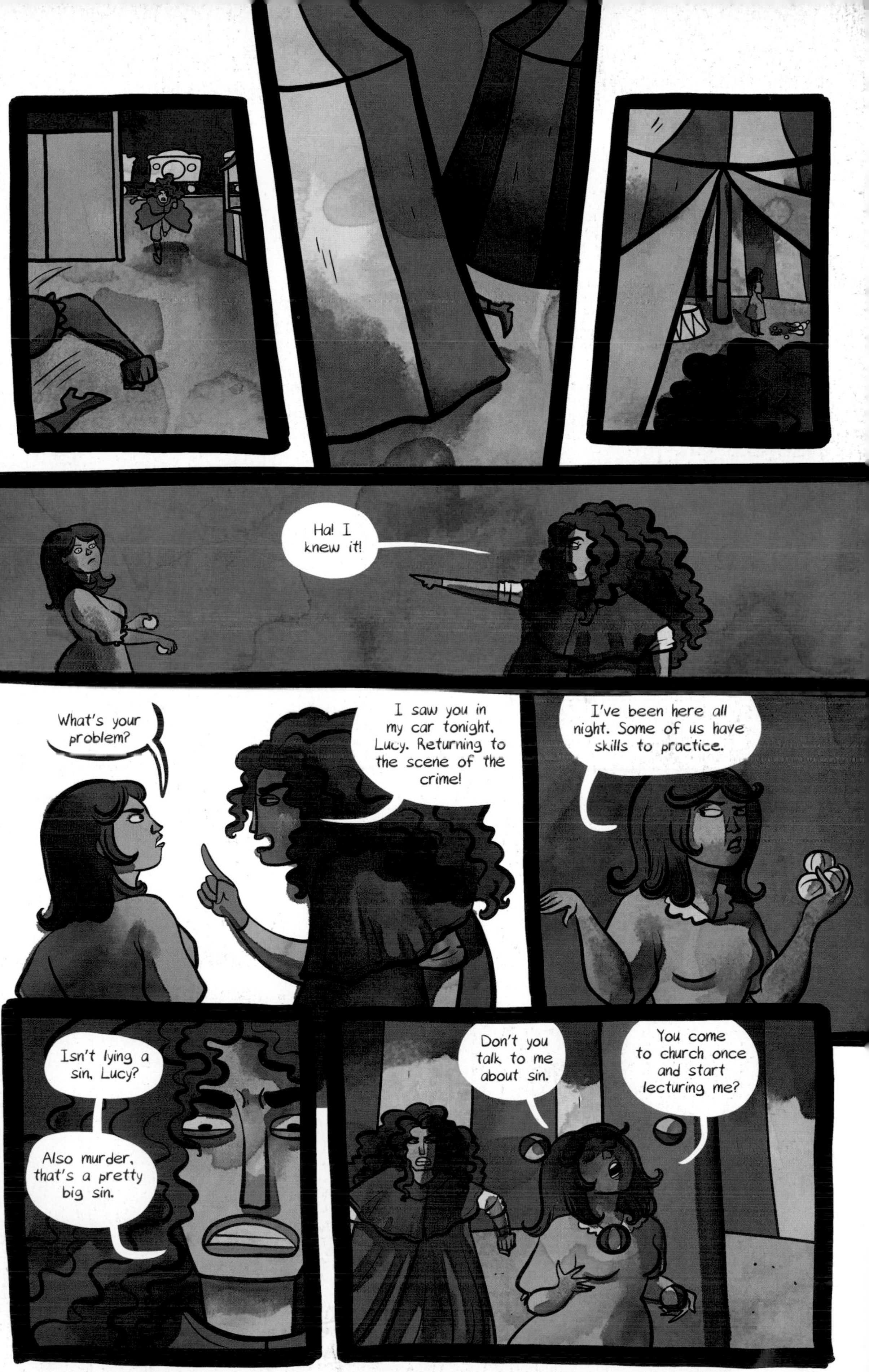
Ha! I knew it!
What's your problem?
I saw you in my car tonight, Lucy. Returning to the scene of the crime!
I've been here all night. Some of us have skills to practice.
Isn't lying a sin, Lucy?
Also murder, that's a pretty big sin.
Don't you talk to me about sin.
You come to church once and start lecturing me?

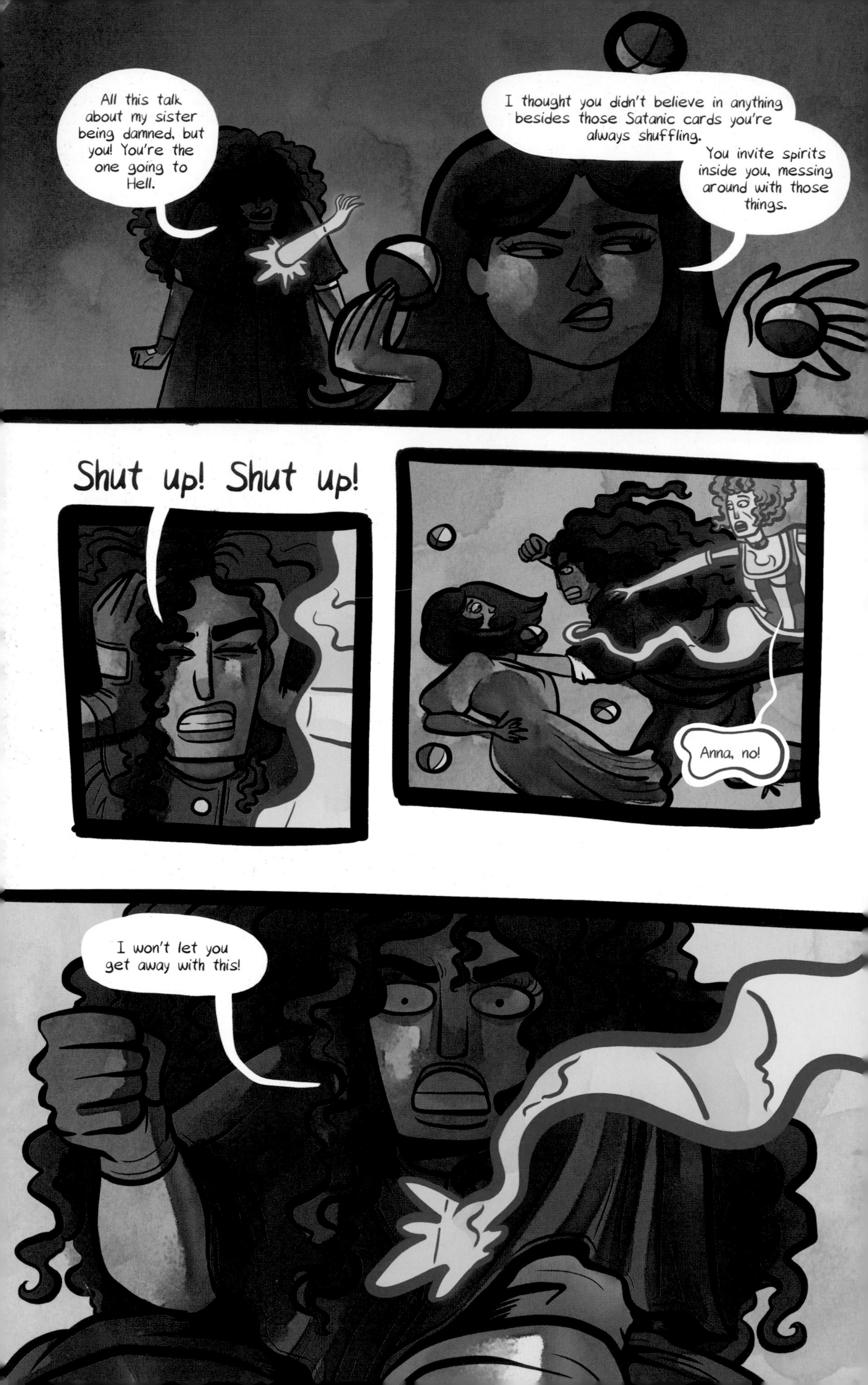
All this talk about my sister being damned, but you! You're the one going to Hell.
I thought you didn't believe in anything besides those Satanic cards you're always shuffling.
You invite spirits inside you, messing around with those things.
Shut up! Shut up!
Anna, no!
I won't let you get away with this!

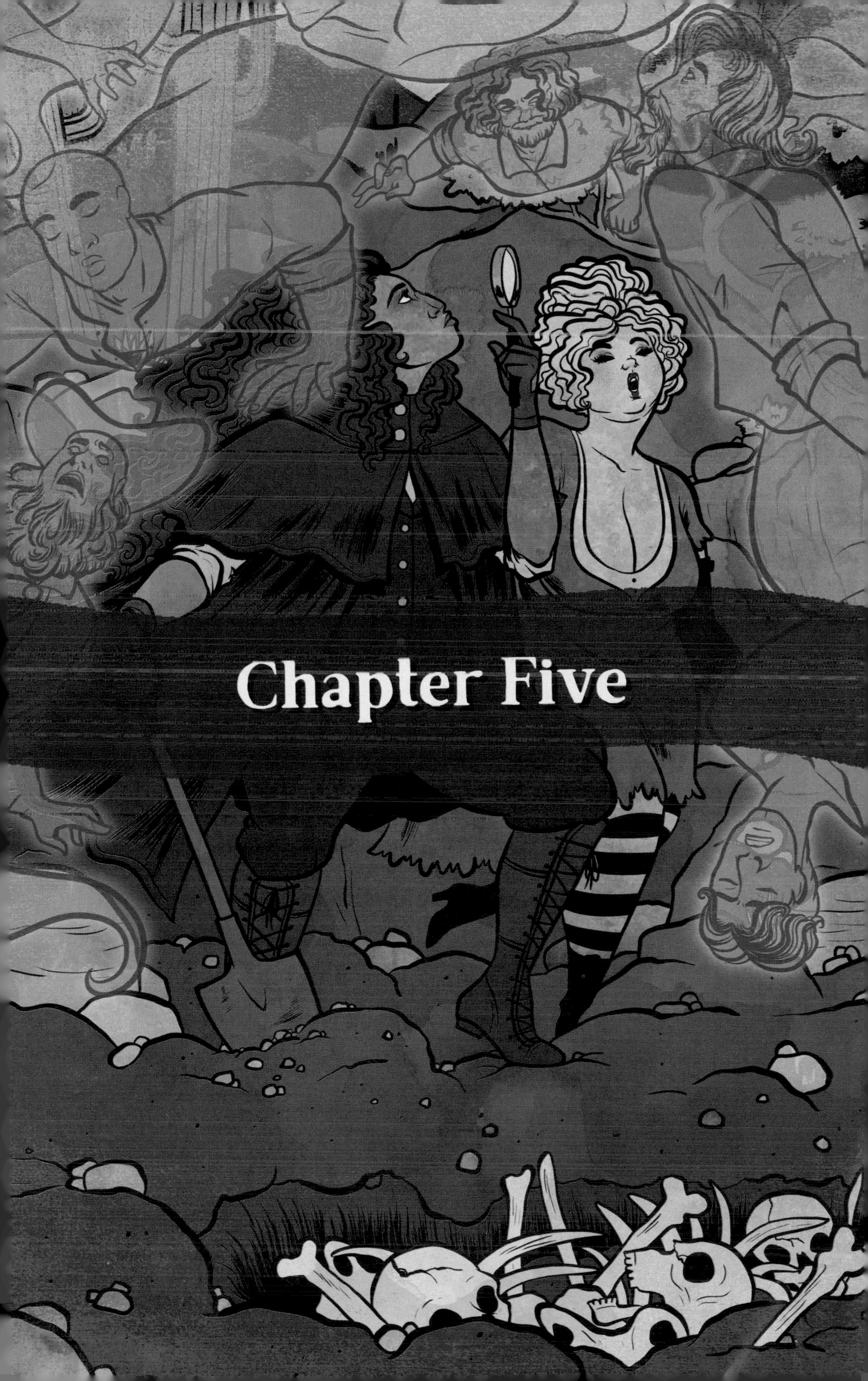

Chapter Five

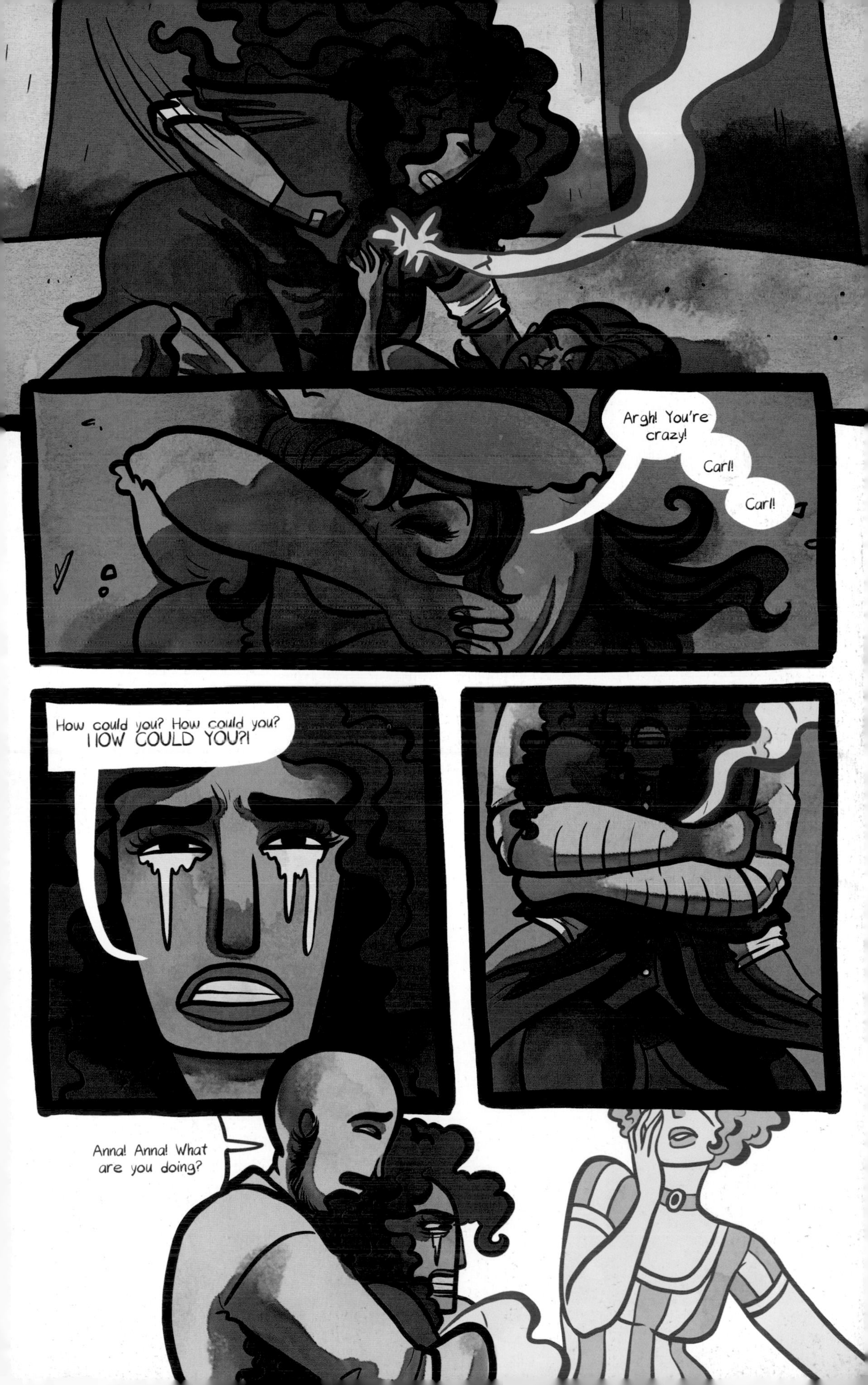
Argh! You're crazy!
Carl!
Carl!
How could you? How could you? HOW COULD YOU?!
Anna! Anna! What are you doing?

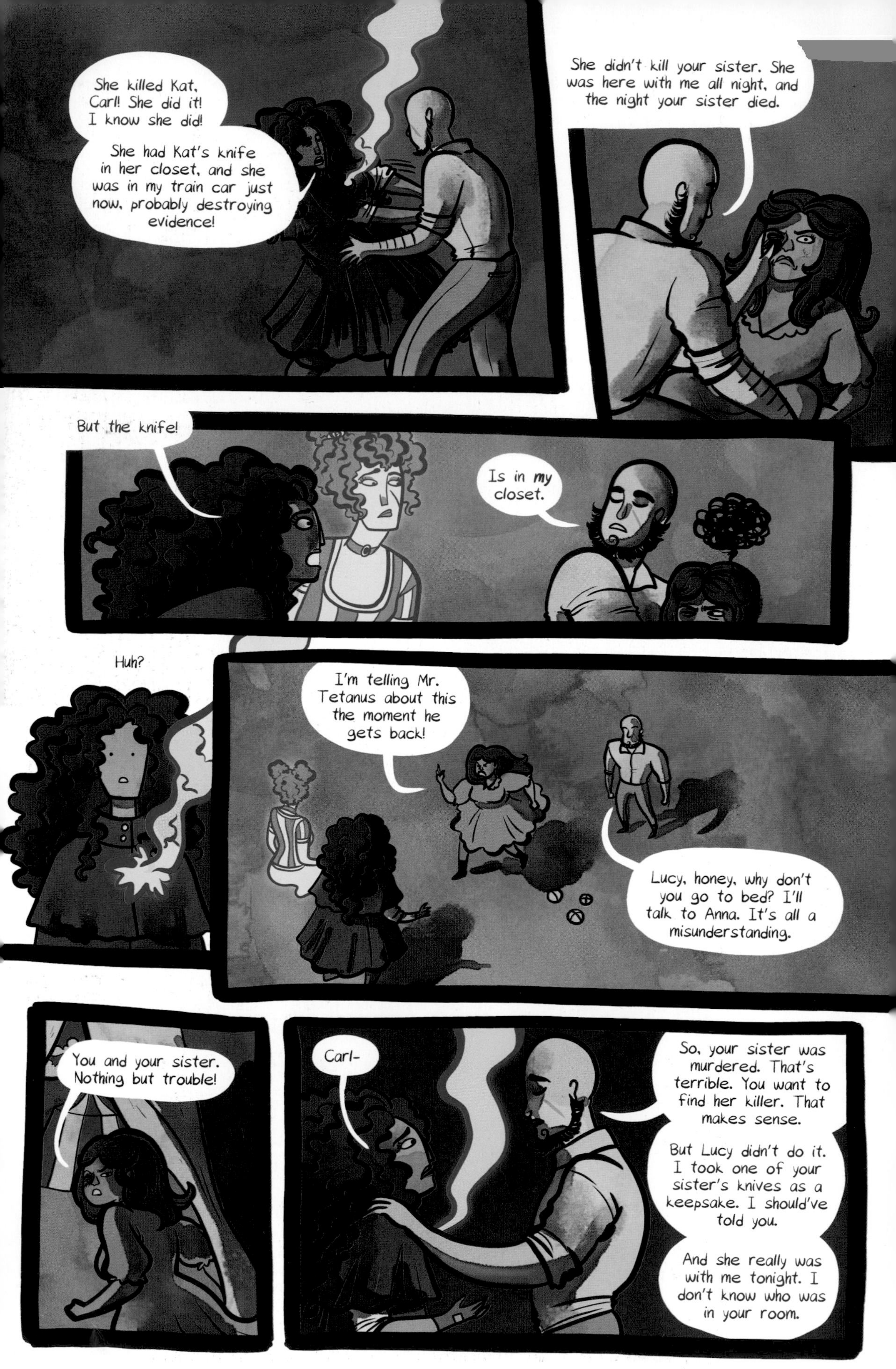
She killed Kat, Carl! She did it! I know she did!
She had Kat's knife in her closet, and she was in my train car just now, probably destroying evidence!
She didn't kill your sister. She was here with me all night, and the night your sister died.
But the knife!
Is in my closet.
Huh?
I'm telling Mr. Tetanus about this the moment he gets back!
Lucy, honey, why don't you go to bed? I'll talk to Anna. It's all a misunderstanding.
You and your sister. Nothing but trouble!
Carl-
So, your sister was murdered. That's terrible. You want to find her killer. That makes sense.
But Lucy didn't do it. I took one of your sister's knives as a keepsake. I should've told you.
And she really was with me tonight. I don't know who was in your room.

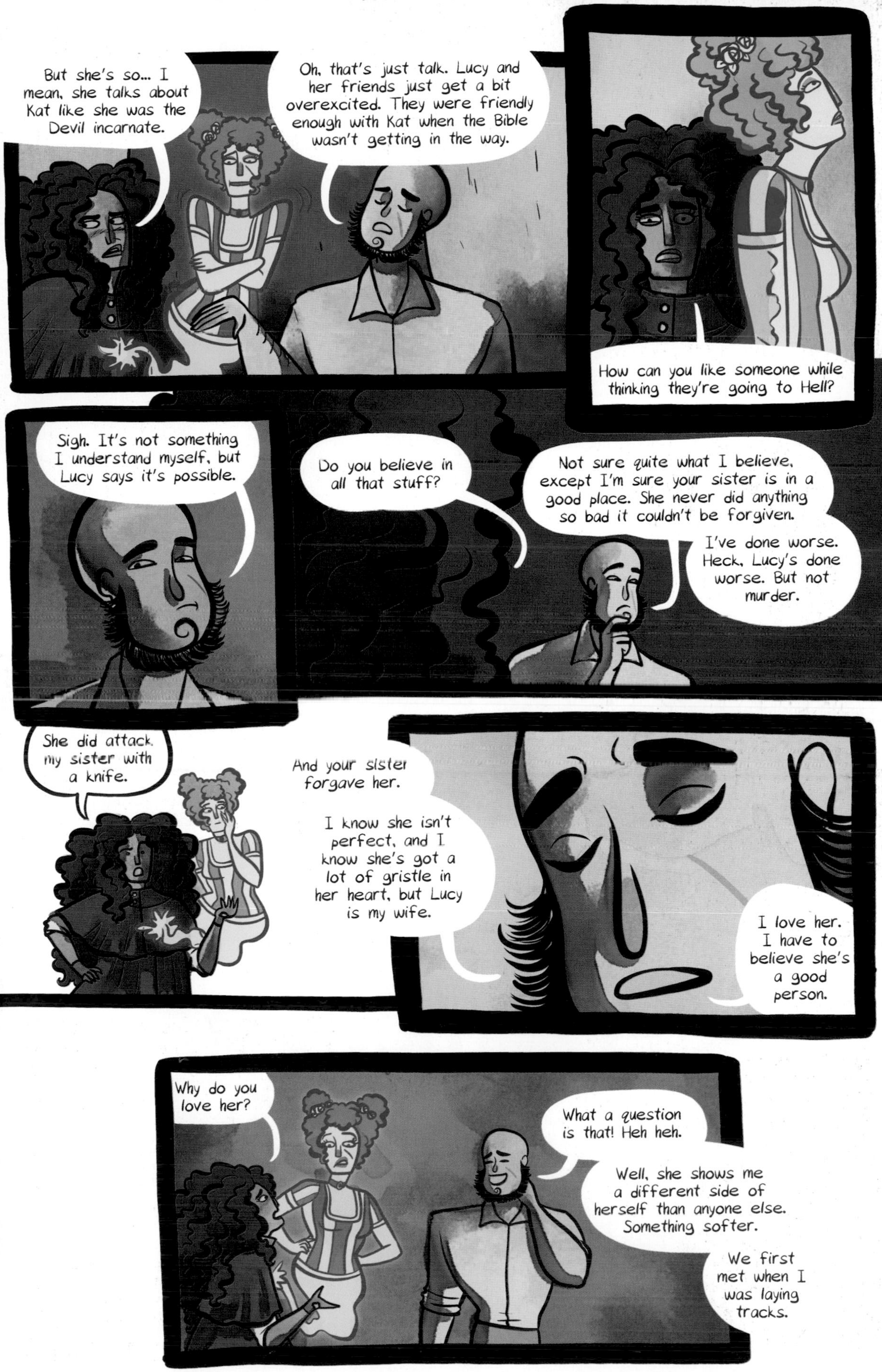
But she's so... I mean, she talks about Kat like she was the Devil incarnate.
Oh, that's just talk. Lucy and her friends just get a bit overexcited. They were friendly enough with Kat when the Bible wasn't getting in the way.
How can you like someone while thinking they're going to Hell?
Sigh. It's not something I understand myself, but Lucy says it's possible.
Do you believe in all that stuff?
Not sure quite what I believe, except I'm sure your sister is in a good place. She never did anything so bad it couldn't be forgiven.
I've done worse. Heck, Lucy's done worse. But not murder.
She did attack my sister with a knife.
And your sister forgave her.
I know she isn't perfect, and I know she's got a lot of gristle in her heart, but Lucy is my wife.
I love her. I have to believe she's a good person.
Why do you love her?
What a question is that! Heh heh.
Well, she shows me a different side of herself than anyone else. Something softer.
We first met when I was laying tracks.

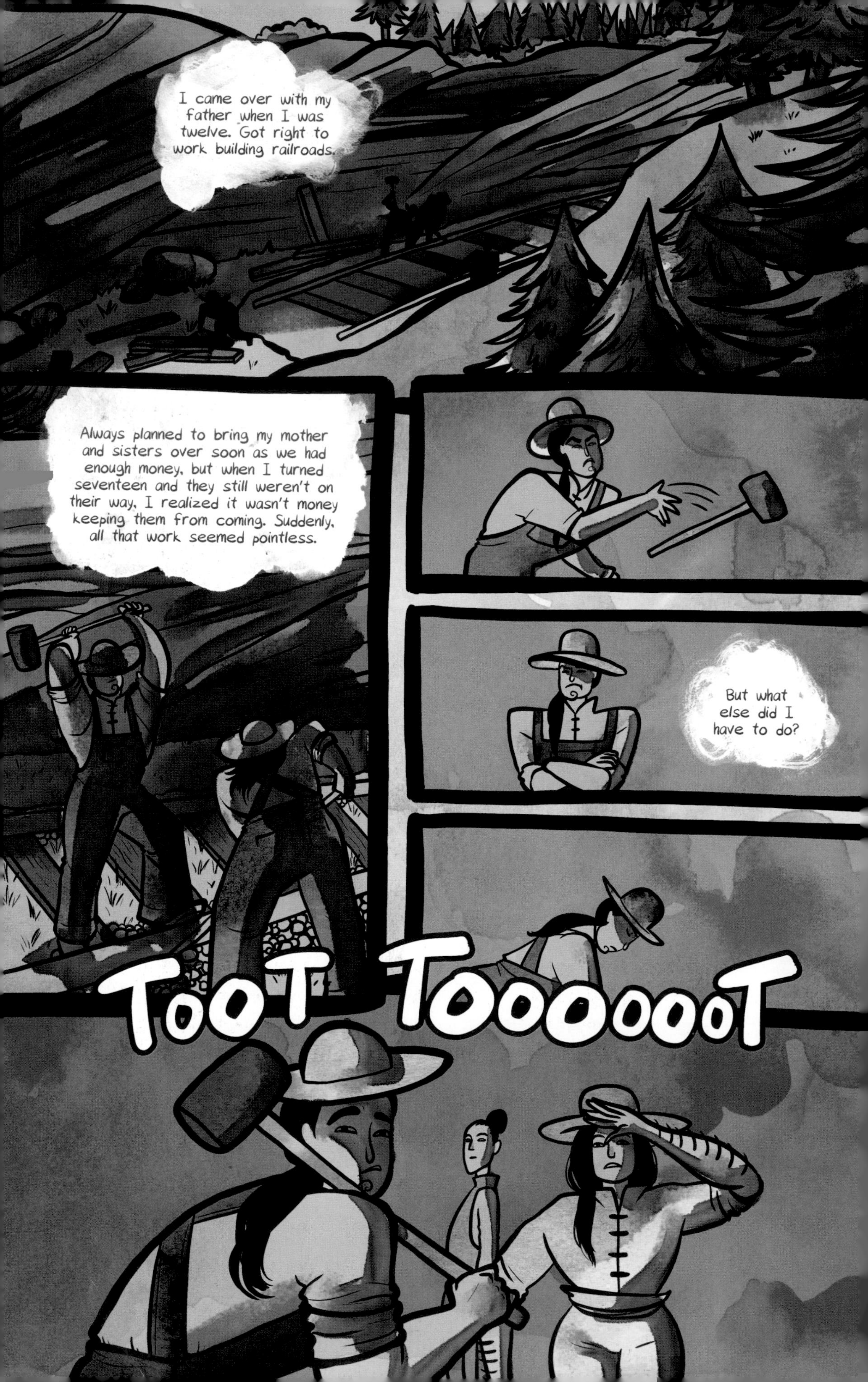
I came over with my father when I was twelve. Got right to work building railroads.
Always planned to bring my mother and sisters over soon as we had enough money, but when I turned seventeen and they still weren't on their way, I realized it wasn't money keeping them from coming. Suddenly, all that work seemed pointless.
But what else did I have to do?
TOOT TOOOOOOT

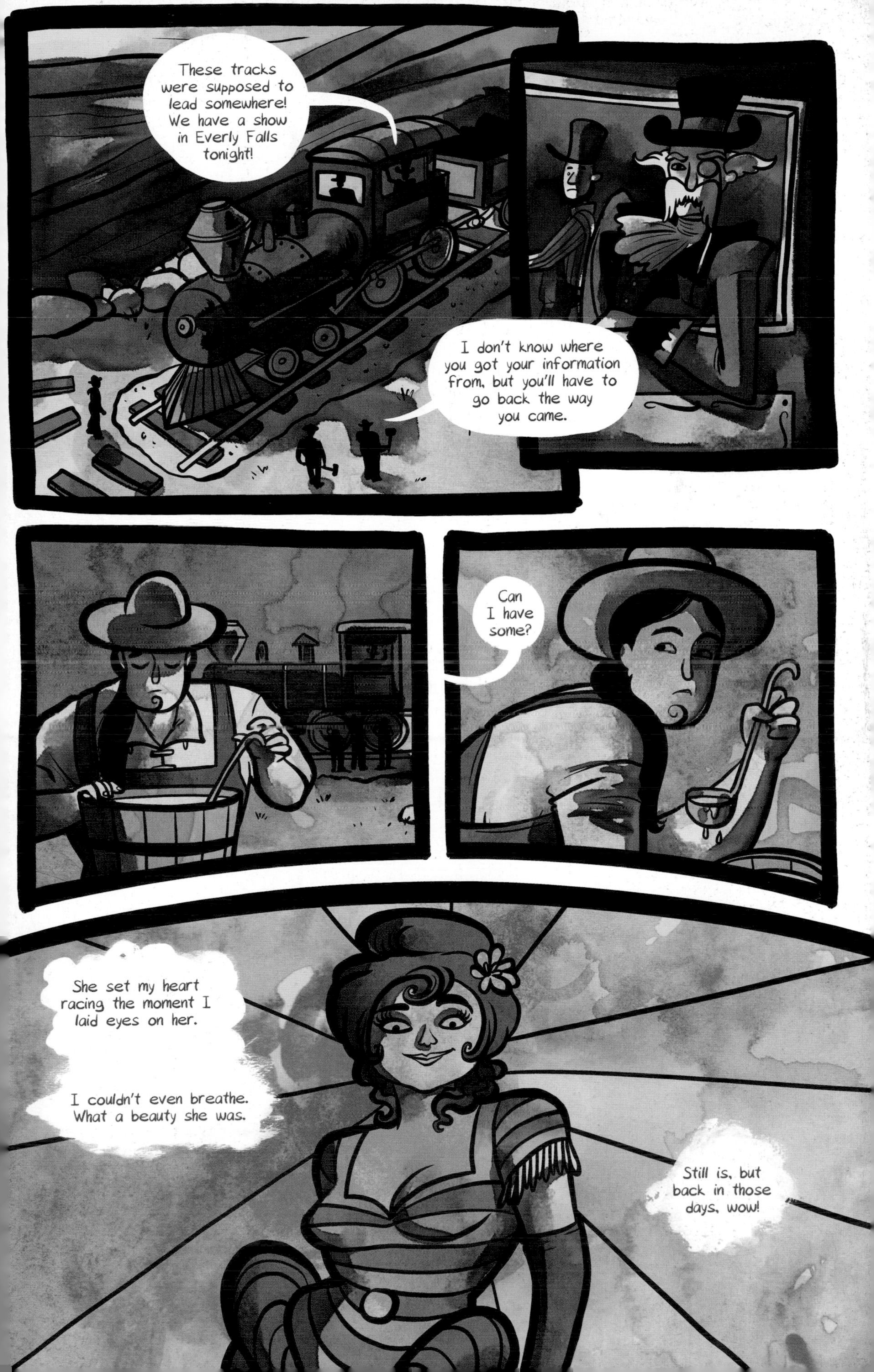
These tracks were supposed to lead somewhere! We have a show in Everly Falls tonight!
I don't know where you got your information from, but you'll have to go back the way you came.
Can I have some?
She set my heart racing the moment I laid eyes on her.
I couldn't even breathe. What a beauty she was.
Still is, but back in those days, wow!

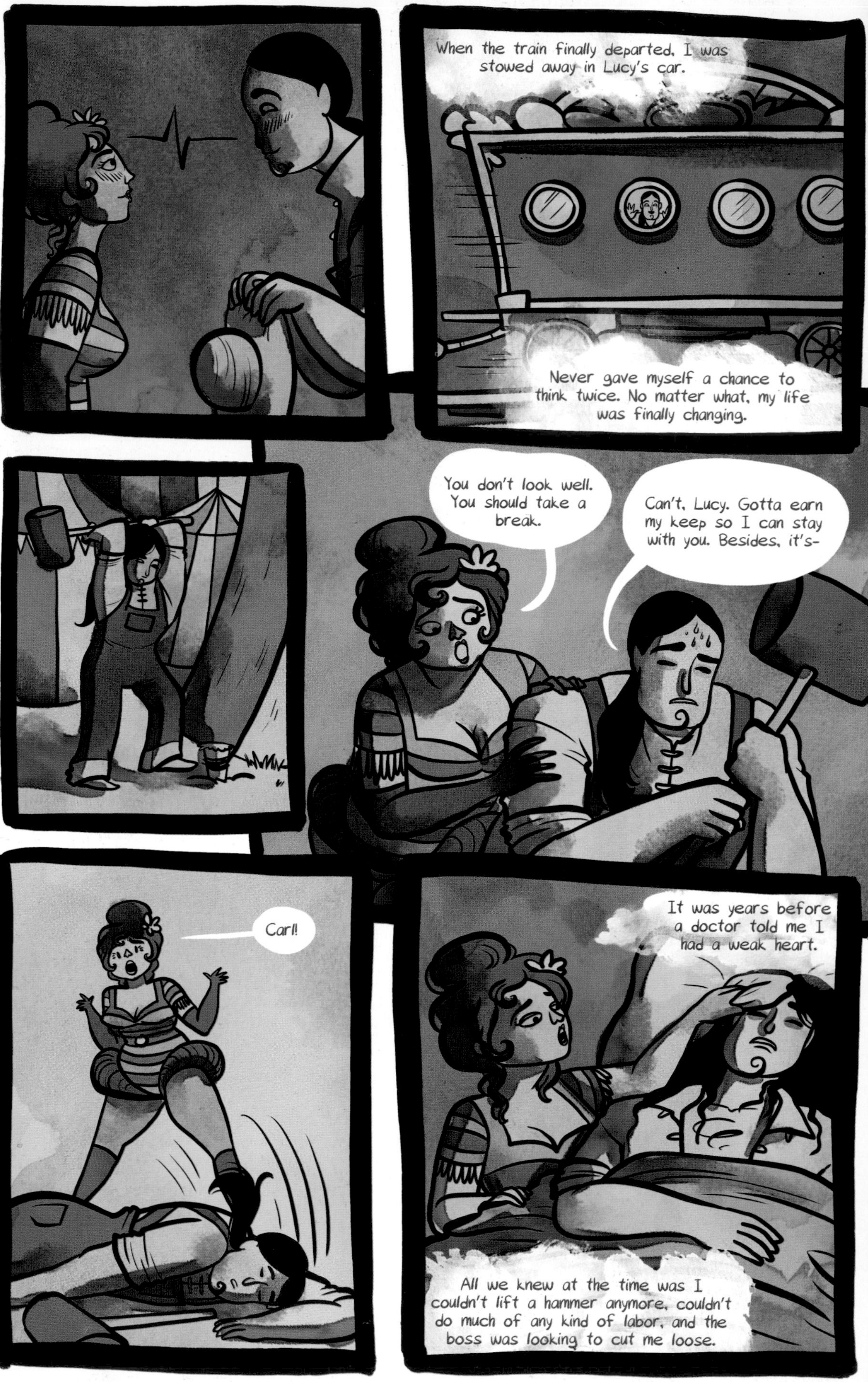
When the train finally departed, I was stowed away in Lucy's car.
Never gave myself a chance to think twice. No matter what, my life was finally changing.
You don't look well. You should take a break.
Can't, Lucy. Gotta earn my keep so I can stay with you. Besides, it's-
Carl!
It was years before a doctor told me I had a weak heart.
All we knew at the time was I couldn't lift a hammer anymore, couldn't do much of any kind of labor, and the boss was looking to cut me loose.

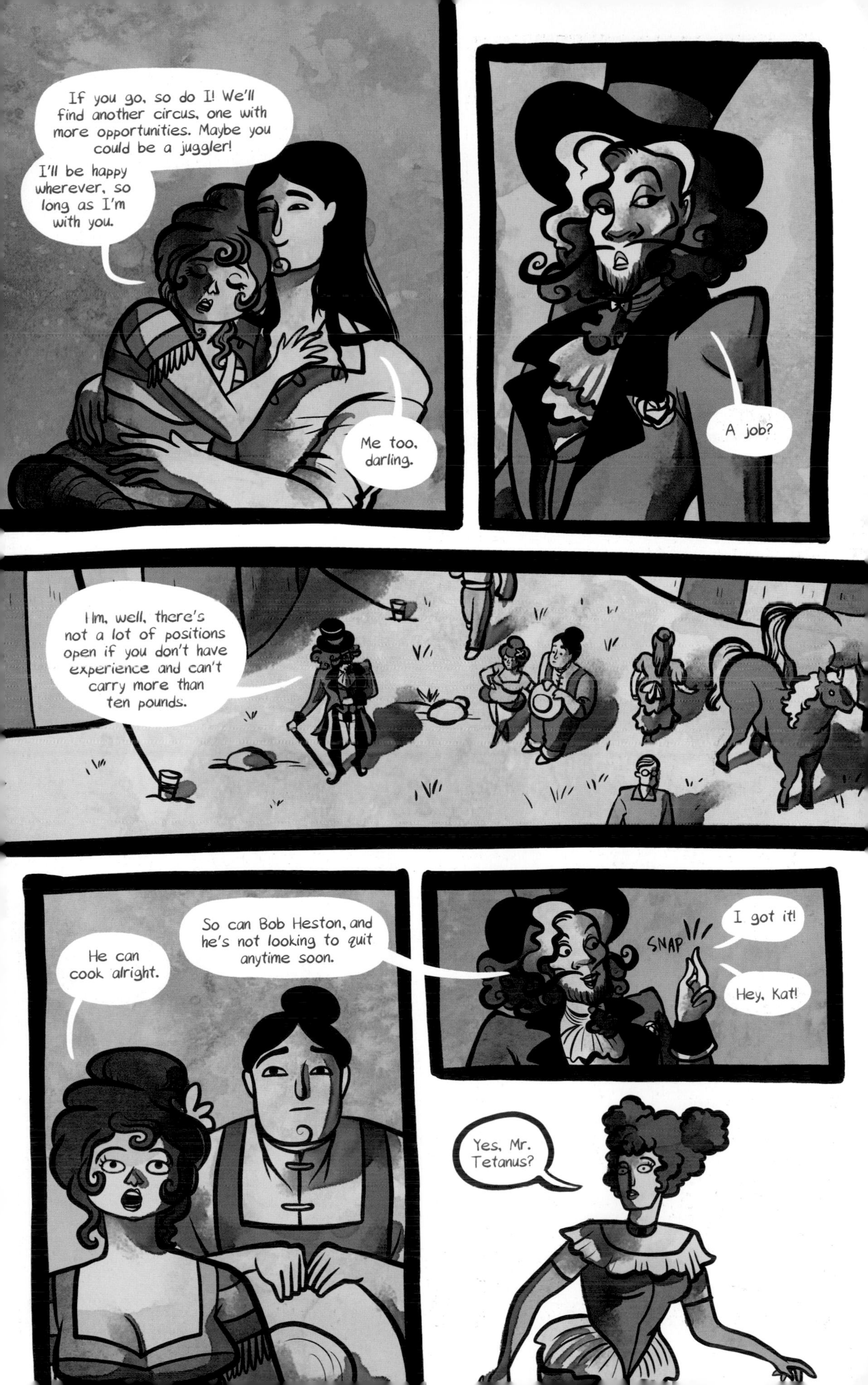

If you go, so do I! We'll find another circus, one with more opportunities. Maybe you could be a juggler!
I'll be happy wherever, so long as I'm with you.
Me too, darling.
A job?
Um, well, there's not a lot of positions open if you don't have experience and can't carry more than ten pounds.
He can cook alright.
So can Bob Heston, and he's not looking to quit anytime soon.
SNAP
I got it!
Hey, Kat!
Yes, Mr. Tetanus?

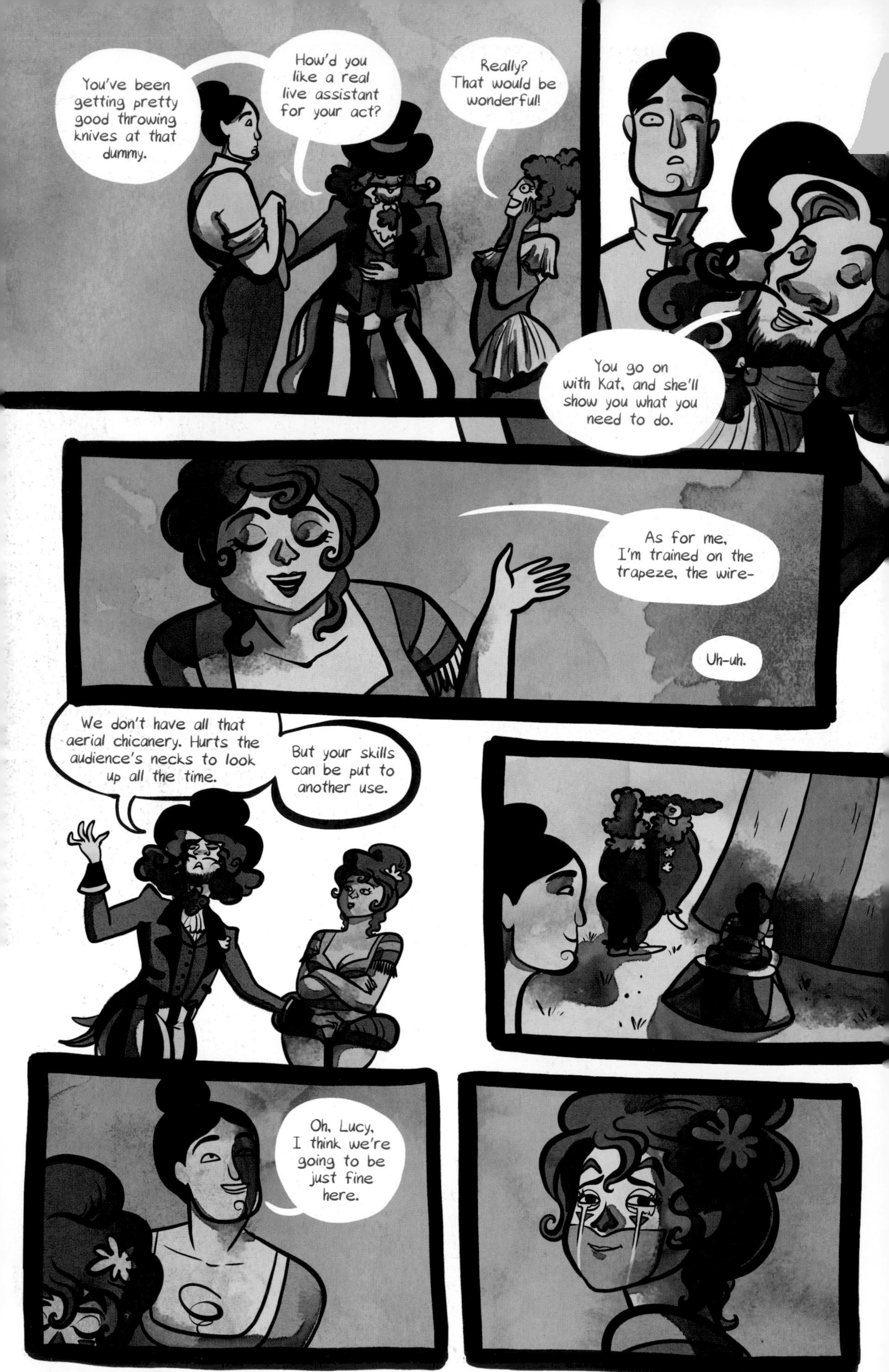
You've been getting pretty good throwing knives at that dummy.
How'd you like a real live assistant for your act?
Really? That would be wonderful!
You go on with Kat, and she'll show you what you need to do.
As for me, I'm trained on the trapeze, the wire-
Uh-uh.
We don't have all that aerial chicanery. Hurts the audience's necks to look up all the time.
But your skills can be put to another use.
Oh, Lucy, I think we're going to be just fine here.

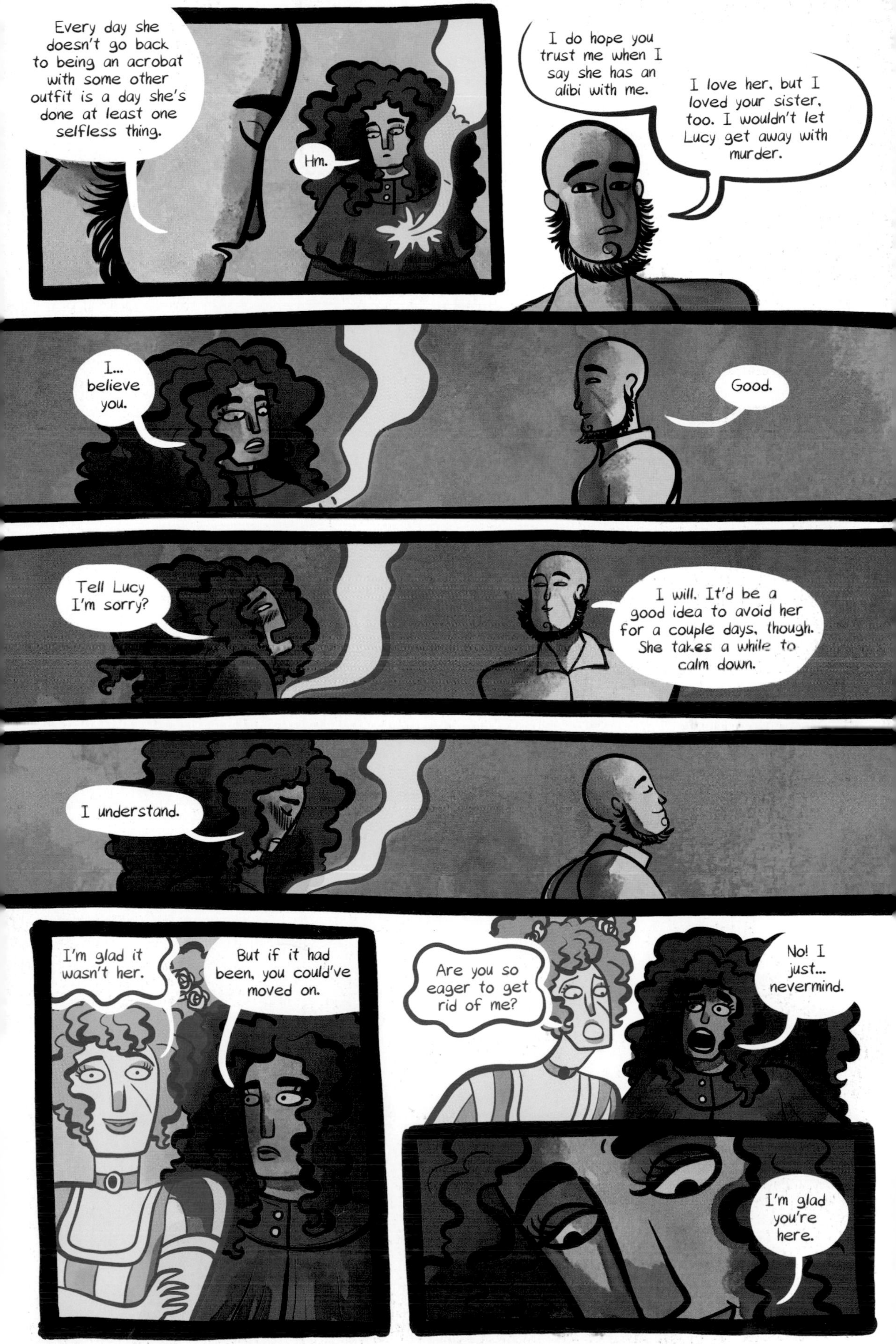
Every day she doesn't go back to being an acrobat with some other outfit is a day she's done at least one selfless thing.
Hm.
I do hope you trust me when I say she has an alibi with me.
I love her, but I loved your sister, too. I wouldn't let Lucy get away with murder.
I... believe you.
Good.
Tell Lucy I'm sorry?
I will. It'd be a good idea to avoid her for a couple days, though. She takes a while to calm down.
I understand.
I'm glad it wasn't her.
But if it had been, you could've moved on.
Are you so eager to get rid of me?
No! I just... nevermind.
I'm glad you're here.

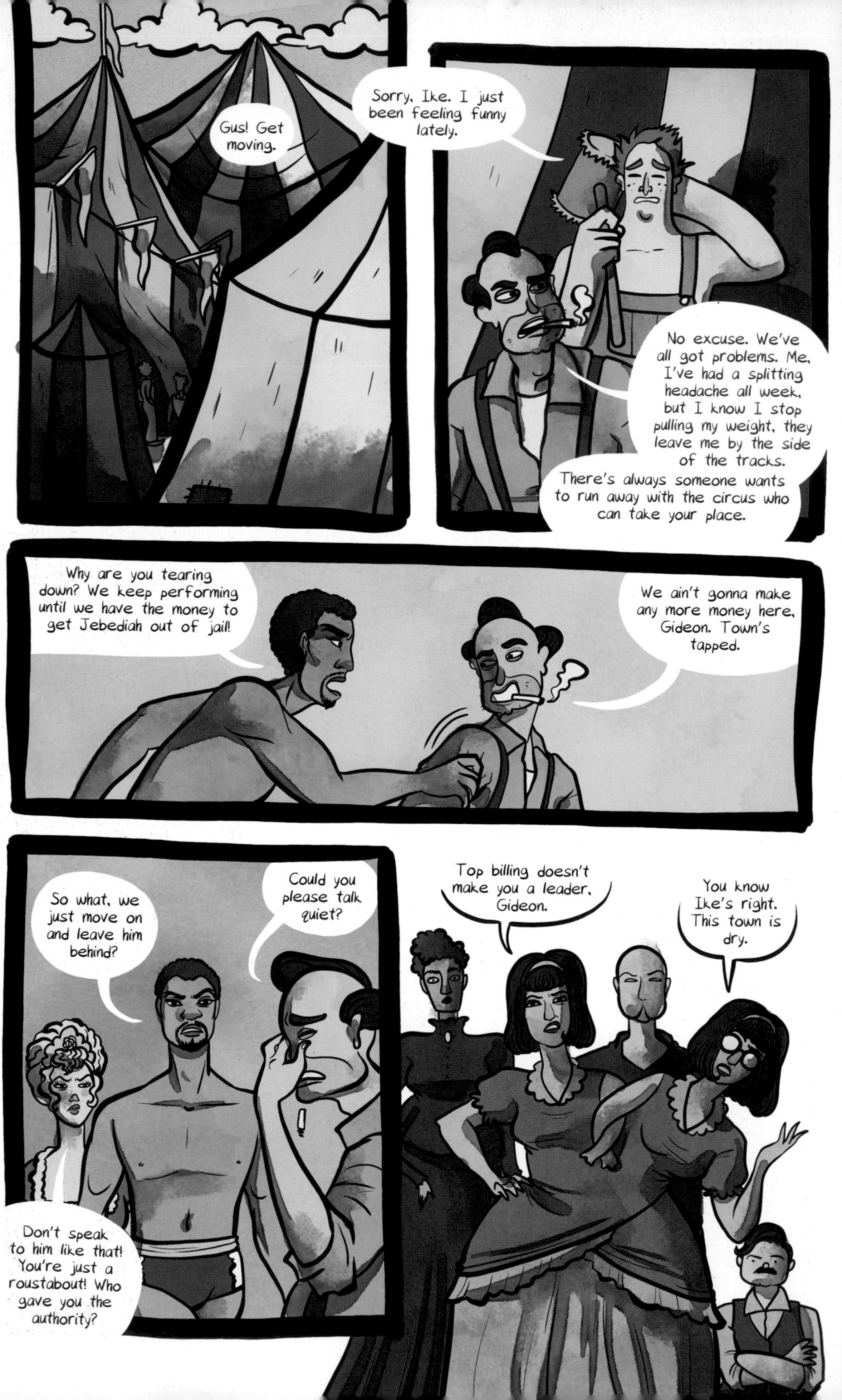
Gus! Get moving.
Sorry, Ike. I just been feeling funny lately.
No excuse. We've all got problems. Me, I've had a splitting headache all week, but I know I stop pulling my weight, they leave me by the side of the tracks.
There's always someone wants to run away with the circus who can take your place.
Why are you tearing down? We keep performing until we have the money to get Jebediah out of jail!
We ain't gonna make any more money here, Gideon. Town's tapped.
So what, we just move on and leave him behind?
Could you please talk quiet?
Don't speak to him like that! You're just a roustabout! Who gave you the authority?
Top billing doesn't make you a leader, Gideon.
You know Ike's right. This town is dry.

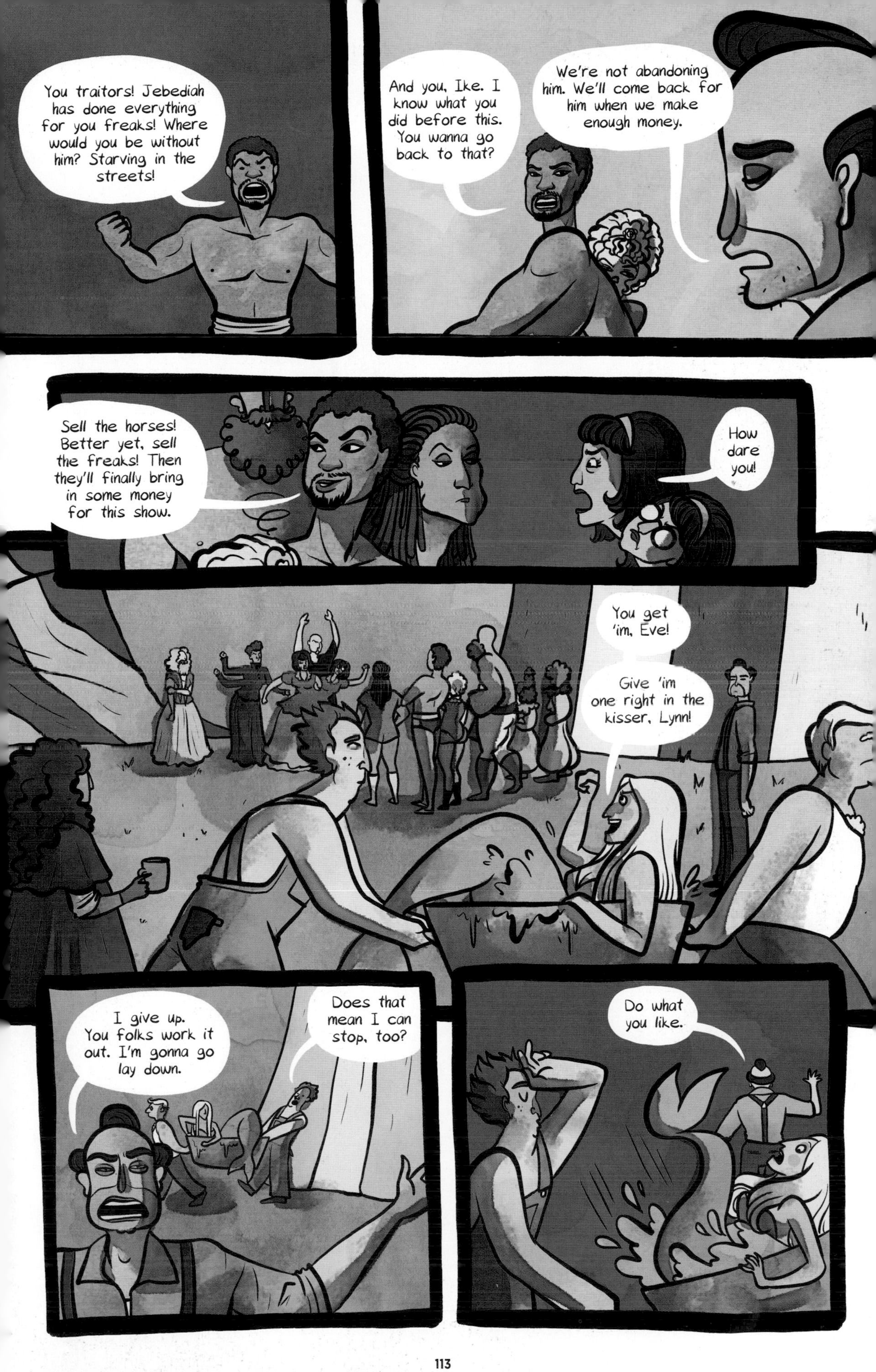
You traitors! Jebediah has done everything for you freaks! Where would you be without him? Starving in the streets!
And you, Ike. I know what you did before this. You wanna go back to that?
We're not abandoning him. We'll come back for him when we make enough money.
Sell the horses! Better yet, sell the freaks! Then they'll finally bring in some money for this show.
How dare you!
You get 'im, Eve!
Give 'im one right in the kisser, Lynn!
I give up. You folks work it out. I'm gonna go lay down.
Does that mean I can stop, too?
Do what you like.

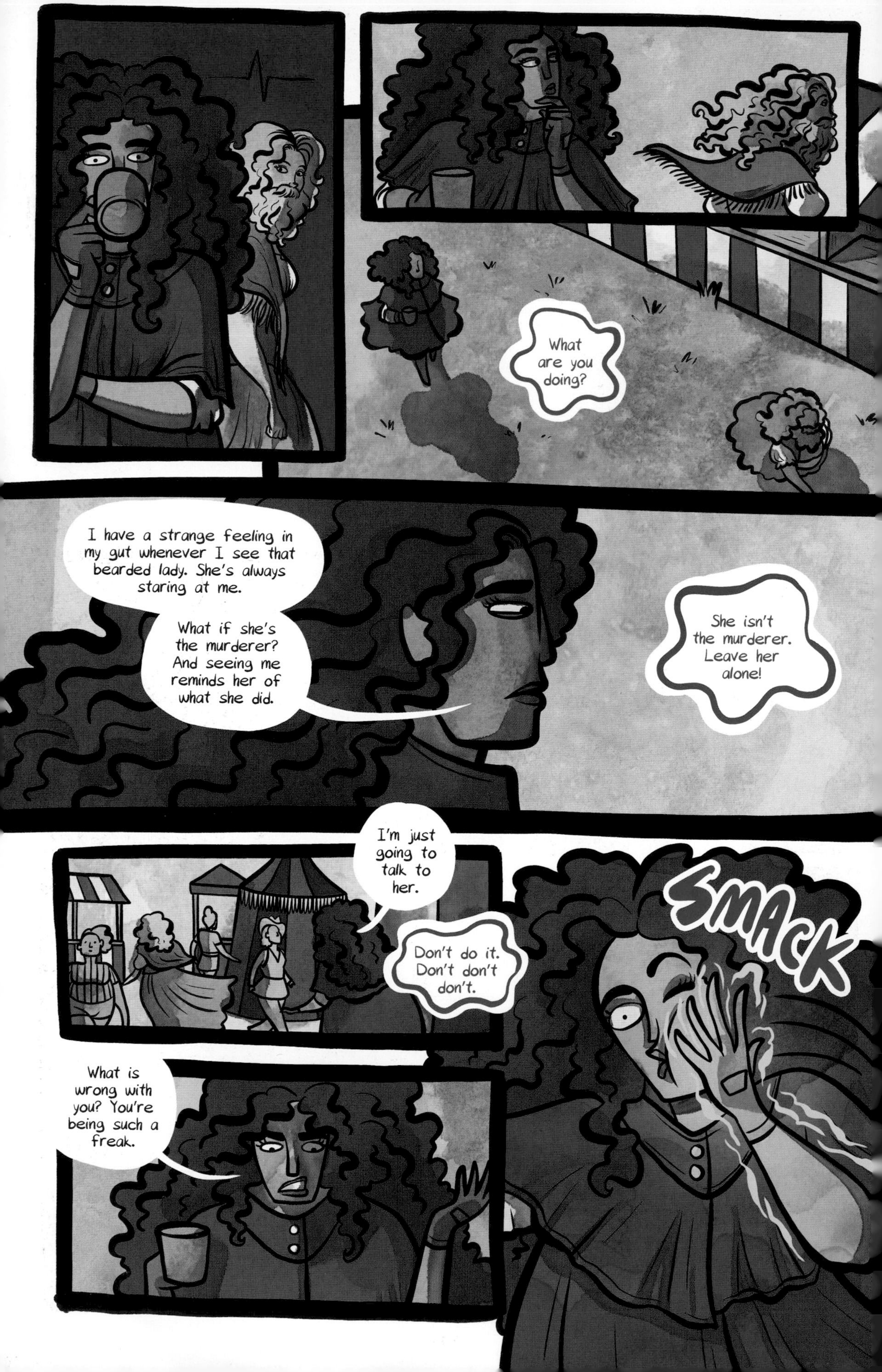
What are you doing?
I have a strange feeling in my gut whenever I see that bearded lady. She's always staring at me.
What if she's the murderer? And seeing me reminds her of what she did.
She isn't the murderer. Leave her alone!
I'm just going to talk to her.
Don't do it. Don't don't don't.
What is wrong with you? You're being such a freak.
SMACK

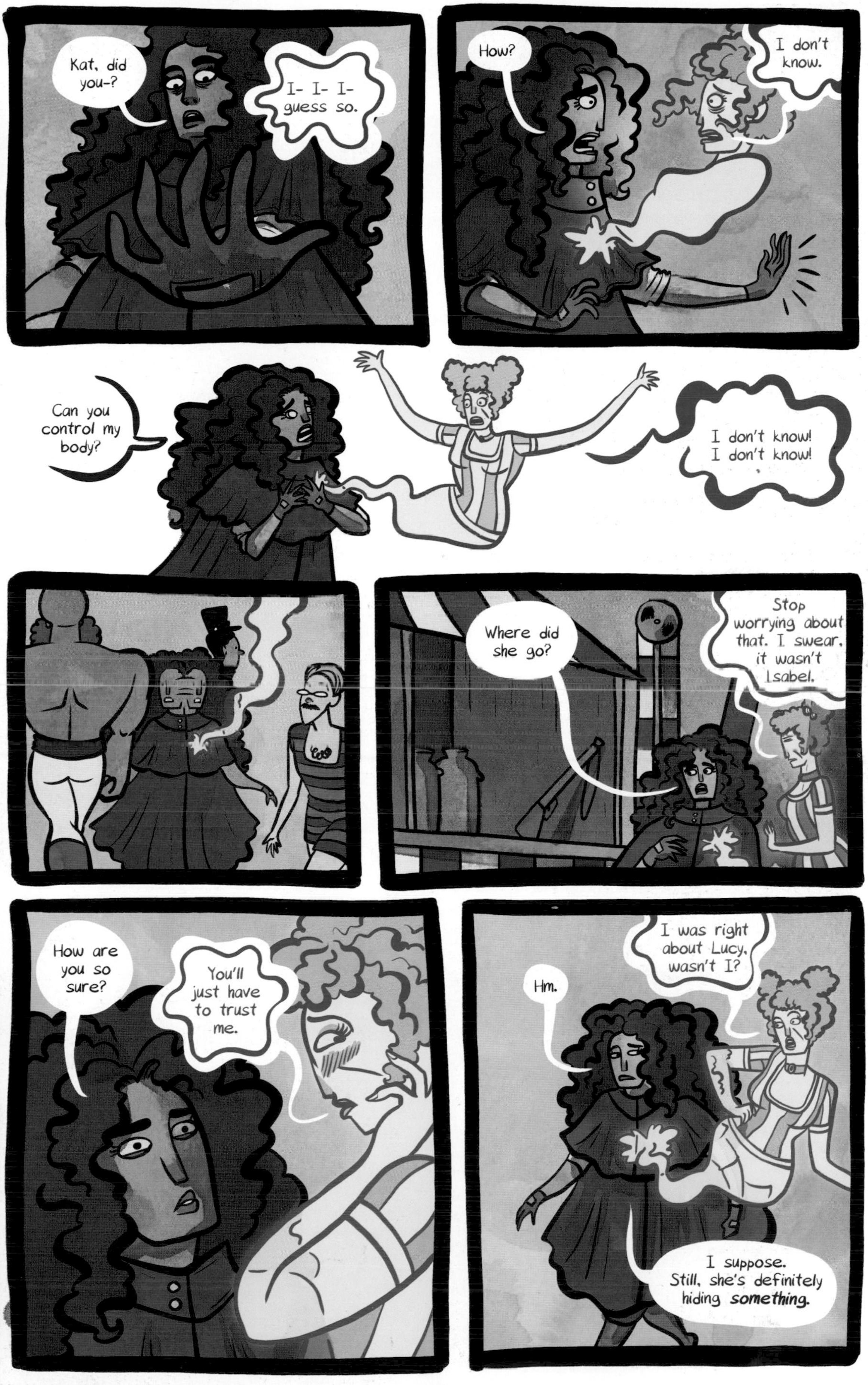
Kat, did you-?
I- I- I- guess so.
How?
I don't know.
Can you control my body?
I don't know! I don't know!
Where did she go?
Stop worrying about that. I swear, it wasn't Isabel.
How are you so sure?
You'll just have to trust me.
Hm.
I was right about Lucy, wasn't I?
I suppose. Still, she's definitely hiding *something*.

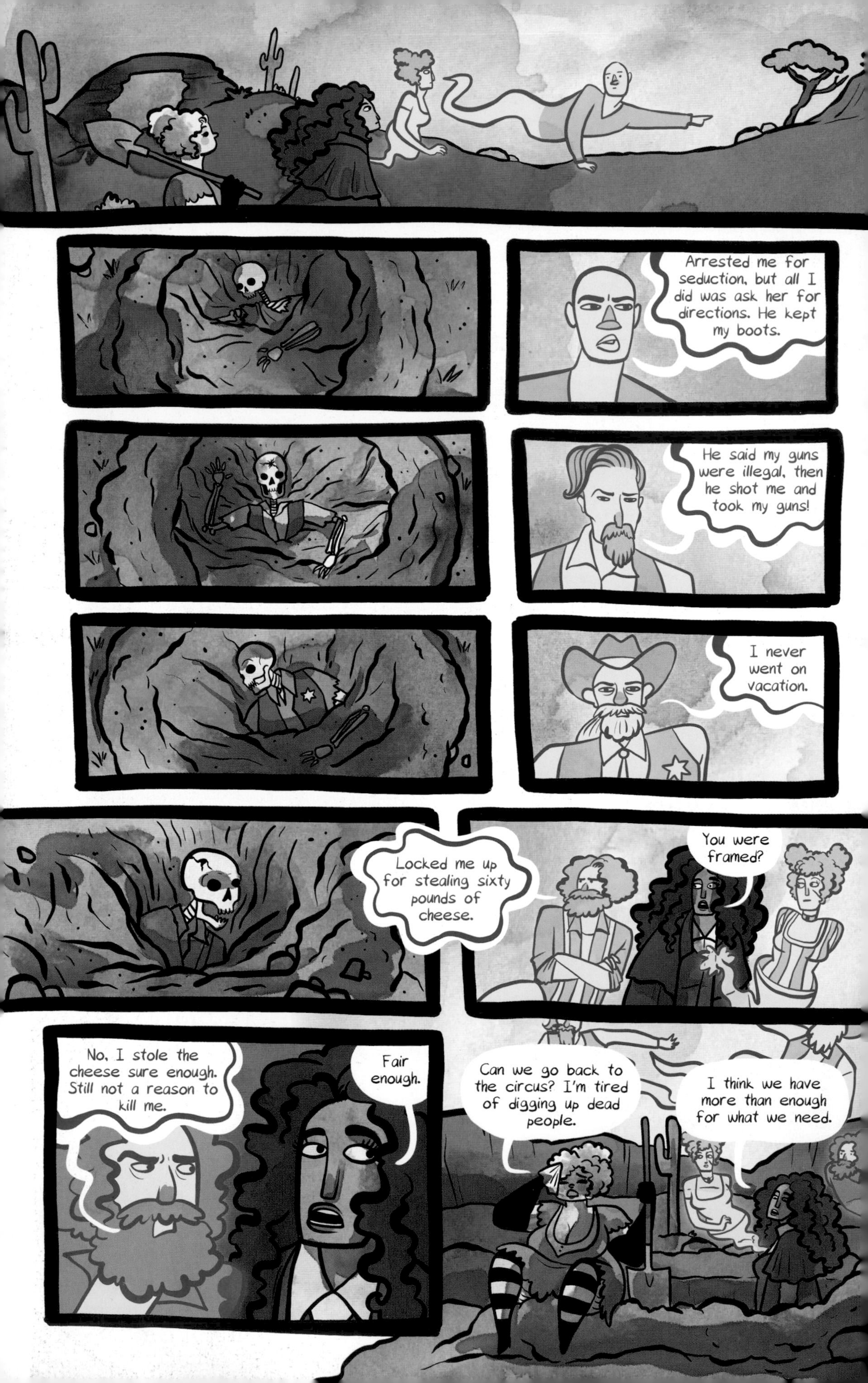
Arrested me for seduction, but all I did was ask her for directions. He kept my boots.
He said my guns were illegal, then he shot me and took my guns!
I never went on vacation.
Locked me up for stealing sixty pounds of cheese.
You were framed?
No, I stole the cheese sure enough. Still not a reason to kill me.
Fair enough.
Can we go back to the circus? I'm tired of digging up dead people.
I think we have more than enough for what we need.

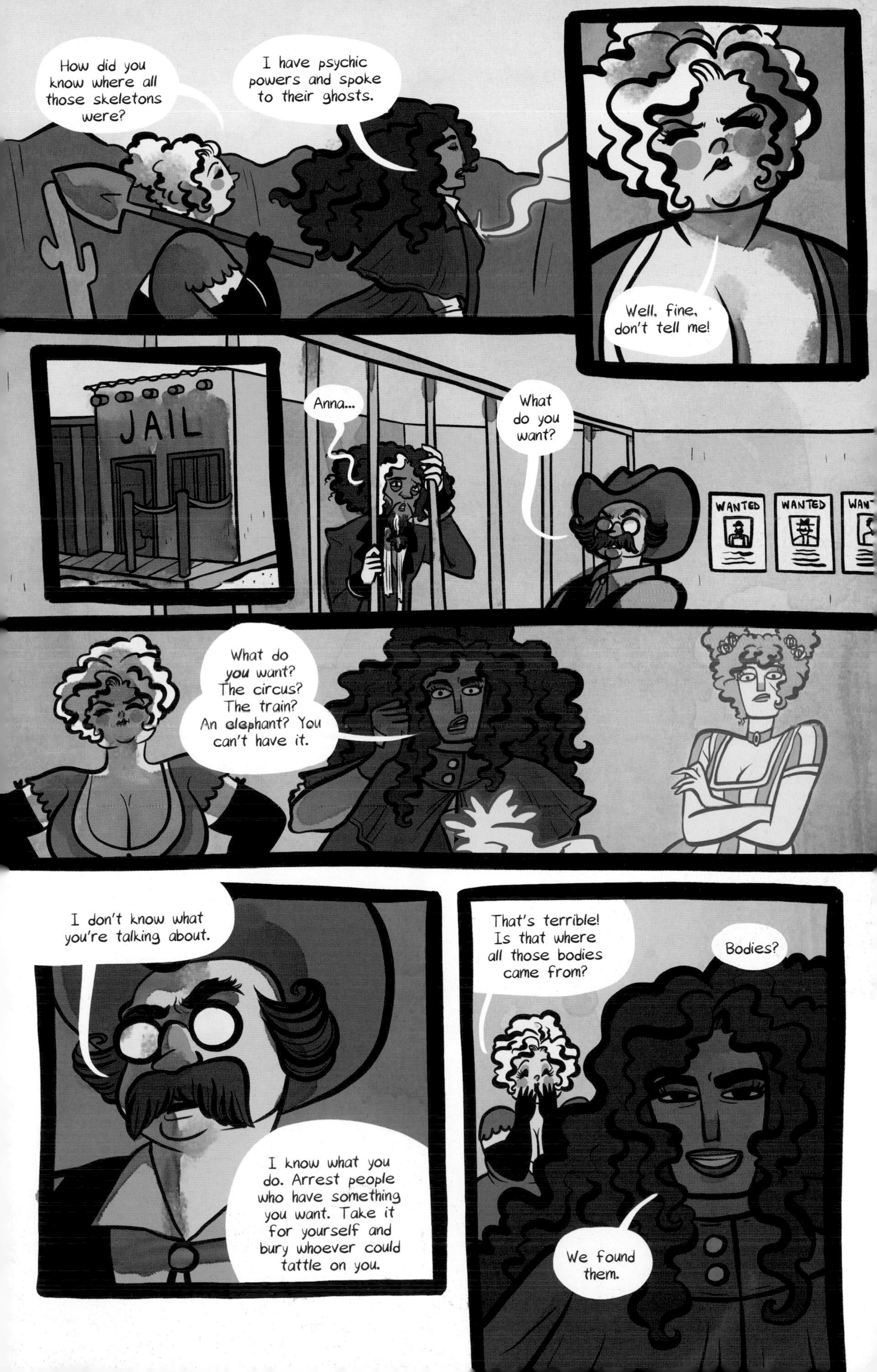
How did you know where all those skeletons were?
I have psychic powers and spoke to their ghosts.
Well, fine, don't tell me!
JAIL
Anna...
What do you want?
WANTED
WANTED
What do *you* want? The circus? The train? An elephant? You can't have it.
I don't know what you're talking about.
I know what you do. Arrest people who have something you want. Take it for yourself and bury whoever could tattle on you.
That's terrible! Is that where all those bodies came from?
Bodies?
We found them.

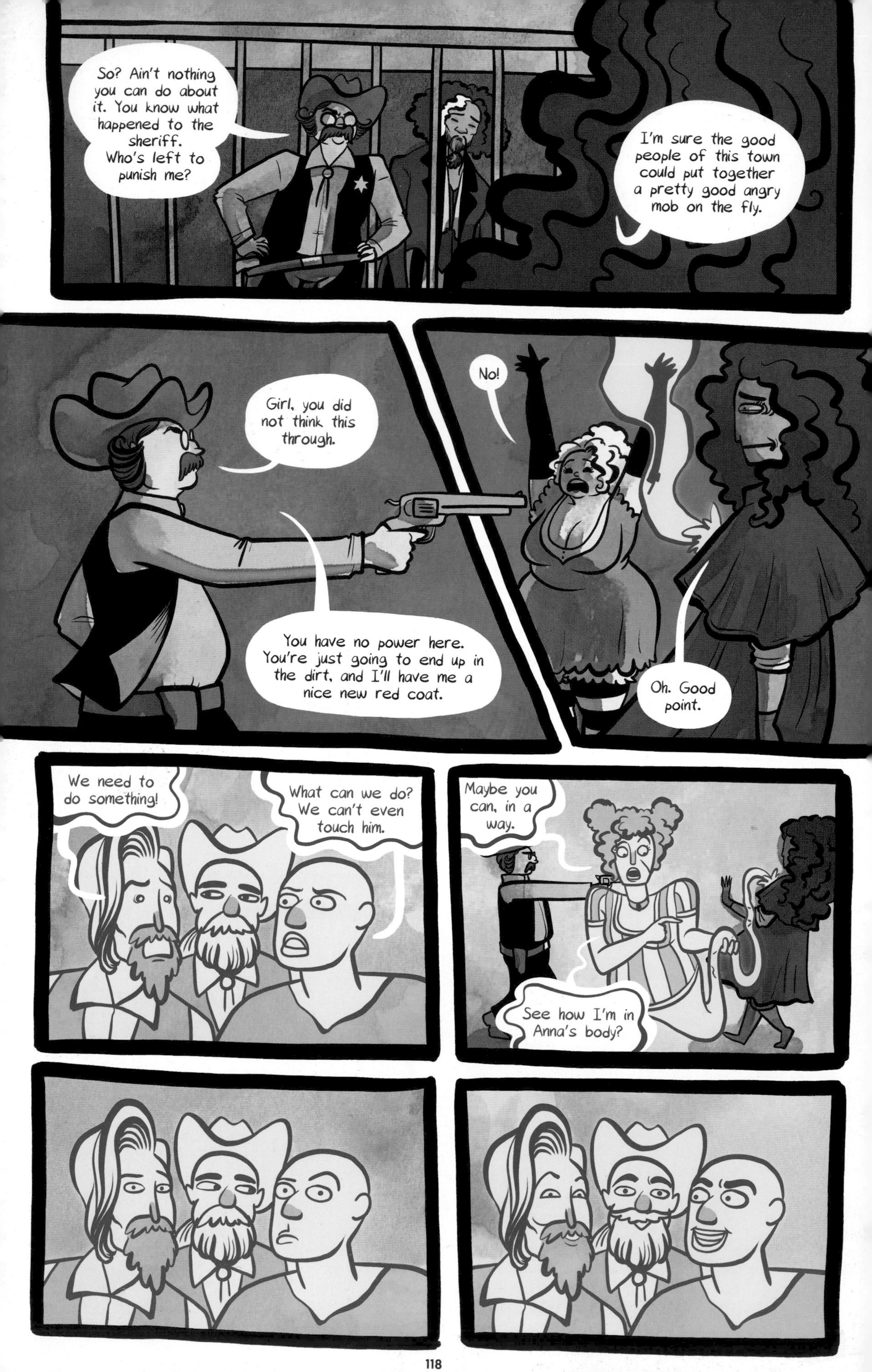
So? Ain't nothing you can do about it. You know what happened to the sheriff. Who's left to punish me?
I'm sure the good people of this town could put together a pretty good angry mob on the fly.
Girl, you did not think this through.
You have no power here. You're just going to end up in the dirt, and I'll have me a nice new red coat.
No!
Oh. Good point.
We need to do something!
What can we do? We can't even touch him.
Maybe you can, in a way.
See how I'm in Anna's body?

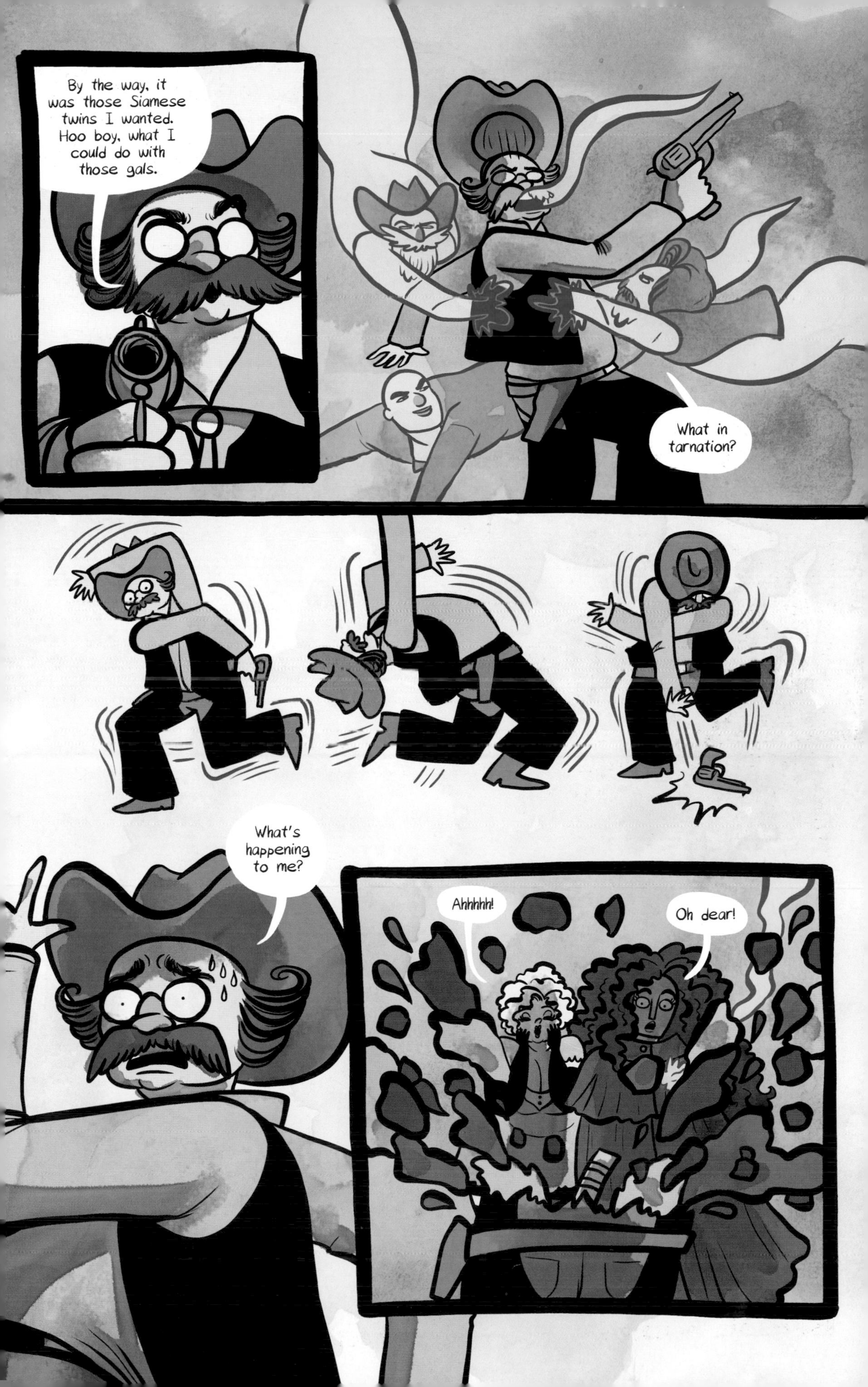
By the way, it was those Siamese twins I wanted. Hoo boy, what I could do with those gals.
What in tarnation?
What's happening to me?
Ahhhhh!
Oh dear!

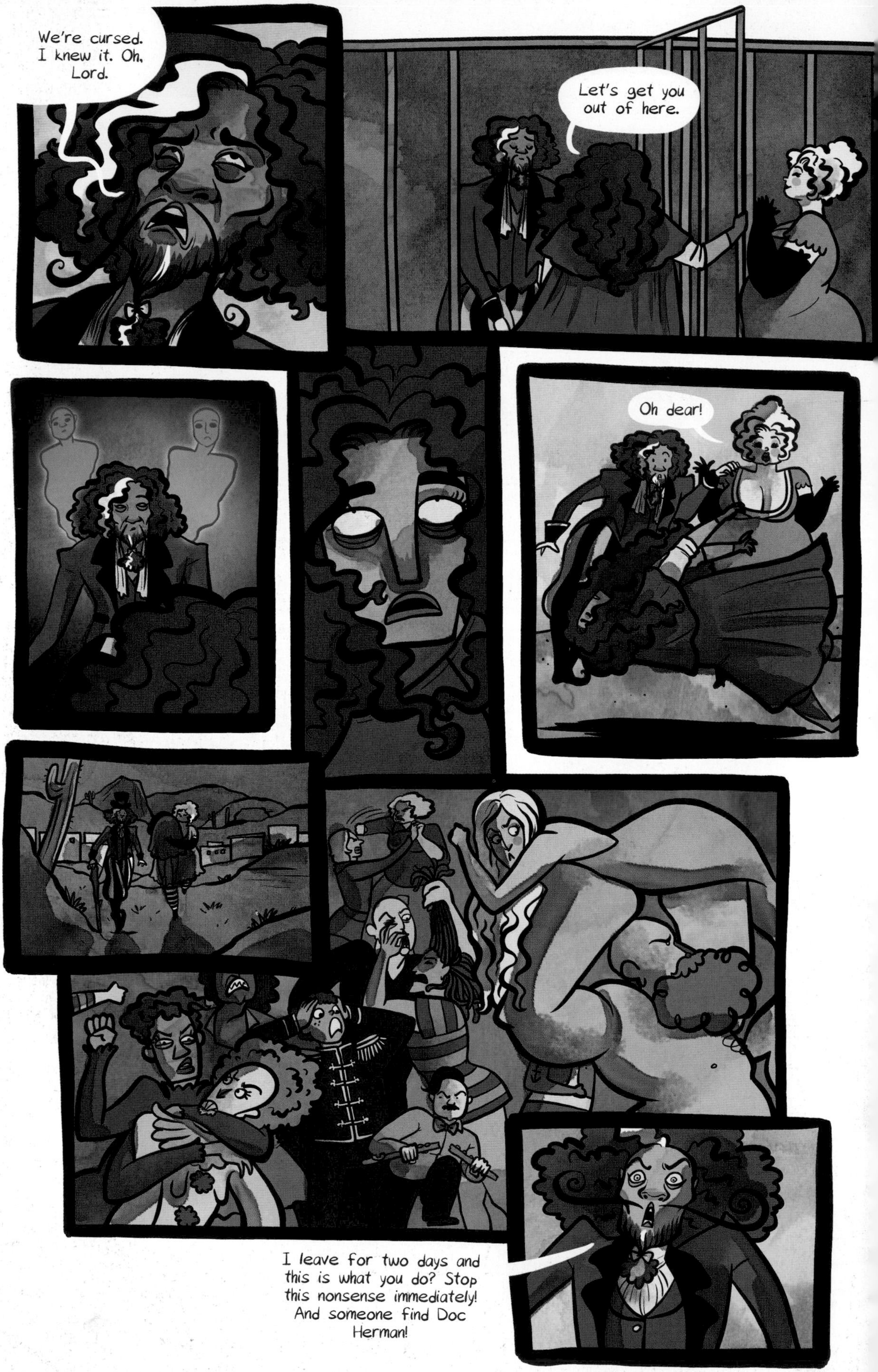
We're cursed. I knew it. Oh, Lord.
Let's get you out of here.
Oh dear!
I leave for two days and this is what you do? Stop this nonsense immediately! And someone find Doc Herman!

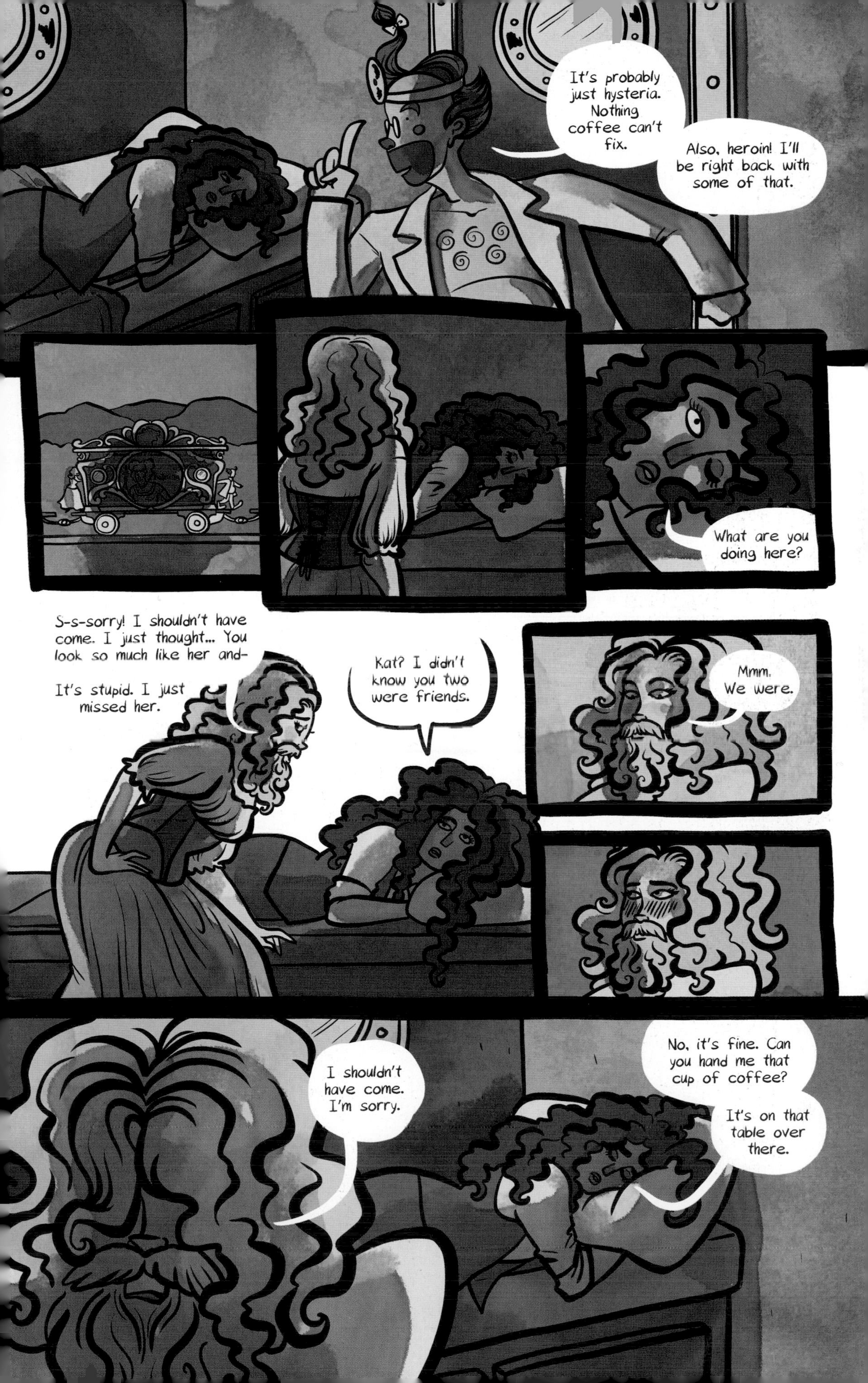
It's probably just hysteria. Nothing coffee can't fix.
Also, heroin! I'll be right back with some of that.
What are you doing here?
S-s-sorry! I shouldn't have come. I just thought... You look so much like her and-
It's stupid. I just missed her.
Kat? I didn't know you two were friends.
Mmm. We were.
I shouldn't have come. I'm sorry.
No, it's fine. Can you hand me that cup of coffee?
It's on that table over there.

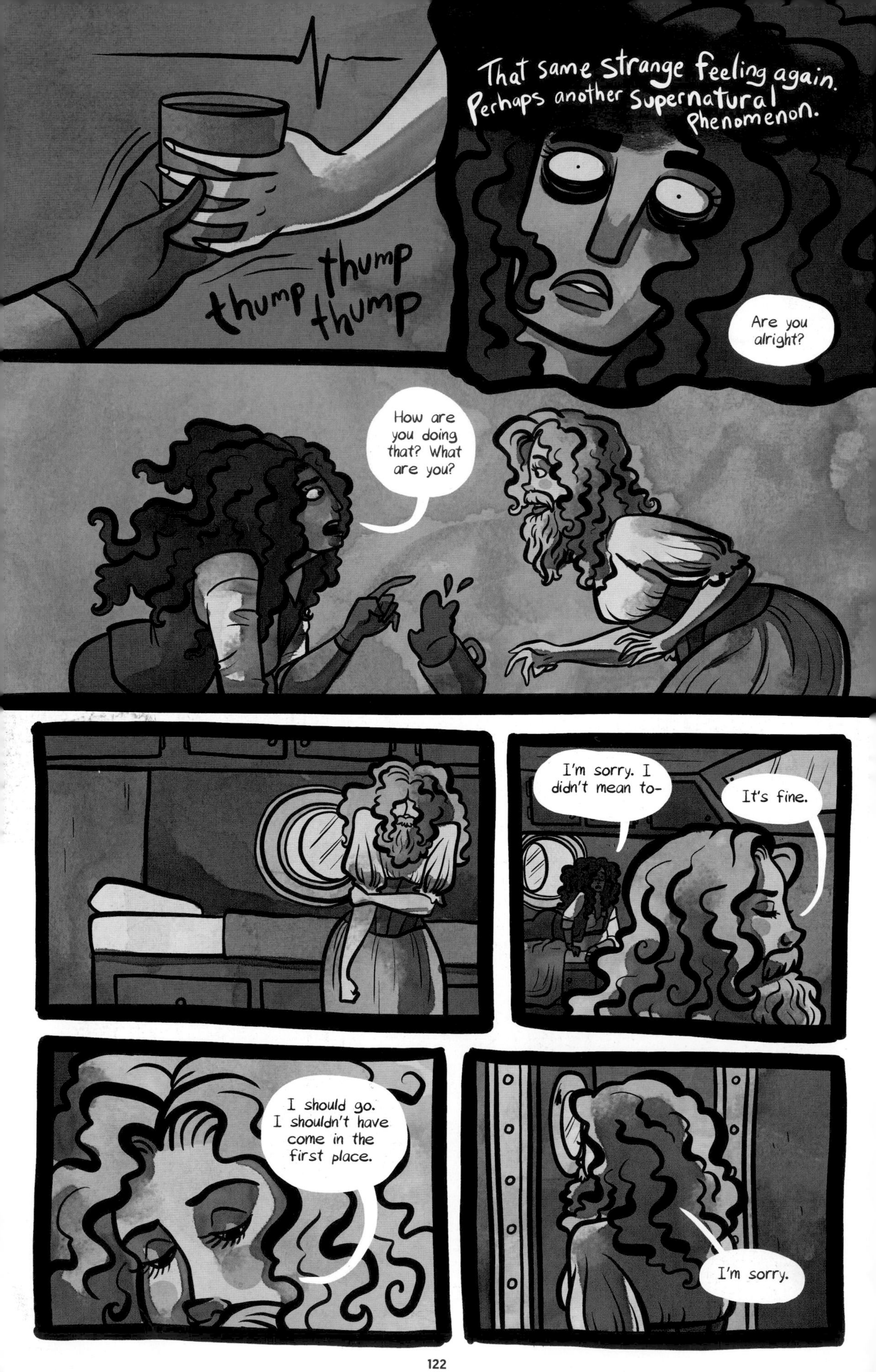
thump thump thump
That same strange feeling again. Perhaps another supernatural phenomenon.
Are you alright?
How are you doing that? What are you?
I'm sorry. I didn't mean to-
It's fine.
I should go. I shouldn't have come in the first place.
I'm sorry.

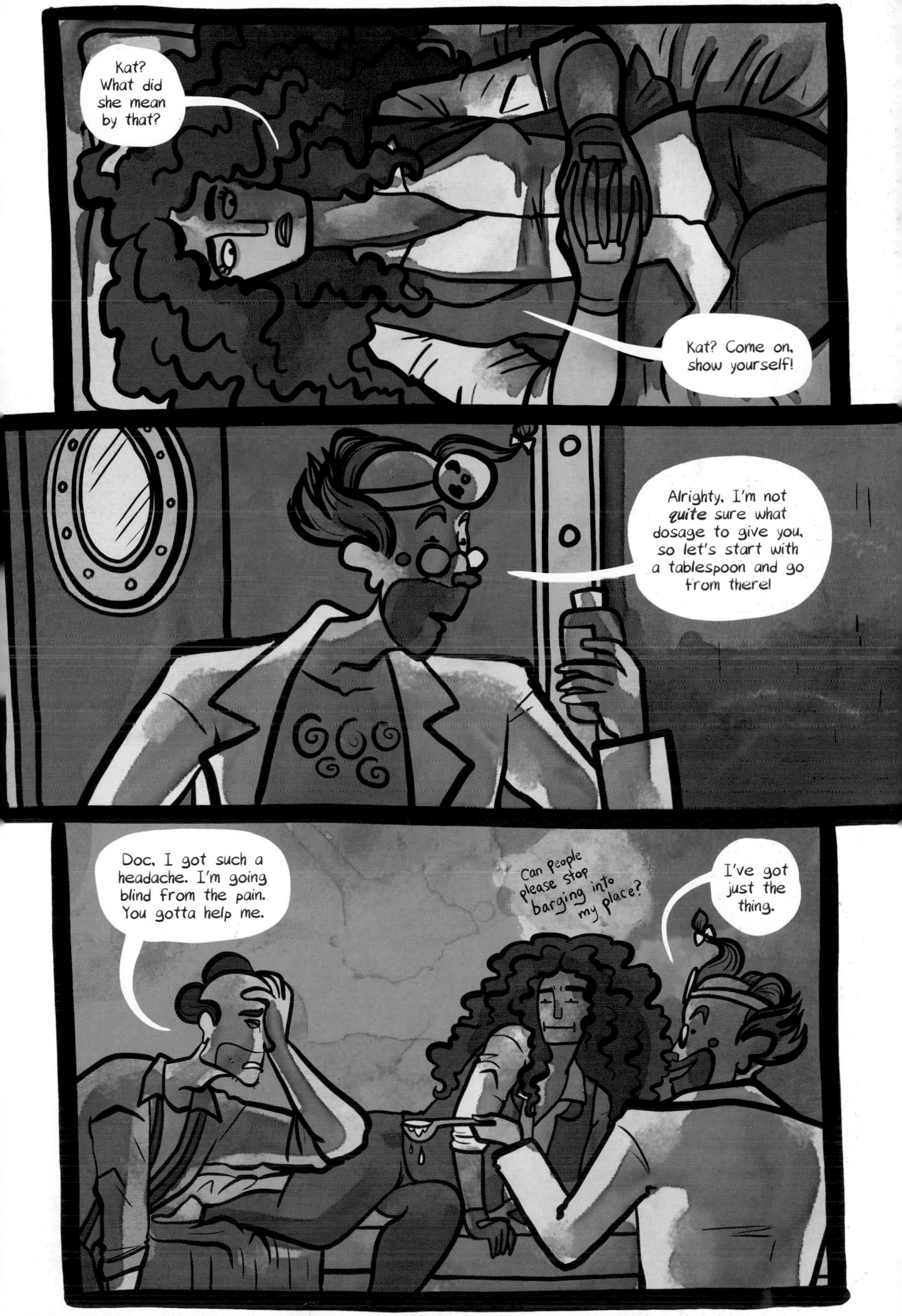
Kat? What did she mean by that?
Kat? Come on, show yourself!
Alrighty, I'm not ***quite*** sure what dosage to give you, so let's start with a tablespoon and go from there!
Doc, I got such a headache. I'm going blind from the pain. You gotta help me.
Can people please stop barging into my place?
I've got just the thing.

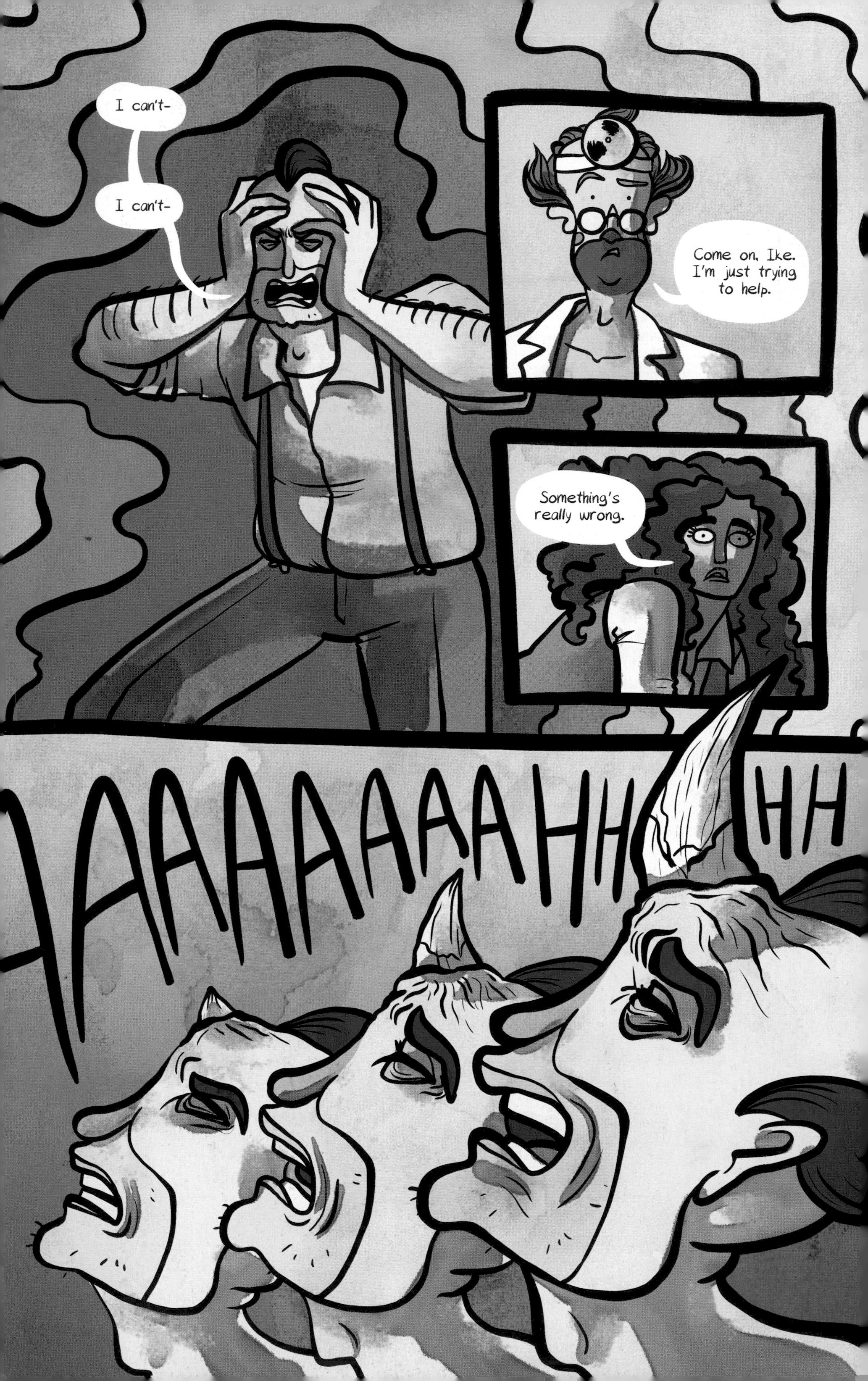
I can't-
I can't-
Come on, Ike. I'm just trying to help.
Something's really wrong.
AAAAAAAAAHHHH

End of Book One

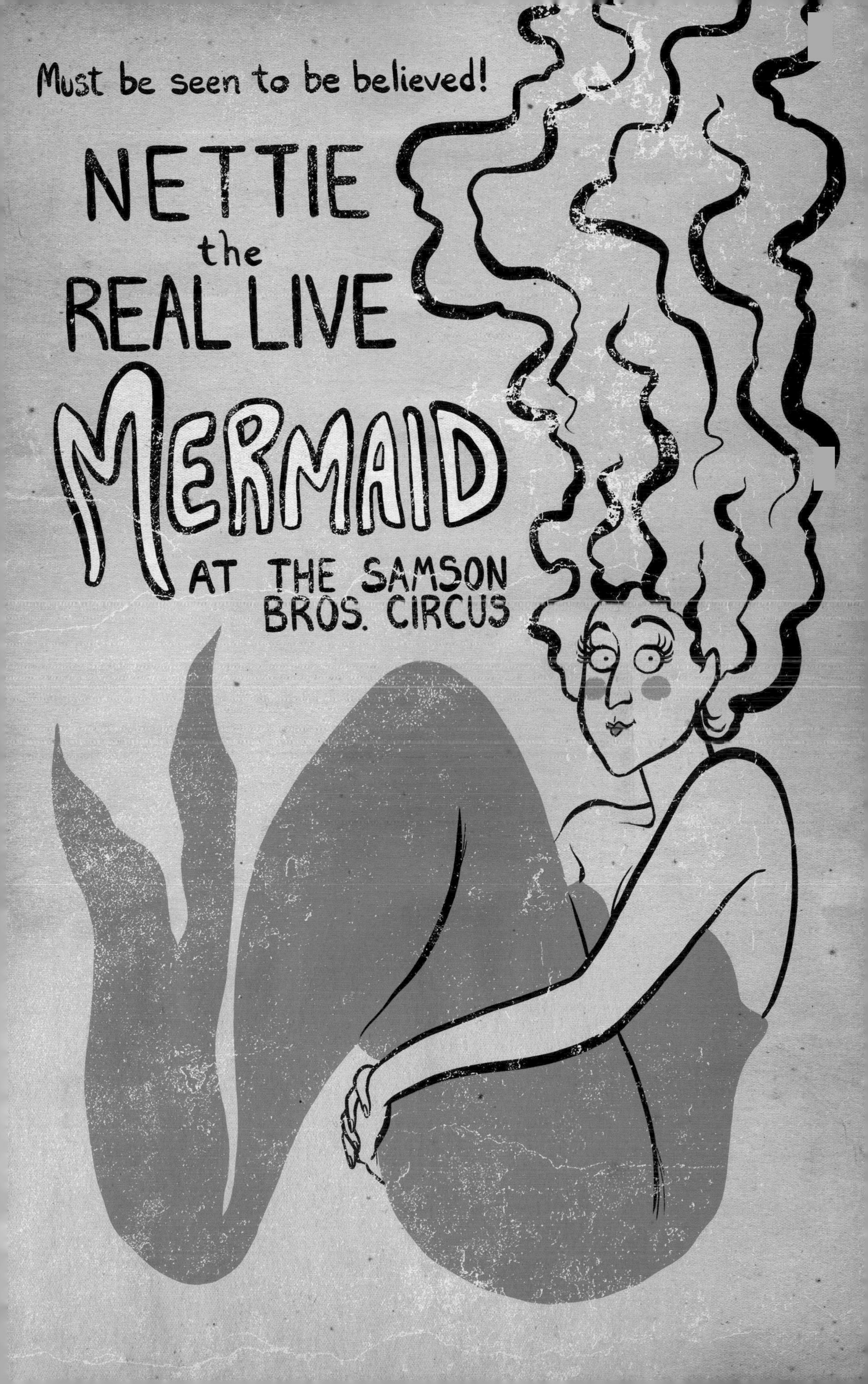
Must be seen to be believed!
NETTIE
the
REAL LIVE
MERMAID
AT THE SAMSON
BROS. CIRCUS

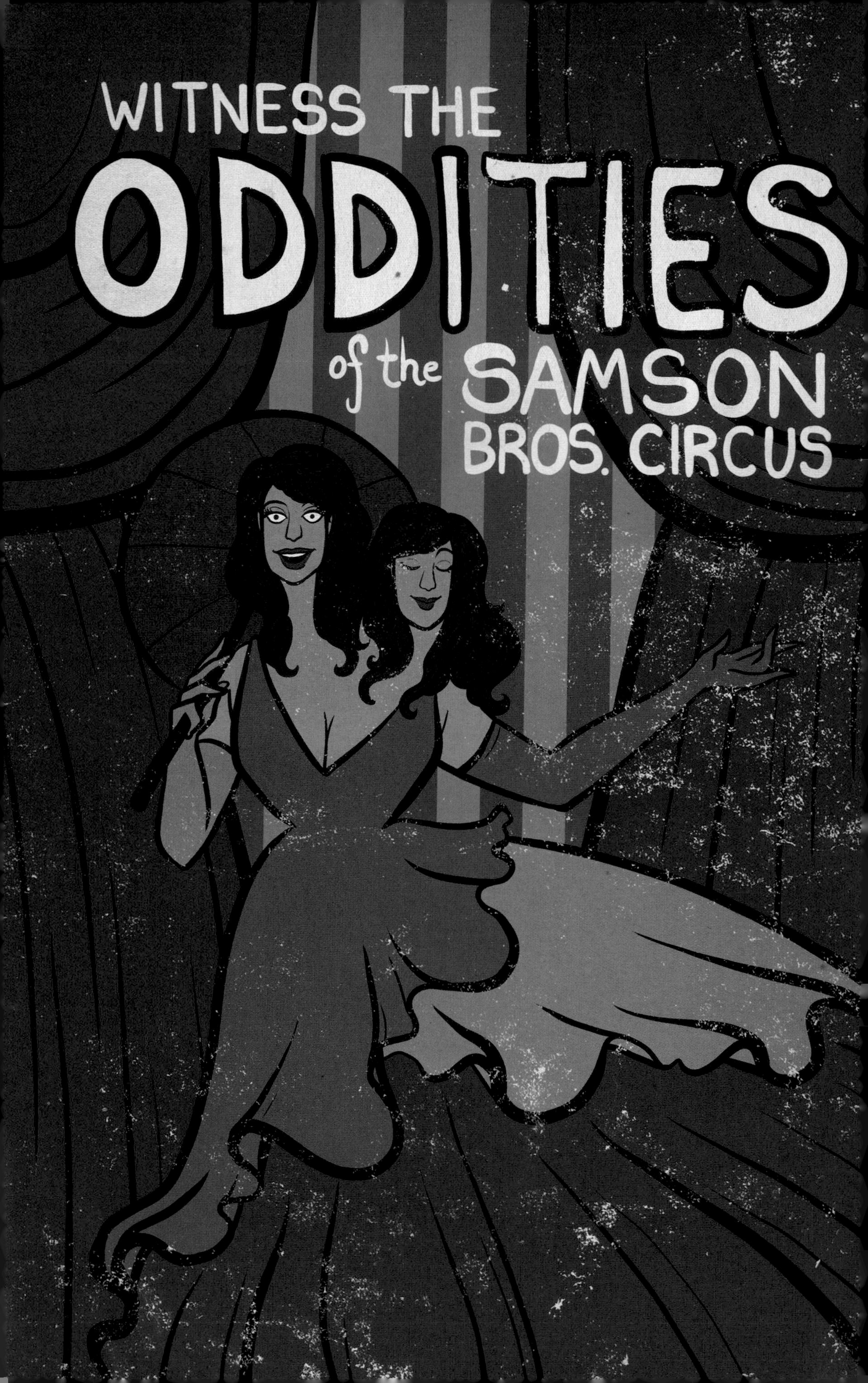
WITNESS THE
ODDITIES
of the SAMSON
BROS. CIRCUS

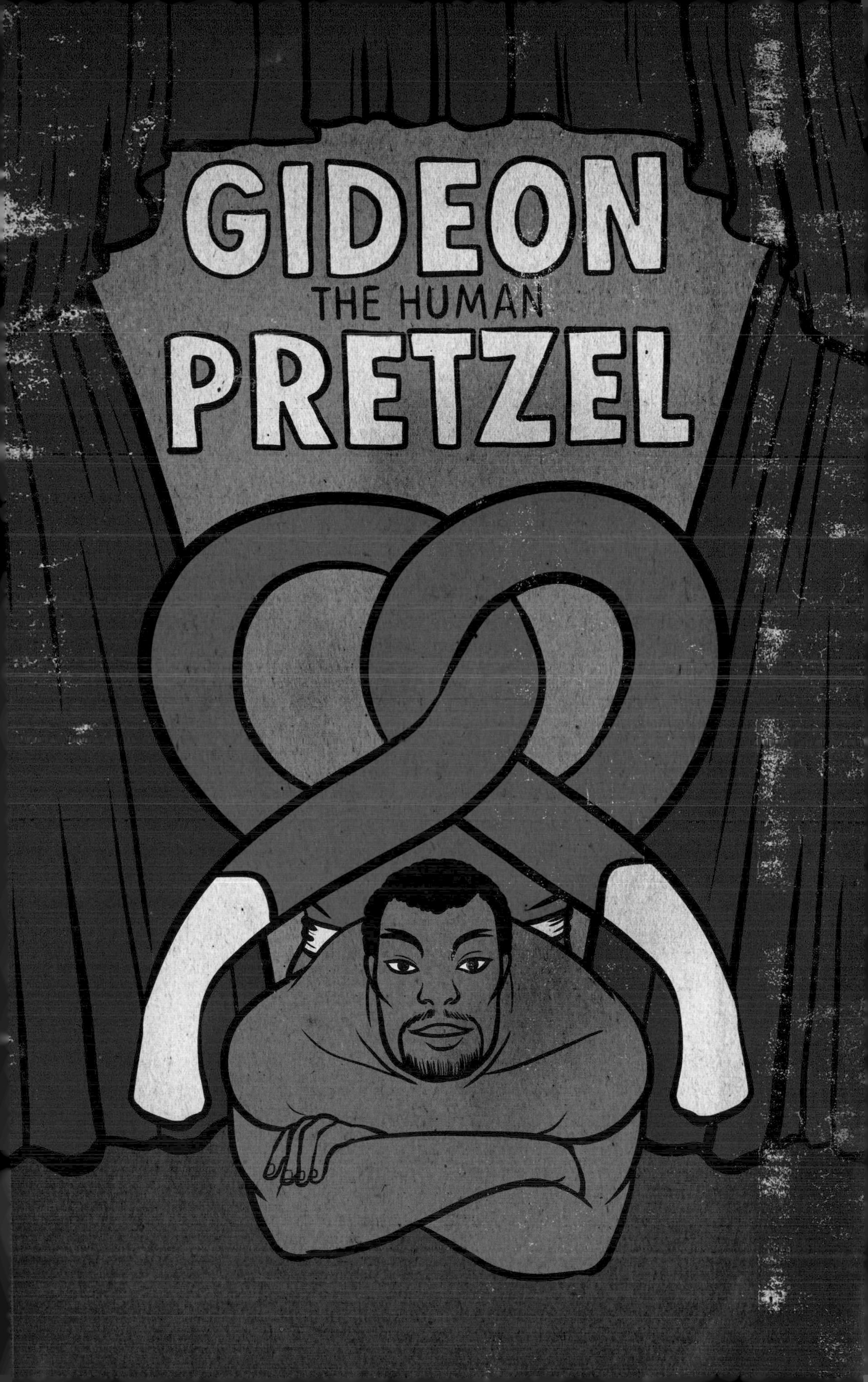
GIDEON
THE HUMAN
PRETZEL

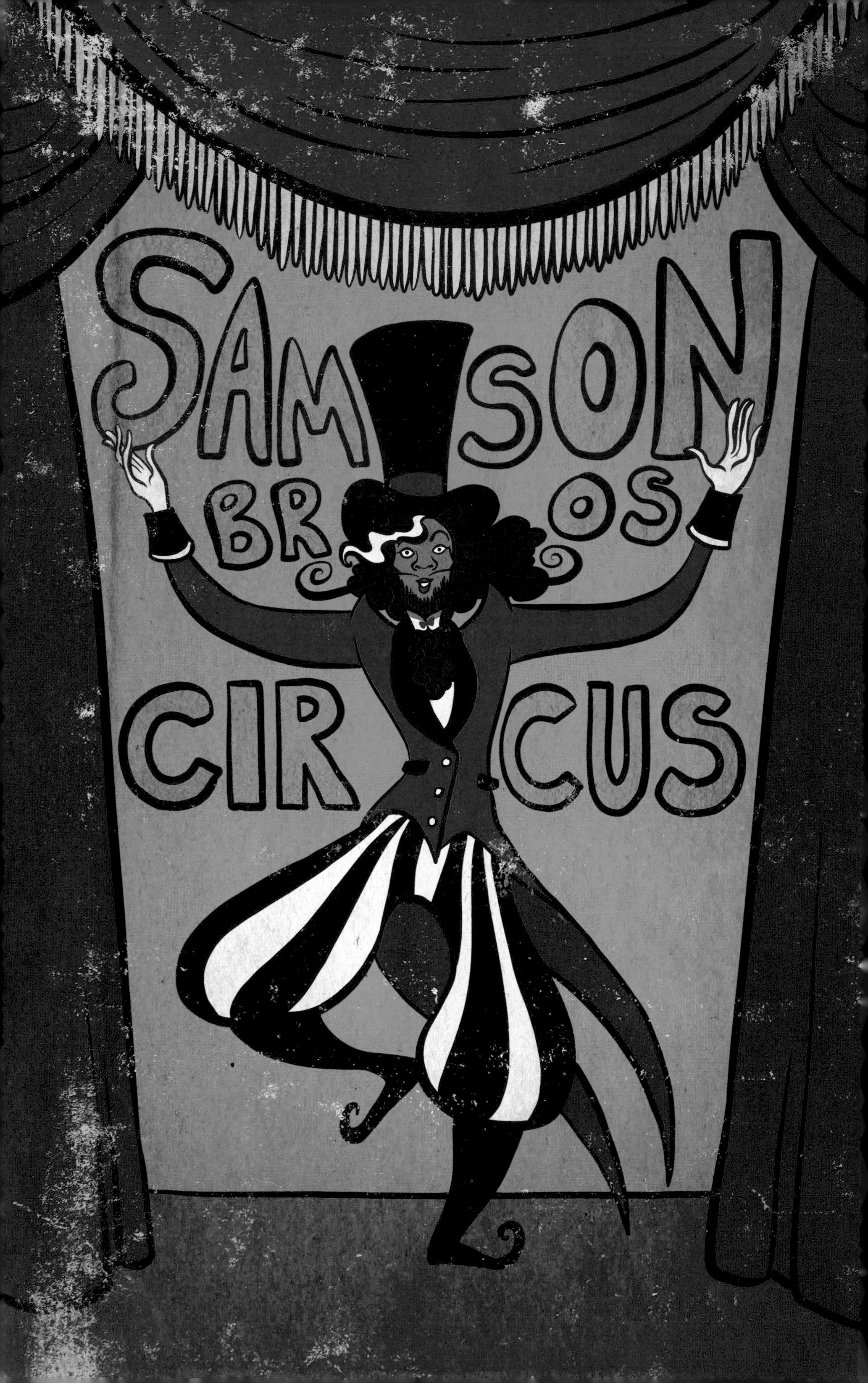
SAMSON
BROS
CIRCUS

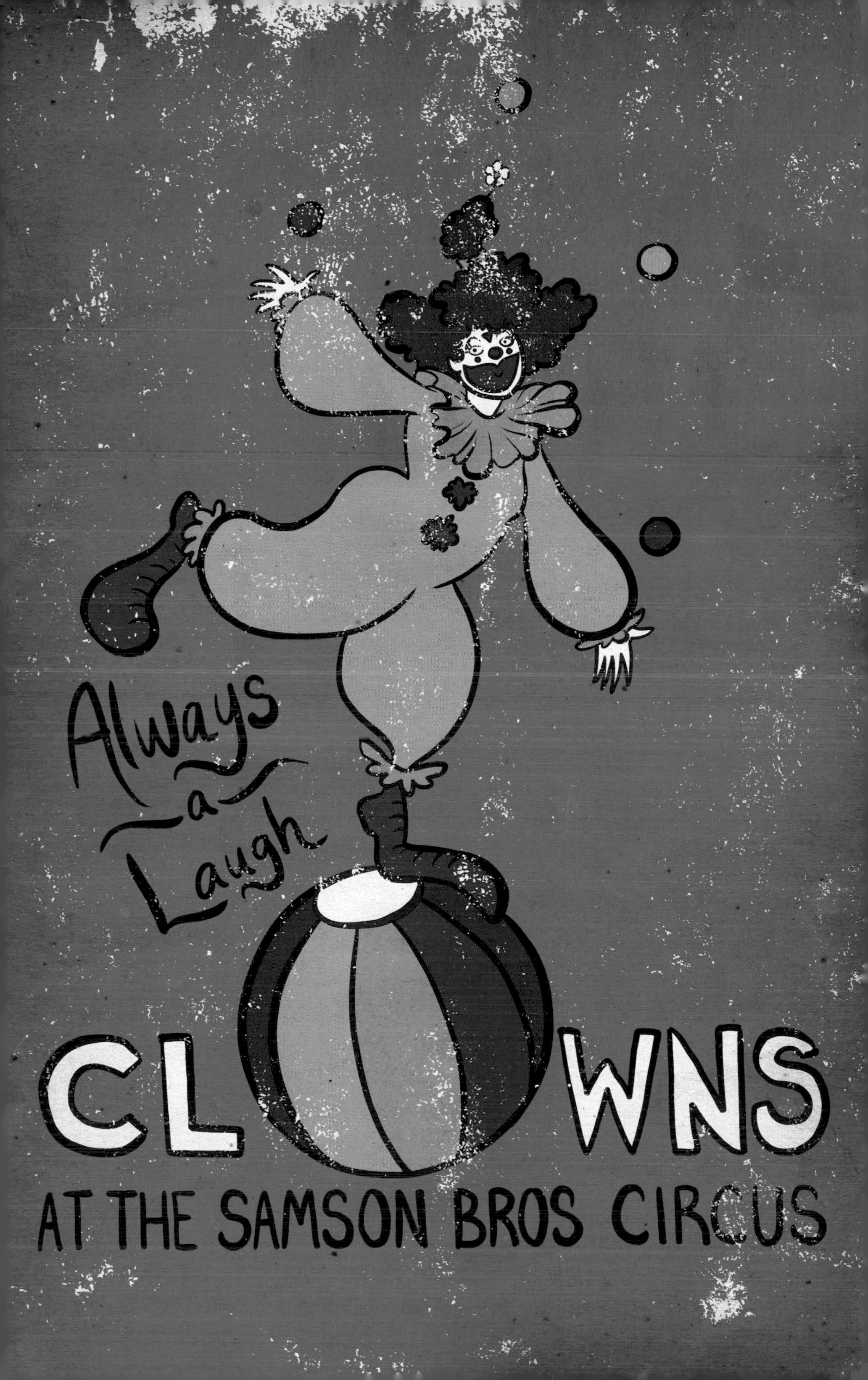
Always a Laugh
CLOWNS
AT THE SAMSON BROS CIRCUS

What WON'T Anna add salt to?

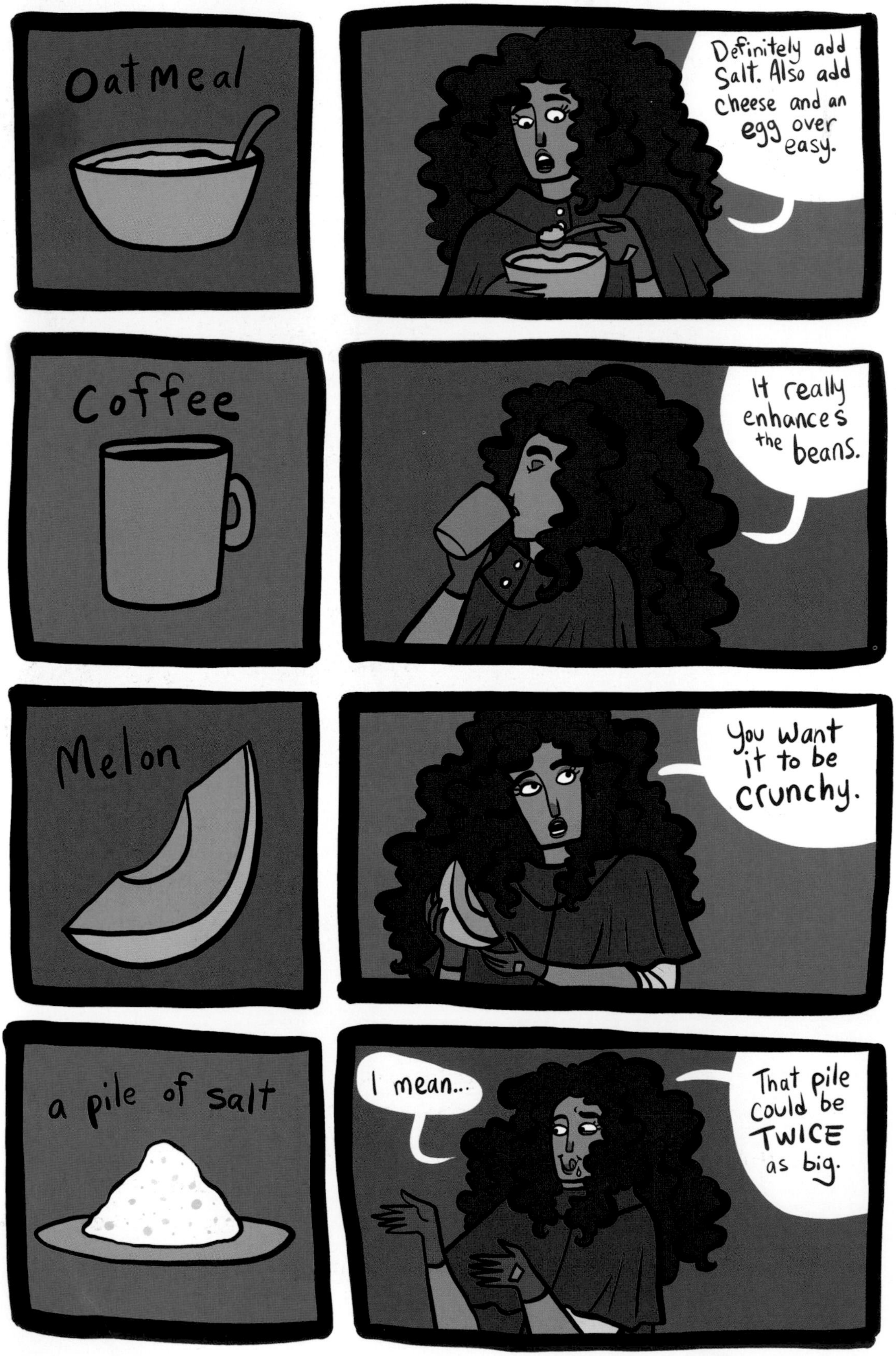
Oatmeal
Definitely add Salt. Also add cheese and an egg over easy.
Coffee
It really enhances the beans.
Melon
You want it to be crunchy.
a pile of salt
I mean...
That pile could be TWICE as big.

ANNA'S COAT

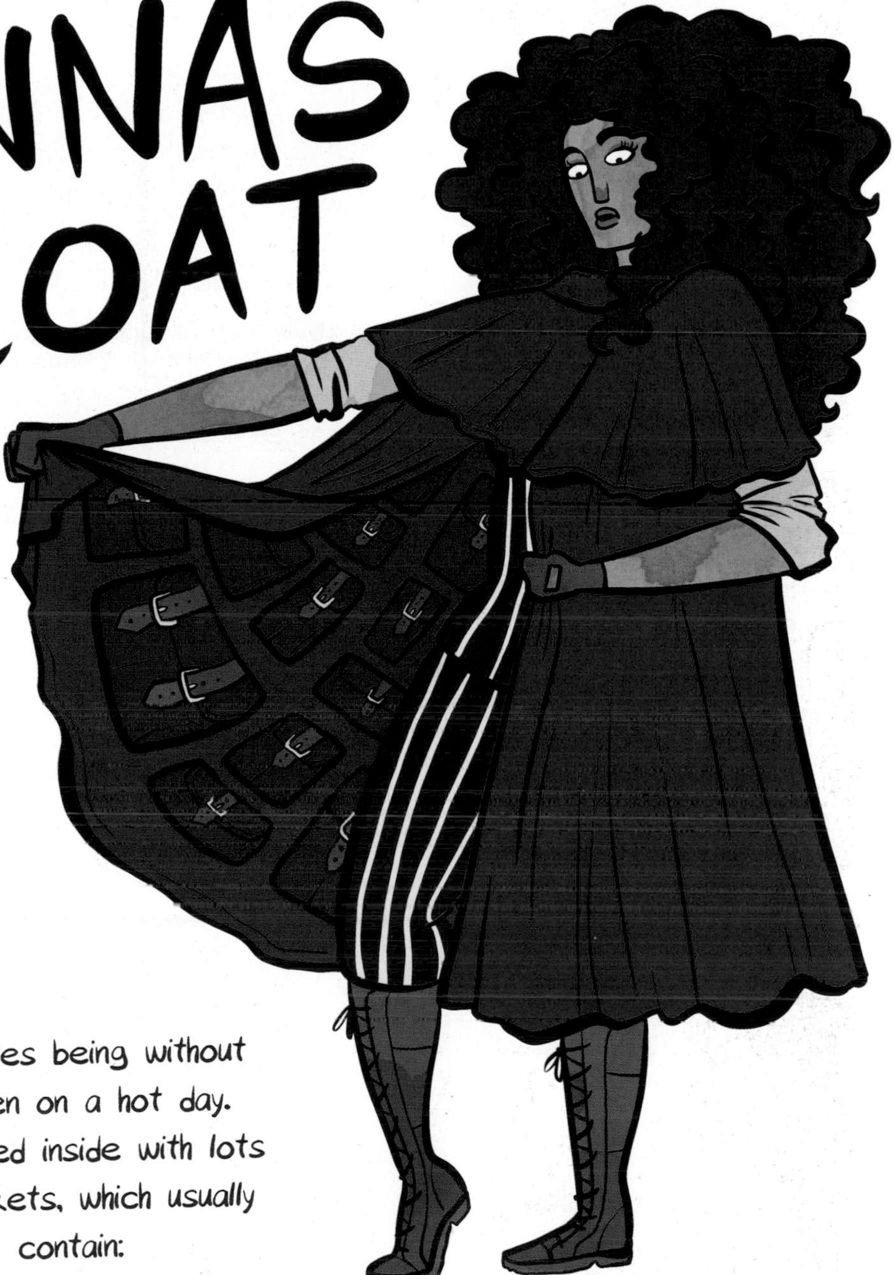

She hates being without it, even on a hot day. It is lined inside with lots of pockets, which usually contain:

Notepads, pencils, Tarot cards, small empty bottles, small rocks, medium sized rocks, magnets, a mirror, a magnifying glass, a book, salt, a pocket knife, spare socks, aspirin, pins and needles and thread (red and blue), matches, candles, small wrenches, screwdrivers, 20 pennies, a pocket watch, and some snacks.

In 2013, I found myself in the middle of the desert.

I had been traveling with a troupe of performers, and our engine broke down in the red dusty back roads of Arizona for four days. Thankfully none of our arguments resulted in murder, though the small motel we took refuge in was filthy, and the bed I was given to sleep on was covered in blood stains. You might notice how much this resembles the first chapter of *Spectacle*. You might think this experience was the inspiration for it.

I wrote that scene in 2011, before I ever joined that show.

Spectacle has gone through a lot of evolution since I started working on it. It started as a novel I was writing to distract myself from how horrible I felt living in a hotel after my house burned down. 30,000 words in, I realized the characters were too spectacular not to draw. Half a dozen rewrites later and you're holding this book in your hands. But the story always started the same. A traveling show, stranded in the desert with a broken engine. If I'd known I was writing prophecies, I would've written something about a lotto winner.

Spectacle isn't directly about my own road stories, but this story is definitely better than it would have been if I'd never took the plunge and signed up for the odd world of touring shows. Performers are strange, especially when you have a group of them living in close quarters. Touring for long stretches of time puts you in a very weird head space. All the problems you used to have are forgotten in favor of obsessing over your next meal, your next bathroom break, and your next shower, all of which will come from a gas station in a town with a population of 17. Some places love you, some places call you witches and shield their children from you as you pass by. Most of my memories of touring aren't onstage, and most of *Spectacle's* story takes place in between shows. Putting on makeup and flamboyant clothing and dancing for crowds is the most normal time you have. Trying to get brunch is where the drama happens.

I don't travel quite as much as I used to. It's hard to draw comics on a bus with a broken suspension bumbling along potholed highways, though I did try, scratching out shaky little tour diaries. It's tempting to leave the world behind and become a full-time performer, but comics have always been my most precious love, and it's probably slightly less likely to kill me. But I do still hit the road every other weekend to go play. Hopefully I'll see you in the audience sometime.

See you in Book 2!

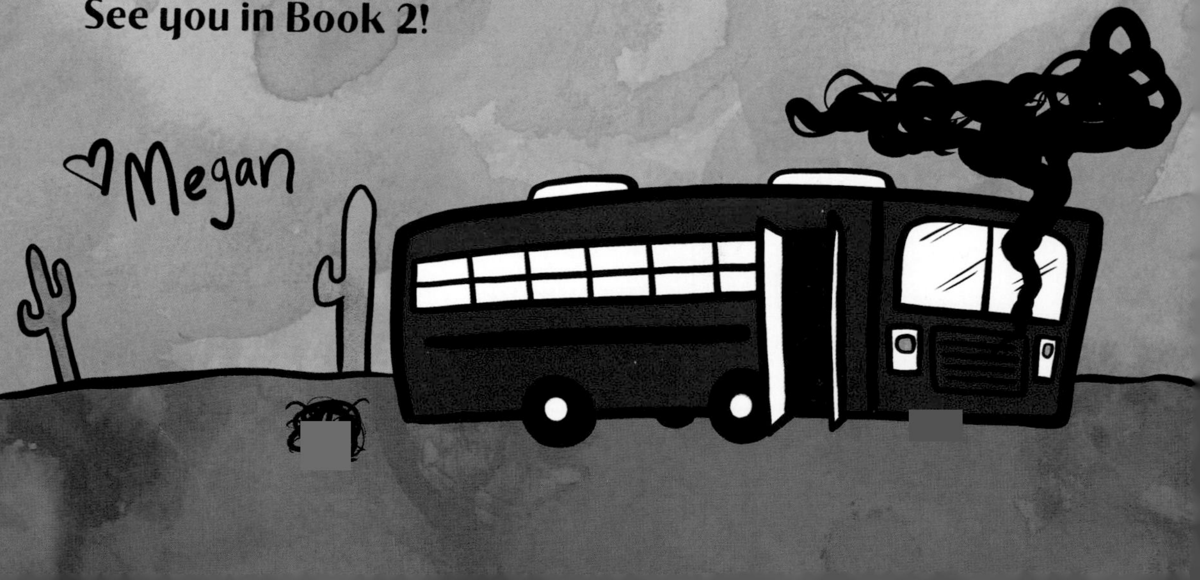
♡Megan

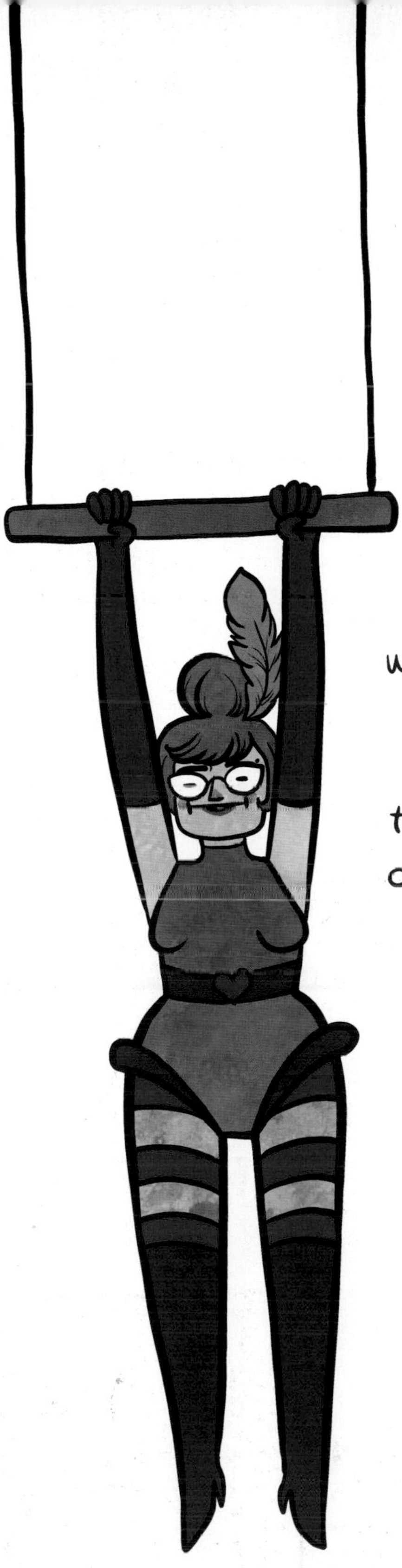

Megan Rose Gedris
was born in 1986 and has been
making comics since 1996.
When not drawing, she is a
traveling performer. She likes
cheese to a worrying degree.
She lives in Chicago.

See more of her work at
rosalarian.com

Read more from Oni Press!

MATT GARDNER
RASHAD DOUCET
ALABASTER SHADOWS

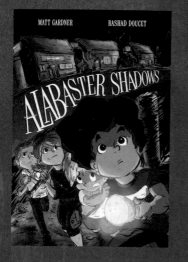

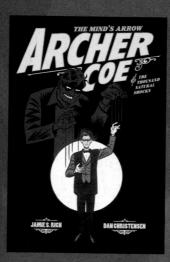

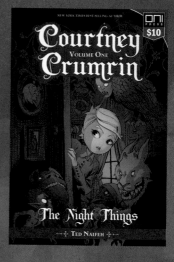

ALABASTER SHADOWS
By Matt Gardner & Rashad Doucet
ISBN 978-1-62010-264-0

THE MIND'S ARROW
ARCHER COE
& THE THOUSAND NATURAL SHOCKS
JAMIE S. RICH
DAN CHRISTENSEN

ARCHER COE & THE THOUSAND NATURAL SHOCKS
By Jamie S. Rich & Dan Christensen
ISBN 978-1-62010-121-6

NEW YORK TIMES BEST-SELLING AUTHOR
ONI PRESS
$10
Courtney Crumrin
VOLUME ONE
The Night Things
TED NAIFEH

COURTNEY CRUMRIN, VOL. 1: THE NIGHT THINGS
By Ted Naifeh & Warren Wucinich
ISBN 978-1-62010-419-4

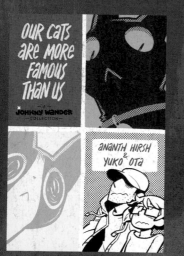

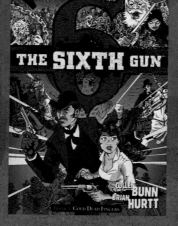

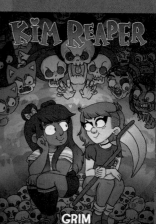

OUR CATS ARE MORE FAMOUS THAN US
A JOHNNY WANDER COLLECTION
ANANTH HIRSH & YUKO OTA

OUR CATS ARE MORE FAMOUS THAN US: A JOHNNY WANDER COLLECTION
By Ananth Hirsh & Yuko Ota
ISBN 978-1-62010-383-8

ONI PRESS
$10
THE SIXTH GUN
CULLEN BUNN
BRIAN HURTT
BOOK 1: COLD DEAD FINGERS

THE SIXTH GUN, VOL. 1: COLD DEAD FINGERS
By Cullen Bunn,
Brian Hurtt, & Bill Crabtree
ISBN 978-1-62010-420-0

KIM REAPER
GRIM BEGINNINGS
BY SARAH GRALEY

KIM REAPER, VOL. 1: GRIM BEGINNINGS
By Sarah Graley
ISBN 978-1-62010-455-2

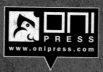

ONI PRESS
www.onipress.com

FOR MORE INFORMATION ON THESE AND OTHER FINE ONI PRESS COMIC BOOKS AND GRAPHIC NOVELS, VISIT WWW.ONIPRESS.COM. TO FIND A COMIC SPECIALTY STORE IN YOUR AREA, VISIT WWW.COMICSHOPS.US.